JO ANDERTON

Suited

BOOK TWO OF THE
VEILED WORLDS TRILOGY

**ANGRY
ROBOT**

ANGRY ROBOT
A member of the Osprey Group

Lace Market House,
54-56 High Pavement,
Nottingham,
NG1 1HW, UK

www.angryrobotbooks.com
Call it civilization

An Angry Robot paperback original 2012.

Distributed in the United States by Random House, Inc., New York.

ISBN 978-0-85766-157-9
eBook ISBN 978-0-85766-158-6

Printed in the United States of America

9 8 7 6 5 4 3 2 1

THE VEILED WORLDS

"Australian first-time novelist Anderton has created a refreshingly original and complex far-future society and uses Tanyana's fall, and subsequent investigation into who was behind it, to examine issues of privilege and poverty, loyalty and betrayal. An accomplished debut."

Eric Brown, *The Guardian*

"Anderton demonstrates a mastery of storytelling and world building in this series opener that is reminiscent of the visionary works of China Miéville. This accomplished debut novel should enjoy a wide readership."

Library Journal

"Jo Anderton's debut impressively combines far-future world-building, conspiracies, and a redemption quest. [She] clearly telegraphs the overall plot arc, but keeps it interesting with Tanyana's strong, proud narrative voice and the complex culture built up around the pions and debris."

Publishers Weekly

"*Debris* is a strong, exciting debut that took me by surprise with its unique setting, interesting main character, and powerful 'fight your way back to the top' narrative. If you enjoy genre-bending fiction with a dark edge, definitely give *Debris* a try."

FantasyLiterature.com

Also by Jo Anderton

Debris

SUITED

Analysis of Past Events

XLIV-A turned his back on the suiting table as another experiment failed. The body lying strapped there belonged to a forty five year old male factory worker. He'd had negligible pion-binding abilities before they'd administered the precise cranial trauma that had replaced them with an ability to see debris instead. Despite intense treatment his nervous structure refused to attach to the suit, and now the pion bonds that held his muscles and bones together were unwinding; the result of an error in the level of suit shielding, perhaps. He'd be dead within minutes, which was a good thing. He was getting louder.

With a twitch of his fingers XLIV-A deactivated the lamps around the table and instigated initial clean up protocols. A moment later his brother, XLIV-B appeared by his side and scanned the results of the experiment, stored in glowing numbers and words on a small slide.

"Another one?" he asked.

"We are having trouble replicating the success we had with Tanyana Vladha," XLIV-A answered. "The weaponised debris-collecting suit takes a toll on the bodies of its hosts.

Only a few others have survived the installation as well as she has."

V-B nodded, and together they left the body to complete its noisy dying. They walked slowly through the laboratory, bright lines of data shining up from the slide. It was time for a pause in the experiments – this had been universally and instantly agreed to – so tables were shutting down all around them, leaving the laboratory dark and silent.

"The Vladha experiment requires proper analysis," V-A said. He flicked his wrist and the data on the slide was replaced by an image. Together, they stopped and stared up as it was beamed into the darkness above them.

Tanyana Vladha; dressed in the deep blue jacket she'd worn as an architect. Small silver bear-head pins shone from her shoulders, denoting the jobs she'd completed for the regional and national veche. A crest embroidered into her collar advertised the university she had graduated from with high honours. Her propensity to dress in trousers and coats rather than skirts unusual, as was her short blonde hair. Most women of status in the city Movoc-under-Keeper – indeed, the whole of Varsnia – kept their hair long. She had a tense, determined look about her. This was her customary facial expression.

"Tanyana Vladha," V-B read out loud as records replaced her image, "was chosen because of her pion-binding strength. She was the centre of a circle of nine binders, and able to gather and command vast numbers of pions." He referred to the tiny, brightly glowing particles that could be used to unbind then rebind matter. "Thus she completed large and complex commissions for the regional and national veche, from buildings to statues."

He paused long enough for V-A to make a short note: *Connection between level of pion-binding ability and suit integration? Confirm subsequent successful experiments had similar abilities*.

"We removed her pion sight," V-B continued. "Through the usual application of targeted trauma to the brain. To do this we arranged for her to work on *Grandeur*, a giant statue commissioned by the veche, and orchestrated an on-site accident in which she was critically injured. As well as the appropriate cranial fractures, she sustained significant wounds to the left side of her body, and will carry the scars for the rest of her life. As a result she is now able to see debris instead, the waste product created through pion-manipulation." They shared a smirk at this, and faint laughter filtered through the darkness around them. Such a quaint definition for something so complicated. "Debris has a weakening effect on pion bonds. If left unchecked it will slow and ultimately unwind any system it interacts with over time. This has necessitated the establishment of a class of debris collectors, and the creation of a debris collecting suit. We installed one such suit on Tanyana Vladha."

A schematic drawing of the suit flashed across the slide. Six silver bands attached to her ankles, wrists, waist and neck, with a truly complex webbing of deep, usually invisible, nervous, musculature and skeletal connections. The bands were complex in themselves. They were divided into sections. The base ring, about as wide as the length of an index finger, was grafted to the host body. It acted like a foundation, above which the secondary, activator ring slowly spun. The space between the two was filled with symbols that glowed and bobbed in response to the electrical pulses generated by the host's brain.

The suit enabled the collection of debris. The liquid silver that bubbled up from these bands was the only substance that could actually touch debris. Otherwise it floated free, sliding through all matter as substantial as shadows, either in solid-looking grain form, or as flat planes.

Tanyana Vladha's suit, however, was different from the usual. That was the whole point. It was the next stage in development, stronger, faster, more closely bonded to her nervous system and brain. This put a far greater strain on her physical and cognitive abilities than most suits did. But it was worth the risks.

"With her suit installed," V-B was saying, "she was instated into a debris collecting team."

"A very particular collecting team," V-A interrupted. "We had already been monitoring certain of its members for some time."

V-B nodded. "Efficiency is the core of productivity."

"Indeed."

They moved on, continuing to read as they walked. Faint lights flickered in the laboratory around them. Lightning flashes of electrical discharge, masses of stored and ready pions, valves, dials and screens.

"Over time, she developed relationships with her new team members. This has helped streamline our monitoring process." Again, the data on the slide changed to images. The faces of each of her collecting team members.

"Kichlan, team leader." A man with a wary expression, dark brown eyes and blond curls appeared. "Ex-debris technician, showed promise before losing his pion sight. Despite initial friction, he is growing closer to Miss Vladha. He is the primary carer for his younger brother, Lad."

Lad looked a lot like his brother, the same eyes, the same

curls, but none of the wariness. He smiled broadly. Despite the uneven stubble over his chin, he had the innocent look of a child. Lines of red, urgent data flashed beneath his image. V-A and V-B shared a humourless, knowing smile.

"Miss Vladha also grows close to Lad," V-A said. "This has been the cause of some concern, but we maintain a waiting pattern. Action has not yet been decided."

Several more images appeared in quick succession. The identical twins, Mizra and Uzdal, thin and pale. Sofia, small, stout, and fierce. Natasha with her sharp green eyes, looking disinterested.

"Suit testing then commenced," V-B read. "Through several staged emergencies we pushed Miss Vladha and her suit beyond the limits usually required of debris collectors. All the while using a debris suit technician, one–" he scrolled quickly through the reams of data to come to a footnote "–Devich to watch and report on her progress." Both brothers made identical sour faces. "The technician's performance in this role was far below expectations. Not only did she identify him as our informant, thus rendering him useless to us, he claims to have developed *feelings* for her and refuses any further assignments."

V-A made an urgent note, *Deal with Devich appropriately*.

"The culmination of her tests coincided with the completion of a secondary experiment – the creation of a sentient semi-physical creature out of altered debris planes and grains." Satisfaction wiped away their sourness. "Success in this area has been a long time coming, but we are pleased with its progress. Debris manipulation continues. The next stage is almost ready for release."

"We digress," V-A murmured.

"We do." V-B nodded. "Let us continue." Together, not

even looking at their feet, they stepped over a series of thick cables that snaked across the laboratory floor. "Miss Vladha successfully harnessed her suit's abilities to combat and ultimately overcome the debris experiment. However, this was not done according to our protocols." Anger on their identical faces this time, a terrible anger that twisted their skin. Thick lines like tearing seams formed from nose to mouth and around their usually impassive, mold-coloured eyes. "There was interference."

"A variable introduced from the beginning without our knowledge. The Keeper."

The darkness around them seemed to shudder, and a hissing sound rose like mist. The Keeper, it always came back to him. All their problems, all their hard work, all thanks to him.

V-B scanned the data. "It seems the Keeper became aware of Miss Vladha as soon as we removed her pion sight. He used the unique nature of her suit to establish communication with her. He gained her trust, and told her too much."

They shared a glance.

"Miss Vladha learned the true nature of debris—"

"To some extent," V-A interrupted. "The Keeper is as interested in guarding the truth as we are."

"True." V-B added a note to the data. Best to be as accurate as possible. "She learned that the Keeper is not the myth her people thought he was. The Varsnians tell stories about the Keeper in which he is a benevolent..." they searched for a word "—deity. He is a saviour who holds back the darkness, pain and death brought by his nemesis, the Other."

"A fascinating interpretation."

"Indeed." How entertaining those stories were. "Miss Vladha, like most people in her day and age, did not believe in the Keeper any more. How surprised she must have been to discover that he not only existed, but he was debris. That what she thought was a waste product was actually a physical manifestation of a – what was that term again? – *deity*."

"And now inconvenient for us," V-A muttered. "For once she learned that the debris she had been collecting, and fighting, was actually parts of the Keeper, her interaction with it changed."

"She became reticent to inflict any violence on it, even after it attacked her city, her companions, and herself. Choosing instead to undo our hard work and return it to the Keeper. She learned that she is able to influence any debris her suit is touching, and can therefore convince it to stop fighting her, become calm and allow itself to be reabsorbed. While she cannot yet understand how she is able to do this, she is certainly growing proficient at the process."

They arrived at a strange looking silver chair shining beneath a single spotlight, and stopped. V-B lowered the slide. More brothers stepped out of the darkness, all nearly identical. They all wore the same crisp, white coat, shared the same features, the same movements and expressions.

"Conclusions?" one asked.

V-A consulted his notes. "Continue suit experiments, narrow criteria for candidate selection based on pion binding ability." A collective nod. "Activate countermeasures against the Keeper's interference in all future suits. We must maintain tighter control on all experiments."

Sounds echoed through the laboratory. The tread of feet, the rattling of metal, a high-pitched, terrified scream. A few brothers glanced over their shoulder. Most ignored it.

"It is time to elevate the Vladha experiment to a new phase. Let us make use of the variables the Keeper has introduced. Intensify monitoring and send a preparatory signal to her suit. If the Keeper thinks to use her against us, he is sorely mistaken. The processes we have started cannot be undone by one woman, no matter how skilled she is."

A general murmur of agreement, and XLIV-A straightened. There, that was much better. Uncertainties removed, plans made, preparations under way. Just the way it should be.

"In the mean time," XLIV-B had to shout over the screaming, coming closer. "Let us continue our work."

As one, the brothers stepped back to make a pathway through their ranks, and turned to watch as their latest experiment was dragged in.

1.

It took me two moons to realise the Keeper was broken.

With hindsight, it should not have taken me that long. But he was the Keeper. He was light to the Other's dark, he was our guardian against the unknown, he stood before fear and death and he protected us. At least, he should have. Two moons of following his call, however, and I was forced to accept that he was none of these things. Not any more.

Knee-deep in sewerage, hand clamped in Lad's vice-like fist, I followed the Keeper through the airless dark of a tunnel far below ground. He seemed to like sewers – anything underground, dark and dank, really – and I was beginning to suspect this was another dead end. My debris collecting team had slogged through so much refuse at the Keeper's command that even our uniforms – that dark, strongly boned material that had never needed cleaning – were beginning to stink. And for all that, he had only led us to small debris caches, not even enough to fill our quota.

"We cannot keep doing this," Kichlan murmured, just behind me. The tunnel was too tight to allow us to walk

2022729239

three abreast, so Kichlan followed his younger brother and me, close enough to step on the back of my boots. I didn't mind. It was reassuring to have him near. "We haven't met quota in moons; how long before the veche come for us?"

I began to agree, but stopped. Lad glanced at me. Neither Kichlan nor I wanted the large, childlike man to know how worried we were about the Keeper. Lad was our connection to him, and Lad was proud of his role.

"I know," I whispered, once Lad's attention shifted away. "But what do you suggest?" This was an old conversation. What else can you do when an ancient, mythical guardian comes to you for help? What choice did we have but to follow him?

"This is getting us nowhere—"

"Quiet, bro." Lad stopped, tensing and tilting his head like he was listening to something the rest of us couldn't hear.

For a moment I heard nothing but the trickling of sewerage somewhere in the distance. Then Lad gasped loudly. He wrapped large hands around my waist and pulled me out of the water as he spun, shouting, "He says to run!" Then he was carrying me back the way we had waded, grabbing his older brother and dragging him along, barrelling past the rest of our collection team and screaming an ear-splitting warning.

From my awkward position clinging to Lad's broad shoulder, I saw the sewer cave in. The walls of the tunnel did not simply crack under pressure, their centuries-old mortar crumbling away, and to my once architect-trained eyes it did not look like the result of a disruption in the pion systems holding the whole place together. Even though I had spent most of my life constructing buildings out of formless stone, I had never seen anything like what was happening in the tunnel behind us. I beat fists against Lad's back – though he probably couldn't even feel me – and yelled at the team to keep up with us, to run.

The tightly laid stones were dissolving. The walls, the floor, the ceiling, the whole sewer tumbled to sand, to mud, to a rush of air that washed hot over my face. And the fetid water we had been wading through for bells first boiled, then steamed, then seemed to dry into nothing.

"What's happening?" Kichlan – still being dragged by Lad and just as unable to escape that vice-grip as I – tried to look behind him as he ran, and slipped and smacked his shoulder against the tight stone walls. Lad did not slow down, not even to help his brother.

"Other's wasted hells!" Mizra held Sofia's hand – the small woman had enough trouble walking through the sewerage, let alone running for her life – and was bounding through the water, his pale face ghostly in the dim, vent-filtered light. "Hells!"

His twin brother Uzdal was trying to do the same for Natasha, but the usually apathetic woman was moving fast, and doing her best to shake his clutching weight from her wrist.

"They'll make it!" I hollered to Kichlan. He slipped again, knocked his knees against a raised ledge and barked a curse.

The roof slid down and the walls fell in and countless tonnes of earth piled in after them. We had come so close to being crushed and boiled in all that chaos. The Keeper had, somehow, warned us all in time.

Then again, he had led us down here in the first place.

Lad stopped suddenly, jarring my chest against his shoulder and knocking the breath from my lungs. "Says we are safe here," he whispered, close to my ear. He was shivering, not only with the exertion of carrying me and dragging Kichlan. There was a terrified cold clamminess to his skin. As quickly as he had collected me he let me go, and I fell unprepared into the filth at his feet.

"Tan!" Strong hands hauled me up. "You okay, Tan?"

"I am." I patted Lad's arms and wiped more of the thick, putrid sludge from my clothes. "Thanks to you."

"He told me." Lad kept his voice low. "Said we had to run." He paused. "Really wants to talk to you now."

I could see the Keeper if I allowed my suit to spread from its six silver bands and cover all of me, but Lad could hear him all the time. He was a Half, belonging partly to this world and partly to the Keeper's, always in the centre of a tug of war between them both. It accounted for his childishness, for the quickness of his temper and the brightness of his smile.

And it wasn't fair. We used him, the Keeper used him, and he never really understood any of it.

"I'm sure he does." But I did not obey the Keeper's summons instantly. Instead – as I caught my breath and wrung water from my scarf – I turned to survey the tunnel behind us.

"What was that?" Kichlan stood beside me. He touched my elbow, the gentlest caress of fingertips, and I leaned against him to let him know I wasn't hurt.

"Why are we standing here?" Mizra, his voice too high and far too loud in this place with its sharp acoustics, was still holding onto Sofia. "We need to get out of here. Now!"

"Is safe now," Lad murmured.

"How do you know that?" Uzdal asked. He sounded much calmer than his twin brother.

"Because the Keeper told him," I answered. "Just as he warned us."

"And we can trust your Keeper." Doubts weighed Kichlan's voice, kept quiet so only I could hear.

I glanced up and met Kichlan's dark brown eyes. *My* Keeper?

"Wants to talk to you," Lad said.

Needs to learn some patience too. But I nodded and released the bonds on my suit.

Silver crawled cool and solid up along my legs, across my abdomen and chest, down arms and over shoulders. The sewer disappeared as the suit enveloped my chin, mouth, nose, and eyes, and was replaced by doors. I hated that moment, that instant between real world and the shadowed, door-riddled place the Keeper called home. But my suit longed for it, and as it wrapped me in its mask, the constant tug, the ever-present discomfort of metal in my bones eased into something like pleasure.

To say it was unsettling would be an understatement.

The Keeper leaned against a cracked and weathered-looking door, watching me anxiously. While he looked like a naked, hairless man with black eyes and thin, pale skin, he was actually debris – but quite a different form to the small lumps of floating darkness we collected.

The door loomed tall above me, curving slightly overhead with the shape of the sewer wall. It appeared to be built from large planks of rough timber, stained mahogany faded by age, with a twisted copper handle turning green. It shook as though battered by a fierce wind, straining its rusted hinges and splintering cracks through the wood.

"This is the beginning," the Keeper said, and I wondered at his emotionless calm.

Features slowly formed on the doors: the real world, bleeding through in faint outlines. Kichlan, by Lad's side; Mizra, Uzdal and Sofia huddled in the sewer's shallow; Natasha, rubbing her wrist. My collecting team, insubstantial, like light projected against the wood.

I glanced around us. So many doors, just like this one, all tall and rattling. They crowded each other, allowing only slivers of darkness between them. This other world, this dark and door world, rumbled with the thumping of wood, the squealing of hinges, and the protest of handles.

"What happened to the sewer?" I had to shout over their ruckus bang-bang-banging. "Why do you keep bringing us down here?" My throat felt dry, the words scraping. "You put Lad in danger."

The sound pounded into me, reverberating through the suit that coated my body. I ached to leave this place, to draw in the smooth metal that encased me so I didn't have to listen to that sound. And feel it.

I held the Keeper's gaze, my silver mask reflected in the liquid black of his eyes.

"I have been looking for one, just the right one, to show you." The Keeper, for all his transparent skin and the dark lines of debris flowing visible through him, still managed a powerfully shamefaced expression. It was a skill he cultivated, each time he used Lad to call me to this world at the back of my collecting suit. "I'm sorry, but the doors are weaker underground, closer to the old city and the places that are even more ancient than that. So I had to bring you down here, because you need to see."

I approached the Keeper and the door, no longer aware of the push of water. The large step out from the sewer to a thin ledge was easy to make with the suit giving strength to my legs and reach to my arms.

"The rest of your team should draw back." The Keeper lifted his hand from the wood and stepped away.

Dimly, I could hear Lad pass the Keeper's warning on, and Mizra's panicked, high-pitched response.

Something tickled a warning in my bones as I leaned forward and peered at the wood I knew wasn't actually wood, at the handle that didn't exist, at the hinges screwed only into darkness. The feeling travelled from the suit's second skin in pinpricks of fear, and a sense that this was very wrong.

"Do not fear. I will close it this time."

I almost missed it. It was the tiniest of cracks, barely wide enough to fit a fingernail through, but the door was open.

"It begins."

A breeze slid through the gap to brush against my face, the lightest touch of air and–

–and it seized the silver that coated my face, it clutched at me so I could barely move, hardly breathe. That soft air drilled down through the layer of impenetrable metal to scorch my skin. I pulled back. It grabbed me, dragged me up against the rough wood so I was pressed to the small crack while invisible tendrils of air like fire, like ice, tore at the suit, penetrated down, further down to my skin, to my muscle and bone and–

–the Keeper closed the door. One handed, with no apparent effort, the gentle twitching of his wrist.

Released, I fell back, crashed onto stone and into water. Around me, inside me, my suit cried and rolled, discordant and painful. It clenched every part of me, like it was patting me down, making sure we were both still there, together, and the breath beyond that door hadn't torn us apart.

Stormwater lapped at my ears. Lying in sewerage, I stared up at the Keeper's sad face. I was dimly aware of Kichlan shouting, of his hands slipping for purchase on my suit-wrapped arms.

The bastard could have warned me, could have just told me, described, not dragged us through shit for moons just to, to–

I thought of the sewer dissolving behind us, the boiling and the steaming of rock. Was that a warning, an illustration? Had he allowed the door to open long enough to almost flatten us, bury us, just to make his point?

Was that what would happen to Movoc-under-Keeper if its doors opened?

I forced control over my body and my suit. My mouth tasted like dirt and blood. I levered myself upright, shook off Kichlan. Lad let out a low, broken moan and I remembered what I had read in a hidden basement library, in an ancient book written with debris instead of ink.

Fear for everything.

Kichlan left to calm his brother, and again I climbed to the unsteady sewer edge.

The Keeper still rested against the wood. Wood, I reminded myself, which was not wood at all. That door was debris, and it had once been part of the Keeper. But now, due to the pion manipulation that built the city above us, it had been stripped from the Keeper's control. He'd warned us, he'd told us that the doors were a gateway between worlds, and he existed to ensure they remained closed.

"That was the other world, wasn't it?" I asked. My voice sounded too loud, my suit and skin both brittle and thin.

"The worlds are divided," the Keeper said. "Dark world, Light world."

Yes, so I had read. And the Keeper alone could maintain the balance.

"So that was darkness from the other world?"

He shook his head. "Not darkness, nothingness. This world is solid." He cupped his fingers as though trailing water. "That world is not. If they come together, both will be destroyed." He drummed a beat on the wood. It echoed through my head. "This is the beginning."

And he was gone.

Feeling thin, strung out, I withdrew my suit, dragging it back into the bands at my wrists, ankles, waist and neck. It resisted, tugging at my muscles and bones, setting my skin twitching.

"What happened?" Kichlan was right in front of me. He grabbed my arm as my suit retracted and searched my face as though he might find the answer tattooed there, his expression frightening and shadowed in the steam-heavy sunlight filtering down from a grate above us.

"Gone," Lad said, quiet and glum.

"It was—" I stuttered, not at all sure what to say to make them understand. I didn't really know myself. "An open door."

"What does that mean?" Sofia hissed. "You should have seen yourself, Tanyana. I thought you were mad, jerking around like someone had you on strings. And when you fell like that, I thought you were hurt!"

I smiled at her. "Worried about me?"

"Of course." She lifted her nose.

"It was scary. And ripply." Lad, eyes very wide, skin very pale, could have been mistaken for a ghost. "I didn't like it."

"Neither did I." I stroked his forearm. "What do you mean ripply?"

He made wave motions with his hands. Ever-helpful.

"The suit," Kichlan translated. "When you started... moving, like that, and just before you fell. The suit did some very strange things."

"Ripply is a good word," Sofia said. Lad beamed his bright smile at her.

"It is." Kichlan wiped sludge from his knees and jacket sleeves. "It looked almost liquid, like ripples in a pond. Except, that's not quite right."

"I'd say sand." Natasha, to my surprise, offered her own interpretation. "Lots of shifting grains of sand."

The hard, pliable metal of my suit changed to shifting grains of sand? "The open door destroyed the sewer. It dissolved it, right down to its pion bonds." Right down to the pions themselves? What had happened to the pions in the sewer, what had started happening to the pions in my suit? Times like this I wished I could still see them. "And it started doing the same thing to me. Undoing me." Turning me to sand, to liquid. To nothing.

Mizra stepped away from me, hands raised, as though the nothingness that had destroyed the sewer and taken hold of me might be contagious. Uzdal scowled at him and shoved him forward.

Cautiously, Lad took my hand. His none-too-gentle squeeze was an unspoken offer of support. I stretched to brush cobwebs from the mess of his blonde hair.

Together, we stared at the rubble that had once been a sewer. Water was starting to pool around the earth and jagged stone. Sooner or later the sewer would flood, and the veche would be forced to employ architects to rebuild it. Would they wonder what had caused it? Would the wrongness of it all – the missing material, the heat-warped stone, and tangled, ruined pion systems – warn them that something terrible was happening in Movoc-under-Keeper, something they needed to stop?

"The Keeper brought us down here to see this." My words sent the heavy, pungent steam coming off the sewerage tumbling away from my mouth. "The door was opening, and he didn't shut it, not straight away. So we could see this."

Kichlan spat into the fetid water. "I knew it." He scowled, face flushed with anger beneath smears of muck and what was left of a spider that had foolishly tried to crawl on his cheek. "Your Keeper is dangerous."

I didn't answer. What, really, could I say?

"Spitting like that is a delightful habit," Uzdal, hand still on his brother's back, made a disgusted face.

"It's a sewer," Kichlan growled. "I'm hardly going to get any dirtier, am I?"

"Can we leave now?" Lad asked. "He's gone." He lifted a leg. "And it's wet and stinks."

"Best thing I've heard all day." Mizra needed no further encouragement to hurry back the way we had come.

I was too weak to push myself through the flow so quickly. Almost as large as his younger brother, Kichlan lent me his strength, one hand on my shoulder, one on an elbow, keeping me balanced and moving.

"There are so many doors," I whispered to him. "And he said this was the beginning. If they all open..." I didn't need to say it.

"Then we need to do something about it." He started to spit again, cast me a guilty look and stopped. "But that involves helping that Keeper of yours. Following him, listening to him. Trying to make sense of what he says."

And that was the problem.

When we emerged – wet, filthy, and fatigued – and returned to our sublevel rooms, the veche was waiting. They stood under the decrepit awnings on Darkwater, creating a rough semicircle around the locked door. Two technicians, one of whom I knew. Two collectors like us, though I recognised neither of them. And two puppet men, pale, expressionless, looking damned near inhuman to me.

Lad flinched at the sight of them and huddled against his brother. I forced myself to keep a steady pace, to show no apprehension, and meet Devich's eyes squarely. I was proud of that. But I did not look at the puppet men, their wooden faces and emotionless, mouldy-green eyes; or the seams I had seen running along their skin, between mouth and chin, jaw and neck, along the hairline, like they were wearing masks, sewn on.

"What do you want?" I didn't even pretend politeness. Not for Devich.

One of the new collectors cast me a surprised glance. He was a broad-chested man, wrapped in a thick leather coat and a head-hugging cap that could not hide an ugly-looking scar running diagonally across his forehead, nose and cheek.

Fair enough, I supposed. The technicians that fitted our suits were employed by the veche and had considerable influence over our lives. They could inspect us on a whim, and even send us back to the horror of the suiting table like machines to be serviced. It would therefore be prudent to be polite to the men who could, if they desired, clamp us down and inject us with the Other only knew what.

And that didn't even take the puppet men into account. They reported directly to the national veche, to the most powerful members of the most powerful families in all of Varsnia. Unless you knew better, you'd think they might deserve some kind of respect.

We, of course, knew better.

Puppet men was not, strangely enough, their official title. With their wooden faces and seamed, ill-fitting skin, they reminded me of puppets. That, and the way they seemed to pull all the strings. They were directly responsible for the debris outbreak that had almost destroyed Movoc-under-Keeper not two moons ago, and they had done so simply to test new collecting suits. Suits like mine. They toyed with debris like vicious cats with damaged mice, and even though the Keeper had warned them not to, had begged them, they continued to do so. With each twisting, screaming, bleeding creature they tore from the Keeper's control, another door grew.

Devich cleared his throat. He looked anxious, and thinner than I remembered him, his skin a sickly sallow colour. Good. I didn't believe his guilt-ridden, remorseful act for an instant, but at least it looked like he was suffering. Lying, veche-spawn bastard.

"The veche has, ah, come to a decision." Something in

Devich's rich green eyes pleaded for understanding. They ached in his formal expression, begged me to understand why he had been *forced* to seduce me, to betray me, and cast me to the claws of the puppet men; why I should forgive him.

Those eyes could swim with emotion all they liked. I wasn't interested.

"A decision about what?" Kichlan passed his brother to Mizra and Sofia. Between them, they worked to keep him calm. The last thing we wanted was for Lad to draw attention to himself.

Because if those puppet men realised he was anything more than the usual collector – that he could hear the Keeper's voice – they would take him away. And Kichlan, I knew, would never let that happen. Not while he was still alive and in one piece.

I really didn't want to see that tested.

"Your team has failed to meet quota for two moons now," one of the puppet men said.

"The veche believes you would benefit from fresh blood," the second said, in the same voice.

"And to this end, your collecting team has been disbanded."

The words hit me like a kick in the gut. If they wore any human expression, I was certain the puppet men would gloat. As it was, they simply watched us impassively.

"Bro?" Lad whimpered like an injured animal.

Numb, I turned. Kichlan had blanched a kind of sickly white, and for the first time since I had known him, he looked afraid. Not snappish, not ruthlessly organised and stoic. He looked as helpless – as frightened – as his brother.

"Your new postings." The second technician held a

small stack of cards. Paper of any kind was rare, because most people corresponded with pions instead. Debris collectors like us, however, who couldn't see those bright particles that everyone else manipulated, could not rely on messages written in their lights and projected from small glass slides.

Where would the puppet men send us? They could disperse us to the edges of Varsnia if they wanted. Or would they send us to the colonies? Did they even need debris collectors on the frontiers?

"Tan?" Lad tugged against Mizra's hold.

"Oh, come now."

I spun. Both puppet men were fixed on me, empty eyes boring through my skin to the suit in my very bones. It seemed to tighten under their scrutiny; the band between my sleeve and glove spun faster, symbols crowding each other and desperately shifting form. I folded my hand into a fist and forced the suit back under my control.

"Nothing to be concerned about." Was that the hint of a smile I caught? The splitting of a seam from mouth to nose?

"Take your cards."

"Return home."

"New teams must meet in the morning."

As one, the puppet men stepped into the street. With a last glance, their faces on the cusp of some terrible smile, they walked away along Darkwater.

The second technician fluttered around us, glancing at the backs of the puppet men, apparently uncertain of the protocol. "Your new rooms have been fitted." He peered at cards, at faces, and passed them out with care. When he pressed the small square into my palm it tore at the corner. Cheap stuff. I peered down at it as though through mist, and struggled to make sense of the words scrawled in already-fading ink.

> *Toplevel, 34 Ironlattice*
> *7th Effluent, Section 12*

Seventh Effluent? Close to the room I leased from an aging and rather food-obsessed woman. Too close to be a coincidence.

Devich approached me on silent feet, and stood near. He leaned forward, and I stepped back.

"You don't need to fear," he whispered. "They have invested so much in your suit they will want to watch you, constantly, so they won't send you too far away."

Did he think – in his twisted, cowardly way – that made me feel better?

"Breakbell," the other technician was saying. "Breakbell tomorrow. Don't be late."

"We know how this works," Kichlan responded, his voice harsh.

The technician flinched, shocked, before handing the last of his cards to the new, scarred collector and hurrying to follow the puppet men.

Devich watched them go for a moment before grabbing at my arm. "Tanyana, listen to me, please I have to show you." I yanked my arm from his grasp and stepped further away, hands raised and suit spinning. He didn't seem to care, just began tugging up his own sleeve, all the while muttering and pleading. "Just look. And listen. You have to believe me, you have to–"

"Get away from her!" Kichlan shouted. Devich's fearful expression darkened into ugly hatred. But in the face of Kichlan so pale and furious Devich did nothing more than squeeze his hand into a frustrated fist, and turn into Darkwater after his fellow. I forced myself to look away from Devich's hunched back, and the furtive glances he cast over his shoulder. He'd seemed afraid, genuinely afraid. But how could I possibly believe anything Devich said? So I pushed him out of my mind.

"That got rid of him." The scarred collector grinned at Kichlan, apparently undeterred by his haggard, grey-skin look. He cradled his card in his palms, strangely gentle. When Kichlan said nothing, the man turned to me.

I found myself fascinated by the scar dividing his nose. Scars were rare in Movoc-under-Keeper; a healer can fix most wounds so they leave no trace. I knew that, because the left side of my face, from forehead to chin and my neck, chest, hip and leg, were riddled with scars of my own. So I smiled back at him and wondered how had he fallen into this low life, and what had given him that scar.

Perhaps, like me, they were the same thing.

"Breakbell?" He rubbed his nose, and I averted my eyes, hoping I had not made him self-conscious. "Well, that'll take an effort. Come on then, Fedor." He gestured to the second collector. A thin man, sickly-looking and staring blankly at the cobblestones. He didn't even notice the card in his hand. "Early morning, I think."

Then he nodded at me, tried another smile on Kichlan, and steered Fedor out into the street. I realised I did not know his name.

"Come on." Sofia unlocked the sublevel door. "I'll help Kichlan, you look after Lad."

Both Kichlan and his brother were shaking. Lad quivered with cold and fear. Kichlan, however, radiated fury. His hands clenched over the board, crushing it. As I coaxed Lad down the stairs, I was aware of Kichlan's presence at my back like a wild and dangerous animal.

Mizra, Uzdal and Natasha followed.

The sublevel was empty. Gone were the couches we had lounged on, gone the shelves and tables for the debris collecting jars. Bars had been fitted to the windows near the ceiling. The fireplace Kichlan and Lad had uncovered, where they had cooked us kasha on cold mornings, had been filled in. All in a day, all while we were following the call of the Keeper.

I did not know this place, not anymore. Lad began to cry.

"They've split us into two," Mizra said. His words echoed sharply in the empty room.

"What?" Sofia was staring at Kichlan. She held her small scrap of board to her chest and her hands were quivering, like she was cold. "In two?"

One by one, Mizra took our cards, read them, gave them back. "Two new teams. One's still in the eighth Keepersrill, different street though. The other's the seventh Effluent."

Kichlan jerked his head up at that. "We should have known this would happen." His dark eyes pierced me, and I knew he and I were thinking the same thing. This was not chance. This was a message. "The veche wouldn't just leave us be."

I approached him, careful and slow. "Show me your card, Kichlan."

He shook as he dropped the torn board into my palm. "What have we been doing, these past two moons?" he hissed between clenched teeth. "Pretending everything is normal? Listening to your Keeper, collecting the scraps he deemed to toss our way? Following his pointless instructions? We knew they would come, and we weren't ready!"

Gently, I pried the card open. I pieced the words together.

"What more could we do?" Sofia whispered.

"Eighth Keepersrill," I read out loud, and my heart sunk somewhere closer to my stomach.

"Oh no," Mizra said, voice defeated. I looked over my shoulder. He stood beside Lad, and held his card. "They split up Uz and me." He face was shadowed, almost expressionless. "They did the same to you."

"What?" Kichlan's voice was little more than breath.

"They split you and Lad up. You're in different collecting teams."

Kichlan swayed. I grabbed his shoulder, terrified he would fall. Lad let out an injured wail and ran to his brother's side. He wrapped arms around Kichlan's waist and hunched over to bury his head in his older brother's chest.

Kichlan stroked Lad's hair. I met his eyes and knew this was my fault. If I hadn't been sent here, if I hadn't disobeyed the puppet men and sided with the Keeper, then Lad would not be in this danger.

"They can't," Kichlan murmured. "I'm supposed to be with him, always. I'm supposed to keep him safe."

"I'll look after him." I mouthed the words, not sure he would hear me even if I spoke.

But Kichlan whispered, rueful, his voice bare. "And who will look after you?"

The veche had divided us with disturbing efficiency. Mizra from Uzdal; Lad from Kichlan. Kichlan from me.

Were we really so fragile?

Kichlan, Uzdal and Sofia had been sent to the new address in the eighth Keepersrill. Lad, Mizra, Natasha and I were to go to the seventh Effluent. The two new collectors had to fit into that arrangement, but we didn't know how.

So we farewelled the sublevel a final time. Kichlan left the keys on the inside doorstep, locking the door before pulling it closed. Then we dispersed, quiet and broken.

Was it really so easy for the puppet men to defeat us?

My collecting team gave me strength. With them behind me I had stood up to the puppet men and refused to become the weapon they wanted. They were more than a substitute for my lost critical circle, more than a group of fallen people I had no choice but to work with. They had given me somewhere to belong, when the rest of the world felt alien.

None more so than Kichlan and Lad.

I watched their backs as the brothers disappeared down Darkwater. They huddled together, two damaged men. And I hated it. I hated that I could not be their strength, when they needed it.

Hunched into my jacket, hands fists in my pockets, I returned home.

Valya knew something was wrong the instant I entered her kitchen. She was a large, old woman, constantly cooking, ever-aproned but with sharp eyes and an even sharper mind. She stood by her kitchen bench, holding a sticky-looking knife and watching the door. Sweetness cloyed the room.

"Pudding," Valya said. "Because I think you need it."

How could she have known that, before I even arrived?

"Sit." She turned back to the bench and I collapsed into a chair beside the large dining table that dominated the room. She fussed for a moment longer before placing a substantial slice of carrot, prune and apple pudding in front of me, dotted liberally with thick cream, and steaming.

My stomach growled with appreciation, but I didn't eat. I watched her serve herself a much smaller slice, then sit opposite me. Pudding for evenbell supper was odd, even by Valya's standards.

"Eat," she said, and picked up her spoon. "Something happened today."

The pudding was moist and sweet, but I barely tasted it. "How do you know that?"

"Knew it was coming." She kept her eyes on my food, followed each spoonful like a cat with string. "Not blind. We have seen the signs."

I stared at her, blankly. "Signs? What signs?"

She made a scornful little noise. "You are not a fool, so do not talk like one. The doors are fragile. We have all felt them."

The doors! "You're talking about the Keeper. The door he showed me." It should have felt strange to me, that the dissolution of our collecting team hurt more than the possible dissolution of an entire city. But it did.

"Of course." She scowled. "What else?"

"How much do you know about him?"

"What we need to know, to keep this world safe." She pointed violently at my half-empty plate with her spoon and I hurried to keep eating. "But what else happened today, what could be more important?"

I swallowed a too-large piece and my cheeks warmed. The scars along the left side of my face tightened, even now. "Those men, who work for the veche." What had she called them? "Their creatures." Creatures was a good term.

She muttered something I was thankful I didn't hear. She knew who I meant.

"They split us up, our collecting team."

She did not look devastated.

"Lad, and Kichlan, you remember them?"

She nodded. "Of course."

"They're in different teams now, Kichlan can't look after..." I trailed off. "It's complicated."

I finished my food under Valya's stern gaze. When she released me to my quarters above her house, I was full and feeling slightly ill from the heavy pudding. The warmth of the kitchen rose to fill my rooms, bringing cinnamon and prune scents with it, which did not help.

I managed to hang my jacket and strip my outer layer of clothes before heavy steps rattled the unsteady iron staircase that led up to my door. I knew that step, and dragged a shapeless woollen shirt and pants over my boned, skin-tight uniform as Kichlan knocked.

I wasn't surprised to see him, but I hadn't expected him so soon.

"Eugeny is looking after Lad," he said, as I opened the door and let him in. He sniffed. "Smells nice."

"Only if you haven't had a piece big enough for three men force fed to you." I smiled at him, but he only twitched the corners of his mouth in return.

"What are we going to do?" He sat at my small, round table, still swathed in his patched-up coat. I guessed he wasn't feeling the warmth from the kitchen below. Perhaps he wasn't feeling anything at all.

We'd been here before. Since we'd discovered the

Keeper, and the puppet men had revealed themselves, we'd asked that question many times. Still, I didn't have an answer.

The only difference was that now we really needed one.

What could we do? Those seamed, expressionless bastards were members of the national veche, Varsnia's highest authority. We didn't even know how many there were – and it was difficult to tell, they all looked the same. How was a bunch of bottom-of-the-social-rung debris collectors – who spoke to an invisible man most people believed was a long-dead superstition – supposed to prove the veche was putting the entire world in danger?

So I hoped, instead, that Kichlan was talking about something I could answer.

"I told you, I will look after him." I crossed my arms over my chest. "I'm not his brother; I can't be a replacement for you. I know that. But I don't want him to suffer either, or be taken away."

Kichlan watched me. His eyes were guarded, mouth set in a heavy line teetering on the edge of a frown. It was always the same with him. He held so many walls around himself, he kept the world at a distance, all to ensure his brother's safety. And after so many years he had trouble recognising the appropriate time to let down those barriers, or the right people to let in.

"You know better than that," he said, and I tried not to take offence at the rough edge to his tone. "He's big, he's strong, what will you do if he becomes violent?"

Yes, I had seen it happen. Gentle, child-like Lad turned to a terrifying and furious man for no reason the rest of us could understand. But I unfurled a hand and allowed my suit to seep solid and silver to my fingertips. It caught the flickering of gas lamps as I slowly turned it. Valya, like Kichlan and Lad's landlord, refused to rely on pion power to light her home, or heat her water, or cook her meals. So she tapped into the old gaslines that ran beneath the city – which couldn't be safe, and surely wouldn't run forever in this new pion-powered age.

Kichlan looked away. He knew that with the control I had over my suit, I was stronger than Lad, and far stronger than Kichlan could ever be.

"We know more about Lad, and what happens to him, now than ever." I tried to sound reasonable, and withdrew the suit. "The voices he didn't understand, the things that used to upset him. We know who that is. We can calm him."

"The Keeper." Kichlan spat the word with the same vehemence Valya had bestowed upon the puppet men.

"Exactly." I tried to be the voice of reason in the centre of Kichlan's storm. "And I can talk to the Keeper too. So I can look after Lad."

Kichlan rested his hands on the table, tapped hard with his fingers, pushed the chair out, stood, and began pacing. I should have known it was only a matter of time before the pacing started. "It's not just voices, Tanyana. How will Lad get to this new address? I can't send him on his own. It wouldn't take much for him to get lost, and then scared, and maybe even angry. I don't know what he'd do–"

Two long strides and I was by his side. I touched his arm and froze him mid-pace. "We will work something out, Kichlan. I'll come and get him, or we'll meet half way."

"This is tomorrow, you realise!"

"I do. And we'll work it out, isn't that why you're

here?" I smiled at him, and was finally able to pry one out of him. "What Lad needs most of all is the support of his brother, like he always has. And you can't give it to him if you're railing and panicking. He needs you to be calm."

"I'm not panicking."

I laughed and leaned back. "Oh really? Doing a good imitation then."

"I'm..." He paused, thought for a moment, then said with a grin, "fretting."

"Well warn me if that's about to change. If this is fretting, I'd like to get as far away as possible before panic happens."

Suddenly his smile was gone. He gripped my shoulders, his fingers pressing hard into the strong, reinforced uniform beneath my woollen shirt. He leaned in close, eyes bright and intense. I wanted to back away, but couldn't move my legs.

"I can't let you go either," he whispered. His breath was hot. "Another team, where I can't be. You and Lad, together. You don't understand, do you? I need to be with you, I need to know you are safe. Both of you."

My heart beat too loud, too fast in my ears. My mouth felt dry and my stomach knotted and something at the back of my mind chimed in with a quiet: "Shouldn't you be more worried about the Keeper, Tanyana?" But I could hardly hear it, and easily pushed it aside.

"Kichlan, I–"

Someone knocked on the door.

For a moment we remained frozen, Kichlan holding my shoulders, his breath on my face, our eyes locked. Then the knock again, harder. We broke away.

Kichlan folded his arms, and turned his back on me as I hurried to open the door. The cold night air was welcome as it rushed inside. I felt too hot beneath my uniform, prickly and uncomfortable.

Valya stood at the top of her unsafe iron stairs, wrapped in a padded jacket and shawl, as though the quick trip up one level required wrapping up. Yicor stood behind her and grinned widely at me as I gaped at them both.

"Time to talk," Valya said, and pushed her way inside. It was her room, after all.

Yicor took my hand, pressed it between fur gloves. "If you would be so kind," he said, an apology and a plea in his eyes.

I let him pass. As I closed the door Valya was peering up at Kichlan – who looked just as shocked as I felt – and nodding. "You are here too, good."

Kichlan caught sight of Yicor, and his surprise slid into disapproval. "What's going on?" He had never liked the old shop owner who had helped me find Valya when I had nowhere else to go.

Possibly because, even though he could see debris, the man was not a collector. Neither was Valya. They had escaped the puppet men and the violence of being suited, when the rest of us had not. Kichlan said collecting was our duty, and doing otherwise was irresponsible. Somehow, I didn't believe that was what truly bothered him about the man. Rather, I think he wished Lad could have escaped too.

"Time for talk," Valya said. She grabbed Kichlan and dragged him back to the chair. "Then time for action. Can't wait any longer."

I fixed Yicor with a stern expression. "This is about the signs, isn't it?"

He gave a sheepish, guilty look. "Ah, I should have known you'd work it out."

"Signs?" Kichlan allowed himself to be seated – though I couldn't see what choice he had – and scowled at us over his shoulder.

"You might know them as being nearly crushed in a collapsing sewer," I explained, as Yicor and I obeyed Valya's imperious gestures, and joined Kichlan at the suddenly crowded table. "And what the Keeper's door did to my suit."

"The Keeper. Again."

"Watch your tone," Vlaya snapped. "Be thankful for him. Without him, we would all be lost."

Would we, I wondered? Could the Keeper really help us now?

"The Unbound have always been guided by the Keeper," Yicor said.

In the old tongue, in a time of legends and stories and myths, that was what we would be. Unbound by pions. Unbound by society. Unbound and outcast. Now, we were debris collectors. I was still struggling to work out if that was an improvement.

"Our predecessors saw the world changing," he continued. "When Novski and his critical circles harnessed the true power of pions and upset the balance, they knew it would be trouble. Since before history our kind has worked with the Keeper to hold the doors closed. And they knew, the more pions are manipulated, the more debris is created. More doors. But the veche would not listen to our pleas."

"Turned us into refuse collectors instead," Valya said with frightening venom.

"They broke us up, they mutilated us." Yicor pointed to the suit bright on my wrist. I fought an urge to cover it with my sleeve. "Silenced us. But some fled, took what relics they could, and hid. Two hundred years we have hidden. So much was lost. Elders discovered, taken away. Halves experimented on, their voices silenced."

From the corner of my eye, I saw Kichlan shiver.

"We few do what we can. Keep the texts, and look for those who can listen."

"Such as you," Valya said.

"We have tried to keep some small memory safe, some small part of a lost history. But with each year there are fewer. With each year, the veche men grow stronger. And now it is too late. If we do not stop them, the doors will be open."

"Fear for everything," I whispered. And shifted my gaze to Kichlan. "Which leads us back to the same problem."

He nodded, grim. "It does."

"What can we do against the veche men?"

Valya smacked the table. "We must do something."

"I know." I rubbed at my eyes and only then realised how tired I was.

"The veche men know about the Keeper," Kichlan said, and all attention turned to him. "He told you, didn't he–" he glanced at me, and I nodded "–and Tanyana saw it with her own eyes, heard it with her own ears. They know, they hear him, they speak to him, but they don't believe him. Or they don't care."

But Yicor and Valya didn't seem to hear. Instead, they both stared at me, almost reverential.

"You have seen the Keeper?" Valya whispered.

"You have spoken with him?" Yicor murmured.

I nodded, wary.

They shared a glance. "Then it was good, that we found you."

Kichlan and I shared a glance. Didn't they understand? What exactly, did they think we could do?

"We will help you," Valya said. "We are already working against them, moving in shadow, infiltrating. Readying to attack. You will join us." She scratched yellow nails across the tabletop to clutch at my hand. Kichlan stared in horror at her wrinkled, bony talons and drew back. "And this time, with you here, this time we will win."

2.

I leaned against a newly repaired brick wall and watched a flock of Strikers glide by. Dressed in white leather, hooded, and surrounded by a ring of crimson-clad Shielders they were a splash of colour against Movoc's grey streets. I could only imagine what they would have looked like if I could still see pions. Solid colour, fierce lights; proud and deadly.

While this area of the city had not suffered as much as others in the debris outbreak two moons ago, it still bore scars. The wall I was leaning against was one. The puppet men had released a powerful fiend created by twisting and torturing a large amount of debris. This creature had critically interfered with the pion systems throughout the city, blocking sewerage ducts, shorting out heating and light streams, and ultimately undoing the foundations of the city themselves. The resulting damage was terrible, and still being repaired.

Several buildings on this street had collapsed when their pion systems unwound. There was still a gaping hole in the ground two blocks away, where a thread of heating pions had torn, backed up and eventually exploded in waves of heat and pressure. I'd eavesdropped on the few people who walked passed me, and learned that light had still not been restored to two large, bland apartment complexes across the road. No matter how many critical circles the veche sent to restore the buildings' systems new bindings refused to take. The pions were shallow and few.

"Unusual," Kichlan murmured, as he and Lad arrived. Lad watched the military men pass with wide eyes. Kichlan and I tried to be less obvious about it.

I straightened, and dusted sand and tiny stones from the brickwork off my shoulders. The veche needed better architects than whoever had constructed this shoddy piece of work. "Maybe there is more trouble on the border with the Hon Ji?"

"Isn't there always?" Kichlan gave a tight little shrug. "Still, Strikers. Seems like an overreaction."

Varsnia's relationship with her largest neighbour had always been fraught. Since Novski's critical circle revolution, few nations could compete with our pion-binding strength. But as the centuries passed, the others were catching up, and the stronger they grew, the braver they became. Hon Ji had established a coalition to lead the push against us. I'd heard of skirmishes in the frontier colonies – arguments over mining land, mostly – spies and intrigue I'd never fully understood, even the odd attempt to assassinate a low-ranking, new-family member of a colonial veche.

But this had been going on for years. It did not justify Strikers. I ran a light finger over the solid silver on my wrist. Neither did it justify the weapon the puppet men had created from me. After all, wasn't that what I was? A weapon that no other nation had, a way to wrest military and technological superiority back into Varsnian hands? That was why they had destroyed my life, my world, why they had tried to break me and very nearly succeeded. All for the glory of Varsnia.

Kichlan touched my elbow, ran his hand down my arm and pried my worrying fingers loose. "Time to go." Just as gently, he placed Lad's palm in my own.

The Strikers glided around a corner. Breakbell was fast approaching. "Yes, we'd better hurry."

"One day at a time." Kichlan patted his brother's back. "Be good for Tanyana, won't you."

"Will, bro." Lad squeezed me for emphasis. I tried not to wince. "You be good too."

I turned my face to hide a smile, as Kichlan's jaw slacked open.

"Let's go." I tugged Lad along. "Duskbell, right here?" I asked his brother over my shoulder.

Kichlan jammed fists into his pockets, hunched against the early-morning chill, and watched us leave.

I couldn't think about him like that, looking so lonely, so lost. I needed to concentrate on Lad.

"Wish we didn't have to do this, Tan." Lad pressed his body against mine. It made it difficult to walk in a straight line, but at least he was warm. "Don't like it."

"Me too. Me too."

With Lad attached to me, I headed back to the seventh Effluent. I noticed more rebuilding along the way. Effluents were generally poorer areas, and the buildings here reflected that. None of the graceful towers found in the wealthier Keepersrills – woven from steel and great shards of light-catching crystal – mostly squat apartments built with cheap blocks of rough stone and lathered with colourless cement. We passed a small factory struggling to produce furniture with most of their roof and half of one wall missing. The entire structure looked terribly unstable, given that we were unable to see the sturdy mesh of bright lights that was no doubt holding it up. Lad slowed, fascinated by the chair legs floating above several six point circles as they were carved by apparently invisible hands.

Thirty-Four Ironlattice lived up to its name. A tall, thin building with long, narrow windows, all wrapped in wrought iron topped with nasty-looking spikes. I baulked at it. Not only because it looked uninviting and almost impossible to get into, but because the old architect in me – never dead, despite Grandeur's best attempts – cried out for a merciful demolition at the very sight.

Lad quailed. "Doesn't look nice," he squeaked.

I craned my neck back to try and find the toplevel. All I found was more iron, and more spikes. "Help me look for a way inside."

Why did a building need so many windows, and why bother with them if you were just going to bar them all up? Together, Lad and I paced the thin strip of street, looking for something other than a ridiculously secure window that might be a way inside.

"Ah, I tried that," came a voice from my lower left. "I don't think it's possible."

I looked down. The scarred collector sat hunched against the dark wall of a neighbouring building. I had missed him. With his knees drawn up and his head lowered and his entire outfit the same kind of mud-brown as the cheap bricks, he was nearly impossible to see.

"Hello," Lad said, peering around me with evident curiosity. "Why are you sitting down there?"

The new collector laughed. He unfolded himself,
grasped the rough brickwork behind him and dragged
himself upright. "Seemed better than standing." He
brushed his dirty-coloured coat, and held out a hand.
"Aleksey," he said, with a wide smile that only empha-
sised his scar.

Lad released me long enough to grab his hand and
give it a far-too-vigorous shake, before reattaching himself to my arm. "I'm Lad," he said, as Aleksey blinked,
probably confused and not a little sore. "And my br–"
Lad hesitated, and looked down to his toes. "My bro's
not here."

Ah well, there went any attempt at pretence. But if
this Aleksey was going to be collecting with us he would
work out pretty quickly that Lad was not a normal man.
Whether we tried to hide it or not.

"Tanyana," I said. "And no, I'm not his brother." Lad
chuckled at my attempt at humour. Aleksey just lifted
his eyebrows. I couldn't loosen my right arm from Lad's
grip, so resorted to twisting my left around and touching Aleksey's fingers, smiling ruefully. "You're with us,
are you?"

"That's what the card says." I caught the roving of his
eyes, the way they touched on my eye and cheek, then
dipped to my neck between cap and coat collar, following the track the scars on my skin. I tried not to mind.
After all, I had done the same to him. "But it doesn't look
like the right building." He turned, placed hands on his
hips and tipped back to look at the uppermost heavily
barred windows. "Oh, actually–"

"Tanyana!" I looked up as Mizra's voice echoed down the street. He was waving a suit-bright hand out of a high window, between two of the bars. "Around the back!"

Ah, the ever-helpful veche and their light-on-the-details instructions.

Aleksey, Lad and I headed down a small side street and discovered a heavily barred – but helpfully unlocked – door. Natasha and Mizra waited for us in the toplevel. It was a wide, carpeted room with a low ceiling and no couches. Apart from the bare shelves awaiting full jars, and a table laden with empty ones, it looked nothing like the sublevel we were used to. Strangely, even with sunlight streaming in from windows that took up most of one wall, it felt darker and colder than the underground ever did.

Perhaps because Kichlan wasn't here.

"They gave *her* the keys," Mizra said in a disgusted voice as Aleksey opened a door at the top of the stairs and we all filed in.

"You can have them if you want." Natasha spun a set of iron keys hooked into a ring around her right index finger. "I couldn't care less."

"It's the principle," Mizra snapped. He folded his arms, cast about for a place to sit, found none and resorted to hunkering against a wall. "Even on my bad days, I'm a better collector than you. I could be asleep and still collect more debris than you do!"

"No offence taken," Natasha said, rolling her eyes.

"Tan," Lad whimpered. "I miss my bro."

Well, this was starting well.

"They also gave me this." Natasha threw a poly-wrapped

parcel at Aleksey, who fumbled with it, dropped it, and sheepishly bent to pick it up.

"What is it?" he asked.

"Uniform." Lad finally let go of me. He hiked up his right sleeve to show Aleksey the black, boned material underneath. "You need to wear it under your clothes, and all the time. Even when you're sleeping." He smiled at me, and I nodded encouragement.

"Why don't you and Mizra help Aleksey into his uniform," I offered.

"Have you been shown how to use your suit?" Mizra asked, as he and Lad stood between the new collector and Natasha and I.

"You mean these bands?" Aleksey said over the sound of torn poly. "Why do they call it a suit?"

"Here, let me show you."

Natasha and I turned our backs and stared out of a barred window in an attempt to give Aleksey some privacy. I felt his confusion keenly. Hardly four moons ago I was just like him. Scarred, alone in a new team, with a new life, and a living suit drilled into my bones.

"They should have given the keys to you," Natasha murmured.

I blinked down at her. Natasha was not usually so loquacious.

"Despite what Mizra thinks, you're the most capable collector among us. He might have been doing it for longer, but you're better at it."

"Ah, thanks." I'd never heard Natasha string so many words together before.

She shrugged. "Like I said, it doesn't bother me."

We stood for a moment in silence.

"Other's farts!" Aleksey hissed behind us, and Lad started giggling. "How did you do that? Where did the metal come from?"

I thought of cables wiggling beneath my flesh and tiny insect legs kicking between my bones. I resisted the urge to touch the silver notch at my ear, or trace the lines of metal beneath my uniform and clothes. They were all injuries the suit had healed, sewing them together with its wire until there were hard and solid.

My old scars were ribbed, white skin. My new scars were suited.

"So, do we have a new quota?" I said, more to hide the sounds of the conversation behind us, and busy my mind, than any real desire to know.

Natasha nodded. "Sixty jars every sixnight and one."

"Not as much."

"Not as many of us."

"Ah, but they don't realise how much Lad is worth," I tried, with false cheer.

Natasha said nothing.

"The metal won't come out." Disappointment in Aleksey's voice was clear, even with my back turned to him. "Does it normally work the first time?"

"For most people, no." Natasha turned abruptly, and approached the men. I followed her.

"Tan did," Lad said. He was tearing the discarded poly wrap into thin, transparent strips. "Hers was big when rocks fell on her and she was all right, even though it was a whole wall."

I smiled briefly, not really sharing his enthusiasm for the experience.

Aleksey's frustration became worry. His dark, tight

uniform stretched over broad shoulders and an even broader stomach that I hadn't noticed when he was wrapped in layers of clothes. It looked uncomfortable on him, like it wasn't really designed for someone so large. "That's not likely to happen, is it?"

My smile broke into something genuine. "Not if you're lucky."

Mizra snorted. "Don't take Tanyana as an example. The woman has the worst luck of anyone I've ever met." His eyes met mine briefly. We both knew it wasn't luck. It was veche machination and an overly enthusiastic Keeper that had dragged me to this low ebb in my life.

But we weren't about to explain the actual truth to Aleksey. And in a way, it was nice to pretend that this was all one big accident.

"Get your clothes on," Natasha said, collecting a thick shirt from the floor and passing it back to Aleksey. "We have a quota to fill. Can't stand around talking about Tanyana all day."

Mizra and I shared a shocked glance. Natasha actually wanted to head out and start collecting? Maybe the Keeper was right, and the world really was ending.

Natasha saw us and scowled. "Try not to act too surprised."

Lad chuckled softly.

We left Ironlattice and stood aimless in the street while Natasha locked the door. A few wrapped-up citizens of Movoc-under-Keeper hurried past. Movoc might be poor this far from the Keeper's Tear River and the city centre but it was not destitute, not shuffling toward death in a haze like the run-down areas at the very outskirts of the city. These were people with some pion-skill, but nothing special: cleaners, factory workers, underpaid and under-valued. We debris collectors rather belonged here.

"Bro normally works out which way we should go," Lad said, trying to be helpful, as Natasha peered along the street.

"Kichlan isn't here though, is he," she snapped.

Lad hung his head, so I took his hand.

It did feel strange to be doing this without Kichlan. He organised us, he kept us going even when the debris was hard to find and the day cold.

"Why don't we start with places that look broken?" Mizra offered. "We can work out a route later. Right now, we should at least get moving."

"This way." Natasha gestured down the street, away from the river.

Movoc-under-Keeper was built around the Keeper's Tear River, and spread out from it in a fan. The further you went from the river, the less kopacks its inhabitants earned. The less kopacks, the less the pion systems were maintained. And it was at poorly maintained pion systems that we were most likely to find debris. Without Kichlan's organisational skills – or Lad and the Keeper guiding us – it was the best plan we had. "Let's do it," I said. I meshed my fingers with Lad's and pulled him into a walk.

Our loose collecting team did not go unnoticed as we headed down the seventh Effluent. We stopped at lamps, we poked drains, we peered over fences and into gaps in walls. Before the debris disaster that had almost de-stroyed Movoc-under-Keeper we had done this, and not been seen. Debris collectors were shadows, invisible to most pion-binders because they simply did not want to see us. But they knew us now; all of Movoc knew it was

collectors who had saved them and that even though debris was rubbish clogging their precious pion-powered
city, it could be dangerous.

So now, we were watched.

A young woman in a thick grey shawl stopped at the
sight of us collecting a tiny cache of debris grains from the
inside of a crack where two buildings joined. She stood
across the street, gloved hands clasped at her chest, and
watched until we turned a corner. We walked by a run-
down coffee house. Conversation stopped. The scent of
burned, cheap coffee turned my stomach even more than
the regard of a dozen or so old men.

I couldn't decide which was worse – when the only
attention we generated was mess-on-the-bottom-of-my-
shoe looks, or this silent awe, this uncertain respect? It
made me nervous. Would it last? And what did they expect from us now? Saviours of the city carried greater
responsibilities than garbage collectors, even if we did
exactly the same thing.

Only Lad and Aleksey didn't notice the attention. Lad
hummed softly, hand holding mine, and scanned the
street for debris as we walked. I could sense his nervous-
ness, how much he hated doing this without his
brother's strong and protective presence by his side. It
travelled in little tremors from the dips and highs in his
tuneless song.

I squeezed his hand back, not sure what else I could
do to assure him that I was here, and I would look after
him. Just like Kichlan did.

Aleksey concentrated on his suit. He held the slowly
spinning, faintly glowing band on his wrist close to his
face. He peered at the symbols that bobbed in the not-

liquid, and scrunched his face into a parody mask of concentration. Trying to work out how to mesh those symbols together, how to induce them to rise and free themselves from the band, to spread across my hand in one shining–

"Tan?" Lad was staring at me, worried. "What are you doing, Tan?"

I glanced down. My suit had spread from my wrist to wrap us both in metal, and had even risen to cover my jacket sleeve. It looked so strange, like that. Bright metal from forearm to elbow, skin-tight and solid, then the thick material of my coat puffed out and wide.

"Sorry." I gritted my teeth and forced the suit back.

Lad disentangled himself. He stretched his fingers, flexed them, and caught my hand again. "It's warm, Tan," he said. "In your suit."

"Sorry, Lad. I didn't mean–"

He stopped in the middle of the street, eyes suddenly wide, expression distant.

I knew that look. The last thing we needed now was the Keeper dragging us on one of his pointless underground quests into who knew what kind of danger. Not in front of Aleksey. Not now, so soon after the door that had almost killed us. "Lad?"

His mouth moved, whispered words, and his gaze snapped suddenly to me. "Tan, he says he needs you, he says it has to be now! Oh hurry Tan, hurry!"

He tried to pull away, to set us running, but I tugged on his hand and he stopped, shocked. "Lad, listen to me."

"But he–"

"Remember yesterday; remember what nearly happened to us."

He ducked his head down, rubbed at his chin. "Saved us because we ran." He squeezed his eyes closed and shook his head. "He is very upset. Very much."

My throat felt tight, restricted. Was this fair on Lad, to turn him into a rope tugged between the Keeper and me? I had promised Kichlan I would care for him, even if that meant protecting him from the Keeper.

"And we will help him. But we will not run into danger again, we will not follow blindly." I paused. "Does he understand?"

Lad sniffed. "He is crying."

Great. "Let's go then, follow him. But we will walk."

Lad's idea of a walk stretched my arm until my shoulder socket hurt, and forced me into a trot. Natasha hurried to keep up, Mizra and Aleksey followed.

"What's going on?" Natasha hissed.

"Keeper." I glanced over my shoulder. Aleksey looked between us, puzzled, his gaze resting on Lad longer than I would have liked. I sighed.

Lad wound a complicated way through streets and back alleys, ducking under fences, pushing through gates, until I wasn't sure how we would find our way back, or even where in Movoc-under-Keeper we were. "Please, Tan," he hiccuped words and tears ran down his cheeks as he forced himself to walk, not to run. "Saying stuff and I don't understand and please, please, if you go he will be quiet."

What did the Keeper think he was doing?

"Is... Is he all right?" Aleksey sounded taken aback.

"He's Lad," Mizra answered, offering no further details.

The crumbling brickwork of the tight alley we were following widened, and Lad slowed. The worn paving stones beneath our feet were old, laced with cracks, puddled with stains and craters. A roof of corroded iron shadowed us from the weak Movoc sun, held up by a latticework of metal beams and stone pillars.

The whole structure looked like it could fall on us at any moment; it creaked and groaned at the slightest of draughts.

Lad dragged me toward a building hidden in the shadows of the roof. More cracked and stained stonework, windows of shattered glass like sightless eyes, broken tubing protruding from gangrenous holes in the walls. Lad pointed to a doorway, curtained by rusted strips of a disintegrated roller door. "Says to go in."

"–good spot for debris collecting." Natasha was explaining in a falsely reasonable, audibly strained voice. "Anywhere pion systems aren't working cleanly."

"But it looks dangerous," Aleksey said.

"It often is."

I turned. Natasha, Mizra and Aleksey hesitated at the end of the alleyway, not quite ready to brave the unsteady structure. "We will go ahead," I called to them. "No point risking all of us."

Natasha and Mizra nodded. Aleksey took a step forward. "Is that safe?" He glanced around. "Maybe I should–"

"No." Mizra and Natasha took an arm each, and guided him back to the relative safety of the alley.

"If we stay here," Mizra said.

"We can help them," Natasha said. "If something goes wrong."

"Need to hurry," Lad murmured in my ear.

I didn't have time to wait for Aleksey to be convinced,

so I allowed Lad to lead me around the sharp edges of the door's remains, and into the building.

It was a factory. Or, at least, it had been, many years ago. The charging machinery for compounded critical circles still remained.

Lad paused beside a nine point loop, momentarily distracted. He waved a hand beside his ear, muttering to himself, but still traced the loop's curling ceramic with his fingertips. "Tan?" He glanced at me, morose, torn, curious. "What is this?"

It was so rare for Lad to ignore the Keeper's pressure, to be able to do anything else than obey his voice. So the Keeper could just wait while I indulged him.

"This helps the people who used to work in this factory." The loop was old and splintered, but the general shape remained. Built of a pale ceramic, thin and delicate, it wound like a ribbon in a flower-petal pattern. Nine circles, all surrounding a tenth point in the centre where the ribbon knotted, thickened, and fed into a tube that plunged beneath the floor. "They work in teams of nine." I pointed to each of the circles. "A person would stand in each of these, and the last one in the middle. They would hold onto the loop." I clutched the ceramic only to feel it break against my hands. With a rueful smile I dusted white sand against my coat. "Then they'd send the pions that they charged along the loop, into the centre and down across the city's systems to warm up someone's home. At least, I think this was for heating."

Lad listened, avid. "Did you use one like this, Tan? Before you came to work with us?"

"No, Lad." I allowed myself a chuckle. "I didn't need one. I was stronger than that."

"Ah." Lad closed his eyes. "Have to hurry, says we shouldn't stop, shouldn't talk. Just hurry, hurry."

The moment was gone.

Lad led us deeper into the abandoned factory. Large, shattered glass sides still hung on the walls; the rotting wooden frames of tables and chairs huddled in a corner, covered in cobwebs and mold. Great holes let in light through the iron-mesh roof; the concrete beneath them eaten away by the elements. We stopped at one such crack in the floor.

"Wants to talk to you," Lad whispered. "Please."

My suit encased me gladly; tight and eager over my skin like a lover's hands. It left me shuddering. The Keeper was pressed up against Lad in his world of doors, begging with him, pleading with him.

"What are you doing to Lad?" I snapped.

The Keeper didn't miss a beat. He disappeared from Lad's side, reappeared at mine. "You need to hurry, now, or it will be too late."

"You have to stop using Lad like this, you don't understand–"

"Tanyana, please. Or she will die."

I shuddered. "Who?"

"Please? She's on the floor beneath us."

"This whole place isn't going to come down on my head again is it–?"

"*They* are with her."

They.

I pulled my suit back in. I didn't want to leave Lad here, alone, like this, but I didn't seem to have a choice. "Can you wait here for me?" To leave a distressed Lad all alone in an unstable and dangerous ruin, and I'd promised

Kichlan I would look after him. Ah yes, there was that famous Tanyana luck again.

He nodded, sniffing loudly.

I gripped the broken concrete and swung down. It was far deeper than I'd realised, but my suit spread over my feet and legs before I hit the distant ground and took the impact of my fall. I didn't fight the suit this time. I let it coat me feet to knees, wrists to elbows, and peered around me, the space lit by the suit's glow.

I was in some kind of tank. Every sound echoed, from the scrape of my booted feet to the rasp of my breath. The walls were white, paint peeling. Ceramic loops curled up from the floor, rising like trees in a knee-high forest from the bottom of the tank, thick as my wrist but flat, and evenly spaced, leaving paths between them. Pion storage? A way to keep heat-charged pions until they were needed?

From the darkness and oppressive stillness, I heard a whimper. I wove a cautious path toward the sound. I saw a light that blinked unsteadily through the ceramic forest. The tank was enormous, easily as long and as wide as the entire building, including the courtyard with its unsteady roofing. Some of it was inaccessible, cordoned off into smaller tanks within tanks, and in places the loops tied into vast and complicated knots that reared above me.

Half-hidden to the side of one such knot, I found a woman, moaning and shaking. Two oil lamps rested beside her on the cracked floor. In their unsteady light I knew instantly that she should not have been here. She was dressed in armour of black leather woven with thick blue thread, and she was Hon Ji.

I crouched beside her. Her straight black hair had been cut short; her olive skin was sun-roughened and scarred. The ferocious Hon Ji dragon twisted across the chest of a narrow surcoat. The material was torn and muddied. She wore two empty scabbards, one at her hip and a smaller attached to her thigh.

It was rare to see Hon Ji in Varsnia, even when tensions weren't high enough to send Strikers gliding through the city. What was this woman? She was too small, too frail looking to be Mob – a heavily reinforced foot soldier, body strengthened by pions. But neither Strikers nor Shielders carried weapons. And why else would she be covered in countless tiny scars, like cuts from many blades, over her cheeks, neck and forearms?

What was she doing here? A member of the Hon Ji military hiding in a storage tank below a long-forgotten factory in Movoc-under-Keeper.

"Hello?" I said, unsure what else to do.

Her eyes opened. Large, dark pupils fixed on me. The whites were so bloodshot they looked dirty, muddy with terror, and pain-wracked. And then she spasmed.

"What's wrong?"

She rattled words at me that I could not understand, while her body shook, thrashing against the floor and the wall at her back. I tried to grab her as her limbs smacked blood onto the ground, but she screamed and kicked at me as her limbs flailed.

I scrambled back. What was going on?

Then I saw it. It wound itself through the mesh of her armour like a snake. Not just one, but many, more than I could count. They writhed with her. In her.

Debris. Pale tendrils of the stuff, no solid grains or

flattened planes but a horrible liquid, serpent-like amal-
gamation of the two.

I pressed my hands to my mouth to hold back rising
vomit when I realised what was happening to the system
of pions that bound her body together. Pions are in everything, after all, even us. The debris in her body would be
interfering with them, just like it interfered with the systems that carried heat and light across the city. Bonds
unfurling, connections breaking, systems failing. That was
why she spasmed so violently, beating her own blood into
the white ceramic floor, her back arching at an impossible
angle. The debris was destabilising the pion bonds that
held her body together and she was losing control. Within
the body of every living creature was a pion system so
complex even the most powerful of healers barely understood it. For all the bone shards they could pry from a
living brain, there were the cuts that had to be sewn back
together, and the deeper wounds that stripped us of our
pion sight that we could not explain. We were all so much
energy, so many connections, all tightly knotted.

Bond by bond, pion by pion, the debris was undoing
that.

The suit tugged at me. It begged for release with a
pressure in my bones and a tightening of my skin that I
could not resist. The Hon Ji soldier woman closed her
eyes as I allowed the suit to encase me again, but she did
not stop screaming. A bottomless noise, all that horror I
had seen in her dark eyes, forced into sound.

Then the Keeper was there, yelling into my face.

"–help her! I can't help her and it hurts, damn you!"
More dark tears down his transparent cheeks. The
grains of debris that surged through his veins rushed like

rivers, they stood out ferocious and throbbing against his paleness.

I pushed him away. "What's happening to her? Why is it doing that?"

"It's killing her! Stop it, Tanyana. Calm it. Don't let her die."

The woman was insubstantial here, but the debris infesting her was clear. A great pallid knot of grains twisted together, joined by something like a moist membrane that quivered as it writhed. It was horrific, disgusting, the filthy insides of some diseased animal given movement and strength. But this one did not attack me, as the other debris creatures had. All it did was squirm within her, winding over and around itself, undoing her, gorging on the broken bindings and growing as it did so.

"How did she get here?" I whispered. I knew I had to calm down; I had no hope of soothing the debris like this. But my bile rose and my suit tightened as horror shivered over my skin.

"They brought her here," the Keeper spat the words through the dark curtain of his tears. "They did this. Like you, like the others."

The woman screamed again, her voice dim in this world. The Keeper added his own cry and clutched at his head.

For a brief, horrible moment I wondered what this was doing to him. The Keeper was debris, and debris was killing this woman. Could he feel it? Did he know what her pion bindings tasted like? And yet, he could not stop it. By turning the debris into this monstrous thing, the puppet men had taken the Keeper's control away.

Ancient guardian he might be. But with so much debris taken from him, tortured and animated into things like this, just what was he now?

How sane could the Keeper remain?

The Hon Ji woman's screaming subsided. The Keeper fell to his knees, still clutching his head. Through the silence I heard footsteps clearly, more than one person but made in perfect unison, walking slowly, echoing oddly against the walls and the tanks and the loops around me. Then voices, carefully loud enough, it seemed to me, just so I could hear them.

"Only an abandoned factory," one said. "This is not what we are looking for."

"Not deep enough," a second puppet man continued. "And not old enough, for a connection through the veil."

"Not a waste of time though." Their voices were all the same. It was impossible to tell them apart, or even how many there were.

"Not at all."

The Keeper lifted his head. His face was in darkness, his eyes spilling as though cut. "She is a Half, Tanyana. Please. She is a Half."

A Half? Which way were those footsteps going? Was Lad still waiting in the factory like I had told him? Waiting, and alone? But they didn't know what he was, did they? If they did, he would have been taken by now. The puppet men had already proven how easily they could step into our lives.

Torn between the puppet men and the muted thrashing of a Hon Ji Half, I wavered. The woman rattled her words again.

"She is begging you, Tanyana."

That returned my attention to the Keeper. "You can understand her?"

"Of course." He turned his weeping eyes to what remained of his Half. *"Please, stop the hurt. Please, didn't mean to. Please."*

"Stop." My whole body wracked. I could hear Lad saying those words in his clipped half-language. And it hurt me to know this poor, writhing creature was the same.

I crouched, shuffled as slowly and non-threatening as I could manage. "Can you tell her I'm not going to hurt her?"

The Keeper said something. She gasped back noises that could have been words. He hesitated.

"What did she say?"

He folded forward, so he was on his hands and knees, and approached us. "I'm not sure. She thinks you are some kind of... Something like the Other."

"I thought you understood her."

"I do. I did. But I have spent so much time in Varsnia and I forget things. Sometimes. There are so many more doors here than anywhere else. So I have to stay here. You see. For so long."

I nodded. "Then please tell her I am not the Other. Or whatever she thinks I am. Tell her I work with you, and I want to help."

As the Keeper and the Hon Ji Half spoke, I tried to focus on the debris. It made no sense. Not quite the usual solid grain, nor the destructive, lightning-like plane. Bound in ways I could not understand, animated yet seemingly insentient, a multitude locked in one terrible purpose. How could I calm something so violent, how could I collect it when it was tied so deeply with her body?

"Does she understand?" I leaned in closer. The debris flickered at me, like a challenged snake, before plunging back inside her.

"A little." He hesitated. "She is in pain, she is scared. As far as I can tell she was taken from her training ground by people she did not see. She was in a colony, she's a foot soldier, but she can't tell me what her rank is. I don't think… I don't think she really understands what it all means. All she remembers is waking up somewhere hard and cold, beneath bright lights and then the debris attacked her. It has been doing this for days."

How many of those days were spent in this tank, with only oil lamps for company, waiting for me?

"Was she taken because she is a Half?" I asked a question the Keeper could not answer.

He hung his head. "It would not be the first time." His shoulders shook.

I needed to get to Lad. But I had to help her first, and fast.

"Tell her I will try to collect it."

"No! You need to calm–"

"I need to get it out of her first," I snapped, and both the Keeper and the Half flinched. Was I terrifying to her, furious in my silver? After everything she had suffered, it was difficult to believe she could be afraid of me. "It is killing her now. She doesn't have time to wait for me to try and calm the debris and return it to you. I will remove it, I will collect it. We need to save her life first. Tell her that."

The Keeper stuttered more words. Ignoring him, I withdrew the suit from my face. I leant forward and extended my metallic fingers into long, delicate pincers. I caught the ridged head of one of the debris snakes and I pulled.

The debris came away from her body. Most of her stomach came with it.

She fell back, ashen, silenced. I stared in horror at the tangle of debris and flesh. Skin. Muscle. Something long and deeply dark.

My suit sprung from my control, it coated my head and the Keeper was screaming. "What have you done? I told you to return it to me!"

"Do you want this back in you? Do you want her blood in you?" We were both screaming now, but somehow, beneath it, I heard her groan. Low, weak.

Lad, I had to get to Lad. I drew a deep breath. I could smell my own sweat. I would not let them do this to him.

"The debris has disrupted her pion systems," I said with a calm I did not feel. "She is coming apart. No matter what we do, she will die." Horribly. Slowly.

The Keeper hiccupped. "I know. But the doors."

"Damn the doors."

The Hon Ji woman fluttered her eyelids and tried to lift her head. I could not let her see part of her own stomach and the writhing monstrosity attached to it. I knew what I had to do.

I dropped the debris. I flattened my hand into a sharpened blade. It was quick, very quick. My suit was very sharp and sliced easily through her neck, through flesh and bone, cleanly to the other side. All it took was a little pressure.

I stood. My legs shook.

I had killed her.

She was dying. It was the right thing to do.

But I had killed her.

I turned and staggered away from the light. I struggled for air in the confines of my suit. It throbbed around me as though awakened by the blood over my hand. For a moment I thought I could still hear her, whispering unintelligible words into my ear. But that was impossible now.

"What about the debris?" The Keeper appeared beside me.

Debris? Did he care about his Halves at all, about Lad waiting and the puppet men walking and the dead Hon Ji woman? Dead. "Other take you!" I ran from him, crashing through the ceramic loops as I went, barely seeing where I was going. I forced my suit away from my face, my neck, my chest.

I couldn't think about blood as I ran. Only Lad. I couldn't think about debris crawling its way through bodies, intent on destruction. Or pulling the poor Hon Ji Half apart, when I had been trying to help her. Or that if I had listened to the Keeper, if I wasn't so terrified for Lad in the hands of those veche puppet men, that I might not have pulled a part of her stomach out. I might have been able to save her life. Except her pion systems were failing. Except nothing I could have done would have reversed that.

Surely.

So I couldn't think about any of that. Only Lad.

My feet echoed loudly through the tank. The ceramic floor cracked beneath me.

All I could hear was my breath, all I could feel was the thud of my footfalls travelling into my legs, my bones, my body. If the puppet men were still here, making their slow funeral procession in the darkness, I could not hear them. If the Keeper harangued me, I could not hear him.

It was me alone in this timeless space. Only me, and my fear for Lad.

And Kichlan relying on me to keep him safe.

Faint sunlight filtered down through the hole in the roof. I plunged my suit into the floor to propel me upward, to Lad, to the puppet men, to whatever I would find in that long-dead factory.

But the suit did not respond. And instead of soaring up I fell onto my face, sprawling across ridges and loops that gouged into my ear and right temple.

Wincing, I pushed myself up. My face tingled cold as silver etched itself into my scratches, healing them into suit. I looked up at the hole. Shadows passed before it. My heart leapt.

I stood and flexed my calves, extending my arms to reach for the ceiling. Nothing happened. My suit still coated me, toes to shoulders, but it refused to obey my command.

Shuddering, I ran fingers through my hair. It was longer than I was used too, and had tangled into knots near the nape of my neck.

I needed to be up there. I needed to see Lad with my own eyes.

"What are you doing?" I hissed.

The suit grabbed me, low against my stomach. Like fingers had grown from the panel against my belly, through clothes and the boned uniform, and raked my skin.

I gasped, staggered on unsteady legs.

It did it again. Harder this time, sharp. I cried out as it cut me, and pressed a hand to my abdomen.

A shadow broke the sunlight above me. "Tan?" Lad. Not a wail, not a whisper, a forlorn and wavering word.

I needed to be up there, with him. To keep him safe.

"Stop it," I hissed, teeth clenched.

Pinching; sore against skin that felt tender and bruised. I hardened my stomach muscles and it eased.

"You will obey me." The suit settled. It withdrew from my shoulders, seeped back into the bands around my neck and wrists. As it retreated away from my stomach I lifted my hand, but no blood welled through my clothing. When it had freed my arms, hands and thighs, I stopped it so my calves and feet remained booted. "We're going up there." I looked to the ceiling. Did I feel it tighten around my legs, or had I imagined it? "Now."

I flexed. Poles sprung from the back of my calves and the bottom of my feet, burying themselves in ceramic and the rock below the floor, propelling me upward. A moment later I hooked my fingers over the rough edge and hauled myself up.

I spun. "Lad?"

A great figure barrelled into me. Arms wrapped around me and crushed me into a solid chest. "Tan!" Lad wailed like a child and held me so tightly I could barely breathe.

When he finally put me down I retracted the rest of my suit, and confined it tightly into the spinning bands. "Lad? Are you all right?"

He sniffed, and wiped a streaming nose with the back of his sleeve. "You were gone, Tan. I was scared."

"But you're all right? Apart from scared? Not hurt?"

He nodded. He sniffed and wiped again.

"Good." And everything seemed to fall out of me – all my fear, all my horror – leaving me feeling weak. I blinked, hard. Everything looked red. And I realised with gut-wrenching certainty how much I wished Kichlan was with us. I was a poor substitute indeed.

"We should go back to the others," I managed to say in an uneven voice.

Another nod and Lad began to shuffle back through the disused machinery. As I made to follow him, I heard them. Clear and echoing, seeming to resonate up from the tank below. Footsteps. Slow, calm, methodical. Three people, maybe more.

I peered into the darkness and saw nothing. But I could feel them looking, the pressure of that inhuman, unemotional, communal stare.

I hurried after Lad, and wrapped my hand in his. He sniffed, perhaps louder than absolutely necessary. "I'm sorry I left you, Lad," I whispered.

"You needed to follow him. He was very upset."

"He was."

I leaned into Lad and knew how wrong it was to rely on his strength and his warmth, when he should be relying on me. But I had to. Without him, I would have curled into a ball as my body ached to do. I had killed a Half. She was just like him.

Lad squeezed me. "Wish Kich was here."

"Me too."

I clambered through the wreckage of the factory door with difficulty. The afternoon light was failing. Laxbell must have sounded, unheard in this strange part of the city. For how many bells had we collected, then followed the will of the Keeper?

We had to be back by Duskbell. I had to pass Lad to Kichlan and try and convince him that nothing strange had happened, certainly nothing that had made me fear for his brother's life. On the first day.

"Shouldn't we go and look for them? How long have they been gone? Something might have happened to them!" Aleksey paced between Mizra and Natasha where they waited at the end of the alleyway. I could see Aleskey's tension from the factory door.

"What, like the ceiling falling in?" Mizra drawled.

Natasha snorted a short laugh.

Aleksey stopped dead. "That's just the kind of thing– Why do you think this is funny?"

"Here we are!" Lad called, his voice echoing too loudly from the rickety roof.

Natasha and Mizra tried to hold Aleksey back, but he shook them off like they were children and ran across the courtyard. "Are you both all right?" He stared intently at Lad, then flicked his gaze to me. I couldn't meet his eyes. Did he see the blood on my sleeve, the death on my hands?

"Glad to be outside." Lad wrinkled his nose. "Was old in there and smelled and there were loops that Tan explained." He paused only to breathe, and I laid a hand on his arm.

"Now, now," I whispered. "Don't say too much."

Lad checked himself, looked away from Aleksey and noticed Mizra. "Miz!" He hurried across the courtyard. "We saw loops!"

I wobbled without his support. Aleksey noticed, and took my arm as we left the factory. "Did you, ah, find– No, *collect* any debris?" He stumbled over the words, unsure what to say, unwilling to let the silence and unexplained absence fester between us. It felt strange. Kichlan preferred to leave things unsaid; he could chew on silence for a sixnight and one and never grow tired of the taste.

"No." I said, hoping he would be quiet. At least with Aleksey in tow, Mizra and Natasha could not push me for answers. I was thankful for that.

A cold Movoc evening wind sliced against my face. The pion-created light from lamps along the street flickered into life, too brilliant. My head hurt. "Lad and I need to go." I thanked Aleksey, and swapped his arm for Lad's. I turned to Natasha. "I have to get him back to Kichlan." My voice sounded so distant, even to my own ears.

"Take him. We'll go back to Ironlattice and put this away." She hefted the bag slung over her shoulder. Metallic jars – most still empty – clanged within. "And see you tomorrow."

Duskbell sounded, and we walked. Lad fretted, inhibited by my failing strength.

Finally, we returned to the street corner. Kichlan was pacing, followed a few steps behind by Sofia. I paused at the sight of her. I had expected Kichlan to be waiting on his own.

As soon as Lad saw his brother he released my arm, shouted, and barrelled through the thin stream of pion-binders making their way home this Frostday evening. A few shocked or irritated glances followed him, but nothing more sinister. I felt thin, strung out by my fear for him, by the day's constant concern. Was this what Kichlan's life was always like?

Kichlan turned to be swept into Lad's arms. I stopped, still on the other side of the street, and considered leaving them. Turning into the stream of people and being washed away by it, allowing it to carry me home. Surely it would be easier than facing Kichlan.

But Sofia wasn't about to let me do that. She pushed her small but solid way across the street, took my hand and drew me through the throng. "What are you doing?" she muttered, the whole way. "He was worried about you. You could at least talk to him."

"He was worried about Lad, you mean," I said, unable to fight her.

She stopped, half way, spun and scowled at me. "All day, he has been fretting about the two of you. We hardly collected anything." She turned, pushing forward. "He hardly even knew the rest of us were there."

Sofia gave Kichlan my hand, and he took it, gently. "What happened?" Stern brotherly and ex-collecting team leader concern mixed on his face with something deeper. Something between anger and relief.

I looked away, only to meet Sofia's red, frustrated face.

Lad answered. "He needed Tan. I had to stay and wait. I was scared." He hesitated. "But nothing bad happened to me. I wasn't hurt."

I allowed myself a small smile for the understanding Lad sometimes showed.

Kichlan kept his face carefully blank. "Another door?"

"Not another one," Sofia murmured. Kichlan glanced at her, surprised, as though he had forgotten she was there.

I shook my head but said nothing. I couldn't explain the Hon Ji Half to either of them. I couldn't discuss my concerns for the Keeper's very sanity. Not right now. Now, I needed all of my strength to get home.

"I think you should take Lad home," I finally managed to say. "He has had a hard day."

Kichlan studied me for a long moment. "And you?" he asked, voice low. "What kind of day have you had?"

"Tan is tired," Lad said. "And white. Was white ever since she came back up, weren't you, Tan?"

Kichlan's eyes widened. "Back up from where?"

"From below the factory," Lad continued, oblivious. "We saw loops. They were old. They broke."

I tried for a reassuring expression, and could tell I failed dismally. "You know how the Keeper likes his sewers. Or anything underground."

Kichlan sighed, rubbed his face. "I don't like this. Leaving you all alone. What if..." a hesitation "What if you need me?"

"Tan looked after me," Lad said.

"I know, Lad." Kichlan stepped close to me, and ran a gentle hand across my face. He rubbed at something on my cheek, and I could only hope it wasn't blood. Please let it not be the Hon Ji Half's blood. "But what about her?"

He spoke so softly I didn't think Lad or Sofia could hear him.

I felt strangely flushed, when he stepped back. Warm, deep inside, even as I shivered. And for all the horror of the day, strangely comforted, by his touch alone.

"Tomorrow morning," he said. "Same bell?"

I had to clear my throat before I could speak. "I'll be here." I smiled at Lad. "Goodnight, Lad. Thank you for helping me today."

Lad released his brother long enough to embrace me. He seemed gentler than usual, as though he could tell I was fragile. But still, it set off pain somewhere low in my belly, a shadowed memory of what my suit had done. I gasped, quietly, and tried not to let it show.

"Let me help you home," Sofia said, her voice a little too loud and falsely bright.

"Thank you. But no. I will be fine, you can all stop worrying." I nodded to Kichlan. "I will see you here tomorrow."

Hunched against the cold, I made my way home. Movoc melded into one great press of noise and dull colour. People brushed against my shoulders as I made my slow and hardly steady way. Each touch jarred me. With each breath something low and sore bloomed inside me.

I did not go to Valya's kitchen when I finally made it home. I dragged myself up the rickety stairs and almost fell through the door to my room. Somehow, I made it to the bed.

For a bell, perhaps, maybe more, I lay half-awake, feet on the floor, neck and back cricked at a strange angle. Dimly, I thought I heard knocking, but even if I could have woken up enough to move I didn't have the strength to stand. It was Valya, I assumed, wondering why I had not appeared to eat as she expected.

Food was the last thing I wanted. Waves of nausea played with the waves of exhaustion like tides within me. All I could do was lie down, keep still, and dream half-dreams of blood, and debris writhing, the Hon Ji Half's voice, and the puppet men walking, ever walking, through the darkness.

Dim, slowly, I woke. Fitful light shone through the window beside the bed from the lamps on the street. Gingerly, I sat up. I was still dressed in the coat and the clothes I had worn to go collecting. Not trusting my legs I eased the jacket off and dropped it to the floor. I shrugged myself out of my long-sleeved, loose woollen shirt, and it fell to pieces in my hands.

The light from the street was dim, but it was enough. My uniform was torn. Great rents, gashes, as though made with claws, ran their way over my stomach.

Lightheaded, I hooked fingers under the edge of the material and rolled it up. My stomach was a mess of cuts and fresh, purple bruises. The cuts were already filled with silver. How deep did they go? What damage had the suit done, only to heal me? I thought of the notches in my ear and face, the new ones I had made this afternoon, and now these. With each wound I was more suit, and less me.

As the nausea rose again I scrambled up to the top of the bed. I lay above the blankets, not feeling the cold, not feeling anything but ill and thin. Taut, and unreal.

3.

Thankfully, the Keeper did not disturb us the next day. It gave Natasha a chance to drag us around in a panic of her own until we had filled all the jars we could carry. She was worried about quota. I understood that. Failure to meet our debris quota would bring nothing but veche attention, attention we did not need. Another excuse to break us up, and take Lad away from even my pathetic supervision. I knew we had to do everything in our power to make sure that didn't happen.

But that didn't make it any easier, or me any less exhausted. So when I returned home that evening I was pining for Rest – so I could, well, rest – but Valya met me at the bottom of the stairs and I knew it was not meant to be.

"Tomorrow, we will leave early." She held a pot out in front of her, hands protected from its heat by several layers of towel. It steamed in the cold evening air, giving her a ghostly halo.

"We will?" Or I could sleep. Actually sleep seemed like a much better idea.

"Of course!" She looked shocked. "There is no time to waste. I thought you understood."

"Yes. I do." But my legs were weak and my stomach rolling and all I wanted to do was lie down. "Tomorrow then."

"You must meet the others. We must begin." She forced the heavy, lidded pot into my hands. Even through the cloth it was so hot I fought the need to drop it. "Must eat." She clicked her tongue in disapproval. "Can't fight if you don't eat."

The pot was full of a thick vegetable soup. I managed a few spoonfuls, fought the need to be sick, lay on the bed, ate a few more. It became the evening's unsettling routine.

Dawnbell, Rest morning, and Valya dragged me from my warm blankets with her knocking. She would not leave until I had returned the pot – empty, and she made a point of checking – then promised to dress. We were outside and walking down the bare, icy streets before breakbell had even sounded.

The old woman did not speak, which was good, because I didn't feel alert enough to hold a conversation. I did, however, slowly realise where we were going.

"Are we going to Kichlan's house?" I asked, slurping the words with frozen, half-awake lips.

She made a sour-taste face. "Eugeny's house, you mean. Your team members merely board there."

I rubbed gloved fingers together, breathed hot air into my palms and cupped them against my cheeks. "So, you know Eugeny." I supposed I wasn't that surprised. Eugeny had sent us to Yicor, when I needed kopacks and somewhere to live. Yicor had sent us to Valya. Eugeny and Valya were similar in some ways. They both seemed to believe soup could cure anything. They both watched and

understood from their quiet place on the sidelines, and
provided warm beds when they were the most needed.

But Eugeny was not Unbound. He was a binder – an
old man who did not like to rely on pions, true, but he
could see and manipulate them all the same. He just
chose not to. What was he doing with Yicor and Valya?

Valya's expression pinched further. I hadn't thought
that possible. She did not deign to answer.

We approached the small house of stone and wood,
surrounded by monstrous concrete slabs of apartments
on either side. I noticed Yicor loitering beneath a still-lit
lamp on the corner. He nodded to Valya.

"Are you well, Miss Tanyana?" he asked, searching
my face.

I made a rueful expression. "Would be better if I was
still asleep."

"Ah." He dipped his head. "I apologise for the early
morning. But time is of the essence."

"I know." I supressed a sigh and tried to forget about
sleep for the day.

"Wouldn't be so tired if you ate properly," Valya muttered as she knocked on Eugeny's door. I ignored her.

"There you are," Eugeny greeted us with a smile. His
unlit pipe dipped at the corner of his mouth. "I was beginning to worry you weren't coming."

Breakbell toned, drowsy and mournful in the distance.
Valya pushed me inside. "Some people are slow."

Eugeny's house smelled of cinnamon, tobacco, and
wool drying by the fire. Those smells wrapped warm and
pleasant around me, touching my face and filling my
lungs, easing the morning cold from my skin. I understood why Kichlan and Lad lived here. It was more than

just accommodation cheap enough for debris collectors to afford. It felt insulated from the harsh city outside, protected from the puppet men and the Keepers of the world.

"Tan?" Lad stood at the top of the stairs, rubbing his eyes. The buttons down the front of his shirt were mismatched and his hair was an explosion of tangled blonde curls. He launched himself down and enclosed me in a brief hug, before stomping into the kitchen and whatever food Eugeny had prepared for dawnbell supper. I assumed it was making that wonderful cinnamon smell.

Kichlan followed him down the stairs, already wrapped in his scarf, hat, gloves, and wearing suspicion like a heavy jacket. He glanced between Eugeny, Yicor, Valya and me.

"We go." Valya was already at the door, ready to leave. "Must hurry. Much to do."

"Kichlan is coming with us," Yicor explained. "Eugeny will care for his brother."

But Kichlan, still standing by the stairs, crossed his arms and pinned Eugeny with a flinty glare. "I will not leave Lad with a person I cannot trust." His voice was heavy and dark and drew Lad to his side almost instantly.

Spoon in one hand, porridge on his chin, almost-empty bowl cradled against his chest, Lad blinked his confusion at us. "Bro? What's wrong?"

Eugeny drew a small, leather bag from a pocket hidden in his quilt-like clothing. He gently pinched dried tobacco from its folds and sprinkled it into his pipe. The whole action was slow, calming, and completely at odds with Valya who had began to rock on her heels and lean toward the door. "I think," Eugeny pressed the tobacco down with a soft fingertip, "Kichlan deserves to know."

"No time," Valya snapped.

"Then I will stay right here," Kichlan snapped back.

"Geny?" Lad caught the front of his shirt into a ball and wiped his chin.

"They can wait a few more moments. After all," Eugeny breathed air in through the still-unlit pipe, "they have waited this long already."

Valya scowled, Yicor shrugged like he didn't really mind how long it took. I crossed my arms and hoped Kichlan would take it as a gesture of solidarity.

"Want me to get your light, Geny?" Lad, porridge now smeared down to his neck as well, glanced at the warm glow of the kitchen fire.

"Wash your face too," Kichlan murmured. Lad blushed – the colour heightened by the warmth of the flame – and hurried back into the kitchen.

Eugeny tapped his pipe against his wrinkled cheek. "I was never a strong binder, too weak even for a light factory, too clumsy to weave calico cloth."

I lifted my eyebrows in surprise and he caught the look. Eugeny chuckled softly. "Hard to believe? As a young man I was employed by the veche as well – but only because no one else would have me. I tended horses, cattle, pigs, and chickens for the city markets. It was dirty, poorly paid work. But at least I didn't starve."

"Doesn't make you a debris collector," Kichlan muttered.

"No, it didn't."

Lad returned, face clean, with a thick twig flickering a small flame on one end. Eugeny took it from him with a nod and touched the light to his tobacco. He drew a few short smoke-filled breaths, and shook the small flame until it went out. "Ah, Lad. My light has died. Fetch me another?"

Lad, who had watched the whole process fixedly, hurried out of the hallway.

"But I was there, dragging a sow through mud and pig shit to the slaughter, when I found them." At this, he glanced at Valya and Yicor. Neither met his gaze. "Hurt, the lot of them. Two were dead, one died as I tried to help him. This one," he gestured to Yicor, "almost joined them."

"What?" Kichlan's intense gaze lashed between the two old men. "I don't understand."

"*This time we will win*," I whispered, remembering what Valya had said. "You have fought the veche before."

Lad returned with a bigger stick, a bigger flame. Eugeny lit his pipe again, breathing smoke deep into his lungs, and sighed satisfaction. "Thank you, Lad. I think that deserves more porridge, don't you?"

But Lad, for all his shortcomings, was not as blind as that. His eyes narrowed. "Could stay here, with everyone. With Tan." He shuffled to my side and wrapped his large hands around my arm. "Tan is here."

"That's very true." Eugeny puffed more heavy smoke, and Lad sneezed loudly. "Suppose you don't want any of my stewed rhubarb then. Fresh. Still warm."

I could feel Lad's indecision through his clutching hands.

"And there's sugar, in the jar. Won't last long."

That did it. With a sigh and an almost inaudible mutter, Lad scrambled back into the kitchen. Part of me wished I could follow him. For the first time in days the smell, the very mention of food wasn't making me feel ill. It figured Eugeny's cooking could do that.

"So why–" Kichlan tried, but Eugeny held up a hand.

"I helped the poor bastards. They'd been beaten, badly, and I couldn't just let them suffer." He smoked, expression thoughtful. "And they came to trust me, even if I was a pion-binder, even if I worked for the veche they hated so much. I learned things from them: how to heal without healers, cook without heat generated by pions, see without pion-created light. I also learned the veche had Mob out looking for them – *Mob*, for the Keeper's sake – and enforcers roaming the streets. I kept them hidden, and kept them safe."

"Eugeny might not be Unbound, as we are," Yicor said. "But he is strong and trustworthy. A true servant of the Keeper."

"Is that why you took us in?" Kichlan asked, teeth clenched but expression uncertain, like he didn't know what to believe or who it was safe to trust.

"Not only you," Eugeny answered. "I grew too old for the sty, too stiff for the stable, too damned slow to chase hens around. I had rooms, and knew there were people who might need them." He tipped his pipe at Yicor and Valya. "Certain kinds of people."

"You have trusted him for so long," Yicor said to Kichlan. "Does this really give you a reason to stop?"

Kichlan's shoulders sagged, he rubbed at his face and for a moment. Shadowed by the fire at his back he looked so tired, so lost, that it tugged at my heart. Then he met my eyes, and I could read the question there. I nodded.

"As you say." He released a great sigh. "Just as you say."

But something niggled at the back of my mind, some doubt not as easily assuaged. Yicor, Valya, the Unbound: what had they tried to do that had brought the wrath of the veche down upon them? And why did they think I would help them do it again?

"I still don't like this," Kichlan said as, huddled against the early-morning wind, we followed Valya and Yicor at a distance. Apparently this was to make sure we didn't draw any unwanted attention to ourselves. "For all their fine words, these are still people we barely know, and we're following them blindly, without any idea what they really want from us." He walked close to me. "I just– I don't want you to get hurt. Not again."

My silver-filled cuts felt strange and heavy. Hard lines against the muscles of my stomach, immobile patches amidst my movement, they jagged into me with each stride.

Kichlan wrapped an arm around my shoulders. He had his brother's breadth, but Kichlan was gentler. His hand cradled, rather than clutched, as it rubbed warmth into my upper arm.

I leaned into him. "What about Eugeny?" I managed, after a moment. "He is someone you know well."

He paused. "I thought I did."

I was about to tell him that everyone had secrets, and not to hold them against the old man who had cared for him and his brother so well. But I caught myself, just in time. I thought about the Hon Ji Half I had killed, what I had put Lad through, and the secret he now carried for me. Secrets and lies weren't innocuous.

So instead, I said, "I know what you mean. But it's important, don't you think, to learn what they have to teach us? Anything that might help us help the Keeper."

Kichlan scowled. "The Keeper. Again."

I said nothing. Better he hate the Keeper than me. I was not proud of that.

Valya and Yicor waited on a street corner for us to catch up. A brave – or perhaps foolhardy – slide vendor dared to approach them. He carried an enlarged version of the small glass rectangles he was selling. Neither Valya nor Yicor could, however, read the words scrawled in bright pions over its surface and projected into the thin air just in front of their faces. I didn't hear what Valya said to make the poor man flinch, turn around and hurry away, but I could imagine it.

"There are places of memory in the city," Valya said when we caught up. She wrapped her old, dust-edged shawl tighter around her shoulders. The old woman did not leave her house often.

"Places where the old world survives," Yicor said. He met my gaze and his eyes seemed to shine with humour, with some wry joke I was not entirely privy to. "Places where its secrets are protected. Hidden."

Like the library beneath his cellar, perhaps? Yicor hid books there, ancient tomes written with debris stitched to the vellum. It was from those strangely fungal-looking, bulging words that I had learned Lad was a Half, and what that meant. It was there I had learned to *fear for everything*.

After a moment of loitering and surreptitiously scanning the street, Valya opened a shop door and hurried us inside. The shop instantly reminded me of Yicor's. Different part of the city, different layout inside and not so heavily blanketed with dust, but still much the same. Instead of shelves filling the wide room this one was occupied by tables. Lined up wall to wall, their scratched wooden tops were covered with antiques. Wooden boxes with glass lids held coins, jewellery, spoons and small pieces of thin-looking porcelain. Large crates contained pottery, silverware, books. There were even clothes, folded carefully in thin paper, or hanging from hooks in the ceiling.

All made, owned and used, I assumed, before the revolution two centuries ago. Or at least during its early days. Artefacts from a time when the city ran on gas and steam, not great threads of bright and colourful pions strung up between buildings. When words were read in books, not in light projected from glass slides. Houses were built by hand, carriages were drawn by horses, and only a few people had enough pion-binding skill to work deep changes to the structure of the world. The descendants of those few, powerful people still made up the national veche today. Debris collectors were not needed, because not enough debris was produced. And the Keeper had no trouble guarding the doors between worlds.

The modern city of Movoc-under-Keeper relied on the augmentation of binding skill through Novski's critical circles: three, six, or nine lesser binders gathering and channelling pions to be manipulated by their circle centre. That was the revolution that changed Varsnia, at first, and then fed through to the rest of the world. Factories full of unskilled binders, working on his principles, could heat an entire city, or light it, or process its waste. Circles of architects built great shining towers. Massive farms were established to grow any kind of food in even the coldest environments. Coaches glided on legs of light.

All this new pion-binding produced so much debris that collecting teams like ours, with our suits and our jars, were established to clear it all away. Too much debris, left unchecked, interfered with the working of a city's new and complex pion systems.

I picked up a small figurine of the Keeper Mountain, made of clear glass, with dots of colour denoting trees and solid white for snow at the peak. It was hollowed out. I ran a finger around the inside, but couldn't work out what was supposed to fit into such a strange shape. "I didn't realise there was such a strong market for antiques in Movoc-under-Keeper."

"There isn't." A man emerged from a door at the back of the room. Younger than Yicor and Valya, solid dark hair slick on his head, and his expression fierce. He scanned Kichlan and me with the same appraisal I'm sure he gave all the merchandise brought into his shop. Beside me, Kichlan bristled. "We use these shops as a cover. You know what they say about hiding in plain sight."

I cocked an eyebrow at him. "I had no idea anyone said that."

Kichlan snorted a tight laugh.

The man scowled, and turned to Yicor. "Are you sure about these two?"

"Of course!" Valya snapped.

Yicor placed a hand on my shoulder, his face set with determination. "Eugeny is. And if you won't trust our judgement, then trust his."

The shop owner softened. "Then come with me." He turned and disappeared back through the door.

Valya and Yicor pressed Kichlan and me forward.

On the other side of the door was a storeroom full of crates. These were, I realised, just cover for a trapdoor at the back corner of the room. Half-hidden by stacks of boxes, it was almost invisible in the dim light.

"What is it with you people and trapdoors?" I muttered.

I caught a fragment of Yicor's smile. "We like buried things," he murmured. "So much of our past is lost beneath the ground; history and memory, crushed by the weight of buildings and time."

A long ladder led down from the trapdoor. Darkness wrapped around me as I followed the shopkeeper, and descended. Only a flickering oil lamp swinging from a hook in his belt and the glow of my own suit guided me. I dropped the last few feet, wincing as the lines of metal across my stomach jarred with the jolt.

It looked like we were in a street. Worn cobblestones at my feet, an eroded and uneven gutter, stone predecessors of pion-powered streetlamps broken and long unused. Broken windows like half-open eyes peered from the remnants of buildings. These houses were stunted things, built of stone, and most had collapsed, forming a base for the world above. Movoc-under-Keeper was one of the oldest cities in Varsnia, and a true child of the critical circle revolution. Hidden amidst the new wonders of Novski's world, slices of her history remained. I had seen the odd wall, built without the aid of pions, still standing after centuries of change. These rare examples were fenced off from the destruction of curious fingers, and usually adorned with plaques listing how old they were and why they had been built. But they looked nothing like this. I pictured the city above us, the wide factories and tall apartment complexes, and wondered how we could have built all that, unaware of the bones of a far older city below.

The foundations of the world above created the roof of this cavern. The light from my suit caught the edges of them and gave me glimpses. Pillars of rock tunnelled into the ancient street and through dilapidated buildings. Steel beams clung to the ceiling like a spine, fanned by a complicated network of pipes. Water trickled down from forgotten and inaccessible drains, hollowing out tunnels in the rock. Light shone in splinters, dulled by distance and iron.

"Buried things," I whispered.

"This is Varsnia." Heavy shadows hid the shop owner's eyes and hardened his mouth. "Before the revolution changed her."

Above us, Valya and Kichlan were descending slowly, the ladder hard on the old woman's joints.

"Lev, by the way." He held out a hand. I shook it lightly, and didn't miss his flicker of a frown as my suit flashed beneath my sleeve.

"Tanyana." I gestured to the ladder. "Kichlan." Valya eased her way onto the stones with Yicor's help, and Kichlan finally made it down. He scowled at his hands as he rubbed them together, blowing small flecks of rust from his palms.

"Let me show you who we are," Lev said, and started down the street. Yicor and Valya kept close to him. Kichlan fell in beside me.

The walls closed in and the ceiling dipped low as we walked. Curious statue-like fixtures protruded from the walls like bolsters, and I began to wonder if they were the only things holding the lot up. I stopped at one. They sparkled in the blue light from my suit, crystalline against the rock.

"What is that?" Kichlan breathed, close to my ear.

There was a face in the rock. A half-decayed mask, features broad and distorted. I could make out an eye, still a faint dark colour, and half a mouth, a similar shade. I crouched. The body was mostly gone, swallowed by time and the crush of the city above. What I could make out – an arm, part of a hand, and something that could have been a leg – were strange. Large fingers, tiny elbow, swollen knee, skeletal shins. The wrongness of it all, the black eyes and the shining stone, made me shudder. These statues had been designed by people who had never seen their subject. They were an estimation, they were imperfect, they were the impossible made physical.

And I knew them.

"It reminds me of the cemetery," Kichlan said. He had crouched beside me, and ran his fingers over the child-like roundness of a thigh. "You know those statues of the Other?"

Half-made, half-decayed, easing their way into the world like they didn't belong. Yes, I knew what he meant.

But I shook my head as I straightened. "Look at the eye," I said, instead, and held my glowing suit as close to the rock as possible. "The lips." Their dark colour was nearly bleached by the light. "These aren't the Other. They are the Keeper."

Our eyes met. Kichlan hadn't seen the Keeper, of course. But he seemed to take my word for it.

"There are more."

Together, we followed the wall. Every few yards we came across another statue, some as solid and identifiable as the first one, most merely suggestions of shape and form.

"Hurry, we're late already," Lev called, and only then did I realise Kichlan and I were being left behind.

"They're the Keeper, aren't they?" I asked, when we reached them. "The statues in the wall."

Lev's eyes widened, and his mouth pinched. Even his surprised expression had an unnerving intensity to it. "We believe so, yes."

"So debris collectors lived here?" Kichlan asked.

"Unbound," Lev answered, his tone bitter. "The Unbound lived here. We did not collect debris then."

"We're not certain," Yicor said, "but judging by the images and the writings we've found, the Unbound lived apart from the Binders, in the old Movoc-under-Keeper. There are even references to an underground city, a whole labyrinth for the Unbound alone."

"Movoc was smaller, then," Valya continued.

"And this area would have been away from the main city," Lev finished. "Not outside the Old Tear gates, of course. The wall has not moved, but we believe the outskirts – between the buildings that crowded around the Tear Bridge, and the wall – was relegated to food production, animal husbandry, and the Unbound."

So, even before the revolution – before we became garbage collectors – we were outcast. Untrustworthy. Different. And yet the Unbound of old had their own language, their own culture, and possessed skills I could not begin to imagine. Yicor's debris books – written in the same indecipherable symbols as the ones on the band in my wrist – were mere shadows of a lost past.

As we walked, I noticed more chunks of the crystalline stone, piled in corners or pressed into doorways. I stopped to pick one up, and found flecks of what looked like gold locked deep beneath its cloudy facets.

"We are here."

The cavern closed off behind Lev, Yicor and Valya, in a tumble of fallen rocks and newer-looking supports built of scrap iron and bricks. The vague outline of a door remained.

"This is the only building that has survived so well intact," Lev said. "Though, as you can see, we have had to dig through the rubble to get to it."

Kichlan and I hesitated.

"It is quite safe." With a smug smile Lev ducked through the door. Yicor and Valya followed.

"*Quite* safe," Kichlan muttered.

I leaned back, inspected the masonry and the rock above us. "If I was still an architect I would probably tell you to run screaming from this place." I tapped the stonework around the edge of the door. More of that strange crystal. It seemed solid enough, but still, I wished for a moment that I could weave a little strength into the pions in this place. Just to be safe.

"But you're not an architect any more, are you?" Kichlan grinned. "Should we run screaming anyway?"

I grinned with him. "It certainly has its merits. But we came this far."

"Then let's see what this is all about."

I slipped my hand down the stone, gripped the edge, and used it to lever myself through the low door.

For a moment there was nothing but rubble to squeeze through. Then the doorway opened up and I stepped into a circular, domed room. Well, it had once been domed. Now only the skeleton remained: thick iron curving above us, gaps between the bones filled in by tightly packed earth. More supports had been set up in here, from a flat steel plate securing an unsteady patch of wall, to a tall, gangly fixture of metal and wood obviously designed to buttress the roof. If the city ever decided to come down on us, I didn't think anything that rickety-looking could have done more than simply fall with it.

There was little left of the structure of the room, but what I could make out was odd. A raised, circular section around the edge of the walls, barely wide enough for a single row of people to sit on, with the rest of the room sunk below what would have been street level. The ground was gritty, layered now with stone and earth. It made me think it might not have been sealed, that even grass could have grown. Had windows stretched between the skeletal iron fingers above our heads, filtering the sunlight and warming this strange place?

Half a dozen people, maybe one or two more, filled the domed room. Most were Valya and Yicor's age, some younger like Lev, only a few younger still. All but one were unsuited, that rare kind of Unbound who had escaped the puppet men, the technicians and their needles.

They milled around on the sunken floor, faces tipped up to watch Kichlan as he squeezed through. He scanned their faces, started to dust off his clothes and paused to say, "Fedor?" in surprise.

Fedor? Then I realised why the single, suited man looked familiar. Not so sickly-looking now, though still thin and pale, he was the second new collector. "Kichlan?" he sounded just as shocked.

"You know him?" Lev asked.

"He is in my collecting team."

A moment of subterranean tension before Fedor stepped up beside us. "We have heard that Eugeny vouches for you." In the sure lift of his head and the firm command in his eyes I saw none of the quiet man who had allowed himself to be herded by Aleksey. From Kichlan's continued surprise, I gathered he was seeing a different side of his new team member as well. "So you are welcome." He introduced his Unbound group, names I was sure to forget: Egor, Kirill, Yan, Anna... I stopped listening after a while. "We thank the Keeper for bringing you to us."

Kichlan snorted, instantly shattering the fragile calm. "The Keeper? That must be a joke, surely. He's led us around for moons now. If he cared about any of you I think he'd have introduced us earlier, don't you?" The scorn in his voice was too clear, his utter disrespect obvious on his face.

Ah, Kichlan's ever-absent tact.

Fedor tensed, as the Unbound behind him muttered darkly. "What do you think you know about the Keeper?"

No point even trying for diplomacy now, was there?

"I know he doesn't look like those statues out there." I jerked my thumb back at the doorway. "Though they got the eyes and the mouth about right."

A moment of silence, of puzzlement. Then understanding sunk in. "You have seen him?" Fedor asked me, his expression a mixture of hope and disbelief.

"We brought her here for a reason," Yicor murmured, and almost sounded affronted. "You should have more faith in your elders, Fedor."

"But that's impossible," one of the Unbound gasped – Egor, I thought.

"Not even Halves see the Keeper, though they hear his voice," another, older woman, said. Anna?

"How is it you can see him?" Lev asked. He remained calm.

I lifted an arm. The suit spun faster, glowed brighter, and all voices within the ancient chamber died.

"The suit?" Fedor peered closer, and then glanced down at his own quiet, dim wrist. "But how does that work–?"

I shook my head. "Our suits are not the same, Fedor." When he looked up again hope had turned to jealousy. Such foolishness. "You're lucky not to have a suit like mine, trust me. Anyway, all that matters is I can communicate with the Keeper, and he with me."

Lev studied me for a silent moment. "So you say. Then you already know what we must do."

"We must close the doors," I whispered.

"We must do more than close them." Fedor grinned, and there was something unhinged in his expression, something that made me shiver and wish I'd never even mentioned the doors. "We must ensure they cannot be created, we must destroy the tools with which they are built, we must splinter the wood, melt the iron, burn the–"

"How, exactly will you do that?" I interrupted and wondered if he realised the doors he was so enthusiastically destroying weren't physical at all and wouldn't, I was fairly sure, catch fire.

"With these." He lifted his hands, and nodded to the bands of suit on his wrists "I chose to be shackled with them. Of all of us, I volunteered. To become a collector, to lose my freedom."

"Why?" I choked. Memories of lying on a silver table, of great needles suiting me with living fire, threatened to overwhelm the dimly lit chamber. Why would anyone willingly give themselves over to the veche and their torture?

"Isn't it obvious?" Lev gripped Fedor's shoulder, possessive, protective. "Fedor is infiltrating the veche."

"The veche?" Kichlan asked, sounding just as sceptical as I felt. "We're not the veche, you know. Debris collectors are nothing. We have no status, no power, and barely any kopacks. What could you possibly hope to learn by becoming one of us?"

It was the first time I'd heard Kichlan speak so harshly about us. He'd always said that collecting was our duty, the part we had to play in Varsnia's complex tapestry. Of course, I'd also wondered if he said that only to justify his own choices, and maybe to stop himself resenting Lad. Kichlan had not been born a collector like his younger brother was. He had chosen to fall, he had dashed himself against the rocks, to keep Lad safe. To be there, always, watching over him.

So, while I tended to agree with him, it was a shock to hear Kichlan speak so clearly.

Fedor shook his head, clicked his tongue, and donned an offensively pitying expression. "You can't begin to understand the opportunities these suits afford us. But that is only because you have not been looking."

"Then why don't you explain it to us," Kichlan said, behind clenched teeth. I touched a light hand to his back, and he seemed to calm a little.

"This is my way inside the technician's laboratories, and the very workings of the debris collecting system. Already, I have seen so much. Already, I know when the full jars are collected, where they are transported, and most important of all, where the debris is stored."

"Fedor will find the debris the technicians hoard," Lev explained. "And together, we shall release it. All of it.

When too much debris is collected, too many doors are opened. So we will undo that."

But we had all seen what happened when too much debris was released all at once. Movoc-under-Keeper had nearly been torn apart by it. "That's dangerous," I whispered.

"We understand why you might not wish to help us," Fedor finished. "We will undo all the work you have done, we will wreck havoc on the pion systems of this city and cast its people down into chaos. But that is the price, is it not? For their lives."

"A moment?" Kichlan asked, with an upraised hand. Then he took my arm and led me out of the domed room.

"What are you doing?" I asked, once we'd managed to squeeze our way through the rubble.

He blinked, surprised. "Discussing this with you. I refuse to stand there and be pressured into making a decision. I thought you'd agree with me."

"Actually, yes. That's a good idea."

Kichlan shook his head at me, but his expression was warm. "Well, I don't trust any of them. Particularly not Fedor. I think this is a terrible idea and we should leave. Now."

"But he's in your collecting team."

"Exactly." Kichlan glanced over his shoulder. "Doesn't that seem a little too convenient to you?"

I was not convinced Fedor was any less trustworthy than the rest of them. And it wasn't trustworthiness that worried me. It was the overall sanity of their plan that had me concerned. It sounded like they wanted to let debris run riot through the city. Didn't they care about the lives of the people who lived here? Did they want more to die in flames, to drown in effluent, to be crushed beneath the weight of buildings that could no longer stand?

That was just what happened when the puppet men let their debris monster loose in the streets. I had fought so hard to contain that creature, and return the city to calm. We all had. Did these Unbound really expect us to help them do it all again?

And yet, if I could convince the Keeper to come with us, and if he could be there as these hoards of stored debris grains were released, he could absorb them just as I had seen him do before. Would that help him close the doors, and keep the city safe? Would that plug some of the holes the puppet men had torn in him? And, perhaps, make him a little more whole?

"I think what they are planning to do is dangerous. It could be disastrous. But they will do it anyway, whether or not we help them. If I am there, however, I can ensure the debris they release goes directly to help the Keeper. And he needs all the help we can give him, before he leads us down any more dark–" I nearly bit my tongue.

"Leads you where?"

"Sewers, like last time."

Kichlan regarded me with a long, level gaze. I didn't think he believed me.

"We should do this, for Lad," I said. "Because until we help the Keeper, he will not leave Lad alone. How much can Lad take, before he snaps again? If this actually works, then the doors will close and he won't need Lad any more."

But even as I said it, I doubted. Would that really

quieten the Keeper? Now that he had found me, now that I had seen him, would he ever really leave me alone? And Lad was his key to me. How long had he existed, with no one to talk to except the poor Halves who could never truly understand what was going on?

"For Lad?"

I nodded. "We don't have to trust them to join them. We don't even have to agree with them – but we can, at least, monitor them."

Kichlan's shoulders slumped. "If you say so, Tanyana."

"Are you sure–"

"We are doing this for Lad. So yes, I am sure."

We pushed our way back through the rubble.

"Done?" Fedor, arms crossed tightly, did not seem to appreciate being walked out on. I couldn't imagine why.

"We will help you," Kichlan answered. "If that is what you want from us."

"I am glad you understand." Lev nodded. He appeared pleased. "More collectors can cover more ground." He glanced back at Fedor. "And I think we already have an assignment for you."

I didn't think the Unbound would let Kichlan and I leave without a commitment signed in blood and sworn before the Keeper himself. But in the end they seemed happy with our word. Or, perhaps, Eugeny's reassurances. Still, we were glad to finally leave, so much we almost ran back to the surface. Valya and Yicor remained there, with their Unbound revolutionaries, in their trapped-in-time world.

Somehow, while we were underground, it had grown to late afternoon.

We passed a group of children, hurried along by governesses in rich dresses. I wondered what they could be doing this far from the Keeper's Tear River. An excursion to learn how poor, less-skilled binders live? Kichlan and I were forced closer to each other in order to walk around them. He slipped an arm through mine in the process, and even when the children were long gone, he did not let me go.

Kichlan headed for Eugeny's house. Arms locked as they were, it seemed I was going with him. I wasn't about to untangle us.

Only when Eugeny's squat building came into view, did Kichlan slow down. "Another few days?" he whispered. "Let me think up an excuse to give Lad first. I do not want him involved in this."

"I agree."

Fedor had given us a scouting mission. Something nice and easy to start us off. Simple. He didn't know where and when yet, but would tell us soon, so we should be ready.

I hoped our role remained that way: simple.

"Let's hope Fedor does not expect us to follow his commands blindly." Kichlan placed a hand on the door's handle, and hesitated. "I'm willing to go along with this, but not if it puts my brother in danger." A pause. "And not if it puts you in danger either."

My heart did a strange little flip. "I know."

But even as Kichlan turned the handle the door flew open. He staggered and almost fell against Eugeny's chest. The old man looked wild, the edges of his face lit by the oil lamps behind him, eyes shining and fearful. Great purple bruises darkened his eyes, his chin, and his cheek was deeply grazed and oozing blood.

"What–?" Kichlan grasped the doorframe to keep his balance.

"Lad is gone," Eugeny said. "He's gone."

4.

"I don't know what happened." Eugeny sat at his kitchen table, in front of a popping fire, cradling a badly bruised arm. "After you left, he seemed happy, his usual self. He helped me with the chores, mucked out the stable – you know he loves that horse." Eugeny sucked air through his teeth as Kichlan tested his wrist.

I stood against the wall, close to the warmth of the fire, so I couldn't see most of the old man's injuries. The black marks around his eyes and cheeks were difficult to look at. Kichlan pursed his lips as he inspected Eugeny's arm, his skin ashen. I couldn't decide if that was due to Lad's absence, or Eugeny's face.

"That hurts, boy."

"I don't think it's broken," Kichlan said, his voice so low it was nearly consumed by the fire.

For a moment, I wondered how he knew. Then I considered a life spent with his strong, volatile brother, and realised he probably had far too much experience.

"Well that's something." A moment of pained tension and heavy breathing. "Started just after we ate. He began talking to himself, pacing. Asking for you both. I couldn't calm him, it got worse and worse. Then he wanted to leave, and I tried to stop him."

Kichlan sat forward, pressed a cloth damped by fire-warmed water against the cut on Eugeny's cheek. I looked away.

"Well, you can see what he did."

A log burst loudly in the fireplace. I watched an ember leap for freedom and wink out silently on the stone floor.

"I should have been here." Kichlan sat back, rubbed his eyes. "I should never have left him."

"Boy." Eugeny touched Kichlan's hand lightly, loosened his tightly clenched fingers and held them. "You can leave this old man be, get out there and find your brother."

"I can't leave you alone again. Not like this."

"I can look after myself."

Kichlan hesitated, until I said, "We will use my suit, the symbols. It will take us right to him. We won't be gone long."

Then the call came.

It blared bright from my wrists, streaming sharply into Kichlan's face and the back of Eugeny's head. Kichlan's came an instant later, and together we turned to direct the shining maps onto the kitchen walls.

"A debris emergency?" The old man turned, and peered at us through swelling skin.

Kichlan and I shared a long, heavy look. We knew where these calls came from. Every so-called emergency the veche and their puppet men had called us out on had turned out to be a test.

"Another one?" Kichlan grated out the words.

"They called both of us," I answered. "Both teams. I don't think that's a coincidence."

He scowled. "We need to find Lad." A flick of his wrist and his map disappeared. "The veche can go hang themselves and their debris. I am going to search for my brother instead."

I slowly shook my head. "Can't you see?" Tension ran tight through my bones, along the lines of my suit, made sharp by the bright light of the debris emergency. It was all so clear to me. I could feel it in the metal deep within.

"See what?"

I flicked off my map as well. Instead, I placed two light fingers on the band around my wrist. I could follow the surging and the dipping of the symbols there, better than any projected map. The debris cipher buzzed violently against my fingertips. Lad's symbol was strange – pulsing, and doubled-up, almost as though there were two of him – and he was right beside the debris.

"The Keeper," I whispered. The words felt like poison on my tongue. "Do you think Lad left on his own? Do you honestly still believe he was talking to himself?"

Kichlan's face closed up, solidified into a dark expression of anger and frustration. "That bastard."

"We need to go. We need to hurry. Whatever is causing this," I waved the blinding suit band in front of Kichlan's face, "the Keeper will be there. With Lad."

"Other's hells!" Kichlan balled his hand into a fist and smacked the stone wall. "Damn him!"

"Kichlan!" Eugeny pushed himself to his feet. "Destroying your hand, and my wall, will get you nowhere. I can look after myself. You need to go and find your brother."

"I should have been here!" He drew his arm back for another swing. I caught him, and he stilled instantly.

"Not you," I hissed. My own anger fought with the suit's tension and between them, something twinged against the metallic scars low across my belly. "Me, Kichlan. The Keeper is doing this to get to me, just like the veche is doing this to get to me. So can't you see? We have to go, now, because somewhere the Keeper and the puppet men are wrecking debris havoc and Lad is with them. Lad! So we have to go, Kichlan, and keep them away from him."

Colour drained from Kichlan's face and I knew he understood. If we didn't hurry the puppet men, waiting for me, waiting to test me, would find only Lad to distract them. "No," he breathed the words. "I can't let them take him."

"Exactly." I turned to Eugeny. His battered face was set and determined.

"Hurry," was all he said.

Still clutching Kichlan's forearm, I dragged him from his home. He sagged like a dead weight behind me, like all the fury and frustration had leaked from him with the colour in his cheeks. I released him only to touch my suit, to follow its instructions. Kichlan did not speak, it seemed like it was taking all of his strength to stay upright.

"Tanyana!"

I spun. Natasha, Mizra and Aleksey ran towards us, their wrists beaming flickering maps on the walls. Mizra stared in horror at Kichlan, but still took his arm from me when I asked.

"Lad is missing," I said, and that was explanation enough. Mizra and Natasha shared shocked glances before peering uncertainly at Kichlan.

Aleksey frowned. "The big guy, right?" he said, after a moment. "Well, I'm sure he can look after himself."

I fought an urge to slap him as Kichlan jerked his head up, and focused. "You're what?"

"Enough," I snapped at both of them. "We need to hurry." I turned on Mizra. "Can you help Kichlan? They've been called too."

Mizra scowled. "Both teams? That's odd, isn't it?"

"I know. Believe me, I know."

Aleksey glanced between us, confused. But I wasn't about to take the time to explain.

"Don't bother," I said, as Natasha beamed her map against the wall. Without Kichlan hanging on to me I could follow the map on my wrist with far greater efficiency.

We ran. I tried not to imagine what was awaiting us, what debris creature the puppet men had summoned to test me with, and what that thing was doing to Lad. Why had the Keeper dragged him from the safety of Eugeny's house?

"What are you doing?" Aleksey ran with surprising ease for a man of his size. He did not even sound out of breath as he matched my pace and peered pointedly at my wrist.

"It's a map," I answered, shortly, and took a sudden corner. He stayed by my side.

"I know, at least, it is on the wall. I know the symbol for me, and I know the one for debris." In the sharp suit glow and the on-and-off light of passing lamps his self-effacing smile took on something sinister, something ingratiating and false. "Natasha explained it to me and I'm glad she did. Can you imagine something like this happening when I've only just started?"

I said nothing, though I could imagine it quite well. After all, it had happened to me.

It didn't deter him. "So I understand it's a map, but you're reading it with your fingers."

I slowed slightly to allow Mizra, Natasha and Kichlan to catch up. With a short sigh I explained, in no real detail, that the symbols on his wrist were the map, and that he could follow them by touch alone. I did not explain that Lad had a symbol of his own. Or that the Keeper was there, with the debris, and that debris was more than a clump wriggling in symbol form in some glowing corner. That it was all around us.

But still, as we ran, Aleksey tested the map on his own suit with his fingers. His eyes widened as he felt bumps in the road before we came to them, and he anticipated corners, gates, and fences in our way.

"Remarkable," he gasped as he leapt over a pothole he could not have seen otherwise. Despite everything I found myself smiling with him, and wondering fruitlessly again what we could achieve if we knew how to read all of these symbols, this long-lost language of the Unbound.

"Kichlan!" Sofia, Uzdal and Fedor appeared at the intersection of a street. Sofia rushed to take Kichlan, while Fedor met my eyes and nodded a guarded greeting.

"What's wrong with him?" Sofia cried out again, tone high-pitched, panicked and far too loud for my liking. She wrapped her arms around Kichlan's chest and stared up into his blank face. "It's Sofia. I'm here now. Everything is okay. Please talk to me."

I let the others explain and, fingers pressed to my suit, continued forward. The debris symbol – that box-like shape, split by lightning with dots on either side – buzzed and shook like a terrified creature. I had never felt anything like it.

Beside me, Aleksey swore. "Is this normal?"

I glanced up at him. The scar across his nose was stark in the suit-light. I must have looked much the same. "Nothing about this is normal."

But when I turned the final corner, when the pull of the map died and was replaced by my suit tugging, aching, demanding to be let free, there was no terrible mass of debris grains growing with each dark and lancing plane. No waves of it rolled over my feet. No creature stalked between realities ready to rip us all apart.

The street opened out to a wide square. I could make out quiet market stalls folded up for the night, their wares visible but secure inside boxes of thick, clear poly. Any signs written in pions that may have given details and prices were probably dimmed, but we had no way of knowing. So too the bright renders – images of bears, usually – that loped through the market for the entertainment of children. Vegetables to be sold raw or roasted were stored at one end of the market, beside frozen meat and long tanks full of dark-scaled Weeping carp. Cheap, factory produced clothing, only available in grey, beige or a sickly kind of green, was piled at another end. Cooking ware, cutlery, small items of furniture and ghastly poly reproductions of the Keeper Mountain were scattered liberally throughout the square.

In the middle of this, beneath a tall, fitfully flickering lamp with ornate, flame-shaped glass, crouched a single person. He wept, long and low, and as a breeze ruffled blonde curls bronzed by the flickering light I realised it was Lad.

Then I saw why he was crying.

"That's him, isn't it?" Aleksey murmured beside me. "Lad?"

"Lad!" Kichlan tore himself from Sofia's gentle hands, shoved Aleksey aside, and ran toward his brother.

My suit pulsed into life. It coated my legs with a quick-silver slick and propelled me forward. Two swift, long strides and I caught him. The suit gloved my arms and my fingers bit hard into Kichlan's shoulders. I forced him down, held him against the cobblestones as he struggled and swore at me.

Lying against his back, I whispered a constant stream of words into his ear. "Quiet, Kichlan. Wait. Just wait. Calm down. Are you calm?"

"What are you doing to him?" Sofia shrieked.

I looked up. Lad turned, face stricken in the lightning flashes of the pion-powered lamp.

"Get off him!" Sofia ran to my side. "Tanyana, let him– oh– Other–" Her words choked off into silence.

A body hung from the lamp above Lad. Headless, sag-ging and disembowelled. But worse – somehow worse – was the way it drooped. Limbs that looked too long, torso twisted out of shape. The Hon Ji Half. And within her, still working its terrible disease, the debris squirmed.

Sofia spun. Her feet slipped and she fell to the stones. Dimly, I heard her retch. Kichlan bucked and fought. My suit demanded freedom, needed to protect me, and some terrible frightened part of me wanted to give in. Because in that world behind the suit's mask the dead woman – the woman I had killed – would just be less real.

Lad cradled the Hon Ji's head in his lap and hunched over it as he wept. And while it was terrible, and while

I ached for the pain and confusion it was causing him, all I could think of was those debris tendrils, those murderous serpent heads. I had to get him away from them.

Aleksey knelt beside me. "What's going on?"

I looked up at him. Mizra, Uzdal and Natasha held back at the corner in a frightened little knot. I glanced over at Fedor. He helped Sofia sit up and wiped her mouth, but his face was pale and sweat-slick in the unsteady light. Aleksey, however, remained composed. He stared at Lad and the body with intensity, but it was not fear or horror. It was business-like and steady.

"I don't know," I grunted as Kichlan bucked. "Can you hold him?"

Aleksey took one look at the large man beneath me, and nodded. "Reckon I can."

We moved swiftly. As I slid myself to the stone, Aleksey took my place. Knee to the hollow of Kichlan's back, elbow at his neck, and Kichlan could barely move.

"You did that well," I said, a question in my tone.

"Ah, yes." He grunted, as Kichlan pushed against him. "I've had practice."

Now was hardly the time for a longer explanation.

My suit began to spread and I did not try to stop it. Its strength seeped through my legs and arms. It pressed against my chest and I breathed with it. Something tickled in my gut, not pain – something heady and far too enjoyable.

Aleksey watched me in wonder. "Lad, did he kill her?"

"No." My shoulders were covered, my neck.

"How do you know?"

The suit covered my face. I blinked. The Hon Ji Half was a chaos of debris, so much more of it and so much worse than the last time. Lad was more solid in this world than he had seemed before, and he cupped a writhing snake-nest in his lap. Above him loomed a great door. Taller than the struggling lamp, as wide as the market square, it rocked wildly on its hinges, ready to break open at any moment.

"Finally!" The Keeper appeared by my side.

I didn't think. Even as the rest of the market was resolving itself – Kichlan and Aleksey, Fedor and Sofia – I spun and smacked him in his white, dark-veined face.

The Keeper's world shook as he stumbled back. The darkness and the doors rippled like cloth in a breeze. He dropped to a knee, pressed his hand to his cheek and stared up at me with shock. "T... Tanyana?"

"That's enough!" I shouted at him, and my own words echoed around the inside of my suit like tremors. "You leave him alone, do you hear me? Never do this to him again!"

The Keeper's expression strengthened and he stood. "Lad is my Half. They all are."

Fury tripped another set of tremors through me. Very slowly, like I was drawing a pair of great blades, I extended my suit out long and threatening from both hands. The Keeper held his ground.

"No," I hissed the word through clenched teeth. "Lad is not your tool. You will not put him in danger, you will not take him from the safety of his home and his family. Not again."

"Tanyana?" Fedor, somewhere distant and dim, sounded incredulous. "Is... Is the Keeper here?"

Kichlan roared and broke free. He scuffled with Aleksey. From the corner of my eye I watched their door-and-dark patterned bodies fight, watched Kichlan go down to Aleksey's tightly controlled fists.

"You don't understand." The Keeper shook his head and ran fingers over his white scalp. "Halves are the only way I can communicate; the only way I can touch any world at all. That is why they were sent here."

I lifted my blades. I felt powerful and strong and more like a weapon than I could dare to think. "Not any more. Not Lad. You will not put him in any more danger."

"What are you doing?" Fedor asked, terrified and outraged all at once. He tried to approach us, but Mizra and Uzdal held him back.

"But that is their purpose!" the Keeper cried.

"Like her?" I pointed to the dead Half and my blade twisted over itself, curling into something intricate and cruel. "Was that her purpose too?"

"What? No." Keeper stumbled back as though I had hit him again.

"That is what happens to your Halves!"

"No I–"

"That is what happens when you communicate with them, when you draw attention to them. She died that way because of you!" Except I knew that wasn't true. I knew she had died that way because of me, but my anger and my suit would brook no argument. "And Lad is not your tool to be used and disposed of. Do you understand?"

The Keeper hiccupped, pressed his hands over his eyes. I could see the throb of his debris pulse as it surged beneath his skin.

"Tanyana! He–" Aleksey this time, strangled and indignant. I turned to see Kichlan knock him aside, leap to his feet, rush at the Keeper – at what must have looked like the empty air I was shouting at.

I blunted my suit, split it, wrapped it around his chest and held him secure. "Kichlan, stop!" His wild eyes snapped to me. Of all the things in that strange, dark space, those eyes were the clearest. "We are coming to an agreement."

Fedor struggled with Mizra and Uzdal, panicked and disbelieving. "But he is the Keeper," he croaked out the words. "You can't just argue with him. You can't–"

I held Kichlan's gaze. He could not see my eyes through my silver mask, but still, I needed him to understand. Then he sagged against my suit like a doll empty of its stuffing, and I hated myself for holding him like this, for keeping him from the brother who needed him.

I turned back to the Keeper. "No more, do you hear?" I kept my tone tight, my voice low. No more shouting, no more screaming. We had to compromise, for Lad. "If you want to talk to me, then talk to me. But Lad is not yours. No more expeditions on his own, no more risks he cannot comprehend. Are we agreed?"

The Keeper lowered his hands, his inhuman face unreadable.

"If you don't agree then you can close these doors by yourself."

He wiped his dark tears away. "Are you are willing to risk the world for him?"

"Of course I am."

His mouth set in a furious line, but he gave in. "So be it."

Gingerly, watching him closely, I unwound my grip on Kichlan's chest. "The Keeper has promised," I said. "No more."

"And we can trust those promises, can we?" Kichlan touched his hands delicately to his forehead, then the back of his skull. Even painted with doors, I saw him wince.

I shrugged.

"You can," the Keeper snapped at me. "Tell him you can."

I said nothing.

Sofia hurried to Kichlan's side, exclaimed over his head, arms, back. Aleksey was rubbing his own jaw, and apologising in slightly slurred words.

But Lad, through all this, hadn't moved. He still sat beneath the lamp – beneath the great debris door – and held the dead woman's head in his lap.

Slowly, I approached him. Debris wormed its way from the clean cut through her neck, questing with stunted, sightless heads out into the world.

Lad's lap was heavy with blood. It hadn't thickened the way I would have expected, if anything, it ran thinner than usual. Diluted and pale, layered like oil. Was her body still disintegrating? The pion bindings undoing even after her death?

"Lad?" I crouched. I tried not to look at the mess that had been her eyes. Something eased above us, something that sounded wet. I glanced up. The Half's body was attached to the lamp by tendrils of metal grown from its copper frame. And while the debris obviously disrupted the pion flow enough to interfere with the light, it was so contained within her, so focused on her bindings and hers alone, that these new and unnatural straps held. Her body sagged against them. It stretched. How long before she came apart like the flesh I had inadvertently pulled from her stomach? And what would the debris do then, without a body to inhabit and destroy?

The puppet men had dragged her body here, hung her up, and then set off an emergency call so we would find her. But I couldn't imagine why.

The Keeper crouched on the other side of Lad. Shoulders stiff, mouth firm. "Do you see what it's doing?"

The wiggling mass of debris had grown. And the pasty snake-heads that rose from her body, that wavered, scenting the air, they were the very things rattling the door.

"You should have calmed it and reclaimed it in the first place. When I told you to."

I released a sigh. "I don't even know if that is possible."

"Of course it is."

"This is nothing like–" I stopped. What was I doing, arguing, while Lad was in such danger?

So instead, I leaned close to him. "Lad?"

He sniffed. "Tan." And the face he tipped to look at me tugged my heart. Riddled with guilt and fear and utter confusion, he shook and began to rock. "I'm sorry, Tan. I hurt Geny. I– tell Kich I am sorry."

"He knows."

Movement behind me. I held up a silver hand. "I think you should stay back." Kichlan, I thought, without needing to look. So I was surprised, when Aleksey said, "What can we do to help?"

I glanced over my shoulder. Kichlan, Sofia and Aleksey stood much closer than I had realised, with Fedor just behind them. Mizra, Uzdal and Natasha had closed the gap, but they were still hazy in the door world. Dimly, I could hear someone else being sick, and clenched my teeth against a powerful urge to do the same.

"Can you see the debris?" I asked them.

"Of course." Kichlan's voice was raw and sore sounding.

"What is it?" Aleksey asked. "I mean, it's debris, but..."

"I know." How, exactly, did one explain such horror? So instead, I talked about pion bindings and disintegration and tried to pretend I wasn't talking about a person, or a Half. "So don't get too close to it," I finished. "We need to be careful."

"What about you?" Aleksey whispered.

"What about Lad?" I thought I heard Kichlan say, but it was so soft I couldn't be sure.

"Tan?" Lad looked up again. "I'm sorry, Tan."

A throbbing tendril of debris, scrawled with thick ridges like scars, flicked itself free of the dead woman's mouth and wrapped around his arm.

Above me, the door banged hard. Wood cracked.

"We have no more time left!" The Keeper cried.

Lad gasped. His suit sliced out from his wrist in a circular blade and cut the questing tendril away. The rest of them, the writhing mass in body and head, stilled. Then, as one, they swivelled to face the slumped, weeping Half.

And attacked.

In one great pale mass the debris reared and ploughed toward Lad. Behind me, Kichlan cried out. Beside me, the Keeper screamed. And with Lad's terrified wide eyes searing my mind I did the one thing I could do. I stood, and I got in the way.

My suit spread out behind me, it fanned like wings that caught the charging debris, then cupped and threw it back. While it battered me I grabbed the Hon Ji woman's head from Lad's lap. She fell to blood and mess between my fingers. Crying, Lad scooted out of the way. I barely felt the gore. Only debris, pressed between my fingers, squeezing and squirming desperately. I spun and threw the strands into the worming mass. My suit-wings shifted, wound their way to my chest and arched above me in a gleaming shield.

"You need to calm it!" The Keeper, beside me, scrambled at my shoulder.

"Right." But I didn't believe it was possible.

You know how, Lad had once said to me. He was no help now. Kichlan and Aleksey ran behind me, grabbed him and dragged him away. He wept loudly, and his sobs seemed to echo from the very doors.

"Right," I said again. In the past, I had used the contact between my suit and the debris to calm it to the point where it could return to the Keeper. I'd held it in thin pincers or silver-wrapped hands, and summoned whatever I could to combat the chaos and the pain the puppet men had imbued it with. From the image of Lad's smile, to the smell of Eugeny's house. To Kichlan. Just Kichlan.

I'd never really understood how and why it worked, only that when I was touching it with my suited hands, the debris could understand me. The Keeper needed me to do that again.

So I closed my eyes. Through the suit I felt each blow, over my skin, though my muscles, and down into my bones. Even as the debris hit me, I reached out to it. I held my hands out, palms up, opened my wing-like shields. It rained thick and heavy against my face, my body, my palms. I tried to make each touch a caress, to respond to each blow with a soothing word.

"You don't need to do this," I breathed. I summoned each inch of love, of protection, that Lad so terrified and lost had brought out in me. I gave it all to the debris. "I know they have hurt you, I know they have frightened you. But you don't need to do this. Let it go."

But the bombardment did not stop, and from somewhere I thought I could hear laughter. Distant, mechanical, unnatural.

I breathed deeply. The air was heavy, it tasted sour. I pushed all that aside, focused on sowing my small seeds of peace. "Listen to me–"

Something twisted my arm. Sharp, burning, like needles plunging into me. And all my thoughts of Lad were shattered. In their place: a cold table, harsh light, and pain, deep piercing pain. They were tearing me, forcing hunger into my being, scouring out an emptiness, a loss I would do anything to fill. And I wanted to scream, because that table, that suiting, was so terrible and so familiar. I had lived it once, I could not live it again. But when I opened my eyes the table was gone and the lights and the needles, but darkness and doors crowded me and for a horrible moment I wasn't sure what was going on.

Then I noticed the debris snakes peeling my suit away from my right arm. They wove themselves in and out of the metal like threads in cloth and from there they pulled, twisted, tugged. And the suit went with them. It split like a deep wound – more tearing, more scarring – and a large section of my arm peeled free. As my skin was revealed, dark and door-textured in this strange world, I finally screamed.

Pain sheared into my arm, and deep into my belly. My wings dissolved, the suit rippled, and sent out hundreds of tiny saws that tore and sliced the debris free.

Shaken, I clutched my arm. What had the debris done? Dissolved the pion bonds in my suit? But it hadn't destroyed it, hadn't liquefied silver as it did to flesh. If anything, it looked like the debris had melded with the suit, joined it, and tried to take it from me.

"Tanyana!" The Keeper was by my side. He touched my arm with his own, pale hands, while the debris rolled over itself, regrouping. "Are you all right?"

I shook my head. "It's not working."

"Are you trying–"

"Yes!" I was having almost as much trouble calming myself. "Yes, I tried. It doesn't hear me, or it doesn't care. I gave it everything I had. It just– it just–" Gave some of itself back. Where I had sent out Lad's love it had forced on me its fear, its pain, its torture. All too recognisable, all too terrifying. "How is that possible?"

"Tanyana!" Kichlan ran to my other side. "What was that?"

"The debris attacked me." And it was strong. Stronger, perhaps, than my suit.

"What will you do?" The Keeper asked.

I glanced between them. "I don't think we can calm it and return it. You saw what it did when I tried."

Kichlan blanched. "So what do we do?"

"The door," the Keeper whispered again, broken and desolate.

The debris looked like it was trying to create a form, to become a creature like the last one that had so decimated Movoc-under-Keeper. A creature which, this time, I knew I would not be able to contain. But it was struggling. It was not one great, single-minded mass of grains, and it was not one sheer plane. So many different bodies, heads, and forms, all folding and fighting over each other. And all so broken, patterned by hard-ridged scars. It surged, it dissolved, elements of it reared toward me only to be drawn back into the rest.

Around it, the door its unnatural presence created was rocking on its hinges. Wild, nearly broken, no small contained gap for the Keeper to trick me into looking through. No sewer wall beneath the city to bear its destruction. That door would burst open and the market square would be consumed by emptiness, possibly this entire Effluent, maybe all of Movoc-under-Keeper.

Would the open door consume everything in this world? Even the debris?

"The door," I whispered, and pushed both Kichlan and the Keeper back.

It was probably a foolish idea. Foolhardy. Dangerous. But it was all I had.

I launched myself through the debris. As it burst around me, as it wrapped its malicious, squirming self about me, I stretched past it. To the door.

I grasped for the handle. My hand slipped right through it.

"Open it!" I cried as wiggling furious fingers slipped into my suit. Into my arms, my legs, torso, face. "Open the door!"

My suit fought back. It churned and rippled, flicking debris from it, smacking it back, pulling it free. Paralysed as the debris and the suit battled, I watched the Keeper from the corner of my eyes. Horrified, he stared at me. His hand twitched once, toward the door.

"What?" he gurgled.

"Open it." My voice was failing. "It's the only way."

Still, he hesitated.

"Keeper!" Lad shouted. He pulled away from Aleksey, stumbled toward me, arm outstretched. "Do what Tan says. Make it stop hurting her!"

I don't know if it was the sight of another of his precious Half flinging himself into the path of danger, or if my garbled words finally drove some kind of sense into the Keeper's pale head. But he flickered, reappeared beside the door, and grasped the handle.

"I hope you know what you're doing," he said, and opened the door.

On the other side was... nothing. Darkness not at all like the night, not at all like the Keeper's world. It was distance, emptiness, nothing. And it made me ache to witness, because it was so wrong, so terrifyingly wrong.

I didn't know what I was doing. But the suit did. As the door opened and that wind, that clutching, dragging, ice and fire nothingness rushed out, the suit gathered itself and rolled one last time. In a great wave, from my toes to my head, it threw the debris from us like shedding a second skin. The writhing mass tried to right itself, but I was ready for it. Even as the debris regrouped I cupped it, wrapped my suit around its unstable form and pushed it right through the open door.

My suit could take no more.

It failed in the wake of the emptiness. As it started to reduce to a ripple of sandy water, it whiplashed desperately back into the bands. The Keeper leaned on the opening door, pushing with all his insubstantial weight against the terrible howling wind, and I strained to help him. But my suit was gone, withdrawn, and my skin touched the rough, splintered wood.

Still we pushed, the Keeper and I, until the door closed, and the wind stopped, and I could fall back, and allow the suit to slip from my eyes.

"Oh, very good." Voices without tone, emotionless, impossible. I had not seen the puppet men. And yet I was not surprised to know they were near.

"Very nicely done."

5.

"Says that was very dangerous. Says that was a bad idea. Says it hurts, Tanyana, hurts and will never heal."

Lad rambled on. I kept my eyes closed, savoured the darkness – the hot inside-my-own-head darkness that had nothing to do with doors – and breathed in the open air.

The city, and the world, had not been sucked into nothingness. So it couldn't have been that bad an idea.

"Says the door will not go away now. The hole will stay forever."

I opened my eyes. The lamp no longer flickered, but when I turned an aching head I realised that was because it no longer existed. The lamp and the Hon Ji Half's body were gone. All that remained were enormous cracks in the cobblestones, spiderwebbing their way from the centre of the marketplace. Even as I watched they inched further, crawled up the sides of a closed-up stall, and dissolved it. Poly turned to liquid, then steam, then nothing at all. The vegetables inside it unwound to thin, floating fibres before vanishing with a breath of icy Movoc wind.

"How much longer will that go on?" I asked, my throat seared.

Someone had carried me from the centre of the market. Without them, would I too have been caught in that creeping emptiness and brushed away like so much dust?

"It's slowing," Kichlan said, close and above me. It took a moment to realise I was lying in his lap, his arms cradling my neck and knees. That explained who had moved me.

I shifted slightly, trying not to feel uncomfortable at being held so close to him. The movement flared up pain, too much like memories of stitches and healing scars. My suit hurt. In the bands, all around them, and deeper, a throb that seemed to travel to my spine. My right hand, I realised, felt the worst.

A grunt and I lifted it. My palm was a mess of countless tiny cuts, all crimson and slowly solidifying silver. Splinters from an unreal door? I shuddered, lowered it, and glanced up at Kichlan instead.

He didn't look to be in much better condition. Blood patterned his temple. His jaw and one eye were already darkening with bruises, and his lower lip was cut.

"Oh," I said, before I could stop myself. "I'm sorry."

"Actually, that was mostly me." Aleksey's jaw was also bruised, his lip swollen and welling up blood. He dabbed at it with his sleeve.

"Oh." It really seemed about all I could manage to say. "I'm sorry."

He tried to smile, flinched, settled into something neutral. "No one warned me collecting would be so violent."

"I'm sorry," I said, yet again. "I didn't have a choice. I couldn't let you get close to Lad – any of you – the debris would have killed you. And then there was a door, and it was open. I didn't want to hurt you, I would never want to–" I sounded pathetic. What kind of an excuse was that? "I'm sorry."

"I know, Tan," Kichlan said. "I really do understand. And thank you for helping my brother." And, so swiftly I could have imagined it, he ducked his head and kissed me.

For a moment, all I felt was his tingling lips on mine. His blood was warm, and did not taste like mine did – not heavy with the metal drilled into his bones. I lifted one of my scarred hands, in something that felt like wonder, and ran fingers down the marvellous angle of his jaw.

Then Lad said, "Says he hurts and you are all ignoring him and you should all stop talking and listen to him instead."

I blinked myself back to reality, feeling flushed and sore and embarrassed. I watched a blush rise along Kichlan's neck, and it was good to know he felt the same. Such a strange connection.

Lad was standing close to his brother, his hand hovering above mine, making patting motions without actually touching me. He looked worn, grey. The hem of his shirt was caked with blood.

There was so much blood. Would we ever truly be clean again?

"I think the cracks have stopped growing," Mizra reported from somewhere I couldn't see. "No more poly failing either."

"Lad," I said. "Will you speak to the… To him, for me?"

He hesitated, placed his bloodstained hand on mine. "Yes." Some of the colour returned to his face. "I will."

"Thank you." I smiled at him, and managed to coax a small one out of him. "I will talk to him, please tell me what he says."

Lad squeezed my hand.

I addressed a patch of air just behind Lad's ear, deciding I didn't much care if the Keeper was actually standing somewhere else. "I couldn't tame it," I said. "I couldn't calm it. And I know tearing it away from you is probably the worst thing I could have done, but I hope you understand that I didn't have a choice."

Lad tipped his head. "Says: the door is closed now, but it is a scar and it won't heal." He paused. "And some other stuff. Sorry, Tan, he talks and talks and I can't understand everything. Some of it isn't real words."

Kichlan's hands tightened around me.

I swallowed down bile through a thick-feeling throat. "Tell him: I wish that was not so. But I couldn't let the debris kill Lad, and I couldn't let it kill me."

"He knows. He is sorry too." A longer hesitation. Idly, Lad stroked the back of my hand with one finger. "He will do like you asked, Tan. Says he doesn't have a choice, he thinks. Next time he needs to talk, he will tell me. Won't ask me to follow. Won't shout. Will just tell me, and I tell you, but you have to put your suit on straight away. Is that okay, Tan? He says: straight away."

"Yes, that's okay. I understand. Straight away."

I watched Lad for another moment of silence, before he said, "Think he's gone away."

Where did the Keeper go to lick his wounds? Part of me wondered if he followed us constantly, just quietly, watching from his dark world.

I was gradually becoming aware of sounds and lights flickering around us. Voices, high with fear or concern. Then, strangely, Natasha soothing, reassuring, sounding very much in control.

I lifted eyebrows at Kichlan. "Imagine that," I said, with a grin.

His hands softened as he chuckled. "Indeed."

And Lad laughed too, though he couldn't have understood us, and tightened his grip on my hand.

For a moment, everything felt right in a way I knew I'd missed, but hadn't realised how strongly.

"Alarms have been sent, apparently." Natasha's head leaned into view. "We've got a small crowd gathering. If it's not too much trouble, and your hands aren't too ah... full, I would love some help trying to keep the crowd away from the sudden crevasse of doom." She flashed a wild grin.

Lad burst out laughing, and pressed his hands to his face.

It was about time I moved, too.

"All right." I flexed, wincing. At least the ache was dimming. My suit still spun, though it did so with a sluggishness I'd never seen from it before. "I can take a hint."

With Kichlan helping and Lad holding onto my hand in a way that was rather less than convenient I eased myself from Kichlan's lap. Standing was a little difficult, but Sofia appeared by my side and gripped my elbow to hold me steady. She glared at Kichlan and Aleksey.

"Off you go, help Natasha," she said. It was not a request.

"Even looking like this?" Kichlan waved a hand at his damaged face. Lad made a little uncertain noise.

"It should give them a pretty good reason to stay back."

Kichlan and Lad slumped away. Aleksey, who seemed to catch onto these things quickly, didn't bother arguing and headed in the opposite direction.

"You need to sit down," Sofia told me, once they were out of immediate earshot.

"But I just stood up." I, of course, hadn't learned that particular lesson so well.

"Regardless." She leaned closer to me. "You're shaking; I can feel it through your uniform and your clothes. Don't try and hide these things from me."

She had a point.

Sofia led me to one of the stalls and helped me sit on it. The hard poly edges weren't comfortable, but it was certainly easier than standing. I watched as Natasha, Uzdal, Mizra, Fedor, Aleksey, Kichlan and Lad formed a rough circle around the cracks and what had once been the centre of the market square. They held back a peering crowd of pion-binders. People who could not know what had just happened here, or what was causing the dramatic holes in the earth, only that it had involved a lot of noise and a group of debris collectors. Since we saved their city we, and the work we did, had suddenly become a lot more interesting.

I shuddered at the very thought of those cracks and the emptiness that had created them. Why would anyone want to stand closer?

"What's wrong? Are you cold?" Sofia touched my shoulders, my forehead.

I shook my head, even as nausea tickled my stomach. "Do you think the pion-binders will be able to fix those holes we made?" I asked, knowing she could not answer.

Sofia stared into the market place. "They'll bring in architects, won't they? Like you were, once?" She waited for me to agree. "Then they should be able to do it in a snap."

"A door opened there. It's not just debris weakening pion binds. The doors destroy everything. Probably the pions themselves." I had no way of knowing that, of seeing it or proving it. But I was certain it was true. That was the only way, surely, the doors could bleed nothingness into our world. By destroying the pions that made us.

"I don't know."

"Neither do I." And suddenly, the nausea stopped tickling, and my stomach rebelled. I was able to twist away before I threw up what little food I had eaten, all over some poor market trader's stall.

"Tanyana!" Sofia rubbed my back. "Is it that bad?"

I lost the battle again, and ended up dry retching. I really hadn't eaten much, and that can't have helped. A few gasps, coughs, spits and I managed, "It will go away in a moment. It always does."

She stilled. "It always does?"

I shrugged, and wished I hadn't actually said anything. I wished I had some water too. "It's nothing."

"That's just not good enough, Tanyana." She did not exactly dig into my back, but the pressure of her fingertips increased noticeably. I didn't like the sound of that tone. "What are you saying? Just how much throwing up are you doing?"

"About as much as you were doing a moment ago, when you first saw that body." I glanced up. Her face was set in a seriously unimpressed expression. "It's only natural. The door, the debris, the body–"

"You said, *it always does*. You should be looking after yourself better than that. Kichlan cares about you." She hesitated.

"Kichlan? What's he got to do–?"

She squeezed onto the poly beside me, crossed her arms and leaned close. Her feet didn't reach the ground. I resisted the urge to lean away. "And Lad needs you, doesn't he? Separated from his brother, you are the one he relies on. What would happen if you suddenly couldn't help him, if you let yourself get so sick you couldn't collect at all?"

I blinked at her, a little shocked. "Oh, that's a bit extreme, don't you think? I'll feel awful for a few bells, maybe, but it doesn't last all day and I'm certainly not getting any worse."

She tucked a strand of her long brown hair behind her ear. Several of them had come loose from their tight bun and floated wispily around her head. She'd have hated that – Sofia preferred neatness and order – so I didn't mention it. She couldn't have done much to fix her hair now anyway. "So you've been feeling, what, generally ill? The usual Movoc winter illnesses?"

"Oh yes, it's probably just that." I tried to laugh it off. "You scared me, bringing Lad into it like that."

"Strange, though, to get them so late in spring. Tired all the time?"

"With the veche breaking us up, and the Keeper dragging us around and yes, taking responsibility for Lad, what else would you expect?"

"How long has this been happening?"

Another shrug. "Moon, maybe a bit more."

"You should take better care of yourself." She patted my knee, but her eyes were sharp, calculating, and searched my face. I was sure she could see every moment of doubt, every scar played in lines and shadows and sallowness across my skin. "And your stomach." She gestured loosely, fingers brushing my jacket over my abdomen, and I could not stop myself from flinching. "Nausea and pain? Have you been eating?"

"You haven't met Valya, have you?"

Another pause. "Have you told Kichlan?"

"No, of course not. He has enough to worry about at the moment don't you think?"

And then the market square lit up, and saved me from the frown gathering on Sofia's face. Together, we glanced up in surprise. Dozens of lights – like little flames independent of the wick – settled across the market square, surrounding the damage. The watching crowd seemed unconcerned, but without their ability to see how these lights were being created it was unsettling.

Lad hurried over. "Lights," he whispered.

I stood using Sofia's shoulder to help me up but ignoring her pointed look, as a small fist of enforcers marched through the crowd.

"Finally." Aleksey and the other collectors abandoned their posts as the enforcers arrived. He tried smiling again as he approached me. "Alarms must have worked. First protocol for an event like this is to bring enforcers in. Control the crowd, ascertain if healers are required. They'll send a pion message back, encoded on the same strands as the original alarm, requesting the appropriate circles."

"You seem to know a lot about the process," I said.

"Ah," he said, sheepishly. "Insider knowledge."

The majority of the enforcers created the same rough circle as we had, keeping spectators away from the crevasses. Three broke away from the group and wandered the site, carrying large slides and apparently making notes, if their twitching fingers were anything to go by. Another, his uniform more ornate and a large roaring bear's head emblazoned above his heart, was already talking to Natasha and Kichlan. I wondered how they would explain the Keeper, the door, and the poor Hon Ji Half of whom nothing remained.

"No healers, unless they think Kichlan needs one," Aleksey continued. He grinned, winced, and touched his lip. "Or me," he added. "Then architects to fix the street, excavators to provide raw materials, engineers to re-establish any broken pion paths. Like that lamp, I'd say. When it is recreated it will need to be connected to the network again, so an engineer would repair the path to allow the pions to get through. The usual."

When I had been an architect I had known "the usual" quite well. In fact, as the centre of a nine point circle I had often organised it. Not when enforcers were involved, however. My circle created, we did not repair.

I mentioned none of this, however, and asked, instead, "Insider knowledge?"

"Ah, yes." He rubbed the scar on his nose. "Used to be an enforcer."

"Before you fell."

He nodded, quiet for a moment, his face folded into shadow and free of expression. But it lasted only a moment, before his half-smile returned. "Life as an enforcer wasn't half as dramatic as debris collecting seems to be though."

"Like I said, this is not normal. Debris collecting is dank, dirty, and tedious. It involves long days of walking, crawling and climbing. We don't usually come across bodies." Or fight for the stability of the world, I wanted to say, but didn't entirely believe it.

The lights strengthened as the enforcer continued to speak to Kichlan and Natasha. Lad, obviously relieved of his initial fear, wandered across the square, trying a little too hard to look casual.

"Bro is lying," he whispered as he passed us, hands clasped behind his back, chin tucked close to his chest. "Not telling them about him, or about you."

"Oh?" Aleksey did not sound concerned, despite his previous employment, merely curious. "How are they explaining this all then?"

"Big explosion." Lad unclasped his hands long enough to make explosive movements. "Like last time."

That sounded like a good approach to me. The debris explosions that had rocked Movoc-under-Keeper would still be fresh in the enforcers' minds. Perhaps it would be enough to prevent any further questions.

"Are they creating the lights?" I asked Aleksey, as Lad wandered away again.

He nodded. "One man has that job. Torchbearer. Always harder to keep the peace in the dark."

"I can imagine."

Finally, the centre enforcer dismissed Natasha and Kichlan with a wave of his hand. They joined us. Natasha looked haggard, Kichlan like he could barely stand. Lad slipped an arm beneath his brother's shoulder, and I was surprised he accepted the support.

"They believed us," Natasha said.

The rest of the teams closed around us, forming a tight knot of debris collectors as the square filled with pion-binders.

"You and Kich are very smart," Lad said, in all seriousness. Natasha smiled at him wanly.

"They don't need us any more, do they?" My throat still stung and my pains were deep. A bed was all I truly needed. "Can we leave? We've done our job, after all." Not all those aches were physical.

"Yes, we have," Kichlan said. "Sofia, can you put something in that?" He glanced at the bag at her feet, carrying the few collecting jars we had not been able to fill. "Yours too, Mizra. The enforcers think we subdued an emergency tonight. I doubt they've ever seen a collecting jar, but let's try and stay on the safe side. Pretend we collected so much we can barely carry it all."

But how would we pretend to the veche, when they came to take the full jars away and found only empty ones?

Sofia and Mizra hunted for rubbish to weigh their bags down. Physical debris – I thought, with a wry smile to myself – pretending to be our debris.

I needed to get home. To lie curled around the sickness in my belly, to peel back coat sleeve and shirt and uniform and see just what the debris had done to my arm when it had torn the suit from my skin. But most of all I needed to get away from the memory of the Hon Ji Half falling to pieces in my hands and from Sofia's too-attentive gaze.

"Ah, Tanyana?" Mizra pulled me from my distraction with a tense, warning tone. "I think you need to see this."

What now? What more would the puppet men throw at me in one night?

I looked up. There, standing beside the enforcer, was Devich, Volski and Tsana. All three were pale in the floating pion lights, and looked shocked.

"Of all the architects in Movoc-under-Keeper." The nine point circle I had once commanded was a well-maintained machine of precision and power. Unless the

remnants of my circle had fallen very far in my absence
– which I severely doubted – they were not the kind of
circle usually called upon fix cracks in a market floor. No
matter how deep.

"What's he doing here?" Kichlan fixed growling-dog
eyes on Devich.

"Good question." An architect's circle was necessary, I
knew that, even one so powerful and so out of place, but
what was a debris suit technician doing here? "It's all a
little convenient, don't you think?"

If anything, Kichlan's expression darkened further.

"That's the lady, isn't it, Tan?" Lad piped up. "The lady
that fixed our ceiling. All on her own, she did it. Didn't
she?"

"That's right, Lad."

Around me, I felt the members of my old collecting
team sharpen. They knew Devich, they knew who he
was and what he had done, and with Lad's prompting
they recognised Tsana as well. I could almost feel their
suspicions rise, their alertness increase, as they scanned
the market crowds for the puppet men.

It was a good feeling. I straightened. I was warmed by
it, and strengthened by it. I was not alone.

"Your architect's circle?" Kichlan whispered.

I nodded, ran a hand through my short and poorly
cropped hair, and approached the members of my once-
circle, taking a wide path around the crumbling ground.
Kichlan fell into step at my left shoulder. Lad tried to follow, but Sofia and Aleksey held him back.

"Tanyana?" Volski noticed me first, and his attention
drew Devich and Tsana's gaze. Devich looked even worse
than the last time I had seen him. He was thinner, the

clothes that had once looked so effortlessly good on him draped loose over his frame. His face was bloodless, his eyes too large and frightened as they met mine. He looked like he didn't want to be there at all.

But he was Devich, so it could all be an act. A lie. A pretty extreme one, certainly, but I had trusted him once and refused to do so again. No matter how he seemed to sway on his feet and dissolve into the market shadows like he was becoming one himself.

Volski and Tsana, however, I did trust. The older man hurried to meet me. He held my hands and peered at my face, sending quick glances up at Kichlan who doubtless glowered down upon him. But Volski was not one to be intimidated, not even by Kichlan on a night as bad as this one. "Tanyana," Volski said. "You look terrible."

I laughed, sharp and sore in my throat, before leaning forward and kissing him lightly on the cheek. I hoped my breath didn't reek. "I probably do." Volski was weathered by years of working in the sun and the harsh Movoc wind, his skin roughly lined and darkened. But even at this late bell he was clean-shaven, his silvering hair immaculately styled, his dark, high-necked jacket – a row of bear-head badges shining from his shoulders – perfectly pressed.

I introduced him to Kichlan, who crossed his arms and nodded. Tsana wrapped me in a light embrace, barely touching me, and her high-necked jacket smelled of cumin and rose. A daughter of an old family with powerful veche connections, she was perhaps not as skilled as someone in her situation should be. After all, it was her mistake that had given me my first set of scars, but she was always graceful, even in the middle of all this chaos.

I tried to ignore how filthy I was, compared to the two of them. But I was aware of every patch in my second-hand clothing, the stench of sewerage and ever-present damp that my life as a debris collector had infused into the cloth, and the blood and vomit stains, newly gained that night.

Before Grandeur fell – before the puppet men and the veche had thrown me from her hand, eight hundred feet in the air – I had been a binder just like them. I had been the best of them. Now we belonged in different worlds. Different realities, I supposed, separated by the silver drilled into my bones.

"Are you hurt?" Volski hissed. He gestured to the great gashes in the ground. "What happened?"

"Debris," I answered. "Debris happened." In a way. I pulled him a little closer. "What are you doing here? Surely this isn't the kind of job you usually do, a patch and repair?"

Volski started to shake his head, but Devich interrupted before he could speak.

"This is not a simple patch and repair." He approached us. Behind him, the enforcers parted the crowd again and allowed the rest of the architect circle in. I noticed two new faces, and no sign of Llada, who had taken over my role as critical centre. "Please set up your circle, lady Tsana. This area needs to be stabilised as quickly as possible."

Too much information to take in, all at once. "Lady?" I said, before I could stop myself. "Tsana, you're the circle centre? What happened to Llada?"

She gave an elegant shrug. "Replacing you, Tanyana, was too hard on Llada. She opted for a smaller circle, and I was made centre." She smiled delicately, before turning away.

I shared my surprised look with Volski, who shrugged,

a decidedly inelegant gesture on him. "I know," was all he said, all that needed to be said. He followed Tsana.

Tsana was not skilled enough to control a nine point circle. But I supposed veche connections could take you far, even after almost killing your critical centre.

"You should leave," Devich said. He didn't try to grab me like he had last time. Instead, his tone was distant, almost defeated. "You've done your job here, and it is not safe to remain."

That didn't sound like the Devich I knew. "Devich? What's wrong?"

Kichlan bristled beside me. "Have you forgotten what this man did to you? Ignore him, Tanyana. Just turn your back and walk away. He does not need your sympathy."

"I know that," I said. "And he won't get it. No matter how good an act he puts on."

Tsana was organising her circle. Evidently unsure of the integrity of the ground she had them form their nine points tightly around her, rather than around the stones they would be repairing. It was less efficient that way. Better to cast your pions across the entire building site then knot them to the side. But she was the circle centre, not me. So I looked away.

Devich, to my surprise, barely reacted to Kichlan and me at all. "An act?" he said, slowly, like he was trying to remember what the words meant. He looked down to his arm and started plucking at the sleeve. A strange habit, and new.

Tsana and her circle began to work. A great grinding noise rose from the ground beneath us, and the entire market square shook. A few of the remaining poly stalls that had survived the debris attack cracked, and sand slid loose from the buildings around us. Clumsy work. Kichlan wrapped an arm around my shoulders, holding me up before I even realised I needed the help. For all the sound and movement very little was happening to the fractures in the ground. A mesh of concrete and iron formed to fill the gaps, but it came out spongy, uneven, and collapsed too quickly into mud.

"Strange," Devich said. He twisted his sleeve into a tight ball of material, revealing an inch or two of what should have been skin. Instead, Devich was silver.

I studied the reflective surface wrapped around his wrist. No swirling symbols or shining lights, so what was it? Then I shook my head at myself. Was I being gullible? Perhaps. But damn, this was a pretty comprehensive deception. "What is?"

At first he didn't answer. The cloth in his fist began to tear.

"Devich?" I laid a hand on his arm, and he flinched, staring at me with a sudden flash of horror. "What's strange?"

"No," he whispered, words little louder than breath. "Please. I tried, I did. So please. Not me too."

"What are you doing?" Kichlan hissed. I waved him back, earning a dark scowl.

"Devich?" I leaned closer. "What's wrong?"

"Pions." Fast breaths and quick blinking. He released his torn sleeve. "The pions are wrong." He gestured to the market square.

Pions? Confused, I followed his gaze. "Why? What are they doing?"

He tapped his forehead, rubbed at his eyes. "Can't tell. Difficult now. I think, I think they're running away." He stared at me in such fear and uncertainty that I was reminded of Lad. And it shook me. "Vanishing. Where could they go, Tanyana? What does it mean? What happened here?"

Vanishing? Pions didn't vanish. They changed, yes, as they created and destroyed at our command. But pions were eternal. What could be happening to them? Were they running away, fleeing to some deeper part of the world where even a nine point circle couldn't coax them into life? Or falling prey to residue emptiness, to the very memory of an open door?

"I don't–" I narrowed my eyes, and stopped myself. Could I really believe anything Devich was saying? Was this all just a ploy to get information out of me? His fear an act, the metal little more than foil wrapped around his arm? I wouldn't put it past him. But why bother? What could I possibly know that he, or his puppet men masters, didn't? "Don't pretend ignorance." I pulled away from him. "I know better than to trust you."

That seemed to wake him up. His eyes sharpened – still too big and heavy with sleepless shadows but much more the Devich I thought I had known – and he laughed, dry and bitter. "Trust? You don't know what you're talking about, Tanyana. You don't understand any of it. You don't understand what they, what they–" He waved his torn sleeve in my face and for an instant, in the bobbing, unsteady light, his arm was longer than it should have been, slender, and elastic like a whip attached to his shoulder.

"What's wrong with you?"

He clutched his wrist to his chest, and sucked in loud, painful-sounding breaths. "I told you, already. But you won't listen to me. Not any more."

"This is ridiculous," Kichlan snapped. He clutched my shoulders and tried to turn me around. "He's lying to you, can't you see that? Manipulating you all over again. This is just another of his twisted games. Don't fall for it. Don't trust him."

A flush of crimson rose from Devich's neck, followed by what looked like ripples beneath his skin. "I promised, didn't I? That I wouldn't lie to you." He released his arm, shook his tattered sleeve free. "There, can you see? I am their tool too, and that's all I ever was. Just like you, Tanyana. And when I failed to complete my task – you, of course, made that impossible – they found another use for me. Piece by piece." As he spoke, eyes wild, mouth loose and dribbling, he scratched violently at the top of his head.

I strained against Kichlan's guiding arm and tried to see. Yes, there was something beneath Devich's shirt. Suit metal? It could have been. But what did that mean? I drew a deep breath, clung to my cynicism, and held the memory of his betrayal close. "No matter what you say, it doesn't mean I can trust you."

A hissing breath, "Is there nothing I can do that will change that?"

"Oh, this gets better and better," Kichlan sneered.

"Why won't you listen to me?"

More tearing, more groaning, and Tsana's circle finally managed to repair the ground. But the work was poor. Instead of the smooth stones the rest of the square was paved with, they had resorted to uneven cement.

"Why won't I listen to you?" I couldn't believe he would even ask that question. "Perhaps you've forgotten manipulating me, lying to me, and tossing me to the veche like so much meat for a pack of rabid dogs! I trusted you, Devich, and you betrayed me. Do you really expect me to make that mistake twice?"

Behind him, Tsana was trying to rebuild the lamp and failing abysmally. A steel pole sprouted, uneven and knobbled, from the iron frames reinforcing her weak repair job. Giant globes like misshapen fruit grew from the top, quickly lost their integrity and slid wet and shapeless to the ground.

Devich laughed at my words. "Trust? I will not, Tanyana Vladha, allow you to lecture me on trust. I have never known anyone with such poor judgement as you."

"What do you mean?"

He was so pale, so gaunt, so much less than the beautiful man I had fallen for so easily. But still he managed to look down on me, to sneer. "Honestly? None of the things the veche have done to you would have been possible if you hadn't placed your trust with people who did not deserve it."

I drew myself up, trying not to feel Kichlan's supporting arm. "Like you."

"Me? I told you, I am just another tool." He jerked his thumb at my once circle. "Think about this, will you? Do you honestly believe Tsana was promoted to the centre of a nine point circle through skill alone?" As if on cue, the makeshift lamp collapsed entirely and ironic applause broke out from the crowd. "You know who her father is; you know who his friends are." Old family veche representatives who were obsessed with debris, and who had orchestrated everything that had happened to me, from my fall from Grandeur to my role as an experimental weapon. Yes, I knew. They lurked in the shadows, pulling the puppet men's strings. "So think about it, for just a moment. Think about everything that has happened to you and how it all began."

I scowled at him. "She has contacts, yes, but that does-n't mean–"

"Glass?" Devich cut through me, just as sharp. "You really think she panicked and accidentally created glass?"

Ice travelled down every scar on the left side of my body. A cold memory of the mistake Tsana had made, when I fell from Grandeur's hand eight hundred feet high and landed on glass. My stomach rolled again, and only Kichlan kept me upright as I swayed.

"That glass gave her the circle centre, as surely as it gave you those scars," Devich continued.

"That's enough!" Kichlan turned me around, started me walking. "Keep away from her."

"Who do you trust, Tanyana?" Devich's voice faded. I felt distant, cold, sick. "Ask yourself, who?"

Behind me the newly stitched ground tore with a long and terrible moan.

6.

Who do you trust?

Devich's words echoed in my head, however much I tried to wish them away.

I couldn't remember how I'd gotten home. Probably under Kichlan's watchful eye. But when the sun lightened my attic room and dawnbell echoed cleanly down from the Keeper's Tear River, I was already awake and unsure if I had even slept.

I dragged myself from my bed. I couldn't stomach Valya's food for dawn-bell supper, or her ever-watching eyes, so tempted a later lecture and headed into Movoc-under-Keeper with an empty stomach; an empty, fragile stomach.

The city felt just as strange as I did, like spun glass in the crisp morning light. Maybe that was because I had almost destroyed it the night before.

Or maybe not. The seventh Effluent was not a wealthy area and as such was never particularly well maintained, but that morning it looked even worse than usual. Weakness ate away at the buildings and roads like a fungus, clear even to my pion-blind eyes. Patchy holes in the cobblestones revealed rusting, unused pipes beneath the street. Cracks ran through walls, and the mortar dissolved between stones. I witnessed two evacuations on my way to meet Kichlan and Lad – enforcers leading poor families out of crowded rooms while three point architect circles fought in vain to keep their homes standing. A small girl, carried by her weeping mother, met my eyes solemnly. That steady gaze seemed to look right through me, to the door I had opened and the Keeper's scar that would never heal, and I hurried away feeling hot with guilt. I paused again at a corner to watch two lamps on opposite sides of the intersection soften and bend forward in a disconcerting, synchronised bow.

Perhaps I was just more aware of the city, of its stones and invisible pion-bindings, since the night in the market square. Or maybe the veche needed to invest in more architects instead of spending kopacks on Strikers, Mob and the puppet men.

Or maybe the pions really were disappearing in the face of the opening doors.

When I arrived Lad and Kichlan were already waiting for me on the corner, which was odd, because I was far earlier than we had arranged.

"Tanyana." Kichlan held my shoulders and searched my face. He didn't look pleased with what he found there. "Did you sleep?"

I started to rub at my eye, but quickly stopped. "Not sure."

"Tan looks very white," Lad whispered to his brother. As usual, his attempts at subtlety failed terribly.

"How is Eugeny?" I asked, trying to head-off the clouds gathering on Kichlan's face.

He softened, for a moment at least. "The old man is

tough. Stubborn too. Woke before us, was already cooking kasha when I got down the stairs and wouldn't let me take over. Typical." He rubbed Lad's back, and some of the guilt eased from his younger brother's expression.

"But what about you?" Kichlan's frown returned with force. "Are you certain you're all right? Maybe you should stay with Valya today. She'll look after you, I'm sure."

I grimaced. "I don't think I could take it. And anyway, who would look after Lad?"

A moment more studying, and Kichlan turned to his brother. "Lad, will you look after Tan today?"

Lad brightened like the newly risen sun. "Oh yes, bro. Yes, I will!"

"You know you have to be careful with her, don't you?" Kichlan continued, as though I wasn't standing right there with them and certainly didn't have any say in this new arrangement. "She might act like she's strong, but underneath she's fragile. You know that, right?"

Lad nodded, expression serious. "Oh yes, bro. Heard you and Geny talking. She is all crystally, right?"

Kichlan coughed, and looked away.

"Crystally?" I asked, an eyebrow raised.

"That's right," Lad explained. "Heard Kich telling Geny. Tan is like crystal but doesn't know it is crystal. But Geny said no, she's too tough. But Kich said, only on the outside, it's so deep even she doesn't–"

"Lad!" Kichlan interrupted, face bright red. "That's enough, Tan understands. Don't you?" He cast me a pleading expression.

Expressionless, I held his gaze. "Oh, I think I do."

"Good." Kichlan, attempting to salvage his dignity from

the situation, placed my hand in Lad's and folded his fingers over mine. "Then I will see you both here this evening."

"Yes, Kich," Lad said, eyes shining.

As we left him, I watched Kichlan from over my shoulder, and maintained my irritation, even in the face of his flushed, slightly pleased with himself grin.

Lad led us to Ironlattice. I was a little surprised that he remembered the way so well. But then, he'd never been given the opportunity to lead before. Perhaps he was more capable than any of us gave him credit for.

"Here, Tan." He opened the back door for me. "Careful on the stairs."

I gripped the wall for support, and focused on not tripping. I suspected he would try to carry me if I showed the slightest hint of weakness. Lad took his responsibilities seriously.

Natasha waited alone in the toplevel. When we reached it, she looked up, her expression hard. "We're in serious trouble."

Silver debris collecting jars were spread out on the floor around her. Four in one neat pile, a good three dozen, probably more, scattered with their lids open. Stones and dirt made up a third pile closer to the windows.

"Morning!" Lad said, and his chest seemed to swell. "I'm looking after Tan today."

"Oh?" Came a voice behind us. I moved further into the room to allow Mizra up. "And why would that be?"

"Tan isn't feeling well and Kich said I should."

"Unwell?" Mizra's expression was a little too knowing, a little too pointed. It unsettled me.

Who do you trust?

"Last night was difficult." I tried to look unconcerned.

But my mind spun webs around Mizra, rolling him over and over, wondering. Could I trust him? Or Uzdal? Even Natasha?

"And she didn't sleep," Lad chimed in. "Said so."

Lad, I could trust Lad. And with him, Kichlan. Maybe that was all I needed.

"Oh dear, looks like I'm last," Aleksey called from the stairwell, his voice echoing. "Sorry about that."

What about Aleksey, this new collector I didn't even know? Could I trust him?

"Not late," Lad told him. "The bell hasn't rung yet."

"That's good."

"So, you were saying." Mizra still watched me, hawk-like. I tried not to feel like some poor rodent about to become supper. "You didn't sleep? Why was that?"

"Why do you think?" I grated out the words, even as my stomach flipped into a knot. "Or did you have your eyes closed all night?"

Metal rang against stone as Natasha, her expression dark and furious, threw one of the empty jars against the floor. We turned to stare at her in shock as the sharp, splitting noise echoed around the close room. "Do any of you even know I'm here?" she growled.

Mizra and I shared a look, stunned that Natasha – *Natasha* – could care enough about anything to interrupt us with such a noise.

"Do know you're here," Lad whimpered. And I didn't blame him. She was just a little frightening, standing over her devastated collecting jars, feet planted wide, arms crossed, face red and scowling.

"Then maybe you didn't hear me," she continued, voice still deep and predatory. "We are in a lot of trouble."

Aleksey cleared his throat. "Ah, excuse me for asking. What kind of trouble?"

One of her arms whipped loose, and pointed sharply at the four neat jars. "Because that is all the debris we've collected. The rest of these jars," she waved that accusing finger wildly at the floor, "are empty. Or were filled with rubbish from last night."

"We have only been collecting for two days," Mizra offered as an explanation.

"We don't even have enough to cover those!" Natasha's tenor and volume rose, apparently in tandem. "Put an emergency in the middle of that and we are very, very behind on quota." She paused to take a long breath.

"And that's a bad thing?" Aleksey ventured again, brave individual that he was.

"It is," Lad said, voice almost too quiet in Natasha's echoes. "If we don't keep up, the veche will punish us."

"They could break us up again, send us away," Mizra clarified.

"Either way," I said. "We don't want that kind of attention. Not from the veche." And not from their puppets. I straightened. "That means we have to work very hard and very quickly. We have no way of knowing when the veche will come to take the jars away. We'd better make sure they're as full as possible."

Natasha crossed her arms again. Lad nodded. Mizra maintained his watch on my face, and Aleksey looked uncertain. All in all, it wasn't particularly reassuring.

"Well, we'd better get moving if we're going to have any chance."

While Natasha scooped some of her empty jars into

the bag, Lad helped me down the stairs. Mizra hovered at our backs like a curious fly.

"Which way?" As Natasha secured the door behind us, Aleksey hunched into his jacket and wound a scarf around his neck. It was a cold morning for the middle of spring – although even in mid-summer Movoc-under-Keeper longed for winter, and spring always struggled to make itself known – the sky clear but the sun insipid. Worn, like the city. Like me.

"Doesn't matter." Natasha ploughed on ahead. "Just walk."

We followed without argument. Lad did not offer to guide us to dangerous and hidden debris, and I was glad for that at least. In fact, it seemed that the Keeper was up-holding our hastily made bargain, and was leaving him alone. Instead, Lad held my hand and warned me about landmarks coming up that I should be careful of.

"There's a hole in the street, Tan. Careful."

I avoided a small crack between cobblestones.

"Oh, water. You could slip. Careful."

I stepped over a small trickle of wastewater from a broken drain.

On my other side, Mizra was just as attentive, though silent. If I so much as blinked, he made a worried face, reached forward to touch my arm, seemed to catch himself and let his hand drop. Between the two of them, I knew I should be finding the whole thing very irritating. But perhaps because Lad was not talking to invisible people and being lured into untold danger, I didn't really mind.

I couldn't say the same for Natasha. She crouched at a broken pipe, scowled inside, lengthened her suit finely and probed. "Nothing," she spat. "Mizra, get over here and help me look!"

Aleksey took his place beside me. He shot uncertain glances between Lad and me before murmuring, "Last night, that was... something. Wasn't it?"

I nodded.

"Was bad," Lad said.

Aleksey's bruises were clear and dark, the cut on his lip swollen. Perhaps he deserved an explanation. But could I trust him? He had helped me, hadn't he? But then again, I had once believed Devich was on my side, and Tsana too. So that proved little. "Lad," I said, with a squeeze. "Would you help Natasha and Mizra look in the pipe?"

"But Kich said—"

"Aleksey will look after me. Only for a moment?"

With a purse of his lips that made him look uncannily like Kichlan when he disapproved of something – which was, after all, more often than not – Lad released me and joined Natasha and Mizra. They had followed the broken pipe to an abandoned heating system, shoved between a rusted gate and the degraded wall of an old building. It looked like the perfect place to find a cache of debris, but Natasha's constant muttering, and the tension I could read in Mizra's shoulders and back, did not fill me with confidence.

"I should thank you," I said to Aleksey. "For helping me last night."

"Not at all." He tried to smile, ended up wincing and touching the cut on his lip. "I'm one of the team, right? It's what we do."

Part of the team, already? Tsana had been part of my circle for years, yet still I had not known her. Not truly. How long did I need to know Aleksey before I could trust him? Before I could tell him what really happened last night, the Keeper and doors and Devich and all.

We watched, in silence, as Natasha pried grains of debris from the old heating system and dropped them into jars Lad held open.

"So," Aleksey said, finally. "I guess you're not going to explain last night to me."

"You were there. You saw what happened." Even as I spoke, I realised how much I wanted to trust him. Scarred, just like me, but smiling and good natured, helpful and concerned. Was I being too cautious, had I let Devich get to me?

"Well, I suppose that's understandable." He even took such rejection with good humour. "Then at least tell me this. What was Fedor was rambling about?"

I blinked at him. "Fedor?"

"After Kichlan and the big one here took you home. He was frantic, kept talking about 'him' and how could she – by which he meant you – how could she treat 'him' like that?" He rubbed his palms together, breathing warmth over his gloves. "Upset the short woman, the one on the other team."

"Sofia?"

"Guess so. She told him he didn't know what he was talking about. It went on like that for a while. I was glad to part ways."

"Ah." Yes, Fedor. Just how much of Yicor's secret books had he read? He knew about the Keeper, but did he know what Halves were too? How much had he heard last night? And could he put it all together? If he'd worked out that Lad was a Half – an intermediary between the Keeper and the world he guarded – surely he would want to involve him in the Unbound revolution. Would I have to protect Lad from Fedor now too?

"Well, as you said, I had left by then. So I'm afraid I can't tell you."

Aleksey worried at the cap pulled tight over his head. "Fair enough. Still, you don't have to tell me anything you don't want to. You're right, I was there. And I certainly didn't have my eyes closed. But, you know, there are still some things I don't understand."

"Oh?" I said guardedly. He had a gentle way of pressing me for information, true, but he was still persistent.

"Like Lad and that body. I mean, I know you said it wasn't normal, debris isn't usually like that. So why was it attacking that dead person? And why did it turn its attention to Lad–"

"Got it all, Tan!" Lad bounded down the street, jar in one hand, looking both proud and relieved all at once. "Were you all right without me?"

I smiled at him, thankful for the distraction. "Yes, Lad. Aleksey has been looking after me."

"Thank you Aleksey."

Aleksey shifted under Lad's warm regard and rubbed the scar on his nose.

"Other's hells." Natasha took the single jar from Lad and glared at it in disgust. "Not even enough to fill one."

"Better keep going then," Mizra said, shifting the bag slung over his shoulder. "Unless, Tanyana, you don't feel well enough."

"Of course I do." I pulled Lad into walking and ignored the twinges in my stomach. Hunger, thirst, only those.

Aleksey fell in beside me, but I did not allow him to try that question again.

"Your scar," I said. "How... How did it happen?" I touched my cheek with a free hand, bringing attention to my own web of scarring. "They are unusual, after all."

His rueful smile returned, and he began to stroke his nose again, an unconscious movement quickly stilled. "I've been building the courage to ask you about yours."

"Tan fell," Lad answered for me, expression glum and his grip tightening to the point of hurting. "She fell very far down and got cut when she landed."

That pretty much said it all. So I said, "Exactly."

"Ouch." Aleksey winced, and Lad nodded in serious agreement. "Well, mine? Someone hit me."

Lad blinked. "They must have hit you very hard."

"They did indeed." Aleksey was silent for a moment, and I wondered if he would elaborate. After all, "someone hit me" was about as detailed as Lad's explanation.

"Oh this is just ridiculous!" Natasha and Mizra had stopped at a sewerage vent steaming into the cold air. It certainly looked like a clogged system; perfect debris collecting ground. But, again, all they found was a small handful of loose grains. "Is it going out of its way to make us look bad?" She almost threw her collected debris at Mizra, who pointed an open jar toward her at arm's length.

"It was a skirmish," Aleksey said as we continued, his voice quiet, his head low. "I was an enforcer, not Mob or anything like that, but we were guarding an old family member of the national veche on a tour of the colony. We must have strayed too close to the border. The Hon Ji got us."

Lad gasped, theatrically.

I patted his hand. "What happened?"

Aleksey cast us another of his self-effacing looks. "Ah,

well, we did what we were trained to do. We sent a call along an encoded pion stream for backup and did what we could to protect the old man. But enforcers aren't strong the way Mob are strong, even Hon Ji Mob. They carried these big… I don't even know what to call it, like a hammer. But so huge, only someone with pions working overdrive in their body could hope to lift the damn things, let alone swing them. One tried to destroy the old man's coach with it, and it looked like it was going to work. Except I got in the way." He traced the gash across his face. It ran from his left eyebrow, across his nose, deep into his cheek and down to the right jaw line.

Following his finger, I couldn't help but imagine the impact, the crush of bone and the slashed flesh, and I shuddered.

Lad stared at him mouth gaping in a wide *O*.

"All I really remember is red. Like the world was full of it, bright crimson like blood. Healers tried to explain brain trauma and hallucinations to me after I recovered, but I didn't want to hear it. So I don't really know what happened after I went down. Only that our call must have been heard, because Strikers darkened the sky and wiped the Hon Ji Mob from the earth. Not that I saw it." He sniffed, ducked his head lower. "When I woke up, my face was a mess – much worse than it looks now, let me tell you – and the pions were gone. But then, you must know what that is like."

I knew, all too well. I remembered that moment of confusion, of terror, of emptiness, when I realised I was alone in a world that had once been full of companions. And then the disgust, when I saw the dirty little specks of debris that had taken their place.

"The healers saved your life though. Scar or no." I knew what that was like, too.

"Yes, the healers." A flicker of a glance from beneath his eyelashes. "I had no face left, Tanyana. No face at all, but still, they, they are the most skilled in the military." He hesitated. "The rest of my Fist were rewarded. Kopacks, status, medals."

"Fist?" Lad asked, voice quiet and expression overawed.

"That's what we are. What they are. A group of enforcers."

"Oh."

"While I had my face stitched up, the suit put on, and was sent here, to collect rubbish for a living and wallow in Varsnia's scum... they were rewarded." And before Aleksey turned his face away I caught a darkness there, a shadow across his eyes. There was rage, hidden somewhere beneath his usual unassuming smile.

"So there you have it." When he looked up again he was all smiles and regretful nose rubbing and I wondered if I had imagined it. "And now I have answered your questions. It's not that hard. You could give it a try."

"Enjoying the walk, are you?" Natasha scowled over her shoulder. "Ever consider, oh, I don't know, looking for debris with us? After all, that's why we're here."

With a guilty look, Aleksey hurried forward to join her. Mizra held back long enough to whisper, "Did someone swap her with an overemotional double while we weren't looking?"

"Mizra!"

Lad and I, however, could not be summoned with the snap of a name, and Natasha knew that. So she allowed us to follow at a gradually slowing pace. I was beginning to feel light-headed, even dizzy, and more thankful for

Lad's support than I would ever tell him. He took his responsibilities seriously enough, and did not need to know
that without the strength of his arm and the grounding
warmth of his body, I could not have kept up even our
slow, slightly limping rate.

Natasha took us down all the usual ways: along dark
alleys, between lampposts, around the back of factories.
But all they yielded were small and sluggish grains, not
even a faint webbing of grey planes. It was almost as
though the city's debris had felt with its pions.

Highbell tolled and faded. Natasha allowed us to stop
long enough to buy hot roasted sweet potato and cups of
chicken broth. The food vendors were having trouble
with their stalls. Made out of clear poly inlaid in parts
with steel, the stalls usually floated above the street, moving gradually around the city on legs of pion threads –
invisible to us, but bright and strong to those who could
see them. But these looked more like they were being
dragged than shepherded as they lurched along, leaving
scratches and dents with their corners in the cobblestones. The three point circles that manned them called
out loudly to the usually helpful pions, a desperate and
unseemly thing to do in the middle of the street. It didn't
seem to help.

I was ravenous, but the smell triggered my nausea
again. It didn't help that the food was poorly cooked –
potato skins burned while still cold on the inside, and
the broth watery and overlaid with an fatty film – but I
ate anyway, aware how much I needed to. The meal sat
heavy, sloshing in my stomach.

The day wore on and the debris grew even harder to
find.

"Only three days," Natasha muttered to herself. "I've only been doing this for three days. Do you think that's the shortest amount of time anyone has led a collecting team before it was disbanded?"

"Maybe it isn't just us," Mizra ventured.

"What difference would that make?"

"Well, if everyone's having trouble finding debris then we won't stand out, will we? And they can't exactly disband every collecting team in the city." He paused. "Can they?"

Personally, I wouldn't put anything past the puppet men and the national veche. But I didn't say so. It was taking all my concentration to keep upright.

When Laxbell sounded, mournful and tired, I knew we had run out of time.

"Natasha," I said, startled by how weak and wavering my voice sounded. Mizra's hawk-eyes returned. Thankfully, I didn't need to say any more. Natasha knew I had to take Lad back to his brother, and she knew she was defeated. Her shoulders sagged. "Yes, all right. Let's go back. And hope they don't come to collect the jars for another few days at least."

Lad stopped pointing out potential hazards on our route. But somehow, his silences were worse. He joined Mizra in attentive, ever-watchful concern, and wrapped an arm around my shoulders instead of holding my hand. While I was thankful, I couldn't stop thinking that it wasn't fair. I was here to look after him, not the other way around. No matter what Kichlan said.

The stairs at Ironlattice were killers. I staggered too many times, and even Natasha seemed concerned about me by the time we returned to the toplevel.

"Not even two." She sighed as she added the jars to the four full ones on the shelves and returned the empty ones to the table. The shelves looked so bare like that, so stark. What hope would we have, when the veche came to collect?

Then Natasha turned to me. "You're taking Lad back to Kichlan, right?"

I nodded.

"And getting home from there..." hesitation "Would you like some help?"

I almost fell over. This wasn't too strange, considering Lad was the only thing holding me up, but even without the now-constant pain and exhaustion, Natasha offering to walk me home would have knocked me from my feet.

"That's it," Mizra said. "I have to know." He approached Natasha, peered at her, head tipped. "Did you hit your head on anything?"

"Pardon?" she asked between clenched teeth.

"You're worrying about the jars." Mizra started ticking things off on his fingers. "Offering to help Tanyana home, bossing us around. It's like you've taken lessons from Kichlan. Is that it? Did the old boy teach you a few things? Haven't got any lectures hidden in there somewhere, have you?"

"Mizra, if you don't–"

"Tan," Lad said, quiet compared to Mizra and Natasha's rising voices, but his frightened tone cut through their bickering like a knife. "He asked if he can talk to you."

In the sudden silence I forced myself to push tiredness and my rebellious stomach aside. This was my idea, wasn't it? So I couldn't tell the Keeper to leave me alone, not when he was keeping to our arrangement.

"All right." My suit was still sluggish, stretched thin from the night before. I gritted my teeth against flare-ups of pain around the bands, and the solid ache within my bones. Not the usual enthusiastic longing for freedom, the suit felt more like it had burrowed deeper inside me and did not want to leave. It spread slowly over my body, encasing my head last. The Keeper stood beside Lad. He wrung his pale hands so tightly the debris within him bulged between his fingers. His dark gaze darted around the room like he was a trapped, frightened animal. But still, he was keeping his word. He did not touch Lad, or crowd around him, or ramble nonsensical words in his ear. The room was small – doors at my feet and at my back – but at least these seemed secure.

"Yes?" I addressed the Keeper, aiming for politeness.

He nodded, too fast, too hard. I thought I heard the cracking of bones in his neck, bones I wasn't even sure he had. "You came, Tanyana. Thank you."

"Are–" I didn't really know what to say. "Are you hurt?"

His hands stilled. "Hurt? I always hurt." He opened his palms, stared at his semi-transparent skin rubbed black, then pointed somewhere behind me. "That's why I need them."

I turned. The jars were difficult to see in this world, they were small and embedded deeply in the patterns of the door at my back.

"There isn't much in them," I answered.

"What?" Natasha, wavering between darkness and the doors, stepped in front of the jars. "No, he can't have the debris. That's all we've been able to collect!"

I turned back to the Keeper. Debris grains bulged in the veins along his neck and shoulders, squirming like insects or snakes beneath his skin.

"I need them," he said, simply. Then he began muttering to himself in a strange, meaningless staccato like the words he had spoken with the Hon Ji, before I had killed her. He shook, muscles quivering, and resumed wringing his hands.

I thought about all that debris I had given over to the emptiness last night, what it must have felt like for him to close the door on part of himself and know it was gone forever. Just how much more of that could he take?

"If we have nothing to give the veche, we put ourselves at risk. All of us."

The Keeper nodded again, and again his neck bulged. "I know. I know. They– they could come. They could be here. Even now. Here." And his eyes darted and I began to wonder if his shivering was exhaustion and grief for the parts he had lost, or fear.

"They?" I whispered.

"Please?" he pleaded, hands wringing, body bent, everything about him desperate and imploring. "I am so weak. They are so strong. And the doors, the doors. You have so little, I know, but you are the only ones I can ask. The only people I can rely on."

I turned back to Natasha. "Doors," was all I said.

She flinched. "But what about us?" she asked. "This will only make us more vulnerable to the veche. That's dangerous. For all of us."

"I think we should," Lad said, his voice quiet. "He needs us, and he hurts, so I think we should."

Natasha hung her head. "The Keeper tell you to say that, did he?"

"No," I answered for Lad. "The Keeper didn't tell him to say anything. Those were Lad's words."

"I promised. See, I promised," the Keeper whispered.

Natasha stepped out of the way.

When I touched the jars they sprung into sudden and sharp focus, as solid as my suited self. I flipped the clasps that sealed them, their lids opened with a soft hiss. The debris grains inside them floated free, aimless in the open air.

I curved my suit into a scoop and collected them. There was hardly enough to fill my cupped palms. I held them out to the Keeper, a small offering, but as Natasha had said, all that we had to give.

He held his own hands over the debris, palms down, while his head tipped back and his eyes closed. The grains were drawn up into him, through his skin. Debris filled the veins in his arms for a moment before being pumped deeper into his body.

He released a great breath. "You do not know what it is like, to have that which was lost returned to you." He opened his eyes. They were calm. His arms hung loose by his sides. "This debris has not been tortured, twisted, or carved into a tool. It is a relief, and I thank you for it." A small twist of a smile played on the edges of his mouth. "And there, do you see what it can do?"

I glanced over my shoulder. The door that made up part of Natasha, part of the wall, part of the table and shelves, was smaller. Not by a lot, but noticeable.

I felt something within me give. Such a small amount, we had just given him, and yet what a difference it had made. His fear, his pain, so obvious a moment before was gone. However brief this glimpse of strength, of sanity, it showed just what the Keeper could be, if only we helped him.

We could not do it with our suits, with our jars and our

quota. At least, we could not do it for long before we were discovered, and punished. But Fedor could. Yicor, Valya and their underground, Unbound revolution. They might not know it, but they and their plans were the only, and most unlikely, thing that could help the Keeper now.

So that was what I had to do. Even if it cost me my safety, even if it put our collection teams in danger. Even if it brought Lad to the attention of the veche, or threatened the stability of every pion system in the city. The Keeper needed our help. How could we have thought about saying no?

"I understand," I said and met the Keeper's eyes.

"I believe you do."

And then I shattered it all, by asking, "Who are they?"

He faltered. "They are impossible," he whispered, eyes darting, hands clasping. Back to where we had started, back as though he had not absorbed any debris at all. "That's what I think. But there are so many gaps, now, so many spaces in my memory. So many spaces in me. Maybe I do know them, maybe I have forgotten. It has been a long time since they sent me a Half who could actually help me, you know. One who remembers. One who understands. One who can connect. So long, and I am old and tired–" The Keeper dissolved into his dark and door-filled world. I stared at the spot where he had been for a long moment, trying to understand any of what he had just said, before pulling the suit back from my face.

The lamplight that lanced in through the toplevel windows was sharp. How long since Laxbell had sounded?

"So that's the new plan, is it?" Natasha said, bitter. She leaned against the shelves with their open, empty jars, and ran her hands through her hair. The bright lights gave her face heavy shadows. "Whatever debris we find, we give over to him?" When she glanced up at me she looked exhausted. "I don't think we will last long."

"I know," I said. Slowly, I dragged my suit back into its bands. After a day of quiet sluggishness it was finally taking up its usual battle of wills. "Trust me, I–"

The suit pinched me. Silenced, I blinked down at my own clothes, at the stomach I could not see beneath all the layers of cloth. Though still not fully withdrawn, the suit was no longer spread across my abdomen, only the scars from its last attack – those solid streaks of deeply woven silver – remained there. How had it pinched me?

"Tan?" Lad leaned forward, touched my shoulder. "You okay, Tan?"

Almost as though it felt him, the suit reacted. It pushed into me, like hands pressing against my belly, while the bands at my neck and on my right wrist slipped from my control, coating my upper body and flicking Lad away with a spasm.

He gasped and started back. I could barely breathe, for all the pressure. Spots of light dotted my vision. I tried to clutch him, as I sagged onto my knees, but I could not move my right arm. It felt like it did not belong to me. It felt like the suit was in control.

"Tanyana!" Mizra hurried to my side, hands lifted and hovering. In response, the suit slipped further down my back and across both shoulders. "What's the matter? Are you ill? Does it hurt?"

"Don't touch me," I managed to gasp. "The suit–"

The suit was jealous. That was what it felt like. Jealous of Lad, as he tried to touch me, so it had taken control –

so easily – and pushed him away. But what was it doing inside me, what was this pressure, this pain, what could it possibly be–

And then realisation trickled over me like ice water. Terrible, drowning. Inescapable.

I thought of Sofia, her piercing eyes, her testing questions. And I realised I had not bled, these past two moons, but with the suit and the Keeper and the puppet men after me – Other's hells! – I just hadn't noticed.

On the last night I had slept with Devich, after I saved him from the violent debris planes that had destroyed his laboratory, but before I learned that he was, in fact, betraying me. The few contraceptive pills I had left had been stolen with my apartment, and my former life, so I simply had not taken one.

I supposed it was possible. But could I really make such a stupid mistake? Could I be carrying a child – Devich's child, no less – and not even notice?

If it was true, then what was the suit trying to do? Rip into me, tear me and whatever new life I might be carrying, then heal me with silver so we could get on with our job as veche weaponry? Fight whatever it was the puppet men had built us to fight?

"Enough," I managed to croak out. "I am not their weapon." I whispered low, chin pressed to my chest, hoping that my collection team – hovering worried but unsure around me – could not hear. "You are a part of me. Not the other way around. So enough."

Some of the pressure eased, and I drew in a deep, ragged breath.

"I am stronger than you."

It was true, for now. This was still my body, more flesh

than bright symbol and liquid metal. And I had to keep it that way, somehow, and hold back the ever-encroaching silver.

Retracting the suit was like a flex of deep muscles. Those muscles were stiff and sore when I tensed them, but no matter how they protested, no matter the pain running deep into my spine or the scalding heat across my skin, they responded. The suit slipped away, slow, muddy and thick, to sulk within its bands. But I knew better than to believe it would stay there.

All I had to do was work out how to control it, before the next time it tried to kill my child.

Child.

My head rang, but that word, that very idea chimed the loudest. Was it really possible?

"Tan!" Lad, wailing, flung himself at me and wrapped his arms around me. He buried his face in my hair and sobbed. "Oh Tan. I'm sorry!"

Gingerly, I loosened his grip and leaned away from his red, wet face. "Why, Lad?" I touched his cheek. My fingers shook. "What do you have to be sorry for?"

"I didn't look after you–" sniff "–not properly."

"It's not your fault." I allowed him to press his face into my neck and held his head, stroking his back in an effort to soothe him.

"What's wrong with your suit?" Aleksey asked, face sickly as thin cloud. My jacket was steaming, where the suit had coated me, and the smell of slightly charred cloth rose about my head, bringing a fresh bout of nausea with it.

"Nothing," I said, shakily. "I'm too tired, I think. Some of my control slipped."

Aleksey lifted his own wrist and stared at his suit with horror. "It attacked you because you were *tired*? It does that?"

"Yes, if you don't take proper care of yourself." Mizra, all scowls and scepticism, took Lad's hand from my arm and placed it firmly in Natasha's. "Perhaps we should have warned you." The thin, usually laconic man had never looked so stern. "Now, Tanyana. Natasha will take Lad back to his brother. I will take you home. After what just happened, you need to get some rest."

For a moment I considered arguing with him. But I didn't really have the strength. So I simply said, "Thank you," and kissed Lad on the cheek.

I caught sight of Aleksey's face as Mizra led me to the stairs. He watched me intently. Horrified, pale, and thoughtful.

"Sofia was right," Mizra said, as he unlocked the door and held it open for me. "We thought she was losing her mind when she told us you might be pregnant. Obviously not. That's what you must have done."

I'd had to guide us here. Mizra had never visited my rooms above Valya's house; only Lad and Kichlan knew where they were. As I tossed my jacket and gloves to the floor I was starting to wish it would stay that way.

"Thank you. I'll be fine now."

But Mizra stepped inside and closed the door with a slam. I winced. Valya would have heard that.

"Who?" he asked, and I wondered at the venom in his tone. Really, he had nothing to be so upset about. None of this had anything to do with him.

"I really don't think–"

"Is it Kichlan?"

I had a small choking fit over the very idea.

"No? The technician. What did you say his name was? Devich."

I nodded weakly.

"Other's shit."

"You're talking about this like we know it's true." I sat in one of the chairs around the table and wished he would just leave me alone. "We don't."

Colour rose from his pale neck to deepen at his cheeks. He undid the top few buttons of his high-necked shirt. "You haven't checked? You don't know?"

"I–" I stared at the floor. "No. I think so, but, no. I haven't checked."

"Given the symptoms Sofia described and your suit's rather extreme reaction, I think you might be right."

I was surprised by that. "Do suits always do this if their body is pregnant?"

"They're not usually as bad as what you just experienced, but yes, suits do some strange things during pregnancy. Something to do with the changes in your body." He shook his head. "Either way, we need to get you to a healer. You need to know for certain."

"Why?" I couldn't stop the word escaping and wished I had when Mizra came a half step forward.

"Are you being serious, Tanyana? Because we need to make sure you are all right. You almost collapsed back there." He pushed up the sleeves of his jacket, obviously getting hot with his growing frustration. "And, because you need to make a decision. What are you going to do about it?"

"Do?" I whispered and felt something cold and hard

tighten within me. I had a pretty good idea what the suit wanted to do about it.

Mizra turned, hunched his back at me. "You don't understand anything, do you?"

"Why don't you enlighten me?" Anger was slowly rising from that knot in my belly. I was sick of Mizra's attitude, sick of his assumptions and his belief that he knew more about what was going on in my body, in my life and mind, than I did. "Why don't you just tell me what you're talking about, or get out?"

He turned, expression teetering between shock and hurt. "Any child of a debris collector has a greater chance of being born a debris collector. Broken. Like Uzdal and me are broken. Or like Lad."

That didn't sound right to me. "Kichlan and Lad's parents were binders. Were your parents collectors?"

He shook his head. "No."

"Then that can't be right, none of us had parents–"

"That's because most children of debris collectors aren't even born!" Mizra approached me, gripped my hands. "Most children conceived without the knowledge of pions are aborted, Tanyana. And even if your baby is not a collector – if it is not broken – how will you raise it? Going to drag a toddler around the city every day, are you? Through sewerage, in emergencies, to wherever the veche decide to send you? And how will you feed them when the kopacks we earn are hardly enough to feed ourselves? How will you teach them to control pions that you can't even see?" He released me, and stepped back. "This is your decision: If it is one of us, will you allow it to live? If it is one of them, will you give it away? For its own good?"

I stared at him, horrified. "That's not much of a decision."

"I know. But that's the reality."

Hesitantly, I placed a hand on my stomach. It didn't feel any different, I had no way of knowing if pions were flowing, teaching, bonding, or whatever it was that differentiated a pion-binder from a debris collector. Whatever it was that bound us, or left us Unbound.

"Rest," Mizra said. "On Rest, we will take you. You need to know."

Numb, I did not meet his eye.

"I'm sorry, Tanyana. I really am. I wish I didn't have to tell you these things. I wish this wasn't the way of the world."

I looked up. Mizra was pale, eyes red as though he had been weeping. "Goodnight," was all I could manage.

He nodded, and left me alone with the beings in my body.

I stripped down to my uniform. When I rolled it back the silver scars across my stomach weren't as bad as I had expected. But as I touched them, ran fingers over their edges and pressed in, I realised they were much deeper than they looked.

Someone knocked on the door. I dragged my jacket over my uniform and opened it, wishing again for solitude and the quiet, quiet dark.

Valya stood at the top of her rickety stairs, a steaming pot in her hands. "You have not eaten."

I took the pot, smelled vegetables and herbs and hoped I did not look as ill as I felt.

"Must be strong," she said. "You are here to help the Keeper, and he needs you to be strong." With that, she turned, and began her slow and unstable descent.

I closed the door, placed the pot on the table and watched it cool.

7.

Two days later, when I returned Lad to his brother's care, Kichlan took my hand. Natasha had accompanied me for the second day in a row, apparently still uncertain about my health. And while Lad was distracted, saying his goodbyes to her, Kichlan whispered in my ear, "tonight."

I tried not to let anything show on my face, and only gave him a small nod of acknowledgement. He did not need to see my constant exhaustion, my confusion or worry. The old binder part of me – the architect who had worked so hard to rise to the centre of a nine point circle – had grown quite vocal since I realised I could be pregnant. She criticised me constantly, like the buzzing of an irritating insect somewhere at the back of my head, making it even harder to sleep. How could I have been so foolish? I knew better than this. And, worst of all, what would Kichlan think when he found out?

So I nodded, expressionless, and tried to silence her, to push her down until she was little more than a memory. Faint, like a scar.

"Wait for me at Evenbell. I will meet you outside, by the stairs."

To my surprise, Kichlan's closeness, the brush of his breath on my ear and the warmth that radiated from his body, shut her up instantly.

Despite everything I felt a strange delight as I waited for Kichlan outside the home I shared with Valya. I had even changed into clean clothes: a fresh scarf, pale shirt beneath my jacket, and the best pair of pants I owned – only two patches on these, hidden at the hem. When he appeared, grinning, bounce in his step, I realised he must feel the same.

"Lovely evening for a little reconnaissance, wouldn't you say?" He produced a parcel from his coat with a flourish. Still warm, wrapped in cloth. Eugeny's cooking. Valya had, of course, already fed me for the night. But something in Kichlan's closeness set off my hunger anew.

"Do you know where we are going?" I unwrapped as we walked. Thickly stewed plums encased in pastry, rich with sugar and cinnamon.

He nodded, and I offered him a bite of the pastry. He tucked his hands into his jacket. "Oh no, Lad and Eugeny made that one for you."

"But I would like to share."

His look turned sheepish. "I've already had three."

"Three?" I laughed, and devoured it. "How could you possibly eat three of these?"

A wink, a cheeky grin. "Practice."

Kichlan led the way, keeping to well-lit streets rather than our usual back-alley haunts. But then, we weren't hunting for debris. It felt strange, to be following him like this, without any jars in hand.

"What did you tell Lad?" I asked. "How did you convince him not to come?"

"I didn't need to." He stopped beneath a rusted but legible street sign, before glancing at the old bronze numbers mounted on the walls of nearby buildings. Most signposts in Movoc-under-Keeper were written in pions now, not bronze or smooth, painted enamel. It made navigating around the city difficult for people like us, who couldn't read them. Some of the richer Rills maintained the old signs and numbers – like this one – as a kind of quaint, historical decoration. Though not well enough to stop them from crusting over. Still, it was better than nothing.

Kichlan had led us closer to the Tear River, down a Rill rather than an Effluent, so the buildings here were of better quality. Apartment complexes built onto the foundations of old, pre-revolution warehouses, contrasting the rough, hand-chipped sandstone blocks with large sheets of river stone, wide reflective glass windows and small balconies hidden by intricate latticework. Little engravings of the Keeper Mountain patterned each of the ancient, sandstone blocks, and had been copied in garish crystal flecked with gold on the new doors and the corner of each street.

I paused briefly to stare at one of those stylised mountains. It was melting, spilling shining, liquefied metal all over the street. Kichlan took my hand and helped me step clear of it. A bizarre sight, especially in what was obviously a wealthy Rill. I'd have expected such a blatant disruption of complex pion bindings to be fixed as soon as possible. But the street was dark – a quick check down and I realised half the lamps weren't even working – and empty, apart from Kichlan and me. Stranger still.

"Lad didn't even want to come." Kichlan stopped and pointed to a door. As gaudily decorated as all the rest, it took me a moment to realise that instead of the usual crystalline screen of a pion lock mounted on the wall beside it, this door needed a key. "This must be the one. Fedor said it would stand out." He glanced around, then herded me across the street. "Now we wait."

We huddled together on the stairs of an opposite building, hidden in the darkness of a malfunctioning lamp. Kichlan dug into his jacket again, and this time he produced a small flask. "To keep us warm."

Mulled wine, so heavily spiced I couldn't taste the original quality. That was probably the point. I almost choked over the first mouthful, and covered my face with my hands trying to stifle the sound. Kichlan chuckled, took the flask and drank heavily. "There's nothing like Eugeny's recipe."

"I hope not," I managed to say, around coughs and tearing eyes. "Lad didn't want to come?" I asked, when I could breathe. "That's unusual, isn't it?"

Kichlan offered the flask again. This time, I sipped delicately. "He just said 'You and Tan should go by yourselves,' and then told me to make sure you ate your pastry."

That didn't sound like Lad. At the very least, he'd want to make sure he fulfilled the duty his brother gave him, and look after me. "Did you tell him what we were doing tonight?"

"Oh, a bit." Kichlan skirted the edges of any real answer. But he leaned against me as he did so, and the warm pressure of his body was so pleasant in the evening chill that I quickly decided I didn't care. Time alone with Kichlan was rare. Extremely rare. No Lad, no Unbound, no Keeper or lurking puppet men. Just Kichlan. "Although," he said, and pressed closer still. "If I realised how enjoyable revolution could be, I think I would have joined the Unbound a long time ago."

I didn't think this was really what revolution looked like, but decided not to make that comment. I was far too comfortable to do that. "I thought you didn't trust the Unbound?"

"I don't." He wrapped a gloved hand around mine, entwined our fingers. "But it's a nice excuse to spend an evening with you. Good food. Good wine–"

"I wouldn't call that good wine."

He just grinned "–and you."

Heat flushed up to my face. He held my hand tighter. He rested a clean-shaven cheek against my hair. He must have shaved before coming to meet me, Kichlan's jaw was never so smooth by this time of night. What exactly was going on here? I thought we were helping the Unbound return enough debris to the Keeper to seal the doors closed. Why did I get the impression that Kichlan's mind was on other things?

And should I really feel this relaxed? With my suit trying to control me, and the baby I may or may not be carrying, and the broken Keeper, and the quota we could not fill. But all I could really focus on was Kichlan. He made it easy to forget all those things, and I was more than willing to give in.

"Look." He tucked the flask away, but did not release my hand. "This is it."

On the other side of the street, a small group of technicians were unlocking the gold-adorned door with a set of large, iron keys. The two bored-looking enforcers with them didn't seem to notice us, hiding in the shadows, but Kichlan drew me against him anyway. He pressed my face into his chest and held me there, embracing me for far longer than seemed necessary. Finally, when he released me and whispered, "We need to follow them," I couldn't care less about the technicians, their collecting jars, Fedor and his Unbound. I would have quite happily remained in Kichlan's arms.

The technicians loaded their jars into a long black landau that floated low to the ground and travelled Movoc's twisting streets at high speed. So Kichlan and I ran after them, still joined by our hands, from corner to corner, hugging what shadows we could find. Every time the carriage slowed, even a little, we hid, bodies pressed up against walls, arms wrapped around each other, my face on his chest and his mouth in my hair. Soon, I could hardly breathe, but not from the running, and he was smiling, eyes flashing, wild, excited. Free.

Finally, the landau halted beside a wide, fat-looking building. For all the prodigious colourless wall space the building had only two large doors, their glass windows a pale green. In the moonlight and unsteady glare from a nearby lamp, it looked ugly and sluggish. And familiar. A debris technician laboratory, it had to be.

Kichlan's smile faded as we watched, still hiding, while more enforcers emerged from inside the laboratory to unload the jars.

"This is what Fedor wanted to know?" I whispered, wishing our frantic chase had not come to an end. I didn't fully understand what Kichlan was doing, why spying for the Unbound had involved food, drink and his body so close to mine. But I had enjoyed it.

He nodded. "Fedor wanted to know where the jars were taken, and how many."

I hadn't counted any jars, or been paying attention to the street names or building numbers as we ran, and could only hope that Kichlan had. "You will tell him to-morrow?"

Another nod, this time silent.

We watched until the landau was emptied, and glided away. Then Kichlan took me home. He did not offer the flask again, and did not speak, but at least he held my hand.

"Will Fedor have another task for us?" I asked, as we approached Valya's stairs. I had no idea how late the bell was, but no desire to climb those steps quite yet, at least not on my own. "Soon would be good, don't you think?"

Kichlan glanced at me in surprise. "I'm not sure. He didn't say. You– you would like that?" He swallowed loudly. "To spend another evening with me?" He coughed, looked away. "For the revolution, I suppose. The Keeper and the–"

"No." I released Kichlan's hand, and stepped so close to him our chests were touching again. At first he hardly seemed to breathe, then drew air deeply, slowly into his lungs so the very movement pressed us closer together.

The feeling made it difficult to speak. A lump in my throat, just like his. Foolishness. I was hardly new at this, was I? But with Kichlan, it felt different, unstable. Since he found me wandering Darkwater all those moons ago, lost, bandaged, and swearing at inanimate objects, I'd known many different aspects of Kichlan. From the hu-mourless man who'd judged me before he even met me, to the possessive but loving brother to Lad, the strong collecting team leader and, finally, a friend who believed me when no one else would. I rather liked where we'd ended up. A place of closeness and trust. If I took this down the paths I so very much wanted to tread, I could lose it all with a single misstep.

Like, say, if he learned about my pregnancy. *Possible* pregnancy.

So I shivered, not just with the Movoc chill. It was terrifying, to think that I could lose him. Far more frightening than it should have been. But then I glanced up to the curve of his jaw and the arch of his neck, and before I could stop myself I was touching him, his skin soft and hot beneath my fingers.

"I couldn't care less about revolution," the words spilled from me, uncontrollable. "Right now, I just want to be with you."

He held his breath until I dropped my hand, then said, "Well, then, perhaps we should just spend another evening together anyway." His voice was very deep, and I could feel it echo through me. Chest to chest.

"I would like that. So very much."

Kichlan kissed me.

His lips tasted of sweet pastry and spicy wine, and he shook, ever so slightly. I kissed him back, wondering what I tasted like. Not – oh please not – like the suit's metallic tang.

We kissed beneath a lamp's weak light. We kissed in Movoc's cold night air. We kissed until nothing really mattered any more, not revolution, not the Keeper, not the doors, not the life or the death within me. There was Kichlan, only Kichlan, as he always should have been. What I'd wanted for so long, I realised, but not been able to admit to myself.

When we said goodnight, eventually, at the base of

Valya's stairs, I could still feel him on my mouth, my chest, my hands. I carried him with me, and slept well for the remainder of that night. For once, without worry.

The remainder of the sixnight was slow, burdened by Natasha's ever-increasing concern over the small amount of debris we collected and brightened only by those few moments when I passed Lad over to Kichlan's care, and our hands touched. Even the briefest brush of his gloved fingers against mine set me shivering. Kichlan smiled at me then, a small, shy smile, and I knew I replied with just the same expression. Fedor had thanked us for our information, but did not give us any more assignments. At first I chaffed for another excuse to spend the evening together, for the closeness it had brought us. I wanted more of it, so much more – like Kichlan was food and I was starving. But exhaustion dogged me as the days wore on, and Kichlan's shy smile grew to worry as Lad whispered in his ear. What was he repeating? How many times I had almost tripped over my own feet, saved only by Lad's constant attention and steadying hand?

When Rest finally came, I got none of it. Early morning light had just woken me when Mizra, Uzdal and Sofia came knocking.

"How are you feeling, Tanyana?" Sofia asked with a don't-even-think-about-lying-to-me expression.

I sighed, and tried not to think about how the day would have been spent if Kichlan had appeared at my doorstep instead. "I could have done with more sleep."

That look deepened. "You know what I'm talking about."

I balled my hands into fists and tucked them deep inside my pockets. "I'm exhausted, I feel sick most of the time, and I'm sore just about everywhere. Answer your question?"

"It's early on," Mizra said, where he and his brother walked ahead of us. "Maybe things will settle down."

I thought of the suit, and didn't think that would happen.

"You look absolutely terrible," Sofia said.

I glared at her. "Well, thank you."

"And Mizra told us about your collapse a few days ago. It worries me, Tanyana."

For a long moment we walked in silence, the scrape of our boots against icy streets the only sound. It sent shivers up my spine. "It worries me too." More than I would say.

"I'm sorry we have been so forceful about this." Sofia even had the decency to avoid my gaze when she said that. "But your health is important to us."

"And the health of–" unable to say it, I gestured to my stomach.

"Yes," Uzdal answered. "And the health of your child."

"Possible child."

With a sad look over his shoulder, Uzdal nodded.

Sofia, Mizra and Uzdal did not lead me to the Tear River. This surprised me. I had assumed that we would catch a ferry up the Tear to the centre of the city and a university or healer's college. Instead, we marched further from the river, down the stark and dirty streets of outer Rills and Effluents.

"This, ah, healer," I murmured. "He is accredited, I assume?"

"Of course." Sofia flashed me a disdainful look. "But you're a collector now, remember? Collectors don't go to colleges under the bluestone of the bridge. Collectors take what help they can afford."

"Well, yes. But still." I glanced up at the blackened windows of a rundown block of apartments. The entire western side of the edifice had crumbled, crashing into bricks and broken mortar on the street. It left the steel framework and windowpanes naked like bones, bare in the face of the wind whipping up from the river down the narrow streets. "If I'm going to let someone prod at me, I'd rather they knew what they were doing."

We stopped at another complex a few doors down. This one was not in quite so bad condition, but cracks still wound their way through the walls. Mould coated the walls of its airless stairway, the steps littered with the desiccated corpses of unfortunate insects.

A short, round man with thin stands of dark hair and unkempt stubble over his chin opened the door to an apartment on the top floor. An unhealthy pion lock by the handle buzzed constantly. Of all the lights down the long hallway, only two worked, and they were faint. "Sofia," he said. "Not having problems, are you?" When he spoke, he reeked of something like very old onions. I reared back, but Mizra and Uzdal at my shoulders kept me from turning around and giving up on the whole idea.

Sofia shook her head. "No, I am well. I am here for a friend." And she pointed to me.

The healer looked me up and down with red, tired-looking eyes. He coughed loud and wetly into a hand. "All right," he said, fishing out a kerchief and spitting into it, "you'd better come in." He turned, and lumbered away into a dim room.

I didn't move. "And this is your idea of a bad joke, right?"

Sofia gave me a sorry shake of her head. "Edik might not look it, but he is a good healer."

"We would not bring you here otherwise," Mizra said.

I allowed myself to be led inside.

Edik's apartment was large, larger than I would have expected so far from the Tear River. But that was where any resemblance to luxury ended. The windows were all shuttered. Dust floated in the few narrow beams of light that crept past them. The room was filled with old furniture: leathers split, fabrics unravelling, wood stained and peeling. Slides were piled haphazardly in corners, some cracked, most heavily burdened by dust. I wondered when the words and images stored by pions inside their thin glass had last been read. Sofia led us down a hallway, just as dusty and rubbish-filled, to a wide room with a tiled floor. A tap dripped over a stained sink in one corner. A hard bed on wheels, covered with dirty blankets and surrounded by trays and metal instruments, took up most of the space. It reminded me of the metal table on which the puppet men had suited me, and I stopped at the sight of it.

"So, what's the problem?" Edik sat on a stool that looked far too flimsy for his weight, and it creaked worryingly beneath him. It seemed he was alone in this apartment, that he did not belong to a circle – not even a three point – and did not care much about basic cleanliness. "Not another one like her, are you?" He unwrapped a handful of seeds and nuts in a paper bag, and started chewing, spitting out any husks on the floor.

"Like her?" I tried not to gag as I spoke. The room stank of drains and stagnant water and not enough air.

Sofia sighed. "Yes, Edik. We think she's pregnant too."

"Think?" he asked.

"Too?" I turned to Sofia.

She couldn't quite meet my eyes. "I told you Edik was a good healer. I can personally recommend him."

"Do you remember when she fell?" Uzdal said, his voice quiet. "Your first emergency, all those moons ago. She was hurt, came here, found out something more than a fracture to her wrist."

I did remember. That first time I had tried to tie us all together in a circle, when we had stood against an enormous mass of debris grains and planes, and worked as a team to subdue it. It had lashed out when we tried to control it, knocking Sofia to the ground. She had looked so pale, almost dazed, for many sixnights after. But I had not known why.

"Why didn't you say something?" I asked her, mind reeling, trying to understand.

She flashed me an angry look. "Because it didn't have anything to do with you."

"Oh, like the way this has got nothing to do with you?"

Edik chuckled. "Please, keep this up. I started charging you the moment you stepped in here."

Mizra touched my arm, lightly. I realised I was breathing hard, fast, and that the bands on my wrists – where I could see them – were spinning in time with my hammering heart. "Sofia was not alone. She had us to help her. Just like you do."

I held Sofia's indignant gaze. "So you removed it, did you?"

She nodded, but beneath her hard expression I thought I saw pain, hurt, and something I could barely understand. Relief and grief, acceptance and guilt, all at once. "It was broken."

"Broken?" That word made me sick.

"Sometimes that's the best option. For mother and child both." Edik levered himself off his stool and approached me. "There are pions present in every living creature, and a developing child is no different. A relationship between the pions in a child's body and those within its mother's body is vital for the creation of a fully functioning individual. However, if the woman is a debris collector, this connection can be hindered. Her child's pions are unwilling, or unable, to interact with her own. We don't fully understand it, but whatever it is that debris collectors lack – that which prevents them from communicating with pions – interferes with the way the pions in their body interact with others. In some cases, such as Sofia here, mother and child appear completely severed. Blood still travels between them, true, but it's like a wall is raised along the edge of her womb and pions simply cannot pass through it. Children who develop without contact with their mother's pions are rarely born whole."

Whole, broken. Who was the filthy man to determine what either of those words meant?

"Such children do not grow up in the usual way. Though their bodies mature their minds are left behind. They might struggle to grasp language, to interact with other people, or function in society. Sometimes they can be violent and difficult to control. While they have suffered no obvious, physical trauma, they will never be able to see pions or communicate with them in any way."

I stared at him in horror, then glanced at Sofia, Mizra and Uzdal. Did they understand what this man was saying? He was describing Halves.

"In such cases, termination is often the most humane choice."

They were killing Halves.

"So you understand why it is so important to know what's happening in your body, in advance. You need time to make a decision." He patted the edge of the bed. "Just sit here and I will have a look at you." He smiled. His teeth were stained. "It won't hurt."

Feeling numb, I sat on the edge of the healer's bed.

"Could you remove your jacket? Your shirt?"

I lifted an eyebrow at him. "Why? You should be able to see pions through my clothes quite clearly."

"Ah, not born a collector then, were you?" He was looking at my scars, probably putting cause and effect together in that cunning little brain of his. "Look, I'm a healer, yes, but one without a circle. Let's make it easier for me, shall we? There are pions in your clothes, and they can make it difficult to differentiate the pions in your body."

I scowled at him. Not only was this man disgusting, he was untalented. He was also all I could probably afford. "Fine." I shrugged off my jacket, unbuttoned the shirt and let it fall. Then I peeled away my uniform top, until I was dressed only in a light shift.

His eyes widened at the twisted lines of jagged scar tissue down my left arm. "Nasty." He sucked air in through his teeth. "And the shift."

I baulked at that. He did not need to see the metal crossed over my skin; the new, deep scars, and the older nicks and scrapes the suit had been steadily filling in. My hair hid the notch in my ear and the new grazes across my forehead. The shift, while thin and hardly dignified, at least hid my abdomen.

"It stays," I said, and placed my palms flat over my

stomach to emphasise the point. Sofia, Uzdal and Mizra were worried enough about me as it was. And I couldn't have them carrying tales of new scars back to Kichlan.

"Now really–"

"I said, it stays." I held his gaze firmly. I wasn't sure if he recognised the nine point circle centre still deep within me, that power and authority I had once worn so well, or if the spinning of my suit as it increased in speed convinced him. Or maybe he just wasn't being paid well enough to take on battles with his clients.

"As you wish. Roll down the top of your pants then, at least."

I unbuttoned my loose woollen pants and eased them – and the uniform underneath – down a few inches. The shift was long enough to keep me covered. As Edik dragged his stool across the floor Sofia leaned down and whispered in my ear. "Why are you making this harder for yourself?"

I made a disgusted noise. "If he is skilled enough to tell me whether I am with child, and if that child will be a debris collector, then he has the strength to see pions through a thin layer of clothing. I think he just likes watching women undress."

Uzdal turned away, covering laughter with a fit of coughing as Sofia – bright red – leaned back.

"Now, let's look at you." Edik perched on his stool and stared intently at my stomach.

It was disconcerting, to say the least, made even worse by his constant murmuring conversation with lights I couldn't see and the perilous way his stool complained so loudly beneath his weight. I knew what he was doing, knew he was watching and coaxing pions, but I struggled to stop myself fidgeting. While I waited I placed my hands on my knees, spread the palms wide and watched the suit on my wrists, ready to catch any unruly activity.

"This isn't right," he said, after a long inspection that seemed to stretch – heavy with the sense of lost kopacks – for bells.

It was hardly encouraging. "What isn't?" And I wasn't about to remove the final layer of my clothing, no matter what he said.

"Isn't she–?" Sofia stammered. "Is there a child?"

Edik shook his head. "I think so, but I can't say for sure. It's difficult to see." He scanned my torso, down my arms, almost fell from his stool to look at my legs. "This simply isn't right."

"What do you mean?" I asked, keeping my voice as reasonable as I could manage. My suit spun faster with frustration, whipping up a need to wrap a silver-coated hand around his podgy neck and force answers from him. "What can't you see?"

"You." Edik leaned back on his stool and stared at me down the short length of his nose. "Well, parts of you."

"How is that possible?" Mizra asked. He touched my shoulder. The suit convulsed in its bands in response, but I held it down. "I mean, she's right here, she's real."

"It isn't possible." I was amazed at the calm in my own voice. "It's ridiculous. So explain it to me."

"I might not look like much to you now, collector, but I have been a healer for many years." Edik sighed, stood, lumbered over to his collection of seeds in their split paper bag and started chewing them again. "I know what I should be seeing. But instead, there are gaps. I can see your heart working, your lungs drawing in air, but anything below that is fragmented. Like, ah, I don't even know how to say it, like something came in and cut the pions away."

All I could feel, for a terrible moment, was the spinning of suit and the tugging in my bones as I wondered, yet again, just how much of me was left.

"But that's impossible. If your pions really were gone somehow, then you simply would not be here. Yet, there you are. And it's not just your abdomen. Your head, I can hardly see any of your brain! There should be countless pions there, frantically working to keep you living and thinking. But I can't see them. Forearms, some of your legs." He ran a hand over his face. "It's impossible, but true."

Gaps within me, breaks in the pions that made me?

"You mean, like, holes inside her?" Uzdal asked, voice strangled.

Another shake of Edik's head. "I don't think so. If there were holes, if the pions really were missing, then you'd see the damage. She wouldn't have a head, for one. Rather, I think there is something else – something that isn't made of pions – in the way."

Something not made of pions? But everything, surely, was made of pions. They were the foundations of our world, the raw materials.

Everything, that is, except for debris. And the Keeper.

Slowly, I lifted my hand, stared at the spinning, begging, tugging suit.

Was it even possible? There was only one way to be sure.

"Watch my hand, please," I said. My voice sounded distant, even in my own head. "Watch the pions. Tell me what happens."

I released the suit gradually. Already aggravated, it pulled for freedom, wanting to coat more than just my upraised hand. I held it in tight check, the memory of its last attack still fresh and sore.

As it slithered its slick way over my palm, the back of my hand, finger by finger to the very tips, Edik gasped.

"What do you see?" I asked, but I was already certain of the answer.

"That's it," he whispered. "It smothers the pions. I can't see through it, I can't see past it." He fixed his gaze on me. "You don't think much of me, miss. I know that. But I was once greater than this filthy place attests, and I am telling you the truth. Your pions are not too deep for me to see, it is not my lack of skill that hides them. That, that *stuff*. It wipes them away."

I reined the suit back in.

So what did it all mean?

I wished Kichlan was here.

"The suit is in your way?" Sofia frowned. "But you could see me clearly. You could," she hesitated, "operate. It doesn't make sense."

"It does," I answered for him. "My suit is not like yours, Sofia. You know that, we all know that." My suit was tied to more than my bones, my muscles and my will. It filled me. It made me. And now, it was trying to control me.

Oh, what a weapon it could be.

"I have a question." Mizra lifted a hand. What kind of class did he think this was? "I thought everything," his raised hand waved around the room, "was built from pions. Us, the room. The suit. So why can't the healer see it?"

I was beginning to understand something, as impossible

as it seemed. "Why do we wear these suits?" I asked, a rhetorical question, but Mizra took it up.

"To collect debris," he answered.

"Why do we need them?"

"Because they are the only things that can touch debris," again, he answered promptly. Too much the attentive student. "Nothing else, not our fingers, not our tools... Oh."

"Oh, indeed." The strange mixture of liquid and solid, of light and symbols that swum in the bands and deep beneath my skin, I had always wondered how it worked, what its pions were doing to create something so strange, so unlike anything I had ever seen. Anything pion-made.

"Isn't that impossible?"

"What?" Sofia glanced between us. "What's impossible?"

"The suit," I said. "It's not made of pions, that's why Edik can't see into it, why he can't see past it. The suit doesn't only collect debris. It is debris."

Edik laughed. It sounded a little strained. "Now that is impossible! Everything is made up of pions, to begin with. And debris is just rubbish. It certainly can't be used to create anything, particularly nothing as complicated as your collecting suits."

I shared a weighty, silent look with Mizra, Uzdal and Sofia. One thing we knew about debris was it certainly was not the inanimate waste product everyone else believed. So was it really that implausible? After all, the ancient Unbound had written books with debris. The puppet men had created monsters with it. Who could say they didn't also create weapons with it?

Other, I needed to talk to Kichlan.

"What about the child?" Uzdal murmured.

I felt a guilty pang. I had forgotten about that.

"Well." With another awkward laugh Edik drew a kerchief from his pocket and wiped his face "As I said, with that, whatever it is, in the way like that, I can't be sure. But I think, yes, very probably, you are pregnant. The pions I could see have clustered toward your abdominal region, and the division of energy leads me to believe your body is currently sustaining another life. But I cannot tell you what kind of child grows within you. A binder, or a collector."

Strange, but it didn't take a moment to digest such news. Maybe it was because I had already come to believe it. Or maybe it was because, compared with what I had just realised I was carrying around, bearing a child sounded so normal.

"Right then." I slipped from the edge of the bed and began dressing. "Just don't expect to be paid the full amount."

"But–"

I turned, held a finger up and silenced him. "You don't seriously expect me to pay for something you didn't do."

Edik wiped away more sweat. "One hundred kopacks."

I snorted. "Fifty."

"That's robbery!"

"One hundred is extortion."

"Seventy-five!"

"Sixty, or nothing."

Sweat ran in rivulets down the side of his neck to stain his already dirty collar.

"Fine."

We touched rublies, and Edik led us out of his filthy home. "I am sorry I couldn't help you. Believe me, I am."

I nodded, unsure whether I believed him, unsure whether I cared.

Back on the streets all I could think about was Kichlan. He would be home with Eugeny and Lad. Surely he wouldn't mind an unscheduled visit? As long as I didn't turn up injured, freezing and newly evicted it would be better than my last surprise appearance at his door.

"Tanyana?" Mizra stopped me as I began to stride ahead.

Surprised, I met his concerned expression. "Yes, what?"

"What are you going to do?"

"I was thinking I would ask Kichlan. I mean, he has a history with suits." I blinked. Maybe they didn't know that. How much of his past had Kichlan told the rest of our old collecting team? "Well, he's been doing this for a long time. I think I should run this theory past him."

"The baby, Tanyana!" Sofia snapped, grabbed my arm and shook it. "Not the suit! What are you going to do about your baby?"

Something sharpened within me as I stared at her, as I met her frustration and disgust. I breathed deeply. The suit stilled.

"I don't know," I said, and meant it. I really didn't know.

"Edik didn't say it would be a collector," Mizra said. "And he certainly didn't know if it was like– Like Lad."

"I heard him."

"So I think aborting it could be a mistake, don't you?" Uzdal finished the thought.

"But the choice is yours." Sofia still held me. "Whether or not the child is a collector you will have to deal with the consequence of its birth. You will be responsible for its life. Do you want that? Can you handle it?"

I stared at them, one at a time. "You realise, don't you, what Lad is."

Silence.

"He is a Half. Broken by our standards, maybe, but vital – absolutely vital – to the future of this world." I pried Sofia's fingers from my sleeve. "And you two," I glanced at Mizra and Uzdal, "think I should kill this child if it is like Lad. If it is a Half."

They shook their heads with a slightly unsettling synchronicity. "We didn't say that," Mizra said.

I turned to Sofia. "And you think I should kill it regardless?"

"No!" Sofia said. "I am telling you that your choice will impact not only your life, but the life of your child. And you should think about what kind of life that would be. What kind of life Lad has had."

"Halves are–"

"This is the modern world, Tanyana." Uzdal stepped forward, his expression like cold stone. "You might have contact with the Keeper, but most people don't even believe he exists."

"But–"

"Let him finish!" Mizra snapped.

"It's all very well to stand here discussing higher purposes and the good of the world, but this is a person we are talking about. A life!" Uzdal took a deep breath and lowered his voice. We were starting to attract attention. "In this world Halves live in danger, in fear. You know what Kichlan has gone through to keep Lad safe! Is that what you want? Another scared creature who cannot understand why they are forced to hide? And do you want to be just like Kichlan?

Always worried that the veche will come and take your child away?"

I remembered what Kichlan had said. That people like Lad, people we now knew to be Halves, would be taken by the puppet men and never seen again.

"We don't know this child is a Half," I whispered. "We don't even know if it is a collector."

"Exactly." Sofia crossed her arms. For some reason, that made me feel better. Like we were back on solid ground, relating in a way I could understand. "That's why you have to weigh up the risks and make a decision." She glanced away. "Like I did."

Together, Mizra and Uzdal looked to the ground, and suddenly the weight of what Sofia was saying hit me. She must have felt like this. Confused and hurting, but hopefully not alone. She'd had Mizra and Uzdal's support, and maybe that of the father, whoever he was.

I baulked a little at that thought. I couldn't even imagine Sofia – sturdy, hard working Sofia – enjoying an irresponsible romance. She didn't seem to care about anything other than debris collecting. Well, that, and Kich–

Kichlan? When I first met her, I'd watched Sofia follow him around like a loyal puppy. I hated myself for thinking that now, but it was true. And even now, the way she questioned me about him, the way she looked at me, she'd even waited for Lad with him on an evening or two.

It, it couldn't be. I could feel myself blushing. Did she know the way Kichlan felt about me, the way I felt about him? Did she hate me for it? Had he kissed her too, beneath unsteady lamplight? And had it led to… to this?

I didn't believe it, not really. But I needed to know. "Your child. Who... Who was–" I couldn't bring myself to say it.

She met my eyes and her gaze was flinty, her expression closed. But she knew the question I couldn't bring myself to ask. "Oh, don't worry," she said, her voice soft. "The father was no one you know. There is more to my life than debris collecting."

I tried not to feel quite so relieved.

She looked away. "He never saw me that way," she whispered so softly I didn't think she expected me to hear. "And now, he never will."

But where did all this leave me? I still didn't know what to do. "I can't make that decision. Not yet."

"Don't take too long," Sofia said. "Or it will be made for you."

I nodded. "I'm going to talk to Kichlan."

She looked away again, her bottom lip caught between her teeth. "Do whatever you need to do. Just make sure you think about it."

"I will." I turned, and hurried away from them, already thinking about the suit, and debris, and whether Kichlan could shed some light on the whole thing.

The trip to Edik's surgery had taken up only the morning's bells. I made my way through the back streets toward the eighth Keepersrill. Until I turned the corner, and almost collided with Tsana.

For a long moment I stared at the woman who had ruined my architectural career and taken my place as the head of a nine point circle. She stared right back at me, squinting as the light from the band peering out at my neck shone brightly in her face.

"Tsana," I said her name through clenched teeth.
"What are you doing here?"

She was not alone. Behind her, my once-circle wove
pion patterns over the supporting wall of a collapsing
factory. On Rest. Why was my critical circle working
on a Rest day? Not even debris collectors worked on
Rest.

My surprise must have shown. Tsana straightened, her
expression firmed into superiority, and she waved little
dismissive gestures at me. "All circles are busy at the moment, just like us. Movoc-under-Keeper needs us. We
don't have time to take a day off."

Behind her, the repair wasn't going well. Of course, it
can't have helped that the circle's so-called centre was
not guiding the gathered pions at all, but rather stopping
for a conversation. But it was more than that.

I approached them. The nine binders were clustered
closely together, ringing the wall in an inelegant semi-
circle. Not how I would have arranged the circle, certainly
– pion threads could get tangled that way, and extricating
them was nothing but a waste of time and energy. They
were attempting to reconstruct sandstone blocks from the
broken shards cluttering the ground. But every brick they
made slipped quickly into mud, and from the pleading,
rambled words and frantic expressions, it seemed they
were having trouble simply attracting enough pions to
work with in the first place. I crouched, close to the bottom of the ragged break in the wall, and scooped up a
handful of mud. As I watched, it dried to sand, thinned
until it was almost transparent, and then seemed to dissolve into air.

I'd seen that before. I glanced around. No frantic Lad,

gibbering the Keeper's words. No flashing alarm from my wrists, ankles, neck and waist. What was going on?

"Tanyana?" Volski caught sight of me and lowered his pion-guiding hands. "What are you doing here?"

"Isn't that my question?" I asked him. "I don't recall ever working on a Rest day." I glanced around the street. "Particularly in a place like this." However much I now belonged in these Movoc-under-Keeper backwaters, my nine point circle certainly didn't. Muck from leaking drains coated their expensive boots. Sand from the dissolving factory clung to the fine fibres of their tailored, woollen pants. Even the bear-heads decorating the shoulders of their jackets, denoting status and veche-employment, seemed tarnished in this place.

"Ah, well." He sniffed too loudly. "Things change."

"What are you doing?" Tsana cried shrilly behind me. "Stop distracting him. Volski, keep working!"

Expression pinched, Volski turned back to the wall.

Setting a tight, false smile in place I retreated, and leaned close to Tsana's ear. "I know what you did to me." A thrill pulsed up from my belly with the words. I found freedom in the truth and power in the scars she had given me. "I wonder what your precious circle would think, if they knew too."

A silence so deep I could hear every last grain of sand shifting from the disintegrating stones, settled between us.

"What do you think I did?" Tsana stammered, finally.

"Don't try it." I wrapped fingers around her wrist and dug them in. "Don't even try to deny it."

"How–"

"And don't ask any more questions." Something more than freedom was rousing through me, something I was coming to know too well. Oh, how my suit enjoyed its power. It revelled in strength, in aggression. It egged me on closer to the fire. What would it feel like, to give in? To be a weapon, just for a moment. To be truly powerful? "You're going to stop interrupting and let me talk to my people."

My people. Unfairly ripped from me. But they would always be my circle of nine.

"And if you don't, I will tell them the glass you created for me to land on was not an accident."

"They won't believe you." But she shook beneath my grasp.

My false smile became real. "Oh, I think they will. You are not strong enough to be a centre of nine, you are not skilled enough. I think it will explain a lot of things."

Tsana breathed heavily, close to my ear. I held her tightly, and waited.

"Fine." She pulled, and I let her go. "Fine."

"Knew you'd understand."

I approached the wall again. The more I looked at it, the more I was certain a door was open here. The stones the architects were creating disintegrated into powder faster than they could build them, and that dust itself was fading away.

But if I was right and a door was open here, where was the Keeper to help me close it? And was I willing to risk another confrontation with the suit to attempt to do it without him?

"You might as well stop trying to rebuild this," I said. "It's not going to work."

Volski – who had been watching Tsana and me – lowered his hands and left the semi-circle before I even stopped talking. "Why? What's happening here?"

I smiled at his earnest face, at that mix of curiosity and trust I knew so well. Volski had been a member of my circles since I had first earned a circle of three. We worked well together. But as I glanced between him and the mess of a wall at his back I realised I didn't know him as well as I, perhaps, should. I had not stood by his mother's grave, as I had with Kichlan and Lad. I had not let him into the most private parts of my life, as I had Sofia, Mizra and Uzdal. He had never opened up to me the way Aleksey – a man I had only just met – did so spontaneously.

What different lives they were, what a different person I had become. The architect, the debris collector. I tightened my fist against my restless suit. And what next? What now, with this silver filling me?

I pushed that all aside. "Remember the marketplace?"

Volski lifted an eyebrow. "I'm not that much older than you, Tanyana. Don't treat me like I'm going senile."

I chuckled. "Fine then." I broke into the half-circle and lifted a hand to the collapsing wall. "I think this is the same."

"So what is it? Debris?" Tsana – unable to hang defeated and sulking in the background – stood between Volski and me and waved imperiously at the terrible job her circle was doing. "Can you get rid of it?"

What anger I had felt toward her, what fury at her petty jealousy and desperate scramble for power, was falling away. Falsely tall, back rigid and nose tipped high, she looked ridiculous. She was just as powerless as I was, I realised. As much a puppet of her family, of the veche, maybe even the puppet men. So I did not hate her. I pitied her.

"It's not debris." My suit spun. "Not quite." I released

it slowly, kept it on a very tight leash. "And it is not that simple."

As the suit spread across my body and face, Tsana backed away. I heard her gasp – the sound distant and muted on the other side.

In the Keeper's dark world, this lowly backstreet was crowded. Doors pressed at my feet, low above my head, and squeezed me from either side. It made me shiver, so much ruin so tightly packed. And no sign of the Keeper. That was disturbing enough on its own. Where was he, while this door leaked emptiness and undoing into the world he guarded?

Sure enough, the door in front of me was opening. The smallest of cracks, even thinner than the one the Keeper had used to prove to me just how vital he was. A draught of caustic air blew in from whatever was on the other side, enough to send the suit on my hand rippling like water.

"What is it?" Volski asked, his voice surprisingly clear. What was it that made some people stand out in this place, when the doors and the darkness covered everything else? Lad was like that, but he was a Half. And Kichlan, sometimes. I couldn't begin to imagine what Volski could have in common with the two of them.

I didn't know where to start explaining doors to a pion-binder. So I simply said, "It's difficult, and dangerous. You should probably move back." Wasn't sure about that either, but it couldn't have hurt.

Could I do anything here, without the Keeper's help? The last time I tried to open a door my hand had passed through the handle. But I had touched it in the end, hadn't I? With my bare skin. In a moment of panic in the market square I had added my weight to the Keeper's and together we had closed the door. I carried its scars in tiny splinters of metal across my palm. Perhaps I could do that again.

So I tried.

The first time, my hand passed through the wood like it didn't exist.

I rubbed at my face. I felt insubstantial and tired and not at all sure this would actually work.

"What is it, my lady?" Volski had not retreated like I had asked him.

I was not a lady, had not been for a long time. As the centre of a nine point circle, when I was employed by the veche for vast sums of kopacks and a healthy dollop of respect on the side, then I deserved – at times demanded – the honorific. When I had lost those things, then I had lost that right.

But this time, I did not correct him.

"I can't close it," I whispered, even though I knew this was pointless because he could not understand or help me.

"What can't you close, my lady?"

I glanced over my shoulder in shock. Almost hidden in the mottle of wood grain and darkness, Kitai had broken away from the half-circle and approached us. A small woman, wispy-thin and pale, she was a much stronger binder than her appearance suggested.

Something lump-like formed in my throat. I was glad she could not see my face.

As I watched her, Kitai solidified in this realm, as though my very attention was all it took to give her form.

"The hole." Door seemed like such a foolish thing to say. I gestured to the wall to cover up my hesitation. "It's something that debris, well, it's like a side effect." Ah, how eloquent and authoritative.

"Is there anything we can do to help?"

Tsana laughed, a hoggish, graceless sound. "Have you all lost your minds? She's not a centre any more! She's a debris collector. And just what do you think you can do to help her? You like the thought of picking up garbage, do you?"

The movement was subtle. My once-circle, the tattered remains of the nine skilled pion-binders I had handpicked and trained into a forceful team, closed ranks. They tightened their semi-circle around me, leaving Tsana fuming, isolated at their backs, and did the thing she hated the most. They ignored her.

Well, most of them did. Savvin held back, as did two new members whose names I did not know. But it was enough. It was more than enough.

"What are you doing?" While Tsana did not quite exist in the Keeper's world, her screeching certainly did. "Stop! She's not– Stop!"

"Can we help you?" Volski's arms were crossed tightly at his chest, the only indication that he even knew Tsana was there. "Is there anything we can do?"

Use pions to collect debris? That was impossible. I turned back to the door, and sucked in a sharp breath. The crack was wider.

"I am your centre! Listen to me!"

But could I use pions to close a door?

The door was debris. My suit was debris. If I couldn't touch it, what hope did my circle – my *ex*-circle – have?

"My lady?" Zecholas this time. "Tell me what's happening.

We must be able to help." What a sharp mind that boy had. No knot of pions was too tight for him, no binding too complicated.

With a fiercer need than I had ever known, I wished that I could find something for them to do. That I could command them, wrap myself in their beaded threads of light and power, and work miracles again. Even if all I could see of those miracles was the waste they created.

Which made me think.

The door was debris torn from the Keeper's control. And we all knew how that debris was created in the first place, didn't we? I glanced back at my once-circle. Who had sent them here, on Rest, to try and patch a hole in a wall in the middle of a backwater effluent? A hole they had no hope of patching, a problem they could very well be making worse with each pion they bound, each thread they strung, each complicated knot they wove. Because those manipulations generated debris, and a nine point circle created the most waste, particularly when a single binder was all it should have taken to patch a simple crack in a wall.

I stared hard at Tsana. She was speaking to Savvin, hunched over, face hidden, though I couldn't have read something as detailed as her lips. The veche. Did they know what they were doing, sending her out here? Did they know a nine point circle would only make the situation worse?

But why would anyone – even the puppet men – want that? What could they gain by saturating this world in emptiness?

"Maybe you can help." The words slipped from me in a daze. "But not in the way you'd expect."

I turned back to Volski and Zecholas, put Tsana and her shadowy backers out of my mind.

Volski grinned so broadly it seemed to shine through the darkness. "Tell us what we need to do, my lady."

We were all enjoying this too much.

"It's a matter of imbalance," I said, and faced the door again. "Too many pions, too much debris."

"The debris created is proportional to the level of pion manipulation," Zecholas provided.

I nodded. "As the do– ah, hole, is directly caused by all that debris, using pions to attempt to correct it only makes the problem worse."

"I see." Zecholas whistled lowly. "So we are useless here."

I allowed myself to smile. It should not have felt this good, to be surrounded by them, to be their focus, their centre. And maybe I had more important things to worry about than trying to recapture my lost glory. But it felt so good, it felt so right. I had thought I was beyond this, that I had accepted my life as a collector and the new people it brought. But this was my circle, and not so easily let go.

"You're a pion-binder, aren't you, Zecholas?"

He even gave me a soft chuckle. "Yes, my lady."

"So why don't you tell me what you have to do."

"The pion system creates the waste–" Kitai began.

"–the waste is the problem–" Volski continued.

"–so close the pion system down." Zecholas finished.

And I bathed in them.

"So you want us to destroy the wall to fix the wall?" Volski wasn't arguing, as such. I knew the tone. He would do whatever I asked of him, he was just curious about my reasons.

"Once I have fixed the hole, you can rebuild that wall in a moment." I stared hard at the dull chrome stretching across my palm. "But until I am able to do that you are useless here, like Zecholas said. Worse than useless." I re-arranged my suit as I spoke, directed as much of it to my hand as I could, thinning the rest. It resisted, it liked to wrap itself around me nice and evenly, but as the centre of this circle, wallowing in memories of authority and skill, my suit was no match for me. Not now.

My hand thickened. The fingers meshed together, it began to look more like a basic scoop shape than the complicated body-hugging form. That didn't matter. All I needed was something strong enough to touch the door, to push it, and to close it.

"Good enough for me."

I couldn't see the pions slow as my once-circle started to work. I couldn't see bonds unravel, free pions dart away into the throng that was Movoc-under-Keeper, but I knew it had to be happening. A wall was a simple con-struction. The mesh of sandstone bricks, the ties of mortar, and the broader framework of stress and weight distribution that held the lot together. It would not take much, three distinct stages. Convince the pions that maintained the bonds to stop working so hard, undo the threads that tied them together, and set them free. The whole structure would return to the sand and cheap gravel that had created it.

I couldn't see the process happening, but I knew as soon as it did. Because Tsana recommended screeching, and because the debris changed.

I hadn't been entirely convinced this would work. The difference undoing the system would have on an opening door was entirely theoretical. So when the door gave a strange rattle – not like something was trying to push through, more like the whole structure was settling – I was too cautious to do anything about it. Until it shrank. One inch, another. Nothing more. But still. It shrank.

"The wall is down!" Volski called, but I could barely hear him. I was focused solely on the door.

"Right." I held out my hand, though I felt like I had a club for fingers. "Right." What had the Keeper always said? Touch it, calm it. The door was debris. I could do this.

I took a step and pushed against the door.

Like the other door, it was rough and splintery. It pushed back at me like there was something on the other side doing everything it could to come through. I pushed harder and my suit responded. It was so thin, taut from skin to bone, but it hardened my legs, it sent a rod of steel along my back and across my shoulders. Together, we pushed. The door groaned, the sound reverberating through me. It started to move.

As the door closed, my suit rippled. How long could it push against this wood before its strength failed? And if this was what it took to close one door, just one door, what hope would I ever have to do it again?

Fear for everything.

How we needed the Keeper. How we needed him sane, and whole.

The door closed with a click, and with that my suit withdrew. I could not have stopped it if I wanted to.

I blinked against bright sunlight as the suit freed my face. An inglorious pile of rubble lay before me. I had even begun to smile when my withdrawing suit pressed against my abdomen. I could almost hear the sharpening of countless tiny, internal knives.

"Is it done?" Volski asked, behind me.

"Looks the same to me," Tsana muttered.

I touched my stomach. I felt like my feet were welded to the ground, part of the stone.

"No," I whispered to the silver and the squirming, kicking wire inside my blood. "I won't let you kill it." For a moment, my suit resisted, and I couldn't move as we fought for control over my body. But the door had weakened it, and I was surrounded by the support of my critical circle, so I was stronger. This time. The suit sheathed its knives and withdrew.

"It is done." I was able to turn, and to smile, and wondered at myself for doing so steadily. "You can rebuild the wall now."

I was right, it only took them a moment. The rubble solidified, churned into blocks of smooth sandstone and grew into a wall. Nothing wavered; no invisible door weakened the very integrity of its foundations. The whole process appeared so normal, so simple.

"Strange," Volski said, when the wall was finished and Zecholas was running his hands over the stone. Double-checking their work, searching for deep faults not immediately obvious.

"What is?" I asked. What wasn't strange, at the moment?

"The pions, their behaviour." He adjusted the buckles on his solid blue jacket, and dusted loose particles of sand from its thick weave. "This has been happening a lot, recently."

My stomach was in knots. I tried to let none of the discomfort show.

"Don't make excuses for your own incompetence," Tsana snapped as she strode past us to inspect the wall. She clicked her tongue. "This will have to do, I suppose."

I laid a hand on Volski's arm as I felt him tense beside me. "Ignore her," I whispered.

With a deep sigh, Volski nodded, but shook me off.

"Done for the day?" I asked, louder. "Surely you don't have any more work to do on Rest."

Tsana refused to even look at me. "Of course we don't. This was a special case, after all."

"Of course." I turned back to Volski. "I was on my way to meet someone. Don't suppose you have time to walk some of the way with me?" I tried for a winning smile.

Volski, of course, could see right through it. But he still said, "I'd be happy to."

And as she stood there, inspecting the wall she had not helped build, Tsana's ill-gotten circle left her.

Kitai gave me a smile as she left, the others – short Kieve, proud Nosrod, and even quiet and reserved Nikol – shook my hand, murmured that the circle was not the same without me, and watched as Volski and I went on our way. Savvin seemed to have disappeared. The two members of the circle I didn't know hovered behind Tsana, evidently unsure what they should do next. Zecholas followed Volski and me and I was happy to let him.

"Tell me what has been going on," I said, when we had turned enough corners and threaded our way down enough side streets to leave Tsana well and truly behind.

"You know about Llada, already." Volski shook his head. "Sad business. She was not the centre you were, but she did not deserve to be pushed out like that."

He did not need to know the truth about Tsana.

Neither of them did. That matter was between me, her veche puppet masters, and the glass. So I said nothing.

"But I don't think that's what you're asking about," Zecholas said. Always a sharp boy.

"True," I murmured.

"This is not the first Rest we have worked," he continued. "And that fiasco at the market square was not the first time we have been dragged out to try and fix the impossible in the middle of the night. Something is wrong in this city. We know it is."

I was leading them to Kichlan's house, but not entirely sure why. Except that this was all part of one big bad puppet show that we seemed powerless to stop. Me, my collecting team, the Unbound revolutionaries, even my old circle and Movoc-under-Keeper herself. We were involved, whether we liked it or not. And I was tired of having my strings pulled.

"Is this a result of the debris emergency two moons ago?" Volski asked. "The one that forced the veche to evacuate the city, and cost so many lives?"

"In a way." I wasn't sure how much to tell them either. "Please, tell me what has been happening."

"The city is..." Volski hesitated. "Collapsing is not quite the right word."

"Pretty close though," Zecholas muttered.

"Well, things are falling apart. But slowly. Not like the last debris outbreak, this is piece by piece, wall by wall, system by system. And when they send us to fix it, we rarely succeed."

Zecholas tightened the fine wool scarf around his neck. Thin veins of gold thread shone from its intricate weave in the bands of sunlight flickering through to the alleyway. "It's almost like the pions are leaving us. I know, that sounds ridiculous, but—"

"It doesn't," I murmured, silencing him. "It's exactly what I expected you to say. I have seen it: this city is rotting away from the inside, from very deep inside." It made me shiver. "And we need to do something about it. All of us."

I stopped outside of Kichlan's door. This was not just a debris collectors' problem, not any more. We could not fix it alone, either.

"I want you to meet a few people," I said, and knocked.

8.

"This is not just about us any more," I said into a cold silence of crossed arms, stony glares, and general discomfort. "And really, it never was."

I stood in Eugeny's hallway with Volski and Zecholas at my back. The old man crossed his arms in front of me, flanked by Kichlan and Lad. Kichlan glared at me; I couldn't bring myself to meet his eyes. Lad watched Volski and Zecholas with curiosity, but had picked up on enough of his brother's foul mood to remain subdued.

Eugeny wore disappointment and anger beside the scars on his face. His bruising remained only as a faint yellowing If I had not known to look for it I would not have seen it. But the cut on his cheek was still raised, angry and swollen, stained with his goldenroot concoction. I wished I was not responsible for the flint in his eye. The mistrust. But still, I pressed on, well aware that I might not be welcome again in this house, a thought that filled me with dread. But I was certain this was the right thing to do.

"The Keeper is failing, the doors are opening, and we cannot fix them all on our own. No matter how many

Unbound you might gather in the streets of ancient Movoc-under-Keeper, this is bigger than debris–"

"Enough," Eugeny bit off the word. "You should not have brought these people here. I thought you would know better, talking like that in front of pion-binders. I don't care who they are."

He had allowed me to get as far as introductions, to set foot inside his home, close the door, and explain who I had brought to meet him. But no further.

"They understand what is happening to this city, Eugeny," I hissed back, angry for insult to the honour of the members of my circle. "Better than you and your Unbound friends do. They have to deal with the consequences of every door that opens, just as much as we–"

"Get out." The old man would not listen.

I turned to Kichlan instead and wished for courage in the face of his stony expression. "Kichlan, please listen to me–"

"Why did you bring them here?" Kichlan interrupted. "I thought you were one of us now, not them. I thought you didn't need them any more, because you have me. And Lad. Us. Is your circle still that important to you? Am I really – are we really – not enough?"

What was he talking about? He hadn't even wanted to join the Unbound in the first place. Then I thought about following the technicians, spying for Fedor. Kissing him. Did he think I wanted the company of my old circle, more than him?

"You should listen to Tan," Lad spoke so softly that I thought, at first, that I had imagined his voice. He watched us all with increasing intensity, with a firmness to his lips and a determination in his eyes that looked so very

strange on his usually child-like face. This was the Lad
who had cared for me so diligently, who took his responsibilities so seriously. Not the Lad who followed his older
brother around like an infant.

"Lad?" Kichlan snapped, harsher I'm sure than he intended. "Be quiet."

"No." Lad didn't shout. He didn't lose his temper or
begin to cry. Softly spoken still, but determinedly resolute
in his gentleness, he met his brother's furious gaze. "No,
bro. We should listen to her."

A horrible thought occurred to me. "Is the Keeper telling
you to say that?" I almost breathed the words; aware that
with each one I spoke, I took Volski and Zecholas closer to
a place they could never return from. "Remember, he
made a deal with us. You don't have to talk for him."

But Lad shook his head. "He is not here, Tan. I–" he
hesitated. "This is what I think. Bro and Geny are wrong.
They need to listen to you."

I could have knocked Kichlan over with the flick of a
finger, if he'd let me get that close.

Eugeny, however, was not so easily shocked and
shook his head again. "Hush, Lad. You should not comment on things you do not understand."

"I do understand." Lad pushed past Eugeny. He shook
off the old man's clutching hands and even Kichlan, as
they both tried to stop him. He stood beside me. "He –
the Keeper – needs help, and you want to help him. That
is good, but he didn't ask you to. He asked Tan." He
wound his fingers with mine and gave a reassuring
squeeze. "He needs me and he needs Tan. Everyone else
is just–" he looked up at the ceiling, searching for a word
"–they are extra."

"Lad—"

But again, Lad cut through Eugeny. And I was so proud of his calm, of the words he used with such straightforward, Lad-ish eloquence, that I squeezed him back. "He trusts Tan. If you want to help him, then you should listen to Tan. Stop making it difficult with 'those people' and 'us'. Just listen to Tan."

"Oh, Lad." Kichlan sniffed loudly and rubbed at his face. "Lad." He seemed to be having trouble with his words, with his breathing, his eyes. I stared at the floor, rather than embarrass him.

"Fine." Eugeny spun, and stalked into the fire-glow and food-smell of his kitchen.

I glanced at Volksi and Zecholas, and mouthed an apology. Wearing identical and utterly confused expression, they shrugged together.

Kichlan had not followed Eugeny. He was watching his brother with trepidation and awe, and Lad shifted uncomfortably beneath the scrutiny. "You said that very well," Kichlan murmured with a smile that seemed to tremble on his lips. "Very well."

"Not angry?" Lad whispered, his hand so tight around mine.

"No." Another sniff. A small cough to clear his throat. "Not at all."

"Not angry at Tan?"

Kichlan shifted his gaze to me. I fought the need to look at my shoes again, to touch my belly, to apologise, to turn around and leave and never come back.

"No, Lad," Kichlan answered. "Not angry at Tan. Just a little confused."

When we entered the kitchen Eugeny was standing

before the fire, glowering as it silhouetted his face and stroked faint touches of crimson light in his eyes. Arms still crossed, he cut a dark and commanding figure. Lad slowed at the very sight of him. It took a squeeze and a tug on his hand to keep him moving.

"Explain, then," the old man grated, his mouth a shadow.

Kichlan sat at the table, indicating for Volski and Zecholas to do the same. They did so with obvious misgivings. Lad and I remained by the doorway, between Kichlan and Eugeny.

I glanced at Volski, hoped he could see the apologies and the plea for patience in my eyes. "Please tell them what's been happening in the city."

By the time Volski explained walls they could not fix, streets falling in on themselves, buildings condemned by a single, unaccountable fault that no circle centre could find, Eugeny had unwound his arms and was rubbing at his temples.

"Fear for everything," I said, and Eugeny's rubbing ceased. He lifted his head, his expression haunted in the flickering reflection of flame. "I know you know what that means." My eyes felt grainy in the smoke haze, my clothes too heavy and warm this close to the fire. I tried to ignore it, to focus. "Your Unbound friends might be slightly delusional, but they're right. We need to do something about the state of this city. We need to stop more doors from being built. But did you listen to what Volski said? This is bigger than any binder can fix. Likewise, this is too big for debris collectors, or Unbound. Alone, we are helpless. We need to do this together."

He shook his head. "This has always been the realm

of the Unbound. Collectors. Whatever you want to call them. It is your role to serve the Keeper. Your place to help him. Not ours."

"What about you?" Kichlan watched his fingers as he spoke. He traced the whorls and patterns in the wooden tabletop. "You're helping the Unbound, aren't you?"

Eugeny sighed. "Just because I have seen the truth doesn't mean you should turn around and trust every pion-binder out there."

Trust. Another word I was coming to hate.

"What's the difference?" Kichlan asked.

"These are not random people I picked off the street, you know," I muttered.

"The difference is I don't use my binding skill, not any more." Eugeny pointed to Volski and Zecholas. "Could you really say that even if they knew the truth, if they understood the consequences, that these two would be able to live without using theirs? No light, no heat, no clothes, no food… Nothing that has been made with the manipulation of pions."

"Well, that's a little hard to say." Zecholas rolled a smooth beat into the wood with his fingertips. "Without knowing what this supposed truth is."

"And who this Keeper is either," Volski added.

Both were watching Eugeny with hard expressions. Not anger, although I would not have blamed them. Members of a nine point circle were not accustomed to being spoken to this way, and neither did they deserve such disrespect. No, they watched the old man with something closer to stubbornness, with strength born of hardship and experience. I couldn't help but feel somewhat proud of that. They were my circle members, after all.

I averted my face, unable to suppress a smug smile. Eugeny really had no idea who he was up against.

"But why would you even want to know?" the old man snapped. "You are comfortable, well-paid binders. If what Tanyana has told us is true, and judging from your bear badges, you are employed by the veche themselves. If you join us, like she is asking you to, then you risk losing all that." Eugeny's arms knotted themselves again, his shoulders hunched. "She's not your circle centre, and she collects garbage for a wretched living now. Is it really worth risking all of that for her?"

"Just for Tanyana?" Volski said with a sad smile in my direction. "Probably not."

"But we are not as blind as you think we are," Zecholas continued.

"When Tanyana fell from the statue we were building, she told me she had been pushed. I did not believe her. I regret that now." Volski caught my eye as he spoke. "There is something happening in this city that I cannot explain. Tsana has dragged us from collapsed wall to broken street to disintegrating factory, one after the other. We used to build masterpieces, now we're lucky if we can complete a basic patch and repair. And it's not only because she is a terrible centre–"

"Which she is," Zecholas interrupted.

"Or that our skills are growing rusty. There are so few pions now, and the ones that we manage to gather aren't doing what they are supposed to be doing. So I've started wondering, the pions that Tanyana said she saw, the ones that pushed her off Grandeur, they weren't doing what they should have been doing either. Maybe I shouldn't have been so quick to dismiss her. And then she shows up today, in the middle of another failed patch and repair job, and she knows what's going on. She can help us do what no other circle has been able to do that successfully for so long. This is why we are following her. There is something going wrong in this city, and I think Tanyana can help us fix it."

"Not to mention what this is doing to our careers," Zecholas muttered. "I have never repaired this many walls, not even as a three point apprentice! Not even for practice. And I'm tired of it."

"Fine," Eugeny said again. "I see you will not listen to reason. Tell them what you want." And he turned on his heel and left the room.

I disentangled myself from Lad and touched Kichlan on the shoulder. He seemed to be hovering on the edge of following Eugeny. "Can you explain it to them?" I asked. "What debris really is, about the Keeper, and the doors? I'm not sure how many times I can do that without losing my mind."

Kichlan agreed with a smile, and my sense of relief was palpable. His expression was the brush of cool air on hot skin. "I'm not sure if I understand it all myself."

"Me neither."

But he consented, and I left Lad sitting next to him – keen to fill in any gaps, although I wasn't sure how helpful he would be – and hurried after Eugeny.

I found the old man hiding in his forest of drying linen, of countless blankets strung up from the rafters in a fire-warmed room. How I'd grown to love the scent of damp cloth and trapped smoke.

"You don't know what you're doing," he said, before I had even brushed my way through the large cloth to find him.

"Neither do you," I answered.

He stood before the low embers of his drying fire, anger lined in his face with heavy crimson and shadow. His bruises were clearer, as though the argument itself had deepened them. "The Unbound have been doing this since–"

I held up a hand, and was surprised when that managed to silence him. "There are no Unbound anymore, despite what your friends think." I tilted the light on my wrist into his eyes. He squinted, and turned his face away. "See this? This makes me a collector. That is what we are now. And we need to accept that."

"No–"

I released the suit just enough to coat my hand. Eugeny stepped back.

"This is the modern world." The words felt like they did not belong on my tongue. Stolen from Mizra, Uzdal and Sofia they carried with them the burden of a decision I refused to make. "It doesn't matter how things were done. They have been changed, torn from our control." By the veche, by its puppet men. "We need to face the way things are now, the reality." I shook my hand as I pulled the silver back in. "Your Unbound believe that by releasing the debris stored by the technicians they can reverse time. This isn't true, Eugeny. The world will never go back to the way it was before Novski's revolution. But that doesn't mean we can let it continue as it is, and lead us into chaos and emptiness."

"So what would you have us do?"

"Compromise. What Fedor is planning worries me; I must be honest about that. But, for now, it's the best – the only – plan I have heard. So I want to help him. And we need Volski and Zecholas to do that."

Eugeny hesitated, eyes riveted on the band at my wrist. "Your suit frightens me. The fact that you can see the Keeper frightens me."

I nodded. "It frightens me too."

He glanced at the hanging linen, but I knew that he was looking further, to the kitchen and the collectors he cared for. "Can we really trust these people you have brought?"

That word "trust" again. "Yes," I answered, even as I thought of Devich, of Tsana, and began to doubt. Maybe this hadn't been a very good idea.

Too late now, though. Too late.

"I will hear what you have to say." Eugeny wove his way with expertness through the drying sheets.

I stared into the embers for a moment in his absence and wondered what I was supposed to feel. Should I mistrust myself the way he seemed to? Given recent history, it was starting to sound prudent. Should I detest the suit that was becoming more a part of me, day-by-day, scar-by-scar? I would never give into it, never become the weapon the puppet men wanted. But, no matter how I turned my back on it, and no matter how much it fought me for control, I had to admit one thing.

The suit made me strong.

It gave me the physical strength of a machine. But there was more. The suit gave me the Keeper. This was surely an unintended side effect, but it gave me truth, it gave me authority, and it gave me a reason to be. I was no longer able to build beauty into my city and my world, yes. But maybe I could make sure no more of this beauty was destroyed.

I followed Eugeny, aware of my suit through every last inch of my body, and feeling strong.

Volski and Zecholas were looking decidedly less comfortable than they had a moment ago. Kichlan shared a rueful look with me, fully aware of just how much he had taken away from these two men I trusted so much. Lad hummed happily at the back of his throat and tugged at a wide splinter lifting from the tabletop. Eugeny had resumed his place by the fire.

Volski looked up at me as I returned. "So what do you want us to do?" His voice cracked a little. I could see how much he wanted me to tell him this was all a vastly inappropriate joke. I would have liked to do that for him, and take that weight from his shoulders. I knew how it felt. The Keeper, after all, had placed it first and firmly on mine.

I glanced quickly at Lad. Well, maybe not first.

I smiled at these two points of my old circle, and wasn't in the least surprised that they would offer to help, even after everything they had just learned.

"We need to help the Keeper hold the doors closed." If only it was that simple.

"Which is what the Unbound were going to do all along," Eugeny murmured.

I nodded, acknowledging him. "Sabotage a technician's laboratory, yes. Fedor's sacrifice and Lev's grand schemes."

Kichlan frowned, but kept quiet.

"So why do we need your binders?"

What I was about to ask could ruin Volski and Zecholas. It could devastate their careers and possibly cost their lives. But this was the strength that came with my weapon, wasn't it? This was the purpose I needed so much.

"Because without their help, the Unbound are going

to fail. And when that happens, a lot of them will die. Just like last time."

"You've certainly thought this through, haven't you," Kichlan said, as he walked me home. I had lost track of the bells, wasn't even sure if it was still Rest anymore or very early Mornday.

We had left Lad soundly asleep on the couch in Eugeny's drying room. He had tried to stay awake with us and follow the conversation, but more than once I caught him hiding a yawn behind the back of his hand or distractedly picking at a loose thread on his shirt. By the time Volski and Zecholas had called for a landau and been driven away, Lad had well and truly lost the battle and snored softly, a soothing undertone to our words. He'd looked so peaceful, so contented, that I wished I could join him. But never had I felt more awake, more sharply focused, more ready and needing to do something.

"Not really," I answered with a grin. "I haven't thought it out at all, actually."

Kichlan blinked at me, eyes bright in the light from a streetlamp as we passed beneath it. "For a such an apparently wonderful circle centre you're not exactly inspiring me with confidence."

There wasn't much I could say to that.

Kichlan and I walked slowly through the night-heavy streets, comfortable in our silence. I wasn't entirely sure why he'd deemed it necessary to accompany me, what exactly he thought he was protecting me from, or why I needed it, but I was happy for his company and had not complained.

"You were a technician once," I said, before I could stop the words and allow myself to simply enjoy his quiet presence. "Do you know what the suit is made of?"

Another surprised blink. "It's a metal alloy, intricate, complicated and highly charged. Quicksilver, I'm certain, iron too. And more. Clay is mixed in at an early stage. But the details…" He shook his head. "I'm not sure of them all. It is developed through several different nine point circles in many separate stages. The metal that is finally strapped to us has travelled most of Varsnia to get here: it is dug from quarries at the very edges of the colonies, melded in one city, shaped in another." He clasped his hands behind his back in his classic lecture pose, and I averted my face before he could see me grin. "It is a convoluted process. Technicians study and apprentice themselves for decades simply to become one point in one of those many, many circles."

Complicated, I could believe. But it seemed strange that a department directly supervised and funded by the national veche was not more centralised. Was it truly necessary to ship half-formed suits from city to city? If I'd tried to construct a building like that – one wall here, the other in Karakov-by-Sea, the roof in a colonial border town – I'd have been dismissed in a less than a sixnight and one. "So no one person, no single technician, sees it from beginning to end. From convict-dug rocks to the glass tubes?"

"Of course not." He frowned down at me. "Why?"

I slowed the spinning on my wrists, sped it, soothed it. The suit was responsive tonight, perhaps as eager for activity as I was. "I've just been thinking about the suit: wondering what it actually is. Why can it touch debris when nothing else can? And the jars, they're the same, right? So what are they, where are their pions sourced from and how are they bound?"

Kichlan looked to his own wrist. He had to concentrate harder to get it to respond the way mine did. "I told you, I was not a technician for very long before Lad– before I had to stop, to look after him. So I didn't learn much. I filled tubes, I set the machinery, I measured width and depth and volume. The suit came to me already made, packaged and ready for implantation. I just kept the machines working."

Well, there went that particular avenue of information. "And say, if I went to a technician from each stage of the process, from the supervisors at the mines, to a machinist like you, each of them would tell me essentially the same thing, wouldn't they? They could only tell me about the part they play. The way the suit arrives in their care, and the way it leaves. They couldn't tell me about the whole."

He nodded, slowly. "Yes. What are you getting at?"

"That means that no one actually understands how the suit is created. No one knows everything that goes into it. No one, really, understands what they are made of."

A hesitation. "There are a few people."

I glanced at him, tingling with a sudden and unexpected hope. "Who?"

But his expression banished it instantly. "Those who oversee the whole process. The veche. More specifically–"

"The puppet men," I breathed.

"Yes, your puppet men."

I had the certain sensation we were going around in circles. And I was getting damned sick of that.

For a moment I considered explaining to Kichlan why I had broken our pleasant silence. My fingers twitched to touch the hard scars I knew were padded beneath coat, shirt, and uniform. Something stopped me. A self-aware suit was one thing, but what would he think of me if he knew I carried Devich's child? Would I lose him, when I had only just realised how much I needed him in the first place?

"Lad told me something was wrong."

"He looks after me," I whispered.

"Is that why you ask? Is it the suit?"

I realised I was holding my breath and tried not to release it in one gasp.

"He said the suit was hurting you, he said it was fighting you."

Lad could be far more observant then any of us gave him credit for.

"Listen to me, Tanyana." Kichlan stopped, held my shoulders, and turned me to face him. His touch was light but seemed to burn through my many layers of clothing. When I looked up into his eyes he was fierce again, bright with that breath-catching look. "You are not a weapon. You are not theirs–" *theirs* carried such weight "–to use as they want. And I know you are strong, I know you could carry this burden on your own and not let the strain show. But you don't have to. Tan, you have me."

His hands slipped from my shoulders, his arms wrapped around me and his strength pressed my face against his neck. I breathed in smoke and food and drying clothes and closed my eyes.

"Please tell me you understand that." When Kichlan

spoke, his voice rumbled low. It vibrated right through me and shook away all those questions I knew I had to answer, but couldn't. "I hope I am enough for you. I am not a pion-binder, not like those two you brought tonight. I am not powerful or wealthy, and I don't have much to offer you except Eugeny's food and drink. But I will give you what I can. I will give you everything I am."

I looked up without leaning back. Fine, pale hairs roughened Kichlan's chin, not as haphazard as Lad's tended to be, all short and even. I ran a soft finger along his jaw line. He shuddered, a movement that felt as deep as the one his voice had elicited from me. His breath was hot on my forehead. Movoc-under-Keeper's night chill receded into insignificance compared to his warmth.

Did he really think I needed anything other than him? Did he really think that was why I had brought Volski and Zecholas to his home tonight? Kichlan wasn't that stupid, surely.

"Tan," I whispered against him. "You called me Tan."

His chuckle was just as resonant as his voice, only richer, deeper, quivering and full. "I'm sorry."

"Don't be." I lifted my face. He lowered his. We rested cheeks together, as I slipped my arms around him in response. "I do understand. I didn't want to think about it, just in case I was wrong, and you didn't feel the same way. You have done so much for me since we met, and I have brought you chaos in exchange. I wouldn't be surprised if you'd rather get as far from me as possible."

I felt him smile. "How could you think something as foolish as that?"

"Oh I'm the foolish one, am I? How can you say that

after the way you behaved tonight?" I pulled back. "And you're not exactly mister 'here, let me express my feelings clearly', you know."

Kichlan chuckled again, and kissed me. This time, he tasted like salt and ash. "What about that, then? Is that nice and clear?"

I pressed my face against his chest. "Well, it's a good start."

"A start?" He breathed deeply. I listened to the rush of air in his lungs. "Well, you know, I don't like to leave things unfinished."

"Neither do I."

But the scars.

"How deeply does that old woman sleep?" Kichlan whispered against my hair.

"Deeply." Actually, I had no idea. And the scars. But Kichlan was here, Kichlan was warm. He wasn't Devich, ready to betray me. He trusted me with his brother, his only beloved brother. I looked after them and they looked after me and this was right, so right. This was all I'd wanted for a very long time, longer than I had even admitted to myself.

Kichlan bent to kiss me again. In this, I could forget it all. The veche, the puppet men, the Keeper and debris. In Kichlan. For a moment I worried that was selfish of me. But his hands pressed against my lower back and his mouth moved down to my neck and I decided he probably didn't mind. Not really. Perhaps he needed the same thing. A way to forget his constant worry about Lad, his mistrust of Volski and Zecholas, the pressure of Fedor, and his new collecting team.

Maybe we both deserved nothing but each other, for a little while at least.

We climbed Valya's rickety stairs one at a time, just to be safe. I asked him to remove his boots and we crept across the floor on soft and silent feet. I had no way of knowing whether Valya was even asleep. Considering the amount of food that woman prepared I wouldn't have been surprised to find she stayed awake for most of the night to cook it. But I decided to take the chance. I wasn't going to stop now.

Kichlan hung both our coats on the hooks on the other side of the door. He arranged our boots neatly beneath them. Then I took his hand and led him to my small bedroom.

"I never liked this place," he whispered, as I sat on the bed and patted the mattress beside me.

I ran a hand through his soft curls. Always shorter and neater than Lad's, they were still tangled and knotted around my fingers. I eased them open, gently. "Yes, I remember. Changed your mind?"

He extricated my hand. "No, not really. I always thought you deserved a place to yourself. Without Valya downstairs constantly monitoring you."

"Really?" I grasped his shoulders and swung myself over to straddle him. He started undoing the buttons of my blouse, his expression serious.

"You used to work for the veche. You were the centre of a circle of nine." He slipped the blouse from my shoulders and hooked his fingers beneath the hem of my uniform. I stopped him, started undoing his shirt instead. The scars. I could not let him see the scars. "I know what that means. You don't need any old woman to look after you. You don't need anyone to do that at all."

"Oh, I wouldn't say that."

Kichlan lifted his arms and allowed me to remove his shirt. The dark, boned uniform was tight across his broad chest and I had trouble taking it off him. I shuffled back so he could squeeze himself out of it, then laid a hand on his bare chest and pushed him down against Valya's patchwork quilt. I traced the faint pink lines the boning left on his skin with gentle fingertips, and he quivered.

He held my waist, but again I stopped him from removing my uniform. "Don't worry," he whispered. "I don't care about your scars."

For a moment, I panicked. He knew, how could he know about the child and the suit? And it shattered my certainty, my need. Maybe this wasn't such a good idea.

"I've seen those before, remember?" He tried to sound reassuring. "All collectors have their scars."

I released a large breath. He was talking about the raised, white lines Grandeur had given me, not the silver the suit was steadily filling me with. So I smiled, and slid down the length of his body. I flicked out the mismatched buttons at the top of his heavily patched pants, and drew them and his uniform down together. He protested, but I kissed him on the way down, small licks with my tongue and gentle touches with my lips until he dropped his head and all he seemed to be able to do was breathe. Great full, long breaths.

I stood, and drew curtains over the lamplight flickering through the single small window. Not as dark as I would like it.

"No," Kichlan said from the bed. "I want to be able to see you."

"Why don't you feel me instead?" I slipped out of my pants, pulled off my uniform top and bottom, and fingered the strips across my stomach. I could see them, if I peered hard enough, glowing their dull suit metal glow and seeming to gather every loose beam of light that made its way inside. With a little thought I dimmed the light shining from the slowly spinning bands on my ankles, wrists, waist and neck, and hoped it was enough.

"Tan?"

I returned to Kichlan, and straddled him again. I tried not to feel guilty as I took his hands in mine and guided them. Not because I didn't trust his touch, but because this way, and only this way, I could be sure he wouldn't find hard metal where he expected soft skin.

Kichlan could not stay the night with me, he had Lad to look after. As I'd expected. I kept my back to him as I pulled my uniform on.

"I always liked the way you looked in that uniform," he said, and held me again. Not skin to skin, but almost the same thing. The uniform was like that. "And now can you tell me why you're keeping so many secrets?"

I unwound my arms and stepped away. "What?"

He smiled. "Don't give me a look like that, you know I don't deserve it."

"You didn't…" I swallowed. I had a horrible sense that somewhere, Devich was laughing at me. "You didn't do that with me just so I would answer you? Did you?"

His smile became disappointment, a kind of weary sadness. "I thought you knew me better than that, Tan."

Tan. Uncertainty tugged at me like it was a suit itself.

"I–" I had lied to him all night, lied in the worst way possible. Surely Kichlan deserved truth. But that made it even worse. I really couldn't tell him now.

"Never mind then." Before I knew it, Kichlan brushed a light kiss against my lips. I waited for the demands, for the questions, for the promises he would expect me to make. None came. "I should get back. I need to be there when Lad wakes up. And I could do with a bit of sleep myself."

I felt my cheeks redden.

He chuckled. "Why so bashful now?"

True, I was the one guiding his hands.

"Don't think this means I'm going to give up," Kichlan continued. His eyes were still fierce, his body and breath still close enough to warm me. But in his smile he held onto that gentle sadness. "You aren't alone. And one day, I'm sure you'll believe me. Although I don't know what else I could possibly do to show you."

He made to turn. I grabbed his hand, pulled him back to me, and kissed him deeply. "I do believe you," I murmured, then kissed him a while longer.

I watched as Kichlan dressed, then descended Valya's rickety stairs. He lifted a hand and turned into the dark night, hunching his shoulders against the sudden cold.

With him gone, I pressed fingers to my abdomen. He was Kichlan. I could tell him, couldn't I? I could trust him, couldn't I?

The bands on my suit spun faster.

9.

"Damn it to all the Other's black hells!" Natasha railed as she lifted the flimsy grain of debris she had just spent half a bell crawling on her hands and knees to collect. "This is ridiculous, this is impossible! Where has all the debris gone?" She stalked toward Lad and me, with her debris brandished high like a weapon, and her face dark as thunder. "Where?"

Beside me, Lad shrank against my shoulder, quite a feat for someone as large as he.

I shook my head. "We don't know, Natasha." I understood the worry, bright with fear in her eyes. Yesterday – Mornday – we had managed to fill another jar and a half of debris. It was already Highbell on Thriveday and we hadn't done much better. Time was running out. We had collected so little that it didn't matter that the Keeper had not returned to receive his share. We would never make quota.

So I understood her concern, even if I wished she would stop shouting at Lad about it.

Natasha growled an inarticulate noise and snatched a jar from Mizra. She shoved the debris in, forced the lid down and continued along the street. "Get moving!" she called from over her shoulder. "We're not finished yet."

Mizra let out a low sigh, something closer to a groan. "I'll be glad when this day is over."

"What makes you think tomorrow will be any better?" Aleksey asked, his voice strained.

"A man needs something to hope for."

"What are you doing?" Natasha yelled, already far ahead. Too many curious faces glanced in our direction at the noise. I wished she could keep her frustrations to a slightly quieter level.

We hurried to keep up, and Mizra watched me critically. "How are you handling this, Tanyana?"

"Better than you might expect," I answered, and it was the truth. Ever since Rest night the pain and the battle of wills, had quietened. I'd even managed to eat my dawnbell supper two days in a row. Valya was delighted.

Mizra narrowed his sharp blue eyes at me, obviously sceptical. "And have you made a–"

"No, not yet."

"You should–"

"I know, Mizra. I know."

Aleksey listened, trying to be unobtrusive about it. Lad, it seemed, was too frightened of Natasha to pay attention to much else.

"You certainly seem to be feeling better," Aleksey murmured, as Natasha set us to work on a street lamp. The driver of a cheap coach with unsteady wheels had stopped her in the street, complaining of faults in the steering mechanism and an uneven acceleration that no amount of maintenance seemed to be able to fix. Lad and Mizra crawled beneath the chassis while Natasha climbed to the driver's seat and started digging up the upholstery.

I knelt, and was able to bend forward and scrape a long, thin strip of suit into the gap between lamp base and paving stones. "Yes, I am feeling much better actually."

"So suddenly?" He focused on extending his suit into a pointed, narrow implement as similar to mine as he could make it. Aleksey had not yet mastered his suit, but he learned quickly, and I had to admit the result was pretty good.

"It wasn't that bad to begin with."

"Ah, must have looked worse than it was, then."

"Exactly."

Together, we poked at the greening copper, carefully avoiding each other's gaze.

"Nothing," Aleksey muttered, inspecting his clean suit. "No debris at all." He sat back. "Damn it, I'm starting to understand why this is getting to Natasha."

"Weren't you trained to handle stressful situations?" I asked, with a grin. "To remain calm under attack?"

Aleksey chuckled, instantly good-natured again. "Ah yes, and if we were actually doing something, achieving something, I wouldn't mind. But all this walking and searching has been for nothing! That's hard."

"That's collecting." I glanced up at the light. While it burned steadily, only flickering slightly – like the passing of clouds across the sun – the fact that it was on at all in the middle of the day while its companions along the street remained silent and dark, meant something had to be going wrong. And that something was likely to be debris messing around the pion system.

"Let's try the valve," I suggested.

Lamps like this one, on a public street, worked on an automated valve system spread throughout the city. As evening fell they were activated, all at once, triggering the flow of light-creating pions. With my collecting suit I was able to pry open the metal panel riveted to the middle of the lamppost, which covered the valve and it complex system of pion-bindings.

"Nicely done," Aleksey said.

Sure enough, we found debris inside the valve. A thin splattering of dark grains clinging to the spindle tip and clogging its thread. By the time we had cleaned it – painstaking work involving thin suit tools and lots of guessing – we had collected barely enough to fill my palm. At least it started the valve working again, and the lamp-light above us slowly died.

"See what I mean." Aleksey scowled at the lint-looking ball in my hand. "That hardly seems worth the effort."

"True enough." I returned the plate, securing it to the post with careful blows of my suited hand. The copper bent easily, as though it was as soft as paper. "But you can't tell me there weren't frustrating times when you were an enforcer."

He rubbed his nose. "You're right, of course."

We turned from the lamp. Mizra still squirmed beneath the coach, Natasha held strips of fabric and packed wool in her arms and argued with the driver, Lad hovered between the two of them, looking worried.

I wrapped fingers around the debris to contain it and decided he could do with our help.

"When I started out," Aleksey said, as we waited to cross the street together, letting a sleek black landau pass smoothly by. "They stuck me with guarding the technicians."

I paused, one foot lifted, just about to step into the gutter. "Debris technicians?"

"Yes." More nose rubbing, so vigorous he left the scarred skin pink. "Ironic now, I suppose."

"I suppose." My mind buzzed with possibilities. "What was frustrating about that?"

"Ah, secretive bunch, you know." We wound our way through foot traffic. My suited hand attracted far more attention than I would have liked. I hid it in a pocket. "Can't go into this room or that room, don't look at this, and sign to swear you will keep your mouth shut if you do see anything."

"Really?" I slowed our pace, pretending to inspect the bottom of my boot. "What were they trying to keep from you?"

"At the time, I had no idea. But now I think it must have been the suits. And all those needles." He shuddered. "I guess they don't want too many people to know just what it takes to make a collecting suit work."

"You could be right." I scraped my sole on the edge of the gutter. "So what did you do? How could you defend a building when you weren't even allowed in some of the rooms?"

"That's what I mean." He nodded, apparently pleased. "Worst job for an enforcer, so they always give it to new recruits. Patrolled the hallways, in a Fist of two if you were lucky enough not to do it alone. Most of those rooms were locked, anyway. Biggest, most complicated bindings I have ever seen. If you try to get past them, and the locks don't recognise you, the whole building is locked down. Alarms and Fists summoned from across the city, and every single one of those doors shut tight. So I don't know why we were there in the first place. Nothing for us to do."

"Sounds terrible."

"And dangerous," he looked away from me as he spoke, as though lost in memory. "Well it would be, if you wanted to break in. Most people wouldn't even know about these defences. Deep in the world, those pion locks are. Too deep for most binders to see."

I couldn't decide what he was trying to say. Was this some kind of warning? What did he know? I scanned Aleksey's rough clothes, his messy hair, unsure how to approach this. "Who would want to break into a technician's laboratory?"

He met my eyes again. "No idea. But they'd want to be well-prepared." No nose-rubbing now. A seriousness that sent tingles of discomfort up from the suit-scars in my belly. "And they'd probably want to make sure they've chosen the right side to fight on, you know? Some decisions made rashly, without fully understanding the circumstances, can be the wrong ones."

I held his gaze, breathless. What was he saying?

And then Lad spotted us, and started waving.

Aleksey's expression was swamped by a wide smile, and he waved back. I had to wonder, just what was the real Aleksey like? Smiling and self-effacing; boiling with barely concealed rage; or stern and coldly calm? Had I really jus heard what I thought I'd heard?

Did Fedor know about the enforcers and pion locks and citywide alarms? How, exactly, did he plan to get past them?

And why had Aleksey told me about them? No, more than that. He had warned me.

By the time we reached the coach Natasha had tossed the remnants of the driver's seat into the gutter and joined Mizra under the chassis. Lad hurried over to us. "Natasha is upset and the driver is mad and Miz can't find anything."

"Are you two part of this ridiculous group?" The driver lurched over to us, carrying torn strips of upholstery in his hands. "Do you see what that madwoman has done to my coach? What are you going to do about it?"

Lad pulled away, expression terrified. But before I could say or do anything, Aleksey stepped forward. He took the material from the driver and shook his head over it, expression sorry. "Sir, I must ask you to calm down." There was such authority in his voice, and such a height and breadth to him, that the man did just that. "Now, you understand, I trust, the importance of debris collection and cannot therefore begrudge this woman the enthusiastic execution of her duty."

The driver met Aleksey's reasonable, but firm expression with a blank look I was certain Lad and I were mirroring. "Of– of course."

"I knew you would." Aleksey lifted an arm and his sleeve pulled back just enough to expose the spinning suit band on his wrist. He guided the driver around, toward the rest of his destroyed seat "The veche is reasonable, you must know that as well. There are many avenues for reparation." Then they were on the other side of the coach and out of earshot.

"Tan?" Lad whispered into the silence. "What did Aleksey just say?"

I shook my head. "No idea." Reparations? I supposed that was the enforcer part of him, coming out when he was needed. As long as Aleksey calmed the man down it didn't matter what he told him.

"Nothing!" Natasha growled behind us. Lad flinched. "What about you two?"

I pulled the small ball of debris out of my pocket and deposited it in the jar Mizra held out for me. If anything, Natasha's expression soured further.

"I don't understand it." She grated out the words. "Something is interfering with the pions in that damned contraption." She kicked at the coach. "But it's not debris!"

I thought of pions disappearing, fleeing this city with its opening doors, but said nothing. It wouldn't help us, even if it was the truth.

"Why did you tear his seat apart, though?" Mizra said returning the jar to its bag.

Natasha scowled at him. "I was trying to get to the gear box – where all the steering pion bindings are, of course."

"Gear box?"

Aleksey coughed delicately behind us. "The driver is currently collecting his upholstery – he is under the impression that the veche will repair it for him, as long as he brings it all in to the central chambers. Can I suggest we leave him to it, before he realises just how unlikely that is?"

"How did he come by that idea?" I asked with a smirk.

Aleksey coughed again. "You know, I'm not entirely sure."

We hurried away, through the twisting back streets and alleys of Movoc-under-Keeper.

"I've never heard of a gear box," Mizra muttered, even as he glanced back at the coach and its hapless driver.

"Well, they exist," Natasha insisted. "And they are usually beneath the driver's seat."

"Usually?" I asked.

She blushed deeply. "Not on this one, though."

"So you ruined his coach for nothing?" Mizra said with a grin.

"Yes. But not on purpose."

We found no more debris by the time Laxbell sounded, and Natasha released us with more sighing and muttering about jars. When Lad and I met Kichlan at the corner, he wore a similar expression.

"Bad day?" I asked, as I handed Lad over to his brother. "Have trouble finding anything to collect?"

He gnawed on the inside of his cheeks. I touched his jaw, lightly, and he stilled. "You too?" he asked with a guilty smile.

"Yes," Lad answered. "We didn't find much and Natasha broke a chair."

I shook my head when Kichlan cast me a questioning look. That was too long a story.

"Don't push yourself tomorrow," Kichlan said instead. "Eugeny confirmed it this morning. Tomorrow is the night. Can you contact your friends in time?"

"Yes." Volski had left me with details of his contacts on this end of the river, a way to reach him without the kopacks to catch a landau into the city centre or hire a messenger. Of course, it would mean a long detour on my way home, and I wondered why Kichlan had not mentioned it earlier.

But then Lad's eyes brightened. He took my hand as well and drew them both to his chest, and I realised what Kichlan had given me. A day without Lad's constant, pleading pressure.

"Tan," he said. "And bro." Bright eyes glanced between us. "I want to come."

Kichlan started to answer, "Lad, no, I don't think–"

But Lad cut across him with a twin squeeze of our hands and a firming in his gaze, a determination that – perhaps more than the pressure on his fingers – silenced Kichlan.

"Bro. No. I will come with you." Lad released us, crossed his arms. "I was there when you spoke to Geny and Tan's friends. I know what is going on. I know you are going underground to help Fedor and you are doing all that to help the Keeper." He nodded, as though confirming it to himself. "Yes. And it is tomorrow night."

I hadn't realised he'd paid that much attention to our argument the other night. Kichlan and I shared a surprised glance.

"It's dangerous, Lad," Kichlan tried again.

This time, Lad only needed to lift a hand. "Know that, bro. But–" he lowered it, entwined his fingers with the hem of his shirt and fidgeted nervously "–but that's what I'm supposed to do." He turned imploring eyes on me. "I'm a Half, aren't I, Tan. And Halves help the Keeper."

"Is the Keeper telling you this?" I asked.

A little, frustrated frown. "No! Promised he wouldn't, and you should believe him Tan." He drew a deep breath and visibly calmed himself down.

It was, all of it, quite remarkable.

"Anyway, he has been quiet. For days now. Not saying anything. I want to come with you, because I should. Because I am here to help him." Those arms crossed again and his head lifted and his eyes glinted and for a moment I wasn't entirely convinced this was Lad standing before us, so strong and sure. "And I don't think you can stop me."

● ● ● ●

Fedor thought it was the worst idea he'd ever heard. And he told us that, in just so many words.

"So did Eugeny, at first," I said.

Yicor had met us at Eugeny's house and led us to the half-buried, domed room beneath the city. He'd been surprised to see Lad, clinging to Kichlan's hand and rocking on the balls of his feet with excitement, but had not questioned his presence. The once great, circular room was almost empty; only the few younger Unbound men had gathered, with Fedor and Lev at their head. Lev shared Fedor's expression of affronted horror.

Of course, that was mainly due to Volski and Zecholas waiting in the underground street, where they were quite happily cooing over the ancient architecture.

Only Yicor did not appear personally insulted by the presence of pion-binders in this secret, buried world. But then, he didn't seem to approve either. The old man simply watched – expressionless, silent – and listened.

"And I agreed with him," Kichlan added.

"Not me!" Lad beamed. "I knew Tan was right from the beginning."

Fedor glanced at Lad and his anger slipped away. "You," he whispered. "The Half."

Tingles of worry crawled through me, and I felt Kichlan tense beside me. Fedor knew.

"Half?" Lev gasped, and excited murmurs rippled through the room. "Are you truly? Do you speak to the Keeper?"

"Am." Lad beamed, proudly. "Do! He talks to me and then I tell Tan. It's very important."

Lev turned to Fedor. "They brought us a Half."

"That is beside the point." Deftly, Fedor returned the

weight of scrutiny to my shoulders. "Those two men waiting outside are pion-binders," he hissed, scowling at me. "They do not belong here. This is not their battle. It is ours."

"Yes," I said. "We've heard that argument a few times too." This was going nowhere. "Listen, I know this is your plan and I know how much you've sacrificed for it."

Fedor grunted.

"But that doesn't change the fact that without Zecholas and Volski's help, you will fail."

"You know nothing about this."

I turned to Yicor. "I don't suppose there's any chance you can talk sense into this man, is there?"

"This is Fedor's undertaking," Yicor answered. "Not mine."

"And not Eugeny's," Lev grated.

"That's enough, we are doing this. Now." Fedor pushed past me, and began squeezing his way through the tight gap that was all that remained of the entrance. "And we are doing it without your help." There was no way anyone could exit that room and still maintain a dignified air of injured pride. But Fedor certainly tried.

One by one, with identical filthy glares and insulting words muttered under their breath, the assembled Unbound men followed. Not before smiling at Lad, however. Or nodding to him, or waving. Of course, he couldn't help but smile back.

"That went well." Kichlan released a loud sigh. "You really have a skill when it comes to things like this."

"It was never going to go well." Alone in the chamber with Kichlan, Lad and me, Yicor began to smile. "No matter how you handled it, these boys have worked too long and too hard on this to let a newcomer take over. Especially one with two wealthy binders in tow." The smile widened. The cheekiness, the hidden depths of knowledge I had seen when we first met, returned. "Of course, they can't stop you following them. Section twelve, tenth Keepersrill. It's the large building on Widesign. You can't miss it." And Yicor left with a great breath to suck in a steadily growing gut, and a final daring glance my way.

Follow them?

"Did you really need him to tell you the obvious?" Kichlan glowered at the old man's retreating back.

"He makes a good point," I answered.

"What, to follow them? I could have told you that."

"He told us the address."

"And why do we need that to follow them?"

"Should be quiet," Lad said, and firmly placed my hand in his brother's, silencing us both. "And hurry, or they will be gone." He left us to squeeze his broad frame through the rubble. Not an easy feat.

Kichlan touched his lips lightly to my straggly fringe. I could feel the curl of his smile. "You need a haircut," he said, before leading me to the door and helping me through.

I emerged flustered and hot into the dim underground street.

"They're leaving," Volski pointed out. He was sitting on rubble in the shadows, away from the opening to the domed building.

"Then let's follow them." I helped Kichlan through. He was, after all, almost as large as his brother. Steadying him took longer than it should – my hands at his sides, his on my shoulders – and when I turned, Volski's gaze seemed to have sharpened.

"This is remarkable." Zecholas, however, remained utterly unconcerned by the less than enthusiastic reception to his presence. He was peering into collapsed windows, stroking time-eroded statues, and clambering into unsafe-looking nooks. "I wish you could see them, my lady. The pion bindings are beautiful. Simple and direct, uncomplicated but strong. As close to perfect as I've ever known. I don't think these were built using pions at all."

"No, they wouldn't have been."

He collected one of the chunks of gold-flecked crystal from a nearby pile, and tossed it down to me. "And these – my lady, I don't even know how to classify them. The pions inside them are like nothing I've ever seen. So concentrated it actually hurts to look at, and too bloody bright to see what's going on anyway. And yet, they're not doing anything. It's just stone, as far as I can tell. The statues are like that too, only not as bad."

He swung himself down from a ledge and grinned at me, fiery with passion for his pions. "This place is inspiring. These buildings use none of the complicated, multi-level, heavily-alloyed bindings that are in vogue at the moment. Maybe not as aesthetically pleasing." He rubbed rough stone. "But see how long they have stood."

"Maybe you should pioneer a new design?" My fingers twitched, unconsciously, with the very thought. To make something as beautiful and simple, as natural rock. That was a greater challenge than it sounded.

Zecholas laughed. "Well I might."

"Your friends–" Volski broke in, ever practical "–are getting further away."

I silenced the foolish dreams of another lifetime. "Then we'd better hurry."

We set off back along the hidden street. Kichlan and Lad in front – Lad humming softly, Kichlan trying to pretend he wasn't watching me over his shoulder – Volski and Zecholas on either side of me.

"I take it our offer to help wasn't greeted with the kind of enthusiasm you had hoped for," Volski murmured.

"You heard?" Hardly a surprise in this stone place. The echoes of our own footsteps looped over us, and I could even catch the edge of Fedor's voice. He was, I gathered, still complaining.

"We heard enough." He hesitated. "So why are we following them?"

My smile hardened. "To help them. Hopefully before they realise how much they're going to need it." I quickened the pace.

"You've really thought this through, haven't you?"

Up ahead, Kichlan descended into a coughing fit.

"I wish people would stop asking me that," I muttered.

We hurried down the submerged path, occasionally dragging Zecholas away from more exciting examples of primitive architecture and every single pile of crystalline stones, and up the ladder. Climbing up was a lot harder than down. I clutched at a stitch in my side until I noticed Kichlan watching me, concerned.

It seemed Lev had remained in his shop. He stood behind his desk and eyed us across the merchandise, lit only by a single oil lamp in his hand. "This is not their battle," he said.

I'd had enough of arguing, and pushed out into the quiet deep of a cold Wetday night in silence. Lamplight flickered around us, an unsteady and increasingly common dance. I wondered, as I breathed steam, just what the doors were doing. Just how many were creaking open, moment by moment, while we fumbled, petty and useless?

"Have we lost them?" Without the history of Movoc past, chiselled into stone to distract him, Zecholas was suddenly focused.

I traced fingers along the band on my left wrist, fidgeting while Kichlan coaxed Lad out into the night. They had no symbol, the band of motley would-be saviours we were following. Lad, however, bumped strong and distinct, clinking against my fingernails. How strange, I thought, for debris to clink.

"I know how to get there," Kichlan answered for me.

"You do?" I whispered, leaning close as he led us through back alleyways that I could barely see in the light of struggling lamps.

"We've been there before, Tan. That's where the coach we followed unloaded its jars." He slipped an arm around my waist. "And anyway, I worked there."

"When you were–"

"Yes. Long ago. Before I fell."

A pause in which I could not properly feel us walking, where all I knew was the brush of his breath and the heat of his hand. Then I whispered, "How did you fall?" And though he hesitated, a barely perceptible movement, he did not pull away.

"After Lad... After he hurt that girl, and the veche wanted to lock him away, thinking him unsafe without constant supervision, I was taking the final measurements for a new suit. I told you the kind of suits the veche had me work on, didn't I? Experimental, different. This suit was more than five bands and deep implants. It was armoured, similar to yours, shaped to fit the body of the young debris collector it had been assigned to. But I knew I had to be with Lad, all the time. So I knew, I had to see debris as he did. I had to fall."

"What did you do?" I thought of the silver hand I had seen on his dresser, amputated, wrist a ruin of torn and burned wiring.

"I overloaded the suit. Instead of readying the network to bond with the nervous system of the collector I wired it to itself, linking all its implants into one great circuit."

I slipped my arm around him.

"Then I diverted the room's heating pion flow into the suit and sat against it. So my head was resting against the heap of metal – hands and breastplate was all they had sent by then – when it overloaded. And exploded."

"Your head?"

"I knew what it took to make a collector." He tapped the top of my head, the invisible scars more terrible than those that crossed my skin. "When I woke again, in another floor of the same building, I was no longer a technician. But I could keep my brother safe."

I felt heavy with the knowledge as we continued. The image of Kichlan – a whole Kichlan, talented and un-scarred by bitterness yet to come – resting his head against the suit, calm in the face of what he was about to become, would not leave me. I knew why he had chosen this life, and yet the details made it harder. Part of me wished I had not asked him. Part of me wished I could have been as calm and purposeful as he was, when I fell.

When I was pushed.

Yicor was right, it was not far. When the alley we fol-lowed opened up onto a familiar street the first thing I noticed was Fedor and his group trying to melt into the shadows along the side of the laboratory. After a moment, Fedor broke away and approached the front door. Even from the other side of the street I could see the slick of sweat on his face and the shake in his step. But it wasn't nerves. He had extended the suit on his right hand into a great blade, a sword almost as long as his entire arm. His left was attempting to mirror it, but burgeoning instead into something shapeless and bulging.

Fedor's suit was not like mine. It was designed to pinch, to cut, to scoop. He was not a weapon. So I drew in a hissing breath at the pain on his face, at the tension I knew would be needling itself through the bone in his arms to his spine, his head, his legs, as he drew on every last inch of the suit embedded within his marrow.

"Bro?" Lad whimpered at the sight and beside me, Kichlan shuddered.

"I know, Lad," he whispered. "What is he trying to do?"

I shook my head. "I think he means to break the lock."

"Tell me you're joking." Volski squeezed himself close beside me. "I don't know what those blade-things on his hands can do, but do you have any idea what the pions on that door look like?"

"Yes," Kichlan and I answered at once.

If Volski was surprised by that answer he didn't show it. "Then you know trying to break into them isn't a good idea."

"That's why you're here." I flashed both Volski and Zecholas a grin that felt a little unhinged, even to me. "Let's go."

"Stop!" I hissed to Fedor as we broke from the cover of our alleyway and ran across the street. "You don't know what you're doing. There are locks and enforcers and even more in that building."

He shook his head at me. "Of course I know that, Tanyana. Do you really take us for such fools?"

I paused. "Then what are you doing?"

He lifted his fully formed blade, turned his arm so light reflected down its sharp length. "Watching. I'm better at that than you seem to think. I watched you fight that twisted debris, I've seen how strong the suit makes you. I might not be able to see the Keeper." Jealousy again "But I too can be strong."

"You don't understand," Kichlan snapped. "Tan's suit is different–"

"But not that different." Fedor gave up on his second blade, and let the suit on his left hand settle back into its band. "If I work at it hard enough, if I concentrate, focus, I too can form a blade that will cut through anything in my way." He glanced at the lock. "Even this."

Could he? True, our suits were not the same, but we had the same foundation. We were both built from debris. "I– I suppose you could." Disrupt the pion systems, disable the lock. "But I'm not sure–"

"And that is why you vacillate, unable to do anything. That is why you collect when you should fight. Because you are unsure."

I stepped back from him, stunned. Where had that come from?

"I, however, believe in what I am doing." He glanced at Lad. "You should tell him that. The Keeper. Tell him he still has servants who respect him, and are willing to risk anything to aid him." Fedor plunged his blade into the pion lock's blank, crystalline screen.

For a moment, the lock spluttered and fizzed sparks round Fedor's suit. Hardly what I had expected. "Didn't I tell you," he said with a smirk, "that I had all the strength we–"

The entire laboratory lit up, splattering light across the cloud-laden night sky, and Volski and Zecholas both threw themselves to the ground. "Get down!" Volski cried. "All of you!"

Kichlan dragged Lad to the stones and shielded him with his body. My suit spread into a wide screen of its own accord. And as the laboratory shone too-bright, too-sharp, I closed my eyes and turned my face away. Until Fedor started screaming.

I dragged my suit back in so I could see what was happening. It protested, tugged and pinched and performed all its usual tantrum-like tricks, but grudgingly obeyed. Fedor was strung up in invisible threads, at least six feet in the air, suit torn from the lock, wrists together above his head and legs akimbo. He shook as the air sizzled, and the pion bindings that defended the laboratory attempted to incapacitate him. But something wasn't quite right. A pathetic wailing sound – more like a crying child than an alarm – rose and fell. And the building flickered, the lights that surged apparently sourceless from the very walls, stuttering like a massive faulty lamp.

I grabbed Volski and Zecholas and dragged them to their feet. "Something's wrong with the defence system. Look at it, is that really what you expected from such a complex systems of bonds?" Still, it took some coaxing to convince them to approach the building.

Fedor's Unbound team had lost their protective cover of shadows but still held back, gaping up at him in horror. Only Yicor approached us.

"By the Keeper," he whispered. "What is happening to him?"

"Not here," Lad muttered. "He is not here to help."

"The building's defences are like nothing I've ever seen," Zecholas squinted as he stared deep into the laboratory, far deeper than concrete and steel. "There are people behind that door. Heavily armoured, reinforced."

"Enforcers?" I asked.

"Actually, closer to Mob. Strengthened, lengthened and carrying big knives. But they can't get out." His eyes refocused on my face. "And we should be thankful. The lock is malfunctioning. I think it's trying to shock Fedor, knock him out, keep him there for those boys with their awful anatomy to catch. Instead, it has fused the doors and the walls into one big mess of knots and steel." He shook his head. "I don't know how long it will take for them to get out, or how long the lock will keep doing that." He gestured at Fedor, who spasmed above us and cried out weakly.

"Can't you help him?" One of the Unbound – Yan, I thought his name was – pleaded, his voice constricted.

"Either way, we will have company soon." Volski was scanning the roofs, tracing the lines of pion bindings that I could not see. His sturdy jaw was set, his eyes serious but always so calm. "An alert has been sent. Down the light threads, one through the heating, probably through sewer pipes too. I'd safely assume they are using every binding available to them. Even if I could intercept each one they are too strong, too complicated, for me to unravel without a circle at my back."

"Even you?" I asked, gently. Volski had far more skill than he would ever admit to.

Volski did not smile. "I'd guess we'll have more of those Mob to deal with – or whatever they are – in less than a quarter bell."

We had to get away from the laboratory, fast. It was time to cut Fedor free. I drew a deep breath. "We need to free him."

"I can't undo that." Zecholas gestured to the door. "The two of us together couldn't do it. I'm not even sure your circle could have, my lady." His shoulders sagged. "If this is why you brought us here then I fear you were mistaken."

But I shook my head. "Actually, I'd hoped to avoid this altogether." I straightened, clenched fists and promised the suit a chance to spread its wings. "But we have to deal with what we're given." I turned to Kichlan. "Will you help me?"

He blinked back surprise. "Ah, of course."

Together we closed in on the door. Zecholas, it seemed, couldn't help but follow. "What are you doing?"

"Fedor was right about the suits, in a way." I slid both my hands into blades, small and tight compared to Fedor's overblown sword. "*My* suit can cut through anything, even the pion bonds that are holding him now. So that is what I'm going to do."

Fedor's suit was not my suit, no matter how far he pushed it, no matter the pain he forced himself to endure or the effort he went to, he did not have the strength to do what I could do. If he understood the consequences he might have counted himself lucky.

And lucky was just what he was. Either his suit had indeed disrupted the bindings in the pion lock or, and I considered this more likely, the building's security systems were already weakening, just like everything in Movoc-under-Keeper. How many of the pions in its complicated and dangerous bindings had already fled, just like so many of their bright, energetic brothers?

"How can I help?" Kichlan asked.

I resisted an urge to kiss away that serious frown. "Catch him."

I plunged the suit into the ground beneath me and reared above Fedor. Shuddering with each shock but still very much aware, he watched me with wide, white-rimmed eyes. Even then, I wouldn't call it pleading. Damn him and his pride.

"Right," I whispered to myself and the suit inside me. "No getting carried away. Make it quick, and get out." But I could feel the buzz bubbling up, the need for release, to test the boundaries. It was so strong I rocked on my stilts and below, both Kichlan and Zecholas held out hands to catch me if I fell. If I only gave in, I could do more than cut Fedor's bindings. I could destroy the entire system: lock and door and wall; lights and siren and alarm; sword and armour and strengthened body. What did those paltry binders think they could do against me? Against blades that could disrupt their very bodies, that could scramble their muscles, that could shatter their lives–

–like the Hon Ji Half?

I swallowed the suit down, forced back its urgency, its violence. That was not me.

Never me.

"None of that." My throat hurt; the scratching of countless tiny wiggling worm-like wires?

I had no way of knowing exactly where the bindings were that suspended Fedor, but I could guess. So I extended my blades further, sharpened and narrowed them. Was that envy I could see in Fedor's pain-wracked and incapacitated face? Even at a time like this, for the power he did not have and the price he did not understand?   ·

"Keep still," I whispered to him. And sliced.

The lock fought me, but I had known it would. Nothing, no pion system or debris outbreak or opening door would sit back and considerately allow its own destruction. Gleefully, the suit responded. As I sliced through the apparently empty air sparks travelled down my arms, latching onto my clothing and sizzling against my skin. Then the suit sent up two appendages like an insect's antenna from my neck and absorbed the shocks.

Fedor's arms hung free. His suit whipped back hard and fast into his wrists and he screamed again. But the lock no longer shocked him – indeed, all its energy seemed focused on my neck, and it buzzed and smelled like burning hair, too close to my ears for comfort. But I no longer felt any pain, even as the suit drank all that energy down and filled my bones and muscles with tingling.

"Don't drop me!" Fedor gasped, hands cradled to his chest.

I lowered myself to cut around his legs. "Just be thankful I'm helping you at all." The scratching in my throat muddled my voice, giving it a thick and ill sound.

With his left leg cut loose he hung at a strange angle, suspended only by his right leg and waist. Half folding in over himself, he could still look up at me in mistrust. "How can your suit do this? What are you?"

I freed his right leg, jerked up again, extended my blades and curved them, then cut away at every binding that could possibly exist around his middle. Fedor fell with a strangled scream straight into Kichlan's waiting arms.

"I am not a weapon," I whispered, and I lowered myself far more gently. The blades withdrew, but the suit fought me over its antenna. Only when I stepped away from the misfiring lock did it allow me to draw them back in.

Kichlan carried Fedor back to his Unbound. Yan and Egor helped him stand.

"Our thanks," Yicor said, apparently for the entire group.

"Time to leave." Volski gripped my elbow then cursed as a spark shot from my sleeve. I felt numb with the energy inside me, trembling from over-excited muscles and the ever-present tension in my bones growing stronger.

Wincing, he rubbed his hand. "They will be close by now."

I nodded. "We need to get out of here."

The Unbound supported Fedor and helped him run; away from the laboratory, down a narrow alleyway beside an empty apartment building. It had once been fenced off from the main street, now only a creaking, corrugated iron gate remained. Kichlan helped me drag it across the opening to the alley. The ground was littered with grates. Steam rose silent but pungent from below. I had trouble believing we were walking over a rill or effluent here. Even in the height of summer the water running in and out of the Tear did not boil and stink like this.

Was that debris, contained beneath our feet?

I remembered the crater in which I had found Devich, half-dead. All that remained of his technician's laboratory. How much debris had it taken to create a force that could hurl buildings into the air like toys? Did the same amount boil and steam beneath us?

Running footsteps echoed around us, Volski risked

another shock to grab my shoulder and halt me. "Enforcers," he hissed, "or Mob, whatever they are. Surrounding the building. At the other end of this alley too!"

"Other's rank breath!" Kichlan cursed. "What can we do?"

Fedor stared wistfully back at the laboratory he had tried to break into. I crouched, ran light fingers across the damp ground, and considered the plan I had – apparently – thought through so well but not been able to put into action.

"What are you doing? Yicor asked, and crouched with me.

"We need to get off the streets," I said. "And quickly. Before the enforcers come down here, before we are found."

A round of quiet agreement.

"So we do what we had always intended. We get inside the laboratory."

10.

There was a moment of stunned silence before Kichlan said, "What?"

I turned to Volski and Zecholas. "We're above the storage vats already. Tell me if you can get us down there." I pointed to the steaming ground.

"Tanyana?" Fedor this time. "I don't understand."

"When you tried to break in to that laboratory you triggered an emergency response that has summoned who knows how many enforcers, and alerted the ones inside the building to our presence. It's only a matter of time before they find us here. Not only that, but in doing so you broke the lock. At the moment none of the enforcers inside can get out, but no more can get in either. I say we go inside, where they won't be looking for us, and where there are less of them, and hopefully do what we came here to do in the first place."

"How will we get in, though?" Yan asked.

I couldn't stop myself grinning, despite everything. "That is why I brought my pion-binders." *Mine*.

They were already working, even while we spoke. Zecholas crouched, hands to the ground, eyes distant and mouth moving as he whispered to the particles deep in the earth below us. Volski stood above him, silent. After a moment Zecholas turned towards me and said, "Something is interfering. There are pions here, there has to be, but I just can't get to them."

"Like something that isn't made of pions is getting in your way?" I asked. The cobblestones were pion-made, and the mortar below them. The earth itself should be rich with particles, enough for any decent binder to manipulate. But just like my suit blocked access to the pions inside my body, the debris vats below us meant that no binder, no matter how strong, could influence them.

Zecholas baulked. "Yes. How did you know?"

Not a question I was about to answer. "Debris."

Curious expressions from both of my binders. "We can't get in that way," Volski said.

I had expected this.

"Then how?" Fedor asked.

I flashed a grin at him. "Watch. Watch and learn." I clicked my fingers. Volski and Zecholas straightened instantly, and turned toward me. "Give me a simple formation. There are a lot of pion-binders rushing around here and we don't want them to notice us, keep that in mind. Do nothing that would look out of the ordinary; follow the pattern of the building. Understand?"

Zoklski grinned. "Yes, my lady."

"We are only two," Volski pointed out. "We can't make a circle."

"When did I say you needed to?" I lifted an eyebrow. "I have enough work for both of you. Think you can handle that?"

"Of course."

"So find me a path to the basement."

"I don't see a basement," Zecholas said.

"There is one. Look *around* the grates here: you won't be able to see *through* them. Talk to the building, follow its patterns inside, and then down. You'll find it. It will be hidden, smothered. It will look like something impossible."

After a moment Volski said, "I see it." He wove invisible patterns in the air until Zecholas sucked in a sharp breath.

"Yes, of course. It stands out." Zecholas glanced at me. "Below us, there is a gap. Empty where there should be light, a square-shaped void."

I held his gaze, kept my expression blank. Did he see the same thing in me? If they did, my pion-binders said nothing. Volski and Zecholas were loyal.

"One of you get us down there, unseen. The other keep an eye on the enforcers and the security system. Work together. You've already had evidence of the kind of defences wound into this building. Don't set them off again. Don't give those men inside and outside a chance to find us. And keep me informed. I need to know when we are close to the enforcers, I need to know about every lock or hidden trigger. Tell me if anything strange happens. At all." Because without them, I was blind.

My binders shared a glance and chose the way I knew they would. Zecholas – with his sharp mind and even sharper skill – stepped out into the alleyway and placed a hand on the flat and ugly concrete of the laboratory wall. Volski – always aware of the bigger picture – unfocused his gaze and appeared to stare at nothing.

"This way," Volski whispered, after a moment. "Do

you see the path?"

Zecholas nodded, and the concrete boiled where he touched it. It pulled back, exposing grey brickwork, then the bricks themselves changed. Zecholas was not moving them, not rearranging them to create a hole in the wall large enough for us to pass through, for such manipulation would have been felt throughout the building. Instead, he was altering the very nature of the bricks; removing the air, unbinding then reforming minerals, easing the ties of heat and drying water, so they shrunk into something harder, darker and misshapen. It was an efficient and silent way to create a person-sized hole. But only a binder as skilled as Zecholas could have done it without the help of a circle.

"Why are you doing this?" Kichlan hissed, close to my ear, just as fresh marching and shouting echoed down the alleyway. New, steady lights bobbed into view, and gradually began making their way toward us. That had to be the work of a Torchbearer. The rest of the enforcers could not be far behind.

"To get Lad off the streets. And do it now."

Zecholas's hole became a narrow tunnel that stretched into the building. We would, I assumed, be travelling inside walls where they were thick enough, through empty rooms, and down supporting beams.

"This won't be comfortable," Zecholas said.

"It doesn't matter." Someone kicked the rotting metallic gate at the end of the alley. "Just hurry!"

With a nod from Volski, Zecholas entered the tunnel. And we followed.

Zecholas was right, it wasn't comfortable at all. Such deep and intensive pion manipulation created not only

enough heat of its own to start us sweating, but lined the
tunnel with warm debris. Kichlan, Lad and I scooped it
up as we pushed our way through. The layer was thin,
and we didn't have anything to carry it in, but any we
left would only make it harder for Zecholas to fill in the
tunnel behind us.

It took Fedor a moment before he sullenly started collecting too.

"I thought you said it was safer in here than on the
street," Kichlan whispered, very close behind me in this
small space. "So what are you worried about?"

I couldn't turn to face him. In fact there was barely
enough room to twist my head and look over my shoulder. "Apart from running out of air?"

"I wish you hadn't said that," Yicor muttered, from behind Lad, who was following Kichlan and struggling not
to scratch himself on the walls.

"There is plenty of air," Zecholas said from ahead. "It's
just all hot."

"You concentrate on what you're doing," I snapped.

"Yes, my lady." I couldn't see his smile, but I could
hear it.

"That's not what I mean," Kichlan whispered, even
lower. "What have you got him looking out for?"

"He has a name."

"Tan." How could he scold me that much with a single,
shortened word?

"There are more defences than one lock on a door, you
know that. Volski is making sure we don't run into any
of them."

Kichlan did not respond, but I could feel that he was
not satisfied. Even as Volski directed Zecholas – noting

locks with wide-ranging trigger-threads, a small collection of technicians huddling away from the alarms, and enforcers searching uselessly along the corridors for a way out – I waited for more. I waited for the puppet men.

And what would they look like to Volski's pion sight?

"There is a stairwell ahead," Zecholas said. "As far as I can see it is empty."

"Yes, and unguarded. No locks, no triggers. Nothing." Volski paused. "But it will not take us all the way down." A longer pause. "There is no way to get to the basement. No stairs, ramps, tunnels. Nothing."

"That makes no sense," someone hissed behind us.

"Either way, the stairwell will be more comfortable than this," Zecholas said.

And sure enough his tunnel opened out to a dark, twisting stairway. It was narrow and musty, but vast and fresh compared to the inside of the building's very stones.

Lad breathed deeply and let out a loud and echoing sigh. Yicor shushed him, while Fedor and his troop emerged, and Zecholas reconstructed the bricks to seal off the tunnel.

"I don't see anyone close by," Volski said. "But try to remain quiet anyway."

"Sorry," Lad squeaked.

I took Kichlan's hand, stretched up and breathed into his ear, "Does this seem strange to you? That there are no doors accessing the basement?"

"Strange? Yes," he breathed back. "But not as strange as an empty, unguarded stairwell in the middle of a highly defended building."

He had a point.

"Enough whispering," Fedor spat as he pushed past us. "Let's move."

No matter how hard they try, nine full-grown adults cannot descend a smooth, tight stairwell, and be silent about it. I felt every clang shudder through me, every cough and each footfall. And with each sound my suit tightened inside me, feeding on my tension and nerves. The energy it had stolen from the misfiring lock shivered through me in little cramps and spasms. But worse were the knots of muscle and silver in my abdomen. With each step they seemed to grow, with each breath the suit glowed brighter.

"Here?" Zecholas stopped suddenly and I bumped into him, zapping his back with the suit's stored energy. He winced, and cast a hurt expression at me. I shrugged an apology. There wasn't much I could do about it.

"Yes," Volski added.

"Here what?" Fedor hissed.

"Here is the best place," Volski explained.

Zecholas bent and touched the ground. The concrete was so cold I could feel it radiating up into my legs, through boots, uniform and heavy woollen pants. "There is a beam here, thick enough." He glanced back at me, squinted against the light from my suit, the light I could not control. "This will be even harder, though."

"Hurry," I whispered.

I drew a deep breath and released Kichlan's hand to tighten mine into fists. Gradually, my light dimmed. It was difficult and exhausting.

Zecholas tunnelled again. "Quick. This is unstable, I don't want to hold it for too long."

And I learned just how pleasant the original tunnel had been. Zecholas had cut a narrow tube down the concrete, reinforced by steel, that made up one of the building's supporting beams. We had to squeeze ourselves down, no real handholds, no convenient steps, but I knew it was all he could do to maintain the integrity of the entire building while providing enough space for us to fit through.

I trod on Lad's head more times than I wanted to admit. He and Kichlan shimmied down before me, with far greater agility than was fair. I didn't want to loosen my suit, though it would have been so much easier to rely on the strong and sharp silver. But if I let it out, even a few inches, would I have what it took to draw it back in? So I endured the scratching of rock, the way sharp pieces of steel frame tore holes in my clothing, and Fedor kicking my shoulders at every opportunity.

When I finally made it through and staggered on the blessedly stable, horizontal, tiled floor, Kichlan caught me. Fedor dropped from the ceiling with a grace that no man who had almost been fried by an over-active pion lock should possess.

Even Yicor, even an old man like him, hardly needed Fedor's helping hand. And here I was, aching with each breath, sharp pains slicing through my abdomen.

"Tan? Are you all right?"

I couldn't straighten. Not yet. "I don't know how much more of this I can take," I whispered, and watched fine lines of silver trace their way across fresh scratches in the back my hands.

At that, Kichlan just held me tightly.

"What is this?" Fedor shouted, apparently forsaking

every pretence of stealth. His voice echoed as though we stood at the mouth to a great cavern. "Where have you taken us?"

I glanced up. Zecholas was closing off the last imperfection in the ceiling, and I allowed myself a moment to appreciate just how skilled a binder he was. Volski was still blank-faced, still our ever vigilant pion-sighted lookout. Yicor, however, seemed to have found a panel and turned on the lights.

They shone, small, not particularly bright, and spaced meanly down the long walls of an enormous room. They didn't provide very much light, but it was enough to see that the basement was completely empty.

"There really aren't any doors to this place," Zecholas murmured. "How is that possible?"

"I can't see anything," Volski added. "Apart the ones inside us, all the pions are gone."

Dread added its talons to the pains within me.

I stared in shock at the empty room. It had, I noticed with a numb kind of humming at the back of my head, not always been empty. There were lines on the floor and walls, and holes, where machinery had been bolted. I could distinguish the outlines of what looked like great vats, tubes, and shelves. Scattered with an apparently haphazard lack of consideration, were a few empty debris-collecting jars.

"Where is the debris?" Kichlan said.

"All that for nothing?" Fedor turned on me.

I drew a deep breath, held it, let the air ease away the sharper edges of my pain. Nothing about this laboratory was right, even I knew that. So I held Fedor's furious eyes. "Why here?" I whispered.

He scowled at me. "What?"

Another breath. "Why this place. Of all the laboratories in Movoc-under-Keeper, why did you choose this one?"

He ran a hand over his face. "I don't know why it matters."

"Tell me–"

"If you must know." He interrupted me and dropped his hand abruptly. "Several sixweeks and one of careful observation. Bells spent hiding in the shadows, waiting for the veche to gather jars full of collected debris. Like you and Kichlan, I stalked several different collection teams and followed most of their jars here." He released a deep and resonant sigh. "Even before I allowed myself to be suited I watched, and waited. All that time."

"And after that, you decided on this laboratory?"

He nodded. "Most of the debris was brought here. In fact, over the past three sixnights and one, all of the jars came here. You saw it with your own eyes, you and Kichlan. I thought my reasons for choosing this place were obvious."

So, had he made that decision on his own, based on the intelligence he had gathered? Or had Fedor – had all of us – been led to this laboratory? I wouldn't put that past the puppet men, they rarely left anything to chance.

And where had all those jars of debris gone?

"Tan?" Lad spoke so softly I almost missed it in the ringing echoes of anger and frustration. "I think he is here."

Silence settled over us.

"The Keeper?" Fedor hissed.

Lad's voice hitched. "Tan, please. I think he is crying."

Crying?

I gave myself another moment to become reacquainted

with standing on my own two feet, before I stepped into the vast space.

We were standing on a platform, raised above the rest of the room and fenced in with steel tubes similar to those in the stairwell. There were no steps down to the empty floor. Gritting my teeth I grasped the handrail and used it to swing myself down. Thankfully, the platform was not very high.

I walked down the middle of the empty room. The place seemed to reverberate. As I walked, I imagined the size of whatever had left such deep tracks in the grey painted floor, and had required bolts so thick they threaded into holes almost the width of my wrist. Where had they all gone? And how had they been taken from a room beneath the ground that had no doors?

I released more of my hold on the suit with each step, careful not to loosen the stubborn knot of control I maintained in my abdomen. As the metal crept over my eyes I realised why the room felt so alive and dangerous. And why the Keeper would sit here and cry.

The entire room was made of doors. Solid and so real I could smell newly stained wood and the oil on their iron knobs. I glanced over my shoulder but could not make out anyone else. Not even Lad. There were only doors. No space between them: doors on the walls, the ceiling, the floor. This entire room was nothing but an opening to another, empty world.

The Keeper sat in the centre, legs pulled against his chest, face pressed to his knees like a child. He wept, shoulders shuddering, black tears streaming down his white cheeks.

I ran to him. The doors rattled beneath me.

I crouched at the Keeper's side and held out my arms to him. He turned – so much like Lad in this moment, so large yet lost and vulnerable – and wept into my chest while I held him. Against my firm suit he felt soft and barely real.

"Is this where you have been?" I asked him, when his shuddering had subsided. "Here, all alone?"

The Keeper drew a deep breath and tipped his head back to face me. Ragged streaks of the debris within him traced terrible patterns beneath his skin. His hopelessness, his grief, written in black and white.

"Do you see what they did?" he groaned out the words.

I glanced around us. "I think we should get you out of here."

The Keeper shook his head. Debris bulged in his neck. "No! I must stay here. I must close these doors when they open."

"They are opening all over the city." I tried to help him up, but his weight hung dead and heavy in my hands. "Not just here. You need to close those other doors too."

He hiccupped a helpless sob. "Too many. I can't keep up." He wiped black onto his pale forearm. "They tell me I will fail. Over and over they whisper from the darkness. How can they, Tanyana? Unless they are just like me? But that can't be, can it? There is only one Keeper." He tipped an imploring face to mine and I had no idea how to answer. "What good am I, if I can't stop them? This is what I was built for. What will happen to me, Tanyana, if I fail?"

Built? I blinked. "Who built you?" I whispered, hoping none of the others could hear me. Who had given him this impossible task?

It had never occurred to me that the Keeper was following instructions. I had always believed he simply was; born of debris, part of debris, working to defend us from the beginning of all time. Or something like that.

He ignored the question, or did not hear it. "There is no point trying. I am already failing."

I fought the need to shake him; he felt so fragile I was afraid he would break. "You are not alone," I told him. "I am here to help you. And can you see them?" I gestured with my head to Kichlan, Lad and the others. "They are here to help you too. Collectors, Unbound, pion-binders and a Half. All of us. We came here to help you. We wanted to find the debris that had been collected here, and set it free."

"You can't," he whispered. But at least he had stopped crying.

"I know. It is gone."

He shook his head. "No, Tanyana." And he stood, holding my arms and drawing me up with him. "It is still here. Can't you see what they have done?"

"Still here?" I glanced around us. There was nothing, surely, but the doors.

Then I thought of Zecholas, unable to see past the walls of this place, unable to see through the warm, steam-rising vents. Suddenly I realised how odd that was, how wrong. Steam, even when the debris was gone. "Oh."

Together, the Keeper and I approached the wall. When I touched a door all I felt was wood and a faint but terrifying vibration.

"Let me go for a moment," I asked the Keeper. "The doors are too strong here."

He nodded, firmer now, as though my presence had somehow strengthened him.

I drew the suit in from my face and hands. It tugged against me, fought with a numbing throb deep inside my bones. I pushed it aside. I had far more important things to worry about now.

"Tan? You okay?" Lad asked behind me.

I glanced over my shoulder. He, Kichlan and Fedor had followed me down, while Yicor, Volski, Zecholas and the rest of the Unbound waited on the platform.

"You said something about doors?" Fedor asked. When I didn't immediately respond he turned to Lad. "What's happening? What is the Keeper saying?"

"Leave my brother alone," Kichlan growled.

I ignored them both. "I am okay, Lad." He didn't appear particularly reassured. I turned back to the wall.

My fingers brushed against concrete where a moment ago they had touched wood. It was not, however, the deep cold I was so used to in Movoc buildings, nor the chill that had seeped up the stairwell. It was hot, slightly damp. And if I turned my head just enough, I caught steam rising softly from the walls in the weak pion-generated light.

"Other." I let the suit slip back over my hand and curled sharp claws onto the end of my fingers. It didn't take much, a little scratching, a little digging, and a layer of thin paint and plaster fell away to reveal metallic walls. And not just any metal. Silver and smooth and glowing, faintly, with a touch of blue. "Damn them."

Why would they do this? Create a room out of debris, out of suit metal? What were they trying to achieve?

"What is that?" Kichlan peered into the gash I had made.

"Debris," I answered, shortly. "The debris that was stored in here."

"Impossible!" Fedor gasped.

Kichlan's searching expression deepened into a scowl. "It looks like a collecting suit. It looks just like the same material!"

"That's because it is," I answered, sharply, and covered my face.

Back in a world of doors and darkness the Keeper still stood beside me. His tears had dried, their black streaks fading, their spilled grains and planes reabsorbing through his thin skin. "Do you see?" he asked.

"I do." Useless. That was how I felt, so pointless and helpless and small. "Why have they done this?" I whispered.

He released a great, sorrowful breath. "To keep it from me." He waved a hand at the doors. "Like that, it is beyond my touch. Twisted and tortured into something that was once a part of myself, but is no more. It is debris without my will, the will that tempered and controlled it. It means the end of everything."

Fear for everything.

"Like the monster," I murmured. "Like the snakes." Like the suit?

He nodded.

"But why would the puppet men do this?" I hissed at him. "Surely they are not fools, and I know they are not blind. They know you exist, they can see you too! And they have been warned."

"I– I cannot–" His control, his strength, fell from him.

"You cannot what?"

"Believe it." He clutched his head and squeezed his skin until darkness swelled between his fingers. I recoiled from the sight of it. His veins, his debris, pulsing, his head juddering, his body hunching over itself like a child hiding his face. "Impossible."

"Hush, please. Hush." I breathed out the words, leaving my insides tingling and taut. "We came here to help you. You are not alone."

His fingers eased open and he looked up, eyes empty and desperate. "But I should be. I was created to do this. Just me. Only me. They should not exist."

I didn't know what to do, what I could possibly say to calm him. Maybe I really did need Lad. Maybe he should have been here, with the Keeper, instead of me.

So, I said, "I closed a door," because I did not know what else to say.

And his shivering stopped, instantly. His eyes widened and he straightened, he looked me in the eye. "You closed one?"

"It was only open a crack."

He watched me for a moment of disconcerting silence. "Still, you closed it."

"There are others." The words poured from me. Anything to maintain his focus, to sustain this lucidity. "The city is collapsing. Bit by bit. Door by door. At least, that is what I believe."

The Keeper squared his shoulders. "I must get back to the city, then. I cannot fail them. This is why I am here. Isn't it?"

"Yes. Yes, of course."

"And I do a good job, don't I? You think I do, Tanyana? I try hard. All the time. So hard."

"I do." My throat was dry and my stomach aching. "But, you should probably hurry."

He hesitated. "I won't run away again. Promise."

"Good. Stay where we can find you." I was going to be sick. And that would be very messy on the inside of my suit.

"Thank you," he whispered, and began to fade. "For finding me."

I withdrew my suit as he disappeared, drawing myself out of that door-riddled world and returning to an argument sharply echoing through the empty room. I nearly leaned against the wall for support. Then I remembered what it was made of, and found Lad's conveniently positioned chest directly behind me instead.

"It can't be!"

"It's impossible!"

"I would have known!"

"Unnatural!"

Kichlan and Fedor shouted at each other, but they did not appear to be disagreeing.

"What happened to keeping quiet?" I asked Lad, who had stuck his fingers in his ears.

"Oh, Tan." He gripped my shoulders, pressed his body against my back like I could become a shield between him and his raging, red-in-the-face older brother. I didn't mind. It was keeping me upright. "Please tell them to stop."

"I don't think they will hear me." I cleared my throat, and tried a sharp, "Enough!"

It seemed to do the job. Silenced, Fedor and Kichlan both turned on me. I felt Lad shrink away from those intense eyes, that sweat and anger, and I didn't much blame him.

"Is that why you asked me how the suits were made?"

There was so much more than anger in Kichlan's face. Anger I could deal with. But hurt, I didn't want to cause that. "You already knew they were debris, but you still wouldn't tell me. You need your secrets, don't you? Why don't you trust me, Tan? Even after everything we have been through together?"

I deserved his anger, I knew it. I still couldn't tell Kichlan the truth, but I didn't want to keep pushing him away either. It was selfish of me. I needed his touch, but I had guided his hands.

I nodded. "Yes, I did know."

"How did you find out? How long have you known?"

I couldn't answer that.

"What did the Keeper say?" Fedor snapped, forcing me to focus on him instead. "Tell me what he wants us to do!"

At least it gave me something to concentrate on, other than the look on Kichlan's face.

"We need to get out of here," I said, and placed a finger on the warm wall. "We cannot release this debris."

"Because it has been changed into suit metal?" Kichlan asked. I nodded. He looked down to the bands on his wrists.

I pried Lad's fingers free and led him across the open floor. Kichlan and Fedor hurried behind. Lad helped me clamber back onto the platform.

Zecholas touched the low ceiling. "We will have to climb the supporting beam again, I'm afraid. I can't alter anything else in this room."

Of course he couldn't. Was it luck that one small square had been left in this room, a closed door only an architect could open? I had stopped believing in luck.

"Are we safe?" I asked Volski, aware of the futility of the question but unable to remain silent.

"I am blind here. There are lights within our bodies, and our breath has added some life to the air. That's all." He glanced at the smooth ceiling. "But we should be able to leave the way we came in."

"Well, let's hope so."

Zecholas began drilling us a horrifically difficult passage out. As the first of Fedor's Unbound helped each other up into the tight space, Volski gripped my wrist.

"Wait," he whispered. "I see something."

Together we turned to stare into the empty room.

"In the air. The pions we breathed out, they are... changing."

Fingers of dread clutched my spine. Behind me, Kichlan was pushing Lad up into the hole. I hoped he could not hear us.

"They burn," Volski murmured, trance-like. "They flare like tiny crimson suns, and die. They just disappear."

Crimson suns? Like the pions that had thrown me from Grandeur, those psychotic bursts of fury too unreal, too impossible, for the rest of my team to see?

One by one the weak pion lights that lined the room flickered off. As darkness spread I hurried Volski into the tunnel, accepted Kichlan's help up and tried very, very hard not to scream.

11.

When I collected Lad the next morning, he was waiting at his corner alone.

"Bro said I was big enough to wait by myself." His tone made it an apology. "Tan," he took my hand and together, we headed for Ironlattice. "Is bro angry with me?"

"Oh no, Lad." This wasn't fair on him. "Not you."

He sighed. "Well, he is angry at someone. Maybe it is Geny – they didn't talk at all after we got back – and bro didn't sleep, he kept turning and turning and mumbling." Lad yawned, widely, half-hiding his gaping mouth behind his hand. "It kept me awake."

"Ah, sorry, Lad."

"Not your fault, Tan."

I smiled at that. Maybe he was right; maybe Kichlan's fitful sleep wasn't my fault. Maybe it had nothing to do with the secrets, and the Keeper, and my circle and his fear for Lad – ever Lad – crowding between us, building as sure as a wall. At least, that was how I had imagined them, as I lay in my bed above Valya's rooms, also unable to sleep, the memory of his hands stinging, and Devich's child heavy within me.

"Don't ever blame yourself, Lad." My voice echoed sharply from the stairwell to the toplevel. "Your brother does not blame you."

"I think you are right. But I don't always understand" Lad opened the door to a room full of puppet men.

Lad tried to drag me back into the stairwell, but not before I had seen Natasha's pale and frightened face so small amidst a sea of fake, stretched skin. And I knew we could not leave her to their tortures but Lad was dragging me, keening like an animal or a broken soul. Like a Half.

He did not get far. More puppet men materialised out of the shadows in the stairway itself, three of them, all mould-like eyes and emotionless expressions that did not sit well on the bones of their faces. So we were squeezed between them – Lad still gripping my hand and panicking, searching the bland unbroken walls for a way out – and shepherded back into the toplevel.

Yet, when the puppet men stepped back to allow us to enter the room and stand by Natasha's side, I realised there were only four. Not the countless, unsettling faces.

I clutched Lad's hand tighter. I would not let go, no matter what they threatened, no matter what veche powers or debris monsters they summoned. I would never give him up.

"Your team is late this morning," the puppet men spoke to Natasha and she flinched. I didn't blame her. When one spoke, it seemed like all moved their mouths. When one set of eyes pinned me, it felt like the pressure of uncountable stares.

I reached for Natasha's hand with my fingers, but she shifted her weight so I could not touch her. "There are no more to come–" She tried, but sandpaper laughter floated through the room as the puppet men grinned for an instant – one horrid, synchronised motion.

"Two more," one hissed.

"The twin." It was impossible to tell their voices apart.

"And the enforcer that once was."

Lad whimpered beside me and those eyes snapped in his direction; thoughtful, considering, scheming beneath their false veneer. I had to get him out of here, away from them. I should never have allowed this to happen!

My suit spun as though in answer. I gritted my teeth and held it down. "What do you want?" The words scratched with kicking wires in my throat. When the puppet men turned on me they grinned again and this time I knew the expression was genuine. Did I amuse them, with my battles against the rising silver in my blood? "Are you going to punish us because we have not made quota?" I barely pushed the words free. "This is happening all across the city, isn't it? We aren't the only team struggling to fill their jars. There simply is not enough debris for us to collect!"

"Quota?" An eerily co-ordinated cocking of heads. "No, Miss Vladha. We do not care about your quota."

"Then why–" I stopped. Why? Because Lad was a Half and I was their weapon and poor Natasha was caught in between. That was why.

They had split us up once before, weakened us. Well, not again. I was not going to let this happen.

"I don't care why." The suit slid from my right wrist to encase Lad's hand in an unbreakable bond. "We are not your puppets." It spread out from my left to take Natasha's hand whether she wanted it or not. "And I will not let you divide us again."

With Lad locked on one side of me and Natasha on the other, I lunged forward. Suit-boots gave me strength to crash past the puppet men, to slam open the door and careen down the stairs. The suit kept me from falling – metallic spikes from the soles of my shoes maintaining my footing – and it held Natasha and Lad upright as they struggled to keep up, half-dragged, half-running, screaming and yelling, filling the stairwell and my head with sound.

But when we fell out onto the street I was forced to an abrupt halt.

Mob ringed the building. Not enforcers. The puppet men had brought Mob against us. A dark stain on the cold city morning, they hulked above us, unnaturally tall, wide faces hidden behind helmets. The hilts of swords, knives and other pion-powered weapons I could never understand peeked from their black armour of leather and painted steel.

The suit flared into knots of heat and pain, at each of the bands on my body. It clamoured for release. There, surrounding us, was a challenge like none we had ever faced. I didn't even need to see the pions that bolstered the Mob, that strengthened them, it was obvious in their size, in the way they stood, in the weapons only hinted at in glints of reflected sunlight. And the suit knew it too, and wanted to test itself against them. Weapon to weapon. I hissed, crouched, as the suit released Lad and Natasha. It shone so brightly I was forced to squint, and the symbols whirred, meshing into solid blocks.

Lad crouched beside me. "Tan?" The fear in his eyes set my heart lurching. "Tan, who are they? Tan, Kich should be here! Where is he, why can't he be here?"

I forced myself to stand. What would happen if I gave into the suit? Could it kill the Mob surrounding us? These were not petty thugs come to evict me. If I took on the Mob I would take on the veche. Varsnia itself.

Yes, and we would win, the suit seemed to say in its spinning and the thrill rising up like flames from somewhere deep inside me. It could fight against the world, this weapon inside me. It longed to.

"That's the one." One of the Mob stepped forward. Dark gloved hands the size of bear paws and ridged with sharp claws reached for us. But not for me, not even for Lad.

The Mob took Natasha's wrist, twisted her arm around, and bound her with a thin chain. It looked weak, its loops like thread instead of steel, but then I couldn't see the pions working inside it. She didn't struggle. Something resigned draped over her face. The Mob spun her around and her eyes met mine. Fear there, but acceptance. I was not sure which was worse.

I didn't know what to do. In my confusion, the suit eased a little, enough to allow me to move without the sharp lancing of deep splinters. "What are you doing with–?"

"Miss, step away!" The Mob – gripping Natasha's bindings so that she was forced to stand awkwardly, shoulders strained – lifted a bear-claw hand. Lad shuddered a faulting step back. The suit held my ground.

"What are you doing with her?" And why her, I wanted to scream. Why not me, aren't I the one the veche want? Or Lad. I actually thought that. Why aren't you trying to take Lad away?

"Miss, I encourage you to back down." I caught glimpses of the Mob's eyes through the slits of his helmet.

His iris had been replaced by a kind of mirror, something flat and slightly golden that seemed to glow. And his pupil was moving, roaming wild across the whites of his eye. "Unless you also wish to be charged with conspiracy, collusion and treachery."

Treachery?

"These are troubling times."

I spun as two of the puppet men emerged from the stairs. They walked with a light step, footfalls soft on the cement, arms loose at their sides. Too relaxed, too languid.

"When our own citizens betray Varsnia. When we cannot trust them to do their duty."

"What do you mean?" I had no idea what he was saying with those unsteady, stretched lips.

Natasha was held so tightly she was almost lifted from her feet, but she croaked out a rough laugh. "I asked you, didn't I, I begged you, not to draw attention to us. Not to put us at risk. But you couldn't stop yourself. Of all the debris collectors in this foul city, this whole country, I had to get saddled with you!" She spat into the street and earned herself a ringing clip across the side of her face.

"I don't–"

"Miss Illoksy is referring to her work as a Hon Ji spy," said a puppet man behind me. "Work you do not seem to be aware of."

Natasha lifted her head slowly. Her gaze was unsteady as she stared at the puppet men, and blood dripped from a cut the Mob had opened up at her cheek. "It seems I did not hide it well enough."

"Our nations are at war, miss, even if your Emperor has not deemed to inform you. As such, the national veche has decided monitoring you is no longer safe enough. It is time to neutralise you."

The puppet men stepped past Lad and me, their very presence a chill in the air. My suit tensed and Lad clutched at my jacket sleeve. "You were watching her, weren't you?" I whispered. "It's not just bad luck, it never is." I fixed my gaze on Natasha's unsteady one. Slowly, understanding dawned there. "You placed me in this team, with her, so you could watch us together."

The only response the puppet men gave was the twitch of an almost-smile at the corners of their mouths.

"But that was a mistake!" My mind spun. "Natasha knows what I am and she knows what you have been doing. She would have passed on every detail about your so-called secret weapon! The Hon Ji know all about me, you foolish bastards."

"That's enough." The Mob holding onto Natasha made a signal with his free hand and the circle of armoured and reinforced men around us closed in. "You were advised not to involve yourself."

The puppet men did not seem particularly concerned. One drew a small wooden box from a pocket in his jacket and opened the lid to reveal a horror of a syringe; long and sharp and filled with something that moved. Natasha paled further and attempted to recoil, but the Mob held her firmly in place.

Didn't the veche care about the spreading of their secrets? Or, if they had known about Natasha, perhaps they had long ago intercepted her messages.

Who do you trust?

Devich, curse him, did he know the truth about Natasha too?

"Your team will be one collector short, Miss Vladha." The puppet man raised his needle. "Perhaps another re-distribution of resources is required."

"Please, no," Lad whispered in my ear.

The Mob closed in. Fire lanced through my arms and legs as the suit tore itself from my control, as it coated hands, arms, feet, neck–

"That's about enough, I think." I could only see half of Natasha's face behind the approaching wall of dark ar-mour and golden eyes, but she was smiling.

Then energy crackled through the air. Something like lightening, something like the misfiring pion-lock on the technician's laboratory. The Mob who held Natasha cried out, and was flung back to crash into the approaching soldiers. As they fell and faltered it was enough, just enough, for Natasha – hands still tied be-hind her back – to break free. Head down, shoulders solid and hunched, she ran past us, and yelled, "Fol-low me!"

I grabbed Lad's hand. Mine was still coated in metal and bit deep into his skin, but he didn't even seem to feel it, and together, we ran. But not before I caught a glimpse of the puppet man, needle still in hand, watch-ing us with the closest thing to a shocked expression I had ever seen on their unreal faces.

Natasha sprinted away at an amazing pace, feet nimble on the stones, never slipping, leaping potholes and skid-ding around corners. Lad and I struggled to keep up, as the Mob and the puppet men fell away in a distance of alleys and buildings and streets. Finally, she halted under the eves of a dilapidated shop. Its windows had dissolved to fine sand, its double door fallen inward and low roof collapsed under the weight of Movoc's fleeing pions. She leaned against a cracked wall, shoes crunching glass beneath her feet, and struggled to catch her breath. I released Lad and he sagged into a similar position. I tried to ignore a stitch, sharp and suit-splintered, gathering in my stomach and rising to sting in my chest.

Gasping for breath, Natasha watched me over her shoulder. Her wrists were raw against the tight chain, red with the rubbing of sweat and steel. "Well," she spat, and I noticed the faint pinkness of blood on her teeth "Now you know what I am."

"Yes." Scratching in my voice, rasping in my lungs. I added them to my list of things to ignore, and approached her. "A traitor, a spy."

"That's right." She tipped her head back as far as her awkwardly strained shoulders would allow. "Working inside Varsnia, to bring down the oligarchy. The old families, the national veche." She looked meaningfully at my wrists. "The same people who did that to you."

I sharpened a suit finger, stepped up quickly behind her and severed the chain that bound her.

She winced, kneaded knuckles into her shoulders before rubbing her wrists, and watched me with uncertainty. "What are you doing?"

"What loyalty do you think I owe the veche?"

"Some would say you gave the ultimate sacrifice for Varsnia."

"Those people have obviously never fallen eight hundred feet and woken up like this." I raised my suited hand.

A moment of consideration, and Natasha nodded. "This raises interesting possibilities."

I met Natasha's piercing green eyes and wasn't sure I

liked what I saw there. She seemed far too pleased with herself. "Does it?"

"We have the same enemies, you and I."

Lad pushed himself upright. "Don't like them either," he declared. "Tash is my friend. I don't care what they said." I wasn't entirely convinced he had understood everything that just happened. "I am still her friend too."

Natasha's face eased into a smile and she released her wrists. The chain had rubbed blisters into her skin and torn patches away, leaving them raw. "Thank you, Lad." She glanced back to me. "Anyway, I'm afraid you've gone and put yourselves in the worst possible position. You can't go back to the rest of the collection team, you must realise this." She looked between us and her eyes were saddened, sorry. "You can't even go home."

"Not to bro?" Lad's voice hitched. Somehow I didn't think Kichlan would be particularly understanding about the situation. This was how I looked after his brother, was it?

Natasha shook her head. "What we need to do now is get moving. I have contacts. Higher up than you can imagine. And smuggling routes, ways in and out of Varsnia. But if we really are at war," for a moment her confident calm faltered, "these will be even more dangerous than usual." She gazed down the murky alleyway. "And there will be Mob all over the city by now. The national veche does not take kindly to traitors and spies."

No, the veche did not. But then it wasn't too kind to simple architects either.

"So where should we–"

The sound of running feet silenced me. As one, we tensed. I shoved Lad against the wall, stood in front of him, suit spinning and starting to draw out from the bands. Natasha crouched beside me, a thick, ugly-looking knife in one hand – how wrong that looked – and a strange, flat disk in the other. She caught me looking and flashed a grin, somewhere between fear and a fierce aggression that reminded me of the suit's own urges. The disk was small, it fit easily into her palm, and seemed to be made of two separate circles of metal with clay wedged between them.

"The shock," she said, like I was supposed to understand. "Used one of them on that cursed Mob. Two left." She rolled the disk between nimble fingers.

Never had I seen something as strange as Natasha armed and ready to attack. I supposed it explained her sudden transformation, her determination to make quota and keep the veche from our backs.

But still. *Natasha*.

"They're here." She half-rose from her crouch, disk raised in a clenched fist, when Aleksey and Mizra emerged from the alley-gloom.

Natasha caught herself at the last moment and gaped in surprise as Aleksey grabbed her upraised wrist and forced her into a run. "Mob!" he hissed. "Run!"

Mizra, unable to do the same to Lad and me, waved frantically and gibbered nonsense interspersed with, "Mob, Mob, Other cursed Mob!" until we started moving.

Then we were running again, down more backstreets and alleys, but this time Aleksey led the way. And he did so with determination, with an intense speed and keen eye. He avoided the main streets, favouring alleys covered by corrugated steel or flapping laundry. The entire time, he held two fingers lightly to the tumbling symbols on his suit.

How could he read his map so well? When even Kichlan had not been able to follow my instructions, Kichlan
who had worn his suit for many more years than I. Or
Aleksey.

"I don't know how you did it," he said, even as he ran.
He sounded strangely calm, focused. "But you managed
to escape the Mob. Let's try and keep it that way."

I quickly grew lost. Lad ran close behind me, though he
could have overtaken me easily. He was steady and strong.
He did not panic, he did not cry for his brother or fear
even for his own safety, so focused was he on making sure
I was all right. He had changed. Perhaps it was because
the Keeper no longer whispered demands he could not
understand. Perhaps it was because Kichlan had told him
to look after me, and his responsibility enfolded him so
completely. Whatever it was, Lad was growing.

It both lightened and broke my heart at once.

I lost track of time along with streets I could not keep
up the pace for long and eventually drew to a halt, hand
pressed to my chest, fighting for breath I swayed in the
sharp light of the high sun. Mizra watched me with concern. "How—" I took a deep breath. Why was no one else
struggling just to breathe? "—did you find us?"

Aleksey looked behind me. "We should not stop."

"Let her catch her breath." Mizra rubbed my back.
"Are you all right?" He whispered. I knew what had him
so worried, and forced myself to ignore the pain in my
abdomen.

Aleksey studied me for a moment, then nodded. He
folded his arms.

"How?" I gasped again, louder. "Tell me! Who are
you? Where are you leading us?"

"Tanyana, it's all right." Mizra again. I shook him from my back and leaned against a wall. "We saw what happened."

I heard Natasha shuffle, and glanced at her from the corner of my eye. She had hidden the knife and disk again but watched Mizra and Aleksey with a hawk's intensity.

"Ran into Aleksey on the way to Ironlattice," Mizra continued. "Half a cotton-spinning factory had collapsed. Blocked the streets and we had to go the long way. So we were late. I almost walked into the middle of the Mob, but Aleksey noticed them first, and stopped me." Mizra tried to take my hand. Even as I withdrew to lean against the wall Lad brushed him aside. "We watched when they brought you out. We hid. I'm sorry Tanyana, but I didn't know what else to do."

I looked up to Aleksey. "And then you used the map on your suit to follow us?"

"Like you showed me." Uncertainty in his eyes, and hurt. I felt myself wavering, tried to hold my resolve. "We couldn't let you run on your own. We're a team, aren't we?" He rubbed the scar on his nose.

"What happened?" Mizra hissed. "Why did they do that to you?"

Natasha was ready to start running again, I could see it in her darting eyes, in her bent knees and the way she angled her shoulders forward; readying for another charge, like the one that had broken through the Mob. It would be easier to just let her go, but she was right. We had the same enemies. And she had already proved her strength.

I pushed myself from the wall. "Quota."

Natasha and Lad's shock blended rather nicely with Aleksey and Mizra's reaction.

"They sent Mob after us, because we hadn't met quota?" Aleksey choked over the words.

"That's unheard of!" Mizra spluttered.

Casually, I took Lad's hand. He squeezed my fingers and, as always, communicated so much through touch. Trust, willingness to follow my lead, even if he did not know why I was taking us down such a strange path. "The veche will use any excuse to get to me, you know that. And considering what we have been doing – obeying the Keeper, ignoring their directives – can you say you are really that surprised?"

Aleksey rubbed and Mizra frowned.

"Well, it certainly surprised me," Natasha said, expression carefully blank.

"You did warn us," I said, "of the risks every time we returned debris to the Keeper."

"I did." Natasha straightened, her hands by her sides and weapons so well hidden they might not have existed. "I certainly did."

"And now they are calling us traitors." I shook my head in false consternation. "Which, I suppose, we are. Betraying the veche to side with the Keeper." And, I thought to myself, the Unbound.

Yes, it was strangely fitting.

Understanding settled over us, realisation of just what that meant. No home, no team, no collecting jars or emergencies.

Unbound – I thought to myself – this is what it feels like to be Unbound.

"We should go somewhere," Lad said, suddenly, and

Mizra jumped a little at the sound of his voice. "Take Tan somewhere to make sure she is okay. But where can we go?"

"Ideally, I'd say as far from the veche as possible." Aleksey watched me as he spoke. "Out of the city. And that's just to start with. But I'm not sure Tan would make it that far today."

Was my weakness that obvious? I could breathe again, but each lung's worth of air I dragged inside me set off the fire of the splinters and the scars. "I think you might be right."

"Bro," Lad said, with certainty. "We should go to bro. He can help us. Or if he can't, then Fedor and Geny. They could."

Fedor and Geny? Along with Lev and his Unbound, perhaps. "Why, Lad. That's a good idea."

"We can't just go chasing after Kichlan," Mizra pointed out. "The Mob will be waiting, won't they? Surely that's the first thing the veche would expect us to do."

"We don't go to home, Miz." Lad said, hesitantly at first. Then he squared his shoulders and looked so much like Kichlan I had to turn away and hide my face in shadow so he couldn't see how proud I was of him. "We go underground."

"Underground?" Mizra asked.

Natasha fixed her newly sharp gaze on Lad. "Underground? You actually know how to get beneath the city?"

"Do." Pride swelled his chest even further. "But Tan knew first," he admitted a moment later, a little sheepishly. "And bro."

"Did she?" Natasha asked with a sly smile. "Some people are full of surprises."

I hoped she could read my expression. I'm not particularly fond of irony.

"I don't suppose you'd like to tell me what you're talking about?" Aleksey asked, sounding strained.

"Same here," Mizra muttered.

"Let's go, we need to get underground." I started back down the alley. "We will explain on the way."

"Tan?" Lad caught up and murmured close to my ear. "I don't know where we are."

I slowed. That was a good point. "Aleksey, considering you're so skilled with that suit now, can you get us to the Tear? Lad and I will take it from there."

As we followed Aleksey through the labyrinth of Movoc backstreets, Lad and I explained about the underground ruins. We told the rest of our team about Fedor and his group. We even explained briefly what we had tried to do the other night, and how badly we had failed.

Natasha followed every word avidly. Perhaps she was starting to realise that being posted with us was not necessarily that bad.

Mizra listened in horror. "I can't believe you would risk all that!"

I pushed aside my exhaustion and irritation and tried for empathy. "You can understand why we didn't tell you, can't you? We didn't want to put you all in that kind of danger." I very carefully did not look at Natasha.

"Doesn't seem to have helped, though," said Aleksey. "The Mob is after us anyway."

"Tanyana, that's not what I'm talking about. And you know it!" Mizra leaned close to me, voice low, and clutched at my arm. Lad stepped between us. This time he actually pushed Mizra away.

"I will look after Tan," he said. "Look after her from everyone." He thought for a moment. "From anyone."

From the Tear River we eventually found our way to Lev's shop. Aleksey did not allow us to travel along any street wider than an alleyway, and often called a halt and forced us to huddle in doorways, duck into buildings, and at one point even climb down an open vent and hide in the sewer. Always, all around us, we heard the marching feet of Mob. As they paced the streets any crowds that could have disguised us evaporated. Markets closed early, shops locked their doors. And I caught whispers of war. The military was mobilising, Movoc-under-Keeper filling with their dark forms. What else could it be, but war?

It was only a matter of time before the Mob thinned out, and Strikers were brought in. If we were not underground by then, if we were not hidden from the sun and the skies then truly, we were lost. So we hurried in silence. The day chilled in the shadow of buildings, in the trickle of dirty water and the creak of rotting shutters.

Lev's shop was closed up, but he appeared when we knocked. Shouting carried down the empty street, distant, but still too close. I realised I did not know what I would do if he denied us entry. Could I force him? Or would we turn away?

"Mob on the streets," he said.

"The veche is hunting us," I whispered. "We seek shelter."

My heart leapt when he nodded. "Like last time." Lev opened the door, just wide enough to let us in. It closed with a great turning of locks. Their sound filled his darkened shop. "Are they following you?"

"No." Aleksey's confidence left no doubt. "Although they are certainly looking for us."

It seemed to be enough for Lev. "Yicor, Valya and Eugeny feared this." He held my gaze. "But we owe you Fedor's life. Take this as payment."

Natasha stared around her as he led us to the hidden trapdoor at the back of his shop, her eyes avid, like she was soaking up the place in as much detail as she could manage.

We descended the long ladder to Movoc's ancient bones.

"Amazing," Aleksey breathed as he dropped beside me.

I looked at him, and wondered if it was such a good idea to bring him here. I still didn't know what to do about him. Whether I should trust him, or– or what? But I could barely stand, let alone confront him. I just needed to sit down.

Lev closed the trapdoor behind us and I fought an irrational horror as the sound of wood closing and iron rattling echoed from the domed rock. Had he locked us in? What could we do, if he chose to leave us here?

The combined light of our suits alone lit the subterranean world. I hated the closeness of that light, the way it made the walls tighter, the roof lower, and all the earth above us heavy.

"Just amazing!" Aleksey smiled as his voice echoed, deeply resonate. "I never imagined this existed below Movoc-under-Keeper!"

"I had heard stories of Movoc-under-Keeper's ancient cities, buried deep beneath her in layers." Natasha wandered to the broken down houses, the barely recognisable tumbles of stone and time. "The national veche uses them, apparently. Though no one knows what for." A small frown formed between her eyebrows. "There's not much left of this one though, is there?" The lines were heavy there. Natasha frowned too often.

"What are we supposed to do now?" Mizra snapped. "Wait around in the dark, for what?"

I glanced at Lad. "Maybe we should take them to the meeting room, the big round one? Do you think it would be more comfortable in there?"

Lad blinked at me and cocked his head. I could almost see him thinking. "Yes. But not much."

I grinned. "I agree." I jerked my head at Mizra. "This way."

It took a moment for Aleksey and Natasha to notice we were leaving them behind. They did not hurry to catch up.

The meeting room was not much more comfortable than the street, and the unsteady shadows cast by our suits made the structures keeping the roof up even more precarious. Our collection team – was it an ex-team now? – squeezed through the narrow doorway and sought out what comfort it could find. Aleksey hunkered down against a wall and rested his chin on his chest like there was nothing wrong in the world. Mizra mirrored him, but shattered the illusion with continuous complaints about the cold. Lad spread out his coat on raised stones and told me to lie down.

"Lad, no." I tried to pick up the large and overly patched garment and give it back to him. "You'll be cold."

"Not cold, Tan." He lifted his hands and backed away. "You lie down and rest."

I smiled at him. "Only if you stay near me."

He nodded, and his cheeks flushed. So I lay on the cold, old stone, softened slightly by Lad's generously given jacket, with my feet resting in his lap.

Natasha sat on the lower section so her head was close to mine. "Why didn't you tell Mizra and Aleksey the truth?" she breathed the words softly.

Because I liked my secrets? I'm sure Kichlan would have agreed with me there. Instead, I said, "We have a common enemy."

It was difficult to see from my angle, but I felt the turn of her head, and caught the flash of teeth glowing faintly blue in the light of my suit. "And you would trust me enough to work with me? I am, after all, a traitor and a spy."

Couldn't argue with that. But still, I said, "So am I, I just don't have imperial backing. And you could have left us to the veche, to the Mob, back there. I'm sure it would have been easier to escape without Lad and me in tow. But you didn't. I think that has to count for something."

Silence. I started to doze, and only realised when Natasha woke me, whispering, "What about Lad?"

I shifted to ease the pressure of a buckle from my jacket pressing into my arm. Lad rubbed my ankle, just above the suit there, like he was soothing a fretful pet.

"Trust him," I answered. "He might surprise you."

"Trust, eh?" Natasha leaned even closer. "Well then, there is something I have to tell you. Just rumours, really, from some of my contacts with the veche."

"Oh?" Why was she hesitating?

"Ever since we learned what you really are – what they were really doing to you, I should say – I've been trying to find out more. You are the kind of weapon that could be a serious threat to the Imperial forces so of course, it was my duty. You understand?"

I nodded.

"I only very recently found anyone willing to talk. A member of the local veche with friends in the regional, who have a cousin in the national, whose great uncle is in military exp– well, you don't need that kind of detail. The point is, you're not the only one the national veche has been experimenting on, and they're not only making weapons."

Something in my stomach clenched. "I didn't think I was." Mostly, I didn't like to think about it. "What are you trying to tell me?"

"The biggest fuss at the moment is being made about a man brought in not too long ago. They are using him like, well, like a blueprint. Using his body to try new techniques. Some that worked, some that didn't. Doesn't prove anything, doesn't necessarily mean anything, but the rumour is that he used to be a debris suit technician. Apparently he volunteered. But I can't imagine anyone would do that."

I closed my eyes. "There are lots of debris technicians," I whispered.

"Yes," Natasha shifted away. "And it is only a rumour."

But I pictured Devich, the last time I had seen him. How sickly he had looked, how afraid, and the silver on his arm. He had been trying to tell me something, but I had refused to listen. Perhaps that was a mistake. I placed a hand on the scars across my stomach, and the child he did not know existed.

Only a rumour.

The cold seeped up through the wool and leather and uniform, and the stones were rough and uneven. For a while I was dimly aware of only the half-light and Lad's touch. Then Natasha, as she squeezed her way out of the rubble intent, I supposed, on further exploring the street. I closed my eyes, wondering how she would see anything. I must have slept somehow, because the next minute running feet echoed through the cavern. My legs were no longer raised, and I felt close to frozen.

I pushed myself upright as flame-gold light flickered in through the tight doorway. Aleksey, Lad and Mizra were gone; Natasha sat close to me, one hand tucked inside her jacket.

"What's happening?" My mouth felt cottony. I realised I was desperately thirsty.

"Tanyana?" Natasha peered at me. "You must have been tired." She glanced at the door. "We heard noise."

Then voices shouted, bodies scraped through the rubble, and Kichlan appeared. He took one quick look around the circular room, leapt across the distance between us, scooped me up in arms, and kissed me hotly on the mouth.

I pushed against him, weak and useless with the cold, because my mouth still tasted like wool and it couldn't have been pleasant. But he would not let me dislodge him. His lips moved from mine only long enough to near-crush me against him, before he kissed me again.

When he released me I was warm again, and embarrassed. Behind him, what looked like a small crowd had gathered to watch and smirk.

Lad, furiously red with the light of oil lamps and flickering candles, grinned ear to ear. Eugeny, Yicor and Valya watched the floor carefully. Sofia had her back to us, Mizra and Uzdal shared a scandalised expression, while Natasha and Aleksey seemed to be trying for no expression at all. Fedor looked entirely unimpressed, but that was normal.

Suddenly the great domed room felt too small. Suddenly, there was not enough air.

"Tan," Kichlan whispered in my ear. "Are you hurt? Mob on the streets and then you didn't arrive, I waited and waited and you didn't come!"

I pulled back a little. "You aren't angry with me?" Sounded pathetic when I said it, but I couldn't stop the words. They welled up on a wave of guilt, that the last time we had spoken we had been angry and mistrustful. I should never have let that happen.

He stared at me for a moment, his eyes searching my face. "Oh, Tan." He shook his head. "Of course I'm not. I was so scared. I don't want you to go, Tan. I don't want you to go." He unwrapped his arms, but clasped my hand instead.

"So." Fedor cleared his throat. "You've got a bit of a problem now don't you."

I swallowed on a dry throat and wished again for water.

"Not fair to blame Tan," Lad murmured. "Was not her fault."

I willed him to be silent; to keep Natasha's secret like I had promised her he could. From the corner of my eye I watched Natasha shift the weight on her feet. Nothing changed on her face, though she slid her hand back into an invisible pocket and I knew, if she had to, she would ensure her secret remained so.

But Fedor hesitated, glanced at Lad. "The Keeper. I know–"

"We risked this for him, didn't we?" I grabbed onto his misunderstanding like a lifeline. "And this isn't even as bad as last time the Unbound tried to rebel! The veche might be chasing us, but we have not been caught. They do not know where we are."

Fedor wavered. He looked at Lad again. "Is he, is the Keeper, is he here–"

"I told you to leave my brother alone." Kichlan released his hold on me, took Lad's hand instead.

"But he is a Half. He belongs with us–"

"He is not yours to use!"

Valya, apparently oblivious to the tension, placed her hands squarely on her hips and scanned the room. "You will stay here. Safe here. We will bring you bedding and blankets. I will feed you all. Keep you warm. Keep up your strength."

Unsure what else I could do, I thanked her. Kichlan held his brother and engaged in a glaring contest with Fedor. I wished I could lie down again, no matter how cold the stones.

"This is all fascinating, really," Uzdal drawled. "But would someone like to tell Sofia and me what's going on?"

12.

I paced the dark underground street because the suit would not let me sit still. Keeper ghosts in pale stone watched me from the tunnel walls. Their crystalline skin flashed blue with my spinning light, their dark eyes surrounded me with shadow.

The suit filled my body with its need: to fight, to flee, to do something, anything, other than lie on the bedding Valya had brought us and wait. Weapons did not wait. Weapons were drawn, swung, stabbed, deployed. Weapons acted, architects waited.

"I am not a weapon," I whispered, head down, so my chest absorbed the echo of my words.

The suit disagreed. So we paced.

"Tan?" Lad emerged from the domed building. One by one, my team was checking on me. Lad stammering and worried, Natasha observant and silent, Mizra complaining, and Aleksey, still brimming with wonder, his nose-rubbing smile always on his face.

The suit wanted to leave them here, in the dust of a ruined world. Because collectors waited. Weapons did not.

"Tan?" Lad matched my pace, cast his worrying gaze to

my crossed arms and the fingers digging into my skin. " 'Leksey thinks you should sit down because you must be tired after yesterday." He drew a breath "There is nothing to worry about. Bro is strong. He can look after himself."

Kichlan? Was that what they thought I was doing, fretting for Kichlan all alone in the Mob-infested city above? True, he and his team had returned to the surface despite my best attempts to convince them to do otherwise. Perhaps that would have made more sense. Perhaps that would have made me a better person, worthy of his love. But I tended to agree with Aleksey – 'Leksey, Lad had decided to trust him, then – and believed Kichlan could handle himself.

Or, I could go to him. Just climb the ladder, break the door, then out into the city, Mob and the veche be damned! I didn't even need to climb if I just gave in.

I shook out my hands, tried to make the fight inside me look like nothing but a need to ease sore muscles.

"I am okay, Lad. Tell Aleksey I am just not very good at doing nothing."

He nodded, serious. "He would believe that."

Lad did not leave immediately. He hesitated, half-turned, then remained by my side. "Am I being a good Half, Tan?" he asked, fidgeting as he walked. "Fedor says I'm very important, because there aren't very many Halves any more. He says that long ago everyone, even pion-binders, knew about Halves. People used to listen to them and do what they said, because Halves could talk to the Keeper, and everyone loved the Keeper back then. Halves had power too, all of their own, different from pions and debris. But it's like this street, now. All buried. All broken. Almost gone." His fretful, intense eyes met mine. "But I don't have any power. And bro used to listen to me, and Miz, Uz, Tash and Sofia too, but I don't think I ever told them anything important. What if I'm not good enough at being a Half?"

I swallowed a sudden, sharp anger. Damn Fedor. This was the last thing Lad needed to worry about right now. "Lad." I took his hands, and calmed his fingers. "I think you are a wonderful Half. You always tell us what the Keeper says, even when he is crying, even when he is scared or upset or not making any sense. He is lucky to have you. We all are."

He frowned. "But I don't have power, Tan. What power am I supposed to have?"

I sighed. "I'm sorry, Lad, but I don't know. No one does, not any more. Not even Fedor. That must have been a very, very long time ago. So long no one can remember."

He looked to his feet, his expression glum.

"But we can't worry about that right now. We need to focus on the present, not the past. We need to help the Keeper now, do the best we can. And we can't do that without you. We need you, Lad. You will help us, won't you?"

Lad straightened his shoulders. "I can, Tan. I will not worry about old things. I will do the best I can. I will be a very good Half."

I watched his back as he returned to the domed room. Then I sat by the legs of one of the Keeper statues. I placed gentle fingers over one of the bands on my wrist. The symbols struggled there, surging and crowding under my touch. But I could still feel him. Lad, his symbol so solid and strong.

I wished Fedor would leave the past well alone. What did it matter, really, what Halves used to be and what power they might have had? It made as little difference to us as the old Unbound society did. We had to survive the here and now. The past was gone.

By the time Aleksey and Mizra made their next attempt, I was walking again. Fingers still pressed to the symbols, marching in tune with the flux of the suit, the rise and flow, the tugging.

Mizra came first. I almost did not hear him.

"You need to sleep," Mizra said.

"Concerned for the child, are you?" I asked him, with more acidity than he deserved.

Mizra shook his head. "Tanyana, I wish you could have understood. We were only ever worried about you. Just as we tried to help Sofia, we try to help you."

"Why? What business is it of yours?"

"You are our friend." He placed a hand against his side, against the scar beneath his clothing, where he had once been joined to his twin brother. "The world isn't fair, Uz and I can't fix that. But we will still do what we can, and offer support to those who need it. To those we care about."

I turned away from him. Perhaps I had judged him harshly, seen what I wanted to see, misread his concern for me as a desire to tell me what to do. It was too late now, anyway. I could hardly book surgery with Edik with the Mob on my trail.

Aleksey gave me enough time to start pacing again, before he tried.

"You really should rest," he said, matching my pace.

"I don't trust you," I hissed at him, "and I'm not going to talk to you. So don't even try. Just leave me alone."

"Come now, Tanyana, won't you hear me out? It's for your own good."

I spun, and my suit unwound a fierce, sharp blade before I could control it. But I didn't even get close to him. Aleksey raised one of his own, just as fast, just as sharp. He blocked me.

His expression remained calm, reasonable, despite our swords. "What have I done to deserve this?"

Shaking, I withdrew my suit. It fought the whole damned way. "I don't even know you. And you know more than you should, you work your suit far too well, and I'm not a fool. I won't let another person betray me." Not another Devich, Tsana, or Natasha. "So just leave. Get away from me, and my team. Go or I will– I will kill you!"

Aleksey shook his head, expression hurt. "You don't have it in you to kill me, Tanyana. And anyway, I'm only here because I care about you."

I started pacing again, striding away from him. "Just go! Leave me alone." He was right. No matter what the veche drilled into me, I was no weapon, nor had I ever been trained to use one. Could I really kill him, like I had killed the Hon Ji Half? Would I let him force me to do that again?

"I only care about you, Tanyana. I only want you to make the right decisions, to choose the right side, to keep yourself safe. Please, remember that." Then he left me in peace.

I half expected Natasha to follow in their wake. But although she might be a Hon Ji spy and apparently well-equipped assassin, she was still Natasha. One failed attempt to convince me was enough for her.

I was left alone again, with the suit and the statues. Was he with me, the Keeper? Following at my heels and worrying in his own, otherworldly way? I did not trust the suit enough to check. I feared that if I allowed it to slip metal over my face as I had done so many times before, I would not be able to regain control.

"What do you want from me?" I whispered into the darkness. Into the stones.

Freedom. The answer came in the twitching of my muscles, in the whirring of symbols. Freedom, and dominance.

"You won't get it," I hissed the words, choked over them. My throat was tight. My lungs full. My tongue thick. "Not over me."

Stalemate.

It was difficult to breathe. I placed hands on my abdomen, readying for the attack. But none came.

"This will get us nowhere."

Agreement. A softening. I leaned against a statue of the Keeper, cheek close to his chiselled one and relaxed my clawed hands. "I will not give in to you." And yet, I had never known strength like the suit gave me. There was power in its silver and in its secrets. It tried to kill my child; it tried to take me over. But still...

Thoughts of Natasha came unbidden. Fighting the Mob, the veche. The puppet men. What had I said to her? We have a common enemy.

I straightened. "We are powerless like this. Divided, bickering over one body. Unless you want to stay down here, hiding, we will need to fix this. We need to come to an understanding."

Curiosity.

I stepped back from the statue, ran a hand over the half-face of the Keeper. That poor, broken soul. We had been doing this wrong from the beginning, following the Keeper on his desperate quest to stay alive, returning paltry caches of debris to him. Even joining the Unbound and attempting to raid laboratories. It was doomed from the start. I'd understood that, even while I tried to convince myself otherwise, cursed like a march through the Other's neverending hells.

I should have known this from the moment the puppet men appeared in Grandeur's graveyard. Or earlier, as soon as I'd realised Devich had betrayed me. The first moment the suit drew its own swords.

We could not help the Keeper. I could not close his doors, I could not maintain the balance between worlds. Such grand designs were the products of his shattered mind. I had to accept my role; I had to come to terms with what the puppet men had made me.

I was a weapon. Weapons do not create; architects create. Weapons do not protect; guardians protect. Weapons destroy.

But maybe that was not so terrible. After all, we had a common enemy.

"I offer you a bargain." I turned, stared at the thin sliver of lamplight emanating from the crumbling rock tunnel. Lad was right, wasn't he? I should do what was necessary, risk anything – even myself – to look after my team. To help those I loved. "Obey me, work with me, and I will give you a fight. A true challenge." Could I trust the debris inside me to keep its word if it agreed? "We are a part of each other, we need to get used to that. But if I can trust you then, only then, I will set you free."

A thrill of exaltation. Not triumph. Just pleasure, just loosening, just the need. I gasped as it flooded up from ankle to neck, from wrist to wrist. Oh that strength, that power. The endless silver and the shining light!

It was me; I was suit. Together, nothing could stand in our way.

Not even the puppet men.

"Can you be patient?" Every last inch of me shivered with the effort of drawing the suit in, of forcing it to wait. "Soon. Soon."

I should have seen it from the beginning. The puppet men had made me into a weapon. I was not a guardian, as the Keeper was. I was not a spy like Natasha or a revolutionary like Fedor. I was not a Half, or a protective brother.

So I would show the puppet men just how strong a sword they had fashioned. And I would stop them. Destroy them. Every last one.

When he returned that night, Kichlan brought Volski and Zecholas with him. Fedor brought his Unbound.

Light scattered across the rundown room from several oil lamps hung from corners of broken stone. Yicor, Fedor, Valya and more of the Unbound crowded the lower level. Behind them Aleksey, Mizra, Natasha, and Lad sat on their temporary bedding. With them were Kichlan and his team. The sight of him caught my breath, he looked so haggard.

"The veche has declared martial law," Volski said by way of a greeting. "The city is being shut down. Shielders on barricades along the Tear River. The bridge has been closed to traffic, ferries requisitioned and services slashed. Mob march the street."

"They say we are at war with the Hon Ji," Zecholas said.

"Debris collections have been suspended," Kichlan said. "We are unnecessary, apparently, in a time of war."

"They will start recruiting soon." Zecholas met Kichlan's suspicious scowl with one of his own. "I wouldn't be surprised if they find another job for you. A military one."

Volski nodded. "They will need support units. Metal workers, light and heat binders, even cooks." He and Zecholas shared a look. "Architects.

As a critical centre I had never been called to sapper duty. An architects' ability to construct large, secure structures was crucial during war, as were their powers to destroy. We were also adept at smoothing roads through otherwise unpassable territory, even recognising and clearing hidden, and most of the time explosive, pion bindings left behind in abandoned fortifications or factories. I knew of critical centres who had spent time training with the military for such occasions, adding an extra bear badge to their shoulders in the process, and kopacks to their rublie. But the military tended to prefer circles with male centres, and I had no interest in arguing with that policy.

I had a dim memory that Zecholas, however, had served with soldiers in the colonies. One of his earlier circles – of six, I thought. From the look on his face, something firm but worried, I thought I might be right.

I sighed. There were more jobs for debris collectors in war than he realised. At least those of us with the correct equipment. "So why are you here?" It wasn't the friendliest of greetings, no matter how pleased I was to see them.

Zecholas snorted. "What do you think? So soon after we set off their laboratory alarm, broke in, and found – I'm still not entirely clear on what we found. A day later and suddenly we are at war?"

"We suspect there are ulterior motives to this sudden

military take over," Volski filled in the gaps. "So we came looking for you."

I couldn't stop a grin. "The veche says we are at war, and you think of me?"

"We met Kichlan on the way." Volski allowed himself a dry smile. "He told us what happened. We suspected this had something to do with you. Now we know we're right."

Natasha had slid from her bedding to haunt the shadows between lamps. But I wasn't going to contradict them.

"The veche are forcing our hand," Fedor said. He watched me, eyes clear of hatred and anger. It almost seemed that desperation had brushed that all away. "Either we hide down here until we starve, or we fight back."

"How do you intend to do that?" I asked him. "Stand in the street and shout dire predictions? 'Fear for everything?' The Mob won't listen to your talk of the Keeper and the opening doors. And the few inches of steel in your bones is the only weapon you have."

Fedor scowled. But again, I had the strangest impression that he wasn't angry at me. His fury, his frustration, his suited blades, they all had a new target; the veche occupying the streets.

"Of course not." His hard eyes scanned the room, resting on Volski, on Zecholas and even Kichlan. He stared at Lad the longest, and I clenched my hands into tight fists, my suit bands spinning. "With the tools we have available."

"Tools?" Zecholas tapped his chest and looked affronted.

"What would we have to fear from the Mob if their pion systems fail?" Fedor licked his lips, the corner of his mouth twitching as though he was trying to contain a manic grin. "From Strikers, should they fall from the sky? What use would Shielders be, with nothing to build their barriers?"

"You want to release debris again?" Volski asked, looking incredulous.

"We tried that already," Yicor whispered. "We were very nearly killed."

Fedor nodded to me. "This time, I will listen. We will do this Tanyana's way. With her circle, with her collection team."

"You're a fool." Kichlan turned away and held the rough stone of the wall. His fingers reddened with the strength of his grip, his knuckles strained white. "What makes you think they will not know? That they will not be there, waiting for us, ready this time with worse than a room without doors?"

What indeed? They knew, the puppet men. They watched and they tested and they laughed. But that was exactly what I wanted, wasn't it? A tight room, deep underground and me, and the puppet men. And my suit.

"I will not wait down here to die! I will not give myself to them without a fight!" Fedor railed.

"Then run!" Aleksey snapped. "Are you broken? When the veche send Mob after us we should not wait and we should certainly not march foolhardily into their arms. We run, curse it! We *run*."

"Coward!" Fedor hissed.

"He makes a good point!" Mizra leapt to Aleksey's defence.

"Fedor is right," I said, in between their breaths. And I nodded, and crossed my arms, and drummed my fingers, anything to ease the excitement, anything to smooth away the tension inside. "We need to fight."

Mizra paled and slumped back against the rocky wall. "You can't mean that. Not after everything that's happened."

Aleksey shook his head violently. "Tanyana, haven't you listened to anything I've had to say? This is not the choice you should be making. You don't understand these people and what they are capable of."

"Oh, but I do." Better than he did. "That is why I know." I glanced around the room. "There is nowhere safe from the veche. We can hide, but they will find us. Even here. We can run, but they will chase us. No matter where we go. So we fight." I met the grim triumph in Fedor's eyes. "Because it is all we can do."

"No!" Kichlan released the wall, half-staggered toward me. "This is dangerous, too dangerous."

"You will risk a lot, going out there," Natasha murmured. "Certainly more than yourself."

"Tan is right," Lad said, and I knew Fedor and I had won. Because silence settled over us and Kichlan turned his face away and I knew that if Lad was with me, his brother would have no choice. And where Kichlan went, so his collecting team would follow. "We should have listened to her last time." Lad nodded to himself. "And times before that."

"Thank you, Lad." I felt no guilt for using him like this. The suit grew tight.

He wrinkled his nose. "Don't like it down here, anyway." He leaned close to me. "Smells bad, Tan."

Aleksey slumped. "I won't be able to help you. Not any more."

Natasha watched me from her shadows.

Kichlan paced. He paced, as Lev and Fedor planned in

whispers. He paced as Valya found bedding for Volski and Zecholas and a space to sleep. The circular room seemed suddenly crowded with plotting and muttering and Kichlan pacing feet echoing from the fallen stone and unstable supports.

I allowed Lad to lead me to my makeshift pallet by a tumble of broken wall.

"Tan, you should rest." He patted the blankets.

"You will need it." Kichlan was suddenly close behind Lad's back, his face a mask of oil-lit fury. "That's right, sleep, Tanyana. Nice and peaceful. Need all the rest you can get if you're going to lead my little brother into danger!"

I turned away from the anger in his voice. Guilt battled with the suit's automatic, aggressive response. Kichlan was only trying to protect the brother he loved so much. What did I think I was doing, dragging them both – all of them – into this fight?

But it seemed both of us had underestimated Lad.

He spun and shoved his brother back. Kichlan, eyes wide, tumbled a few steps away. "Don't say that to Tan," Lad said, quiet for once, his words nearly lost beneath the echoing babble of many voices in a crowded room. "And don't use your voice like that. She did not ask me, I want to come. I am a Half, and I am strong, and I can decide for myself!" He drew a calming breath. "You should know that, bro. I can decide for myself."

Speechless, Kichlan and I gaped at him, then at each other, then back at him.

"I–" Kichlan stammered. "I am sorry. I should have realised. I– you are my brother. Sometimes, I just want to look after you."

"Is okay. Forgive you, bro. Just, you should know. I

can look after me too." Lad crossed his arms and didn't move. "And Tan too. Say sorry to Tan."

Kichlan looked down on me. Shock had broken whatever fury he had paced himself into. "Sorry, Tan."

Everything about him softened slowly, he came to sit beside me. Lad turned around and placed himself in front of us like a screen. He was such a large man that he did so quite effectively.

Kichlan touched my chin, my jaw. He brushed back my unruly fringe. "What have you done to yourself?"

Part of me needed to pull away. Because of Devich's child. Because Kichlan was right, and I was using his brother for my own ends. But more, because the notches were yet another scar, another ugly mark and he was close, so close, searching each one of them with prying eyes. I hated myself for thinking that, as though I should care what Kichlan thought of the state of my face. Wasn't I used to scars by now?

Instead, I swallowed my pride. "It's the suit," I whispered, unable to lie, even if I did not confess the entire truth. "The suit is healing me. Becoming me." Was it really so easy to say? "Bit by bit, piece by piece, I am becoming their weapon."

He shook his head. "No, you will never be that."

"You don't know the extent of it. You can only see my face."

"Oh, I think I've seen more than that." He smiled. It only made me feel worse. "It doesn't matter. Tan, you will always be you. Even if you turn into silver, you will not be their weapon. You are too strong for that."

I hoped so.

He kissed me gently, over the gouges in my forehead.

He wrapped his arms around me and I did the same to him. Together we lay down on that hard, cold stone padded with thin blankets, and somehow I managed to sleep.

I woke to a world that wasn't quite real, and the suit thrumming in my ears. Deeper than a heartbeat, stronger than the rush of blood, as solid as bones and taut as muscle. Gradually, I eased myself upright. The room sharpened into such focus that I could see every mark on the walls, smell every last wisp of oil-scent, taste the sweat and feel the heat of close-packed bodies.

Kichlan had left me alone on the hard bed. He and Fedor stood together, faces close as they debated, eyes catching lamplight to flicker toward me.

I caught snippets of words, more than I should have been able to hear.

"–the defences are already weakened–"

"–any front on attack would be suicide–"

"–binders did it the first time–"

I lay back down. It didn't matter how we got there, only that we were ready when the puppet men came calling.

"Bro will work it out," Lad said. He was sitting close to my feet, a stooped figure nearly hidden in the shadows. "He said he would make sure Fedor did not ruin the whole thing."

"Good," I said. And heard the scratching of wires inside me.

Lad cast me a strange glance, worried eyes and terse mouth. "Don't need to worry," he said. "We won't be all alone this time. The Keeper says he is coming with us.

He will tell us if they are following us or watching us or coming for us. Says he will warn us in time."

As long as he did not get in my way. I closed my eyes again. The suit and I slept.

"You're a heavy sleeper." Aleksey, close to my face. When I opened my eyes his scar was long and pale in the darkness, like a crescent moon. He was holding my shoulders, gently rocking me to consciousness.

"She isn't still asleep, is she?" Mizra peered around his shoulder. He lowered his voice. "Is something wrong?"

I stood, rolled out a crick in my neck and shook feeling into my hands. Wrong? No. I had never felt stronger, more powerful. I felt as though I towered above everyone in the room, calm even in the face of their desperation and fear.

"No." My voice was smooth, too smooth. A chime of metal, a great and solid bell. "I was tired. That's all."

"Been an interesting few days," Natasha said from her spot beside Sofia and Uzdal. "I can't really blame you."

"But we need to move," Fedor said in tone that brooked no argument. "Tonight, or not at all."

I pushed past them into the subterranean street. Lad kept close to me, matching my pace but asking no questions, his face as determined as I had ever seen it.

We climbed up into Lev's shop and dispersed in small groups to roam Movoc-under-Keeper in apparently random patterns, which would eventually congregate at a laboratory high along the river on the outskirts of the old city. We were not to attract attention, the small groups ensuring that if some of us were found, captured, and questioned, at least the rest of us could complete the mission – Fedor's plan, with Kichlan's embellishments.

The street lamps, I realised, were dead. The suit saw debris planes in their systems and felt cracks along the pion lines as far back as their factories. Not the Unbound, facilitating their desperate night raid; not the veche, hiding their troops in the darkness; but a city falling, the unravelling of every pion bind, the weakening of valves, the shifting of walls, steel, and flesh into sand.

I did not need the oil-lamps each group carried to see by. I saw the night world with a bluish tinge, as though the light spinning on my wrists, ankles, waist and neck had lit the city for me, and me alone.

"This way!" Kichlan hissed, crossed a blackened street and ducked down an alleyway. I followed, and wished I had bothered to find out where we were going. I could have outrun them all.

Kichlan had made sure to take Lad, Volski, Zecholas and me in his small group. We ran in short bursts, as silent as feet on stone could be. So when the suit heard a single person – small, light-footed, agile – running close behind us, cutting cross our path, darting wall to wall, I stopped.

"Tan?" Lad asked, peering at me from over his shoulder.

Kichlan scowled at us both, lifted a finger and pressed it against his lips. "What are you–?"

"Wait for me," I whispered. The footsteps were fading, their owner getting away.

"We don't have time–"

"Then keep going." I didn't bother to look at him. "I will find you." And before any of them could respond, I was gone. Silver in my bones. I didn't even need to let the suit loose. I was running. Back down the street, a sharp turn

into an alleyway, two easy leaps: lamppost, wall, to roof.
Then I was gliding, the suit light, like invisible wings cupping the icy night air, so soft was my tread across the
shattered tiles of failing rooftops. It was good, oh so good.
The suit goaded me, filled me with its strength. Dimly I
was aware of life in the buildings beneath me: snoring,
the clatter of furniture, the dark spitting of an argument
terrible in the night. They were not aware of me.

And neither was Natasha. She ran so smoothly she
could have been a shadow herself. Away from her allo-
cated group, away from apparent suicide by attack
against the veche, away from the collecting team she had
infiltrated so effectively that Lad and I had risked the
Mob to keep her safe.

So I told myself that was why I dropped from the
rooftops to land in her path, because we had risked so
much for her. Even this foolhardy last stand against a
vastly superior foe was happening, in a way, because Lad
and I had decided to protect her. Running away from us
was a betrayal.

That was a better reason than the feel of icy wings,
than the hunt, the chase, the fight.

I landed so silently that she did not hear me, did not
even see me, until it was too late. Natasha skidded to a
halt, suddenly ungainly, suddenly clumsy, slipping on
night-wet stones only feet away. Her usually green,
sharp eyes widened like dark haloes in a ghost's face.
"How?" she whispered, and I saw true fear there. In the
shaking hand that pushed strands of brown hair away
from the sweat on her forehead and yet – I was certain
– would draw a weapon from her jacket faster than she
could blink.

"Go ahead," I said, in my smoothly metallic voice. "Try one of your little tricks. Let's see what happens." I was grinning. Utterly out of my control, like the bubbling warmth spreading from my bands, coating my legs, abdomen, and torso.

But to my disappointment, Natasha dropped the hand. She stood, arms by her sides, held slightly away from her body with her palms facing me. "This isn't like you, Tanyana," she said. Hardly the begging apology I deserved.

"You're running," I hissed. "Abandoning them."

"Of course." She tipped her head slightly, actually looked confused. "What would you expect me to do?"

"Stand with your team and fight!" I hissed.

Natasha shook her head. "This is not my fight. This should not be anyone's fight. You are letting that man, that Unbound fool, lead his people and your people to their deaths. You must know that is true."

"You understand nothing." I stepped forward. We were close, so close I could hear the blood beating fast with fear in her veins.

"No, Tanyana. Please." Was that it? Was that the pleading I had wanted, the begging she owed me? "I need to return to my contacts. I have a duty; I have sworn an oath to the Emperor himself. I must tell them what the national veche is doing, I must warn them. There is more at stake than you could understand, more going on than your foolish suicidal plans!"

Emperor? Natasha did not look like she belonged with the Hon Ji. She was too pale, too green-eyed, hair too light and curled. But then again, she could not have infiltrated us so effectively if she did not look like this.

Hope sprung up in her eyes, and a subtle change of

breath. "We have a common enemy!" she said. "You want to fight the national veche, Tanyana? Those corrupt old men who did this to you? Then help me escape. The Emperor's army is your only chance, far better than a small group of the ragtag poor and broken. With everything you know – with your very strength in our ranks! – we will break their hold over this nation. No one will ever be subjected to the kind of torture you have known at their hands. Never again!"

Armies? Emperors? It was a nice try, a bold idea. But the suit and I knew what it would take to remove the puppet men. Us.

"Your armies will die." I thought of debris monsters devouring the pion bindings that hold a body together. Had she told her precious Emperor about that? "I will not join them."

Natasha sagged a little, appeared defeated. I was not convinced of her apparent helplessness.

"Why do you spy for them?" I asked, softly, ready to move. "You were not born Hon Ji, were you?"

Her sharp eyes flickered up for a moment. Bitter, unsure. "My Hon Ji mother worked in the colonies," she hissed. "My father was Varsnian Mob. I take after him."

Indeed she did. For she moved, suddenly, with such speed and grace that I wondered just how much of his pion-enhancements her father had passed to her with his looks, or if that was even possible. One moment she was dejected, slumped, and the next she had her blade in one hand and the two remaining metal and clay disks in the other.

Natasha was fast, unnaturally so. But she was not suited, not the way I was.

Silver lashed out from my coated hand. It caught her wrists before she could so much as activate her lightning weapon. It squeezed her bruised and broken skin, twisted bones and tendons until her hands opened in reflex. The knife clattered useless to the stones. I caught the twin disks.

I drew her hands together, wrapped myself around them like I was the chain I had freed her from earlier.

"Damn you," she gasped, but I did not loosen my grip.

"You will stand with us," I said. "You will fight with us."

But as I began to drag her back to Kichlan and Lad, the suit refused to be put away. Uninterested in hibernating in its five tight bands it clamped hard over my skin and clothes and refused to respond to the usual movement of muscles, the normal firing of nerves.

Gripping Natasha's wrists hard, I wheezed a deep breath. "Not now. Not yet." I coughed against scratching, digging, wiggling silver. "Not her."

The suit did not want to be placated. Battle, it whispered somewhere inside my head. Fight. Even Natasha – with her hidden weapons and the deadly grace she had, somehow, hidden from me for all these moons – had been too easy, over too quick. It was not enough, my muscles told me as they flexed, we needed more.

"She is not the challenge, you know that." I turned my face away from the line of Natasha's shoulders, so ready to try and throw me off balance, the casual strength in her stance. And I pushed down the rising need to test her, to see how lithe that back, how strong those legs, and just what she thought she could do against me without her weapons. "And this is not the bargain."

"Who are you talking to?" Natasha asked, voice restricted by pain.

Hesitation. The suit did not understand the difference: a good fight was a good fight.

"A compromise then?" Was I really arguing with my own body – *again* – with my muscles and the deepest of my bones?

The suit agreed to retract, but only so it could slide back over my very skin beneath clothes and boned uniform closer than it ever had. And I gasped, not because it was cold but because it was warm, living yet metal. And I could not tell where skin ended and suit began and it felt right, so horribly right, like we had been missing each other, like this was the way we were always meant to be. Those paltry bands on my wrists, ankles, waist and neck only held us back. We were supposed to be joined all over, ever more.

I hated myself for feeling it. But I could not stop the pleasure.

I convinced the suit to leave my head clear. Although, adding all the scars on my face and scalp, I was silver enough.

"T– Tanyana?"

I glanced over my shoulder. Natasha pulled back, horrified, from the suit-coated hand that extended to bind her wrists. Had she seen it move beneath my sleeve? Had she felt the ripple as it claimed my skin? She did not understand.

"We must hurry." I held the two disks in my free hand, and could feel their energy, their vibrating potential, through the touch of metal to suit. "Try to keep up."

Suited this way, I knew instantly where Lad was. I

could feel him. Not just his symbol pushing insistent against my fingertips, I felt him through all of me. From skin to bone. Lines solid, symbol strong, flowing through me.

So we ran toward him, the suit and I a splash of light in the darkness, with Natasha stumbling, falling, dragging behind us. Quickly, too quickly, we found him. It was an effort to slow down and stop. All I wanted was that sensation of speed, and the flush of wind.

"Tan!" Lad launched himself at us as we rounded the corner, wrapped his arms around me and held tight. "Thought we lost you!"

He rocked me, his touch sending shivers through us. The suit did not like him, the suit did not trust him. Until Kichlan appeared by our side and noticed Natasha; Natasha, weakened, bloodied, fallen against the stones. Still bound by the wrists, still linked to me like a dog on a chain.

Kichlan crouched beside her. Gently, he lifted her head. Her eyes flickered open, and she winced beneath his concern. One side of her face was bruised, scratched by the stones. Her clothing was torn, wet; her arms straining at a terrible angle.

It reminded me of the Mob, too keenly, sharpened with guilt and an underlying horror at what I had done. It was enough to force the suit to let her go. It retracted back to cover my hand and brought with it the taste of her fear, the dirt of her skin, the feel of her blood. I shivered.

"Tan?" Kichlan helped Natasha sit back against a wall. She groaned as he laid her hands in her lap, ran fingers along the bones in her arms. "What happened?" Hesitation, disbelief, played across his face. "Did you do this to her?"

"She was running," I said, as though that explained everything, as though that excused me.

"Running? So you, what, chased her?"

Volski and Zecholas held back. I could feel them behind me, hear their breathing and shuffling feet.

"I can't just let her go," I hissed. "She is one of us!"

Then Lad, to my utter surprise, took my hand. "Tash has secrets," he said. "Tash was the one the Mob was after, not Tan. Tan and I helped her." He glanced at me, hesitating. "So– so she shouldn't go. That's why, isn't it Tan?"

Slowly, Natasha lifted her head. One eye was swollen shut, her lips bleeding, great scrapes and grazes darkened her forehead. "You, Lad?" She spat blood. "Even this suited bitch kept her mouth shut. But you would betray me?"

"Tash–"

"I thought you were my friend."

Lad hiccupped an uncertain sob.

The suit believed this was all a waste of time, and it was easier to agree. So I turned – still holding onto Lad – and strode ahead, leaving Kichlan crouched by Natasha's side. "We should hurry." I rattled the disks against the metal of my hand. It was a struggle not to run.

"My lady?" Volski murmured as he and Zecholas hurried to keep up. "Lady, are you all right?"

I was. The suit and I, together. We were damned near perfect.

I felt the laboratory before I saw it. Or, at least, I felt that which it housed. Debris was a symbol of itself, the strongest symbol of them all. Fiercely bright and connected to me in a far deeper way than Lad was, but connected also to the suit, the city, the sky, the earth. It thrummed through me, a bass accompaniment to the suit's ecstasy, a second heartbeat, an all-consuming pulse.

The building loomed before us. Squat, made of pale concrete rendered inelegant in the lampless dark. All laboratories, it seemed, were built the same. I imagined their security systems were also similar.

Even so, I crossed the street, no hiding in shadows, no skulking in adjacent alleyways. The suit laughed, filling my head with a metallic buzz, with wire scraping and wind rushing and I could not help but smile.

"What are you doing?" Fedor hissed, emerging from the doorway of an adjacent apartment block. "You will be seen! The Mob are everywhere, the veche is looking for you!"

Well, the veche could find me. Wasn't that the whole point?

"Lady, he's right," Zecholas followed, almost as close to my back as Lad. "More of those reinforced enforcers – or whatever they are – are inside. The door and the lock are just like last time. Lady, please, stop!"

In small groups they peeled away from alleys and doorways to follow in my wake. Fedor, Yicor and their Unbound. Sofia, Mizra, Uzdal. Aleksey. Finally, Kichlan, supporting Natasha, and Volksi. Insects, the suit called them, small and crawling.

"Careful!" Aleksey ran forward. "Don't you remember what I told you? The locks, the security!"

"She should remember." Fedor grabbed my arm. "Last time–"

"Don't touch Tan!" Lad released me and knocked Fedor to the ground. "Don't say bad things about her!" There was panic in his voice, and confusion. His trust in me had done that, and his desire to protect me.

Yicor tried to help Fedor up, but the younger man shook him off. Sofia and Mizra drew Lad away, as Kichlan was still occupied with Natasha. Zecholas eyed me, uncertain, before crouching and placing a hand to the cold street.

"There is something here, definitely," he said. "Below us, like last time. But," he shook his head, "it's not the same. Half a dozen small and compact areas of nothing. Debris, I think."

"The collected debris is stored in vats," Kichlan said. "At least, that's the way it's supposed to be."

"And security just as tight as last time." Volski crossed his arms, watched me with a look that mirrored Zecholas's concern, his outright fear. "Are we tunnelling, again?"

"We need to get out of here," Aleksey hissed. "They will see us! Alarms will be sent and the building shut down and there are so many Mob on the street, too many. We should hide!"

But I shook my head. "No," I said in a metallic voice not entirely my own. "We are tired of hiding."

I rattled the weapons in my palm, took a single step forward, and hurled them at the building's pion-lock. The suit's aim was far better than mine, its arm strong and true. The disks hit the lock directly on its small crystalline pad, and detonated.

Energy surged through the doors. A great blast like a lightning strike shattered them, knocking out chunks of concrete and brickwork from the surrounding walls. The ground rocked as fire laced the sky – the weakened pion network overloading, the destruction of thousands of powerful and complex bindings all at once. Around me, the Unbound and debris collectors threw themselves to the ground, covered heads, sheltered fellows.

They cowered. The suit laughed at their weakness, and together we entered the building.

Fire raged around us. It set my jacket alight, it caught embers in my woollen pants and singed the leather of my boots. I felt none of it. The suit was stronger than any fire, than even the backlash of shattered pion-bindings. I allowed it to slither over my face, to shield skin and eyes and lips from the heat, the rolling smoke, and the lightning crackling wild through the corridor.

The enforcers had been crowding the entrance as though they were waiting, as though they had known we were coming. Perhaps we had already triggered subtle pion-alarms; perhaps security had been strengthened in the wake of the war's commencement. Perhaps the puppet men had sent a warning. Whatever the reason, it meant the blast had killed most of them at once. Three burned, two shocked. Four struggling as Natasha's weapons and the overloaded security systems ran rampant through the bindings in their bodies.

No amount of enhancements could help them as the suit ended their lives. Clean strikes with a sharp blade. Certainly faster than being burned alive.

The way clear, I returned to the entrance. A cold wind blew the fire into smoke trails in the sky. So I pulled the suit back from my face.

"Tanyana?" Zecholas leapt forward, exclaimed over the burns in my clothing. "Are, are you hurt?"

I shook my head, gestured into the building. "The way is clear."

"What about the Mob, the enforcers?" Aleksey approached, hesitating. The bands of his suit span fast, in tune perhaps with the frantic panic on his face.

"Taken care of." The suit smiled for me.

He gaped at me, at the door, at the smoke and the faltering lights behind me.

Volski scanned the sky, the ground. "Not all the alarm systems were destroyed." He met my gaze without expression. "Although you took out most of them. Somehow."

I pointed to Natasha. Kichlan was standing again, one arm around her shoulders as she clung to him for support. "Thank Natasha."

Suspicious and uncertain faces turned to her. She hung her head, did not look up.

"Reinforcements will arrive anyway," Volski continued as though he had not heard me. "Given the noise and the smoke, I think they would come no matter how many alarms you disable. I suggest we hurry."

Yes, the suit agreed.

I led the way through the ruins and the bodies, and pretended I did not hear Sofia gasp or Fedor mutter over the corpses. Kichlan transferred Natasha's limp form to Mizra and Uzdal so he could comfort Lad in the face of blood, of burns, of the sharp and ever-present haze of frantic pions.

We found a stairwell and descended, leaving the smoke behind. A tiled corridor stretched off into dimly lit distance, empty, smelling strongly of a caustic cleaning agent. Most of the doors were shutdown, pion-locks squealing protest.

"It's so empty," Volski whispered. "There is no one on the other side of these doors. Another Fist on the floor below us, I think, but that is all I see."

"No one? That's impossible." Kichlan refused to let go of his brother's hand, even though Lad appeared to be trying to block out the harsh sound. He cupped his free hand over one ear, and had resorted to tilting his head, trying to press the other ear against his shoulder. "There's always someone. Newly fallen collectors, surgeons and nurses to tend them. Technicians maintaining the vats or monitoring suits as they are prepared for activation."

"Where are they, then?" Fedor snapped. "This feels wrong, and that's too familiar."

"Military rule?" Aleksey suggested. "Perhaps they have cleared all but the security staff. Is debris really a priority in war?"

The suit was not interested in questions. Together, we followed the symbols. Down the stairs, along another corridor, into the path of an unfortunate group of enforcers. I gave my head to the suit and it felled them, all nine, with one, two, three tight steps. They were mere shadows against doors. I did not feel their deaths.

"Tanyana?" Someone was screaming when the suit retreated. I looked over my shoulder. The debris collectors and the Unbound continued to huddle, all wearing identical expressions of horror. Kichlan had wrapped himself around his brother, holding him back, blocking his view. Sofia was crying, and she was the one screaming my name. But it was Fedor who approached me. I noticed how carefully he avoided stepping in blood.

"What have you done?" he choked on the words.

Curious. "What was necessary."

"But–?"

"But what?" The suit begged me to strike him. He was just too soft, too naïve. I refused. "What kind of bloodless rebellion were you expecting?"

"I–" He paled, and looked almost as sickly as when I had first met him. "Not this."

"Happy to release debris into the city to wreak your dirty work, aren't you? But too weak to dirty your own hands." I shook my wrists loose, sending a small shower of blood to fall on his boots. "You should know what debris does to a city built on pions. You must have seen people crushed by falling rubble, burned by an out-of-control heating system, or smashed at the bottom of a crater where a building once stood. So what did you think would happen?"

Nothing, no answer. The suit was unsurprised.

"We are almost there. You wanted to fight the veche. Let's do it."

"Are you certain, Tanyana?" I thought I heard Aleksey whisper. I glanced at him. Not fearful as the others, but stoic and accustomed to the sight of spilt blood. But he did, I thought, look a little sad. Perhaps, because it could have been him. In another time and a life before his fall, doing his job, waiting for us here, only to die on my blades.

Another level, a tighter corridor, deep below ground now. I forced open a final pair of heavy doors, reinforced with steel. The metal tore like paper, like leaves, so flimsy and weak. The locks squealed, alarms flashed, and all of it for nothing. We were unstoppable, the suit and I.

Lights flickered on. Another long, wide basement stretched out before us. But this one was whole, its machinery still bolted into cement, it debris not plundered and altered into ceiling, walls and floors.

Six vats crowded the space. Great, fat cylinders of suit metal almost as tall as the high ceiling, ringed by stairs and dotted with lights, gauges, and knobs. I could feel the pulse of the grains and planes held captive within them. I lifted a hand, flexed fingers. I was the same, wasn't I? Sheathed in silver – debris inside and out.

A tool, just like these machines.

For an instant, I faltered. For a moment, I wondered what that meant.

"We found them," Fedor breathed. "We actually found them." Then he vaulted over the railing, dropping to the floor below. The Unbound and the collectors took the stairs. "Let's hurry."

We stared around the room. Where were the puppet men?

An easy jump, and I followed Fedor. My reinforced legs did not feel the impact, but left cracks in the cement. As I approached the first vat, others fell in behind me. Kichlan and Lad, Volski and Zecholas close to my back. Behind them Mizra and Uzdal, with Natasha between them, and Sofia. Fedor, Yicor and their Unbound spread out around the other vats.

Aleksey remained on the platform. Again, I glanced back at him. His face was unreadable, but something about him made the suit pause. The very sight of him set the suit shivering.

"Do you know how to open them?" Zecholas was asking Kichlan.

He shook his head. "I worked with suits. A whole different section of technicians maintained the vats." Kichlan tapped on a glass gauge. Lights shone behind it, and something hummed. "And I don't see any instructions."

"It's remarkable," Volski said. "There are pions in here, there have to be, nothing this complicated could work without them. But if they are, they are too deep in all that debris to see, and yet it works! Why isn't the system failing? I can't believe this even exists."

"It shouldn't," Zecholas agreed with him. "By all the laws of pion manipulation we know, it shouldn't work." A pause. "My lady? What do you think?"

I looked away from Aleksey. The lights meant nothing, the gauges, the flickering numbers and balls bobbing in quicksilver tubes. Not to me, and not to the suit.

So I placed a palm on the vat. "Step back." Silver pulled to silver. The vat began to ripple.

Then Lad was shouting, "Oh no! Tan, look, hurry!"

Even as the suit and the vat bonded, as it fed the desire to open, to pull back, just as I had done to calm rampant debris countless times, I followed Lad's terrified gaze to the platform. And lifted my hand.

Aleksey still remained on the platform, and behind him, the puppet men stood. Three, five, it was hard to tell how many, they seemed to blur with the very wall, the very light, insubstantial yet real.

"How did they get in," Volski paused. "It's them! They *are* the crimson pions. Impossible." He raised hands and swatted at vicious, invisible lights. "They flare, brighter than suns, then they just die. I don't understand."

Together, Zecholas and Volski stumbled back.

"'Leksey!" Lad lurched forward but Kichlan grabbed him, hauled him back. "Run, 'Leksey! They are right behind you!"

I turned from the vat. This was why I was here. I lifted hands, blades, and whispered to the suit, low, breath brushing the metallic skin beneath my torn clothing. "You wanted a fight, you wanted your challenge. Well here it is." No longer whispering, shouting now, filled with strength and rage. "Together, like we agreed. Together, we will kill them all!"

"What are you doing, Miss Vladha?" one, or two, or all of the puppet men asked, sounding unconcerned.

"You think you can use me," I growled. "You wanted to create a weapon. Well, you have. And I will show you just what your weapon can do!"

I crouched, ready to leap forward, ready to slice through their bizarre wraith-like bodies, their crimson pion bindings, or whatever they were made of. But Aleksey was changing. His suit bands span fast and bright and spread. Legs, arms, torso, and even up to his face the suit grew like a hardened second skin. Only a thin rectangular strip across his eyes remained bare. His suit pulled at me, I felt in it a kindred, a mirror of my strength.

"I'm sorry, Tanyana," he said. His voice, rather than being muffled by his suit's mask, was sharp and metallic. It echoed through the basement like the scraping of metal.

"'Leksey?" Lad whimpered behind us.

"But you know I can't let you do that."

13.

Who do you trust?

I stared at Aleksey – at his suit, his weapon, just like mine – and realised that, yes, I already knew.

"So," I whispered. "This is who you are." I glanced at the puppet men behind him. "And this is why you are here."

But he shook his head, and the strip of his eyes I could still see were sad, disappointed. No smug triumph, no aggression. "You should not have done this, Tanyana. I warned you, again and again."

"I should have killed you when I had the chance." But that was the suit talking.

"Why?" His shrug was a ripple, the lancing reflection of light, tinged blue.

"You lied to me!"

"No, I didn't. I helped you, I warned you. And we are just the same."

"What's going on?" Fedor pushed forward. He stared up at Aleksey with a mixture of horror and anger. "Your suit, it's just like hers." He glanced down at the rolling symbols on his wrist, tipping his arm. "How did you do that?"

Aleksey's eyes flickered toward him. "I suggest you stay out of this. You do not understand what's going on here, and you cannot hope to be compared to us."

The suit agreed with him. Aleksey was like us; a soldier, a weapon. Far stronger than any of these others, the paltry collectors and soft Unbound.

"Tanyana." Was that pleading in his suit-strengthened voice? "This is why you are here too, this is your role." He lifted his arms. "Join us, fight with us." I could not see his mouth, yet I heard the grin in his voice. He sounded wild, and it spurred on the suit inside me. "We have a war to wage, after all."

"I might be a weapon," I said. "And unable to stop the changes wrought within me. But I am not *their* weapon." I shifted my defiance to the puppet men. "And I will not fight for anyone but myself, and those I must protect. Step aside, Aleksey."

"You know I can't." Resigned, but determined. "I am a veche enforcer and I will remain so, right to the end." Aleksey leapt from the platform. He landed with a crash that ricocheted through the basement. He left a crater where I had only made cracks. "I only wanted to help you, to work with you, until you joined us. But if you will not, then I must stand in your way."

So be it. The suit, at least, was pleased. The clash of swords was far more interesting than simple slicing through flesh.

"Move," I hissed over my shoulder, into silent shock and fear. "Get back."

"No, Tan!" Kichlan had to be dragged to relative safety among the vats. Fedor took hold of Lad – who wept for 'Leksey's betrayal – and did the same.

"No, Tan, don't!" Kichlan shouted. "You're not a weapon! Remember that, please. You are Tanyana, and not what they made you!"

Aleksey straightened, rubbed his fists, and loosened suited shoulders. "Come."

The suit enveloped my head. In that dark plane, with doors wrapping curved around the vats, Aleksey was solid and silver. I glanced down at my body. I was too. But I was an architect, for all the weaponry the puppet men had injected into me. Not an enforcer, not Mob. Behind him, the puppet men were easier to see, yet their skin seemed thinner, hatched with seams, and their eyes even darker than the world.

The Keeper huddled beside me, his debris pulse beating frantic and visible beneath his own thin membrane. "What are you doing?" he said into the darkness. "What about the vats, what about the debris?"

"Stand back," I told him.

"No! I need you to help me, not this! They will kill you, they will tear you like they have torn me–"

Poor, weak debris shade. "Stand back, or you could be hurt."

Then Aleksey came.

He moved so fast I did not see him. Before I could even think to react he grabbed my shoulders, squeezed and bent me back, forcing me to the ground. I landed hard. The Keeper scrambled away. Aleksey kicked, sharp, controlled movements – stomach, head.

I was not as fast as Aleksey. Yet our suits were the same. Each blow was more than physical; it sent shivers of aggression through me, of force. And I realised that Aleksey and his suit was doing what I had once done to debris, what I had started to do to convince the vats to open. His very consciousness was invading my suit with each touch. Debris to debris.

Tanyana the architect could not compete with Aleksey the enforcer. So the suit decided she was holding us back.

And with a wrench I felt in my body and my mind, the suit put Tanyana aside.

I was the suit.

Aleksey's foot came down and I grabbed it. A twist, he fell, and I leapt back to my feet.

"Finally!" he said again, and laughed as he pushed himself upright. "You're ready."

Blades sprung from his arms and he lashed at me. They met my shields, but instead of knocking his blow aside I wrapped him in bubbles of my own, snapped his blades and kicked him hard in the gut.

The blow was nothing. The blades were not.

With a scream he fell backward, holding shattered arms up before him. I absorbed the pieces I had torn from him, my silver burrowing into his, whispering, coaxing, demanding, until they were a part of me. And I was stronger for his weakness, more for his less.

"First point," the veche men whispered. "We are pleased."

I looked at them. "Don't be. I will come for you next." They were the true fight, the real challenge, the battle I had waited so long for.

"Don't turn your back on me." Aleksey recovered, ploughed forward. His shoulder smashed into my knees and dragged me down. On top of me, he plunged hands into the suit over my chest and dug like a rabid dog, tearing chunks away. I gasped, unable to breathe, as he took back what I had taken and more.

"Second point."

Spears lanced up from my abdomen. They plunged into him, lifted him off and threw him to the side.

Still gasping, I pushed myself upright. Aleksey was already on his feet. "You should not have made me do this. You are weak." I could hear his predator's smile. "And I will make you mine, tear that suit from you, and kill the body that hosted it." He glanced at the puppet men. "That will make me stronger, won't it? The strongest weapon ever known."

"Third."

Aleksey nodded. "You should have recruited an enforcer from the start. Allow me to correct the mistake."

I struggled to stand. How had he recovered so quickly? Didn't he feel the pain, the loss, the ripping of muscle underneath and the hollowing of bones?

Blades again. He jabbed at my head, at my chest, but I knocked each blow aside. Quick steps around each other and I swung for his head, fist extended to a club. But he was too fast as though he could read me, as though he knew how I would move before I did. He dodged, swung around behind me, and stabbed low into my back.

I felt his blade slide in. Through silver, to flesh. No pain. I was already repairing the damage to muscle, organs, nerves, but weakness wracked me as his blade extended, roamed, and began slicing me away.

I struggled, twisted around, gripped Aleksey's arm and with a grunt forced him out of me. Without his strength holding me up I slumped back. The body was bleeding. I sucked it in, drank up its life, channelled every spare drop into self-repair.

Blades dripping blood and quicksilver, Aleksey stood

over me. "I always knew you had some strength. Of mind, of spirit, if not in body. I am honoured to have had you as a test, and regret what you have forced me to do. But it is over."

I couldn't move. I ceased healing the body, I gathered all my strength, but it was useless.

"Complete it," the puppet men said.

"No no no," the Keeper whimpered somewhere amidst the darkness and doors.

Aleksey lifted his blades. I had no eyes to close.

"Tan, no!" someone shouted. Fast footsteps echoed sharply through the darkness and I turned my head, still watching those blades from the edges of my vision, to see Lad running toward us.

Aleksey struck.

Lad lunged at us.

"Do not harm the programmer!" the puppet men cried.

Aleksey checked himself, but too late. Lad flung himself in front of me and Aleksey's vicious twin blades plunged into his back.

Stunned eyes stared at me, full of pain and confusion. They were so clear, even in this place, as though Lad belonged here. Like the Keeper did. Like the puppet men.

"Lad?" I whispered.

Aleksey withdrew his blades and stumbled back.

I caught Lad as he fell. Blood washed too red, too real over my hands, my chest and arms. It ran the along the smooth contours of my suit and drained into the gashes Aleksey had made, the gaps he had torn into me. Fire spread from those holes, fire through my bones and across my skin, fire to my head where it roared in my ears and clouded my vision. My suit felt heavy, and tingled with each drop of Lad's blood.

Tan? Lad seemed to whisper, right against my ear. I couldn't tell if his mouth was moving. The world was red, and unreal. *You okay, Tan?* He sounded so close. *I look after you. From anyone. Bro said... bro said I had to look after you...*

He slumped forward, as the Keeper howled. My vision cleared and the suit retracted. It slid away from my face, my hands, and Lad's blood was warm and his skin was soft and he was gone. Lying on me, bloodied and gone.

"–waste," the puppet men were saying. "That was an unnecessary waste."

Aleksey shook, still wrapped in his suit, and stared at the crimson dripping thick down his arms. "No," he whispered. "I didn't mean to."

"Lad!" Kichlan scrambled out from behind the vats on his hands and knees. Like an animal he crawled, slipping, scratching, across the cement. Then he rolled his brother's body off me, held him close, buried his face in those unruly curls and screamed. He screamed until I thought he would tear with it, until I thought I would break under the weight of such loss.

I couldn't feel. There was something wrong with my back. I knew it hurt, but couldn't actually feel the pain and nothing below my waist would move. I felt so heavy with blood. And still above me, above us, Aleksey stood. Bladed, suited, bloody and murderous.

"Finish it," I hissed. "Shouldn't you just finish it?"

The skin around his eyes was white. "I didn't mean to," he whispered. "Not him."

"Only me." And suddenly it wasn't enough to lie here waiting for death. Because Lad had, Lad had–

The suit was moving again, I could feel its pressure, its pulling. But the thrill was muted, the need weak. Beneath the weight of Lad's death, such things were meaningless. And Aleksey had torn so much of it from me – suit, silver, debris – that it simply could not rise up and take over its fragile flesh host. Part of me wanted to give in to it, to let it coat me in that emotionless, invulnerable shell. Because the suit did not grieve, the suit did not understand loss or self-loathing. Beneath it, I would not have to listen to Kichlan, to what I had done to him. But I was not a weapon, not of any kind, not for anyone. I was Tan.

I closed my eyes, bent my head a little. "Heal me," I whispered to something deep inside, to the struggling ruins of a presence. "Hurry, or he will kill us." The suit had to obey.

I screamed as it knitted the wound in my back, as feeling rushed down my hips and legs and my entire body flared with pain. But I could move again.

"You have not completed your test!" the puppet men cried, and it seemed they had discovered emotion. Was I that terrifying, as I laboured onto weak legs, covered in blood? I couldn't imagine so.

Aleksey jolted at the panic in their voice. He focused on me, and flicked the blood away. "Yes," he whispered. "The test." But his voice quavered and he did not attack.

Behind me, Kichlan's screams had dissolved into sobbing, wracking cries.

How much of the suit's strength had Aleksey torn away? Enough, perhaps, to allow me to regain control, but what good would I be against him now? Aleksey was still an enforcer, and he not only knew how to fight while I was struggling simply remain upright, but he was stronger than me. Far stronger.

He crouched, stalked tentatively forward. I stepped back – how it hurt – away from Kichlan and Lad. "Get them out of the way," I hissed, to whoever listened and cared. "Move them!"

Mizra and Volski broke from behind the vats. I caught a glimpse of Mizra's face, red and wet with weeping, then they were struggling to convince Kichlan to stand, to carry his brother's body to the negligible safety of the vats. Kichlan fought them, and Uzdal ran to their aid, then Sofia was there, and between them all they got Kichlan standing, Lad in his arms, half-dragging his precious broken cargo. I continued to draw Aleksey away. He was fixed on my face, almost as though he could not stand to watch the damage he had done.

I could not defeat him. I knew that with utter certainty. In fact, it was ridiculous to try. Even if I had the skills to fight him off, to knock him down, I could do nothing against the suit he wore. Or the suit, perhaps, that rode him.

Was this even Aleksey I was facing? The man who had collected with us, who had helped us flee the Mob, with his easy smile and the rueful way he rubbed the scar on his nose? Or was he more suit than human, just like I had been? Pushed to the side, carried on a body that was no longer his, unable to stop what was happening.

Could I really fight someone like that? I understood what it meant to have the suit infuse your body and take it as its own. He was just like me, here through an accident of fate and the machinations of the puppet men.

Not that any of this helped me.

Aleksey's blades grew. He ran at me, slashed widely. I lifted a thin shield and rolled, pressing against the floor with my suit to fling myself away.

He scowled, turned his head to watch me and did not hurry to follow. After all, where was I going to go? And we all knew how this was going to end.

"Tanyana!" Zecholas shouted. "Step back!"

I flung myself backwards as the ground rocked. Great pillars of stone shot up from the cement, violently jagged and cruelly sharp, they speared at Aleksey.

"Yes!" Volski cried.

But Aleksey simply held out a hand. As the stone rammed into him it shattered, and fell like sand around the strength of his suit.

"What?"

And he turned toward them.

"No!" I grabbed a loose rock from the littered remnants of Zecholas's powerful binding, and threw it at Alseksey's head. It crumbled on him. He did not even seem to feel it. "I'm the test, right? I'm the one you want to fight!"

He paused.

"My lady?" Zecholas dropped to his knees.

"It won't work," I called to them as Aleksey returned his regard to me. "Nothing is stronger than the suit. Nothing pion made, not even debris." Not even debris twisted into a manic weapon capable of incapacitating an entire city. The puppet men had seen to that. The only thing strong enough to fight a suit was another suit. And the only way I could weaken him would be to absorb his suit into mine.

But how long could I maintain control over my own body if I did that?

Death was better, wasn't it, than a kind of half-existence lost somewhere in my own head? But then I thought of Lad, of his confusion and fear as Aleksey's blades slid into him, and I wasn't so sure.

"Fight then!" Aleksey tensed. The suit around his legs began to move, ripple and bunch like muscle. "Complete the test!" He jumped, and his suit sent him so high, so fast, that I could not move in time and he crashed into me. We fell onto rubble, each rock bruising and cutting. As the suit rushed to slide back over my soft and useless flesh, I realised this wouldn't last very long.

"Pathetic." Aleksey punched down, I caught his fist with both hands. Our suits clashed, metal to metal.

Tanyana.

Aleksey did not pause. He had not heard that voice, dim and impossible in this world of light, and yet, right beside my ear.

Come back to me.

I twisted his arm, slid to the side as he toppled, pushed myself to my feet. It was impossible. Only with my head encased in the suit, or holding debris in silver hands, had I been able to hear the Keeper. I spun, staring wildly for something, anything that might explain it.

Please.

Aleksey rolled and stood slowly, watching me wearily.

I released the locks on the suit at my neck and allowed it to smother me. The Keeper knelt where the rubble was, his face streaked with black, skin so transparent he hardly seemed to exist. He lifted a hand; it fluttered like cloth in the wind. I bent to help him up and to my absolute horror he passed through me.

"My Half," was all he said. His voice was as full of grief

as Kichlan's, and flipped something over inside me. Grief. I wished I could sit here and bury my face in my hands and cry and cry until I was empty.

"Lad," I whispered.

"What are you doing?" Aleksey circled us. "Who are you talking to? The Keeper, is that it? Is he here?"

"Ignore it!" The puppet men commanded. "Complete your test."

Aleksey stilled. He pressed a hand to the side of his head. "Yes, of course."

Behind him, the door that curved around a vat full of debris shuddered on its hinges. And I realised there was, in fact, a way to defeat Aleksey. If I dared to try.

"Enough." He rolled his shoulders, shook his head. "Enough. I will end this."

But I could not do it alone.

I grabbed the Keeper – it took three attempts to find something solid – and hauled him to his feet.

Blades and implacable silver, Aleksey advanced. No threats, no grand theatrics or aerobic feats this time. Nothing but his sharpness and the steady tread of his feet.

"Slow him down," I whispered to the Keeper.

He blinked at me. His flickering eyelids were a thin and ghostly haze. "Slow?"

"He is debris, like I am debris. We are both part of you. Surely, you can affect him, alter him, control him, even in some small way! So do what I ask for once and slow him down!"

"I–"

But the Keeper was not the only one who heard me. "Yes, my lady!" Volski, his cry so distant, like an echo or a memory. And then the earth was rocking again, and I could hear crashing and someone screaming, although all I saw was black.

Aleksey stopped in his tracks and was knocked to the side. As I watched, he lifted an arm and buried his blade in something. He began sawing away.

"Your binder has collapsed the ceiling." The Keeper glanced around him. I wished I could see, I wished the debris and the suit hadn't dragged me so deeply into this world of darkness and doors.

"It will not hold the enforcer for long." He ran a transparent hand over his face and smeared his tears. "And it has damaged one of the vats."

I nodded. "Good. If any debris escapes, take it. Take whatever you can. Then help me."

The Keeper disappeared. I struggled to the closest door. Rubble I could not see tripped me up, something knocked then seemed to slip through my head – I tried not to think what that meant. As I came to the door Aleksey freed himself. He stood, shook, spotted me and continued his advance.

"Get back!" I cried.

He shook his head. "I do not have that choice."

But my words were not for him. "Get back, get as far as you can. Now!" I hoped my circle, my collecting teams, and the Unbound could hear. I hoped they did what they were told.

I turned my back on the advancing enforcer. I stared at the door, at its handle, at its slight and almost imperceptible shaking. Like every door in this city, it was weakening. I hoped it was weak enough.

I grabbed the handle. My hand passed right through it. Again, I tried. Again, I could not touch it. Aleksey was closing, his footsteps echoed. Maybe I was not enough suit, not enough debris, to touch the doors. Not any more. Still, I tried.

The Keeper reappeared beside me. "What are you doing?" He hissed, and was more solid, his skin white where it had been transparent, his debris pulse firmer though still visible in his veins.

"This is the only way." I remembered how that emptiness had wound itself into my suit, how it had torn metal from my body and tried to draw it back through the door.

What else could defeat one of the puppet men's suit-weapons, their creatures of debris and bone, if not nothingness itself?

"No." But the Keeper did not sound sure of himself.

"It's the only–"

Then Aleksey stabbed me again, high, so his blades plunged through my chest to emerge terribly bloodless on the other side.

And as his suit sunk into mine, into flesh and bone and silver, we took from him what strength we needed. We drew him in deeper, and I grabbed the door's handle, turned it, and pulled it wide open.

"Help me," I gasped to the Keeper, where he stood staring at the open door with his horrors for eyes, his death mask of a face. Moving hurt, breathing hurt, and all through me was a sense of wrong – the wrongness of Aleksey's blades inside me, the struggle between our suits being fought out in my body.

Emptiness spread through the open door. It rushed over me like a scathing wind, like ice and heat and sand and fire, and I did not know how long I could stand in its storm before I too collapsed into dust.

I called to the Keeper, "Help me!" And he wrapped his pale hands around Aleksey's shoulders, and I gripped the blades that protruded from my chest and together we spun. Stunned by the open door, rocking with the battle playing out beneath our skin, Aleksey did not fight us. Only when he felt the rush of nothingness on his own back, only when his suit began to ripple and retreat did he tense and struggle. But the Keeper grabbed my wrists and pulled me free of Aleksey's long knives.

I cried out weakly, and slumped against the Keeper's pale body. Blood and silver fought over the wounds in my chest. He held me upright, and I lifted my head to see Aleksey, frozen in the black curve of the open doorway.

Black? It wasn't black. Behind him, there was nothing. Emptiness beyond colour, beyond my understanding. And Aleksey wavered in front of it. His suit rippled like grains, like tidal shifting sands, and retreated to its five bands so quickly he stumbled with the force of their movement. He tried to step forward; his leg collapsed beneath him, and disintegrated into something like bloodied dirt littered with flecks of chrome.

He reminded me of the Hon Ji half, and I, at least, had showed her enough mercy to end her suffering quickly. I had not sent her to death by undoing.

Aleksey teetered, fell to the side. His arm dissolved where he landed, his shoulders sank and caved in. He stared at me with that same look of utter confusion and emptiness that I had seen on Lad's face as he died.

"Tanyana?" he whispered. The wires in the mess that had once been his wrists, his ankles, waist and now his neck, fell to sand, to countless tiny specks like stars, and the emptiness whisked them away in a flurry of sparking wind. "I– I'm sorry."

Then the emptiness took Aleksey's body and scattered him too.

"The door, hurry!" The Keeper pushed me upright. I didn't have the strength to fight him as he placed my hands on the wood, hands no longer wrapped in silver; my suit was a coward. Together we pushed. The door shuddered to stay open, the wind wrestled with us in turn. But slowly, too slowly, the door closed.

At that last moment, before the door clicked and the lock snapped and we both collapsed, breathless to the dark floor, I saw something in the darkness. Impossible, I knew, because there was nothing on the other side of those doors; a dangerous, ravenous nothing. But still, I saw flickers of light, like the breeze-swirled remnants of Aleksey's suit, unsteady at first, then blazing into something strong. Stars grouped close together and connected in a tight, curving formation, in dozens of colours from suit-light blue to a dark, warning red. It made no sense, because nothingness did not have a colour and nothingness did not glow. And it did not howl like distant wind or crash like distant waves. And it certainly did not smell like smoke, like gas, like the heady energy of pions.

Together the Keeper and I closed the door on such impossibilities, these figments of my unstable imagination, conjured up by a mind fighting to stay alive.

"Thank you," I breathed out the words.

Lying beside me, the Keeper shook his head. "Every time we do this, we lose a piece of this world. How many scars do you think it can handle?"

How many scars could anyone handle? Too many, I thought, too many to still live.

The exhausted suit retracted sluggishly from my face. Darkness and doors were replaced by the ruin of the basement. Great fissures in the concrete and broken protrusions of stone were all that remained of Zecholas's valiant binding. Half the ceiling had collapsed; I could see hand-shaped scars on the concrete where Aleksey had clawed his way out.

Then faces lurched into view and Sofia was pressing something against my chest – something soaked in blood – and crying and screaming, but I could not hear her. All I could hear was laughter, unnatural, inhuman, manic yet mechanical, echoing over and over in my head.

I knew I should be dead. Aleksey had stabbed me somewhere in my spine, and twice in the chest. I had to fight to breathe around the liquid in my lungs. Yet somehow, I lay there, watching Volski take the bloodied cloth from Sofia while Zecholas peeled away my jacket and shirt, but baulked at the tight uniform beneath them.

"No," he mouthed. Or spoke; yet still I could not hear.

I knew what he must be seeing, what sent him so pale. But even so, I levered myself up and stared down at my chest. Two silver gashes tore their red-edged and puckering way through the dark uniform and into my skin. One above my right breast, the left just below. How much of my blood was suit-tinged now, with each unnatural pulse of a heart that should not beat?

"My lady?" Volski supported my head and shoulders, he helped me sit up, while Zecholas covered me again with my clothes. "How?"

Bent over, I coughed and spat out blood until my

throat was raw. I hurt. Chest, back – everywhere. The suit was weak, its healing slow. "How am I alive?" I could hardly speak.

They helped me stand. Volski beneath one arm, Mizra the other. Sofia wept, and Uzdal shook. I couldn't see Natasha, Fedor, any of the others. Kichlan. Or Lad's body.

Still standing on the platform, raised above the chaos in the basement, the puppet men laughed. They tipped heads back at an impossible angle, opened their mouths so wide I thought their faces would split in two, and clapped while they roared without humour, without merriment, without any real emotion.

"Because of what I am." I spat more blood to the floor. It swam, thick with living specs of silver. "What they made me into."

The laughter stopped suddenly, like a switch had been flicked. Eyes fixed on me. They still grinned so widely. "You continue to amaze us." I couldn't tell which of them was speaking.

I wished I could stand on my own feet, I wished I could have been strong before them and had not needed to rely on the support of my debris collectors and pion-binders both. As it was, I scowled at them and knew that was the best I could manage. "You toy with us, you play with us like dolls."

"Oh no, never dolls." A spate of whispering, and I had the strangest sensation that they were insulted by the re-mark. "A prized sword, polished and sharpened, that is what you are. Named, even, and blessed, inscribed. Whatever ceremonies were once performed."

I did not understand them. My stomach rolled and for a brief and terrifying moment I wondered what had happened to the child within me when Aleksey's blade plunged into my lower back. How far had it gone in? And could this body – little more than death and metal now – even support a life other than its own?

I pushed both thoughts aside. Aleksey dissolving. My unborn child struggling.

Lad, dying.

No, I focused on the puppet men and tried for strength. "I came here to kill you."

They paused. The muttering ceased.

"You threw your best weapon at me–"

"Second best, Miss Vladha," one of them whispered.

"–and yet still I stand. You should run, flee. While you can." But I was all too aware of just how weak I was in my half-dead suit, they could do anything to me and I would not be able to fight back. Not yet. Not until we healed.

Zecholas stepped forward, his fists tight. "Get out of here," he grated over the words. "Or we will see how strong you are without your weapon."

Volski passed my arm over to Uzdal's shoulders and stood beside Zecholas. "Leave." His voice, so quiet, so darkly furious and grieving, sent shivers through me. I hated that he sounded like that, that I had given him such pain, by drawing him back into my life. "And don't come back for her."

Collectively – it was still difficult to tell how many of them there were – the puppet men tipped their heads to the side. Their false and stitched-in grins slid to something smaller, sly. "The sword does not turn on the arm that wields it." A group nod. "But a misused blade is blunt and weak. Return to your sheath, little sword. Apply the oil and sharpen. See how long it takes before you are begging to be drawn." Even as they spoke the puppet men grew hazy. They did not leave through the door behind them, but seemed to turn into mist, and I blinked because something had to be wrong with my eyes, and they were gone.

Sofia moaned. "What are they?"

I shook my head. They were mad, they were impossible, they were like darkness to the Keeper's own broken light. But I was too exhausted, too stunned and aching to know the answer. All I wanted was to close my eyes and wish the basement and everything that had happened within it far away.

"We need help over here!" someone called from the rubble. Volski and Zecholas hurried over, with Sofia close behind. Uzdal and Mizra helped me follow at a much slower pace.

At least one of the vats had been breached. Debris blobbed and floated from a crack where a chunk of ceiling had crashed down on top of it. The basement around it was a ruin: shards of concrete speared up from the floor, water streamed down from a burst pipe, and lights flickered fitfully with the interrupted pion flow.

Fedor and a handful of his Unbound wandered the basement. In the guttering lights and cement-dust cloud the vats seemed to stretch out like trunks of a looming, colourless forest. Blood trickled from a cut in Fedor's forehead, his face was smeared with dust and bruising. He cradled a wrist against his chest.

Zecholas hissed as Volski, visibly shaken, turned his face away. "We did not mean to hurt you! We were trying to destroy that... That thing. I did not mean..." His words faded into helpless silence.

Fedor did not acknowledge him. He just stared at me in horror, skin pale beneath his injuries and dirt. "What happened?" He choked and coughed over the words. "What did you do to Aleksey?"

I couldn't answer. I couldn't even stand.

Volski and Zecholas began putting the basement back together, even though it was a battle for them with the loose debris tangling their bonds, and the residue emptiness from an open door scaring their pions away. The floor Volski and Zecholas remade was lumpy, the cracks and stitching visible, and the ceiling they fixed sagged. They could do nothing for the broken vat.

Their work was slow, and the Unbound aided with their bare hands – lifting rock away before Volski and Zecholas drew it back into the architecture. Not everyone had escaped the rubble with little more than blood and bruising.

Fedor found Yicor's body. The old man lay crumpled beneath a jagged slab of ceiling, pinned to the side of the vat. Fedor wept as his Unbound took the stone away, and Zecholas spread it messily back into the ceiling.

Three more of the Unbound were trapped by rubble. Yan had been hit by a lump of concrete that had ricocheted from Aleksey's upraised hand. He had bled to death. Anna had been crushed when she had tried to help him. The third was alive, Egor, a man almost as old as Yicor, though trapped. I did not stay to watch the Unbound free him.

"Kichlan," I managed with a groan. "Please."

Mirza and Uzdal, transfixed by the scene, hesitated. Then they carried me around the vats, deeper into the basement.

Kichlan lay beside his younger brother's body, on the hard, cold floor. Natasha knelt beside them. In the weakened light it was difficult to see Lad's blood, or the wounds that had killed him; wounds so like my own. He could have been asleep.

"Tanyana." Natasha stared at me in disbelief, still bloodied and bruised by what I had done to her but apparently more mobile than I. "What happened to you?"

I shook my head. What was there to say? "Down."

Uzdal and Mizra helped me to the ground. I managed to prop myself against the vat and find Lad's hand.

He was still warm. I took that hand and pressed it against my cheek. But he didn't move, didn't crush my fingers with his unconscious strength, didn't whisper a strange abbreviation of my name.

Beside him, Kichlan shifted. He sat, fitful light flickering shadows and stark colour over his face. His eyes were empty, his face wet and smeared with blood.

"I–" There was nothing I could say. Sorry? What did I think that could do? Would it bring Kichlan's brother back? Would it change the past, so I'd never made my way into their lives?

Lad had died for me. I knew it, Kichlan knew it. We could never be the same.

Kichlan held Lad's other hand. Together, we hunched in the darkness of the debris vats as cement dust settled over us, as the Unbound treated their injuries, while debris collectors wept and pion-binders did what they could to rebuild this place, and we held his hands. We would not leave him here alone.

14.

"My lady?" Volski, so close to my ear I could feel the warmth of his breath. "My lady, you should wake. We must leave."

Wake? Surely, I could not have slept. Coughing, I struggled to move, to unwind folded legs and straighten a crooked back. Someone touched something cool and preciously liquid to my lips and I drank, and I wondered who had thought to bring water.

I glanced around. They were all watching me. Fedor standing, arms crossed. Zecholas and Volski hovering and concerned; Sofia standing behind Natasha, who crouched on the floor, with Uzdal and Mizra like a guard on either side. The half-dozen Unbound I did not know waited in a loose group, some pacing, some curled or hunched on the ground.

Kichlan had left me by the vats. He knelt before four bodies wrapped tightly in colourless cloth. Judging from the missing jackets and scarfs, Volski or Zecholas had patched the shrouds together with the few pions they could find to help them.

My throat was raw and my head pounding. I leaned on the vat for balance and pushed myself to my feet.

Mizra leapt forward. "Say something before you do that! Let us help—"

But I didn't need it. Oh, I was weak. I shook so hard I could barely control my arms. Numbness and tingling travelled through me with equal vigour, and the newly cut scars in my back and my chest pained me. But I was healing. Somehow, I was healing.

Fedor spat, and looked away from me. "Look at her. Stabbed, crushed, yet she stands, yet she moves."

I didn't blame him.

"We need to get out of here," Volski made to take my arm. Shuffling, pathetic, I moved away from the vat before he could touch me.

"I've lost track of the bells," Mizra said, as he and Sofia helped Natasha her feet. "It could well be dawn. Either way, I don't want to know how many Mob are waiting for us outside."

"We aren't going that way," Zecholas said. Despite the battle, despite the basement repairs and the exhaustion I could see in his unsteady hands as they grasped for pions, Volski was building us another way out. A set of stairs, leading from one of the basement walls, beneath the streets above us, to open up in the lower floor of a run-down building two blocks away.

I had thought, once, that I created miracles from the centre of my architect's circle of nine. But nothing we had once done, no majestic building or symbolic statue, was as grand as what the two traumatised points of my circle were doing now.

"I'm sorry," I croaked. Wasn't there any more water? "I should not have slept."

"I don't think you had much of a choice." Kichlan

stood with a low grunt. He wobbled for a moment, head bent as he stared at the wrapped body of his brother – easy to identify, by far the largest of the four – then he turned his empty eyes on me. "Even you, even that thing inside you, could not have recovered from that fight with Aleksey so quickly."

I wavered, and he grabbed my shoulder. Not that he was much steadier than me. "Careful, Tan."

And suddenly, I could cry. And Kichlan was holding me, and we were weeping together. I was dimly aware of Fedor organising people to carry the bodies, while Mizra convinced Volski and Zecholas to let Kichlan and I be. I cried onto Kichlan's shoulder. Because I would never hold Lad's hand again. Because I would tell him no more stories, or eat his apple pie or allow myself to be swept up in that energy, and that smile.

We wept. Because Lad was gone.

I'm sorry. Please, tell him. I am so sorry.

I swallowed on a tear-thickened throat, and leaned away. "Why can I hear you?" I whispered.

"What?" Kichlan said, but I silenced him with dirty fingers on his lips.

I held his confused gaze. "The Keeper says he is sorry. So sorry."

Kichlan's dark brown eyes turned distant, for a moment. "I used to be so angry with him, I used to think he would be the end of L– my brother. Turns out he didn't need outside interference to place himself in death's path. He made that decision on his own."

Or it was my fault. All a matter of interpretation.

Unblinking, I held his gaze in silence.

"Wait." He stepped from the circle of our broken

embrace and smeared the crimson on his lips with his own, bloodier hand. "You can hear him? But, you're not–" he waved his hand over me in a terribly dismissive gesture.

"Exactly. So, why can I hear you?"

Nothing.

Ignoring Fedor as he fidgeted, his gestures overstated and his shuffling feet loud, I closed my eyes and released a long breath. I had not imagined that voice. I was not as broken as all that.

–only sometimes.

"There you are," I breathed.

I don't understand, Tanyana. There is so much of me inside you now, maybe that is why. But you and I have been connected for so long, and you have heard me before, you must remember that. Even so, I think this is different.

So much of him, in me? The suit was debris, yes, but debris twisted and mutilated and used. Was that really him? And if I was so much of him, then what would that make me?

If I did not know better I would say you were a Half. You are not, Tanyana. Halves cannot be made, they must be born. But I feel you, so close to me. I feel the debris in your veins.

The debris.

I opened my eyes and looked back over the vats. After everything it had cost us to come here, were we really going to leave without doing what we could to give strength to the Keeper, to make him whole or heal some of his scars?

"Tanyana?" Fedor, exasperated, had ordered his Unbound to leave. "You are delaying us."

Kichlan escorted his brother's body through Volski and Zecholas's path, and did not look back. Sofia and Natasha followed. Fedor muttered something and left the basement.

Only Mizra, Uzdal, Volski and Zecholas remained. And the Keeper.

Lad would have stayed with me. He would have understood what needed to be done, and none of his collecting team would have left without him.

To Mizra's shocked cry and Uzdal's spitting curse, I released the bonds on the suit at my neck and wrists and allowed it to coat my face and hands. It did not tug for freedom, it did not demand strength. A tool, a limb, it did as I commanded.

How long would that last?

The Keeper stood before me. His tears still flowed though he did not quiver or sob. "You should go with them," he said. "Be with him. The Half, Lad. He would not want to be alone."

I nodded. "I will. But first, I will do what I can to help you."

I approached the closest vat, the one that had been broken when the ceiling caved in. Its door had shrunk, and it did not strain at its hinges and locks. The result, no doubt, of the debris the Keeper had consumed. "Be ready."

Lifting a suited fist, I withdrew the mask from my eyes and plunged my hand through the vat. I did not try to bond with it – silver to silver – not this time. Two more sharp blows, faster than I should have been able to move, and the vat cracked open. Debris bubbled from the fissure like blood from broken skin.

Ah! Thank you.

Vat to vat, I broke them open, no need for delicacy, surely, or for subtlety now, and released fat and floating grains of dark debris into the air. Strange to say, but they looked healthy. No straining, fierce planes driving them, no twisted humanoid form or murderous, implacable snakes, this was debris. Clean, normal, like I had first seen as I fell from Grandeur's palm, before I even knew what it was.

The vats squealed alarm with every shell I broke. Their cries echoed harsh and painful from the close basement walls. Until Mizra pried a chunk of loose concrete from the ill-made floor and smashed each dial, each glass tube, each flashing red light, and silenced them.

"They're too loud," he snapped into the ear-ringing silence when he was done, and threw the chunk of rubble down hard.

"Thank you," I said.

He ignored me.

With all the vats split and silenced, I suited my face again. The Keeper stood, arms outstretched, head tipped back, while the debris flowed into him like water to a pond. It eased into his body through his very skin, and with piece he grew more solid – his skin white, his pulse hidden – and the doors faded, until there was nothing left but darkness, and random fragments of loose debris, and the Keeper.

"Thank you," he gasped. "This feels – I can't say, I can't really describe – but I am real again."

"Then that is something." Not justification for Lad's death, because nothing was worth that, but something.

"You should go." The Keeper looked at me for a moment. His black eyes were so rich, I thought I saw stars in their depths. "Be with him. Be with them both."

"Yes." Kichlan needed me. I needed to be with him.

As I turned, as I began to withdraw my suit, I noticed a stray grain floating aimlessly past my legs. I bent, gripped it with my suited fingers and went to add it to the stream of similar grains rushing to fill the Keeper. But it wiggled in my grip for merely a moment, hardly long enough for me to straighten, before sinking into my silver and being absorbed into the suit.

I blinked down at my empty hand, rubbing fingers against each other. They were not dirty. There was, in fact, no evidence that the grain had existed at all. I decided I had imagined it, until I felt the debris – a solid, distinct lump – continue its merry way up through my arm, beyond my shoulder, to settle at the growing scars on my chest. It sent quivers through me, a joy so unlike the suit's bloodthirst. In the wake of the debris I felt pure, clean, like I had just drunk deeply of clear water.

A glance over my shoulder and the Keeper had tipped his head back again, his eyes closed. He had not noticed.

I withdrew the suit from my face and hands. Then I followed Mizra and Uzdal out of the basement. Volski and Zecholas came last, sealing the path behind us.

We could not keep Lad's body in the subterranean street with us. I understood that, I knew the reasons, but watching Eugeny and Fedor try to convince Kichlan to give his brother up still made me feel sick. I felt some of his desperate need to hold Lad close, as close as possible, and not let strangers take him away. Even in death, Kichlan protected his brother.

When Eugeny rejoined us he had become a different man. Older in a way that made him thin, his skin like paper and eyes watery, not entirely focused, weak to the point where he was unable to descend the ladder on his own, and shuffled as he walked.

He took my hands, bent his face over them. "He was a good boy," he mumbled, voice hoarse. "I told you, he cared for you. He loved fully, our Lad did. He loved with everything he was." His mouth sounded wet, strangely toothless. So much less than the Eugeny I knew. He was not carrying his pipe, either.

Valya had accompanied Eugeny. She did not stoop, she did not weep. She sat, instead, by Yicor's form, so still she could have been a Keeper statue herself, and stared at him; silent and utterly alone.

And when Valya had done her sitting and Eugeny his weeping, then talk turned to removal, to burial.

"We need to do the best we can," Fedor said. "To say goodbye." His face was ashen, he watched Eugeny with the same disquiet I felt. "Lad was a Half. He deserves a Half's farewell."

A few curious faces looked up at that. Most of the Unbound had returned to the surface, they did not feel in any danger from a veche hunting collectors and spies. But those closest to the dead remained. The mourning remnants of the debris collecting teams could not leave. Nor my pion-binders, uncertain whether they still had a circle outside. We all hid in the domed building for two days, or what felt close to it, for it was impossible to know without the movement of the sun or the chiming of the bells.

"What's a Half's farewell?" Mizra asked, his voice raw, his eyes red.

"They who served the Keeper should be honoured when they die." Fedor cleared his throat. "There are old ways, Unbound ways, to bury a Half. I have read some of them. I think we should perform them, as best we can. For him."

Kichlan was sitting on the floor beside his brother's body. For a long moment, he did nothing. Then slowly, he looked up at Fedor. "Lad was a good Half," he whispered. "And he was proud of that. He tried hard, very hard. I think," he glanced at me, "I think he would have wanted to leave us like a true Half would."

I closed my eyes. What else could we give Lad on this final journey? We could not walk into the regional veche registry to organise a proper farewell and a plot of earth beside his father and his mother beyond the city walls. Perhaps that was part of why Kichlan agreed. Because he could not give Lad what he deserved, not even rosemary for his grave.

First, they built him a coffin. It would not be a real one, because he could not be buried here with us. Really, it was nothing more than a poor attempt to recreate an ancient ritual we did not fully understand. The coffin was rough, just a ragged pile of the quartz-like stones scattered on the street, but Fedor would not allow Volski or Zecholas to help. It had to be done with hands, not pions. I supposed that was only fair.

The real ones were beautiful, the Keeper murmured soft commentary in my ear. *Carved out of large slabs of precious stone, covered with symbols and words and designs. They shone like they were full of stars. So pretty. Of course, not functional, but it's all symbolic, isn't it?. Just like this, it's the thought that counts.*

Functional? I shuddered.

The death of a Half used to send whole towns, or cities, into mourning. Once the Half was laid in their coffin, and as they were readied for the final farewell, mourners would visit. They placed gifts around the glowing crystal. A lot of flowers. The Keeper paused. *I think Lad would have liked the flowers.*

Fedor began painting Lad's face. He used mud and ground up stone and blood to trace symbols across his cheeks, forehead and neck, similar to the ones that bobbed and shone on my suit's silver bands; the ancient language of the Unbound. None of us, let alone Fedor, knew what it meant.

This demonstrates that the Half is changing. Lad is no longer bound by the limitations of his body. He is becoming pure again, returning to his original state. The Keeper's voice took on a slightly pained tone. *I know he is doing his best, but Fedor is using all the wrong symbols. And they should not be written in mud, but silver, or gold. Something treasured. Something conductive.*

That caught me off guard. "You can read the symbols?" I whispered, careful to keep as quiet as I could.

Of course. But these are meaningless. Just snippets, really. Fragments. They do not sum up Lad, all he is, all he has done. The great sacrifice he made for us all. That is what the symbols should do. They should create him. Remake him in words and ideas.

Fedor hummed as he worked, rocking on his heels.

And here he should be chanting, not humming. Fedor should read out all he has written on Lad's skin, and the Unbound, even other Halves, can add their own words to the pattern. It should be loud enough to echo through the doors. But that's symbolic too, you know. Because sound doesn't work that way.

Finally, Fedor stood. He bowed to Lad, and faced Kichlan. "I'm sorry," he said, his voice broken. "That's all I know. We don't have much to go on, and I don't know what it means. But it's something, isn't it? It's something."

It's more than has been done for Halves in a very long time. Fedor should be proud of that. He doesn't have the tools to complete the rituals, anyway. The hubs, for example, are all inoperative, and the Halves that exist now wouldn't be able to help, even if we found them. He sighed. *My Halves weren't always like this, you know. Scared all the time, confused, and slow to understand. They once had strength you cannot imagine. They were once my voice, my helpers. But that was so long ago.*

Kichlan took Fedor's place by Lad's head. He dipped his finger into the simple paint, and traced his own patterns on his brother's skin. He shook so hard they came out as shapeless lines. "Goodbye, Lad," he whispered. "Goodbye."

It broke my heart. Instead of watching, I squeezed through the doorway and made my way to the statues draped in their shadows and time. I ran fingers around the outline of once-dark eyes, over the threaded, crystalline stone.

"What happened to the Halves?" I asked. "What changed them? Where have the powerful ones gone?"

The Keeper was silent, but I could feel his presence beside me. Finally, he said, *I don't really know. But recently, I have started to think it might be... interference. Something, or someone, is blocking them as they are sent to me. Scrambling them, so when they arrive they aren't quite right. Not quite whole. This weakens me, you see.*

And who did we know was intent on weakening the Keeper? "The puppet men?" I breathed the words.

But if that is true, then it has been happening for a long time. How could they have been doing this to me, and I didn't know? Am I really that useless?

Long enough for Halves, and the Keeper himself, to slip out of memory and into myth. Surely, then, it wasn't possible. I swallowed. "Just before before Aleksey killed Lad, they called him something strange. A word I didn't understand."

Programmer.

"Yes! What is that? What did they mean?"

"Who are you talking to?" Volski said, behind me.

I jumped, and turned. I hadn't heard him follow. "The

Keeper." I patted the statue, and he lifted his eyebrows at me.

"So, that's what the Keeper looks like, is it? " He leaned forward, squinting to see in the low light. "Not much left. Do you want me to…?" He flicked his fingers in a light gesture that somehow, I understood. We had been bonded in our circle, hadn't we? And still weren't so far apart.

I shook my head. "No. This was made by the hands and tools and sweat of the Unbound, in Movoc-under-Keeper before the revolution. No manipulated pions should ever shape it."

"Understood." So he traced what remained of the statue's shape and form with his fingers alone. "You should be in there," he whispered.

Guilt trickled through me. "I can't."

"But Kichlan, he–"

"Don't say he needs me, Volski. Don't even think it." I leaned against the cold touch of the stone. "He needs his brother. Do you think I can stand there in his place?"

"You are not a substitute for Lad, you never were. Not to Kichlan."

He did not understand. "Lad died trying to protect me. So what do you think I could possibly say now to make up for that? What could I possibly do?"

A pause. I hoped he was about to leave me be.

But Volski grabbed my wrist and pulled me from the shadow and the chill. He glared at me, eyes brimming with a furious kind of tears I'd never thought I'd see from him. "You are an idiot."

I blinked, too shocked to pull away.

"You are still my lady, you always will be. And I will

JO ANDERTON 369

follow you, even when disaster strikes in your wake. But you are an idiot."

"You–"

"Quiet." He growled the word. He actually growled. "Don't hide behind guilt you do not deserve, don't bandage this pain with self-loathing and blame. Kichlan does not need his brother now. His brother is dead. Did you hear that? Dead."

I tugged away and Volski released me. But his eyes arrested me.

"So he needs you, Tanyana. Like he's needed you since I've met him, though you're so thick or stubborn or just plain stupid, you don't see it. Or you don't want to, maybe. As if I could ever understand you." He crossed his arms and bit his lip to hold back tears. "So you just go over there and be with him, because he needs that right now. He might not know it himself – he's almost as thick as you, isn't he? – but just do it."

I gaped at him. When I was his critical centre Volski would not have dared raise his voice and speak to me like that. But then I had never seen his calm veneer crack so thoroughly.

"Go!" He grabbed my shoulder and gave me a push into the street, just as tight groups of Unbound emerged from the domed building, carrying the bodies between them. There was no way to bury the bodies without approaching the veche so the plan, as I understood it, was to slip them into the Tear River. Let the Keeper's tears wash his dead away. The thought filled me with horror. Kichlan followed, still reaching for his brother, surely thinking the same thing.

I used Volski's momentum and broke into a run. I took

Kichlan's hand and drew him close to me. I held his wrists by my side, I pressed our chests together and laid my cheek on his shoulder. So familiar a stance now, body to body. But this time, he shook against me in grief, not desire, as he watched over the top of my head that slow and sad procession disappear into the darkness.

"I should be with him," Kichlan whispered.

I squinted, one eye pressed closed against his shirt. Volski was gone, Fedor had followed his Unbound, and the street was lit by the struggling lights of our suits alone. No longer that bright and signalling blue, Kichlan and I radiated a kind of sickly, cloud-pressed moonlight.

"He should not be alone."

I knew how he felt. It throbbed within me too: the need to watch over Lad, to guard him, to soften this ugly world for him. With him gone that need left an emptiness, a sense that something was wrong, so fundamentally wrong. Which, of course, was true. Everything was wrong without him.

"He would be scared–"

I leaned back, released his wrists, touched two fingertips to his lips, and said the last thing I wanted to say. "He is gone, Kichlan. Lad does not need us any more." I hated myself with each word. I tensed and waited for Kichlan to shove me away, to shout at me. Any of the things I so richly deserved. But for a very long moment – his short, hot breath grazing my fingers – we watched each other while the words hung between us.

Then he sagged. "I know."

I let my hand drop. His warmth travelled through my metallic patterning to lodge somewhere aching in my chest.

"But I should still be with him. I need to be there. Instead, I am here." He fixed flint-like eyes on me and I slid my gaze away. After all, it was my fault.

Fedor and his Unbound began trickling back along the street, now empty-handed. I wondered how they had got the bodies – Lad, Yicor, Yan and Anna – up the long ladder and through the trapdoor to Lev's shop. I did not really want to think about it.

Kichlan turned his back on them. I continued to look at the floor. And we remained so, long after they had squeezed their way into the crowded, airless domed building.

I needed to get out of there.

But I could not move.

Then the light from Kichlan's suit flared weak in my eyes, and I looked up to find him close to me again, brushing hair back from my forehead.

"What happened, Tan?" He breathed the words. They sent every scar on my face tingling. "When…" His hand stilled, he caught himself, and pressed on. "When Lad died. During your fight with Aleksey. What happened to you?"

I refused meet his eyes. "What has been happening to me from the beginning; I am what they made me."

He began to shake his head, but I did not give him the chance to speak his reassuring lies.

"But I was, Kichlan, so utterly their weapon. Even before Aleksey brought it out of me, I had given up. Given myself to the silver. Bargained with it, promised it battle, promised it blood if only it would help me kill the puppet men. So what do you think that makes me, if not a weapon?"

A small frown flickered over his face. "You bargained with it?"

I supposed it was too much to ask him to understand

that. "Don't you see?" I whispered. "I am alive when I should be dead, I am suit where I should be skin."

"You mean, like these?" His soft touch traced my temple, the notch in my ear, and the countless flecks across my cheeks. Day by day a little bit more of my face peeled away, as though my skin was a costume and silver my natural hue.

"No. They are nothing, they are petty, cosmetic. That is not what I mean."

"Then show me."

And demonstrate just how thoroughly I had lied to him? "I–"

"Show me what they have done to you, what you think you have become. What you have been hiding from me." His voice shook "Why they killed Lad."

I didn't move, not even to stop him as he removed my jacket and began, hands shaking, to unbutton the filthy woollen shirt I wore. So terribly the same as before – in the darkness and the silence – yet entirely different. And I wondered if anything would ever be the way it was in the room above Valya's house again.

He concentrated on my shirt with unnerving intensity, and I watched his eyelids and creased forehead as he worked. So I caught the moment of shock, the way his eyes widened and flickered up to meet mine, but only for an instant.

Finally, I glanced down.

He had exposed what was left of my uniform. Torn by two great rents across my chest, the tough boning splintered and hanging loose in every place Aleksey's fists or suited blades had struck me. I was surprised the garment held its shape at all; surprised it still clung to my body. What use was it now, so limp and broken?

"How–?" but Kichlan stopped himself from asking the obscenely obvious.

Was that enough to shock him? With a grim set of my mouth, I shrugged off my open shirt. I wrapped my fingers around the edge of my weakened uniform and peeled it free.

The shift I wore beneath it was in a worse state and no longer an aid to modesty. But I did not care. Because he was Kichlan, who had touched every part of me that was not suited, and because so little of me was skin any more. Was I ever truly naked, if most of me was suit?

But I stayed my fingers at the top of my pants. The old, deep scars over my belly were still my own, my secret, my dread. And Kichlan did not need to know what might have once been living beneath them, or might still be. Since Aleksey had tried to kill me, since the suit had taken me over, I did not know if the unborn child remained. I'd expected telltale signs like blood and pain to herald its death. So far, nothing. And I did not know what that meant.

Kichlan did not notice my hesitation. His face had drained, became sickly, almost fluorescent in the haunting suit light. His shaking now more pronounced, he took hold of the strips of dirty cotton shift and drew them from my shoulders.

My heavy silver scars reflected his light as Kichlan paced around me, circling. Each brush of clothing, each touch of his breath or the air he displaced with his movement, sent shivers across my skin. I glanced down at myself, because it was easier than watching his face, as pale and expressionless as the marble Keepers.

The scars on my chest had healed. No more red and puckered skin, just smooth, and one with my flesh. They were bigger than I remembered them. I placed a hand on the one over my heart and it filled my open palm. The metal was warm, when I moved it did not jut awkwardly into the flesh around it the way the scars on my abdomen did. These felt more a part of me, less the attack of an invading force, than was comfortable.

"They go right through you." Kichlan stood behind me and whispered. "Are you silver the whole way?"

"Yes." How could I sound so calm?

"And this is because the suit? This is what the veche has done to you?"

I nodded. "And if they had not, then I would be dead too."

He hardly seemed to be breathing. Was he thinking that it wasn't fair? If Lad had worn my suit then he too could have lived. Or was he looking at the ruin that was my body – from Grandeur's pale scars, to the filled-in surface scratches, to the great holes bright in our suit light – and realising that, perhaps, Lad was the lucky one?

That was a terrible thought.

"If Lad had not torn me away from a technician's life, with his violence and his needs, I might have been one of them. One of the technicians who worked on this suit. I might have been like Devich. Lying and manipulating, all to create this weapon. This abomination."

I shivered at the word. If I was the suit and he thought the suit was… No. I would not go down that path.

"If it had not been for Lad," I answered, instead. "Would you have become a technician in the first place?"

He had no answer to that. And it was all meaningless anyway.

I stooped, collected my woollen shirt and slipped it on, not bothering with the remnants of my uniform and shift. The material felt heavy, and strangely itchy. It had been a long time since I had worn anything but the uniform against my bare skin. "There, now you know," I turned as I buttoned the shirt. He was staring at me, his eyes unfocused, his expression distant, "what this is all about."

He blinked. "It has been doing this for a while, hasn't it? Gradually taking you over, inch by inch."

"Yes."

"Are there more?" He glanced down to my stomach, then legs. "Were you hiding them from me? That night, in the dark. Is that why you drew the curtains? Is that why you…" He couldn't finish, just lifted his hands and rubbed his palms and took a deliberate step back. "Even then, you couldn't trust me."

I said nothing, because really what was there to say?

"Why are you still here?"

I drew back, unsure. "What do you mean?"

That expressionless, statue-like look returned to him, and he crossed his arms. "You should not be here, with us. You know what they are trying to do to you, you have known for so long, and still you remain in Movoc-under-Keeper. Right where the veche can find you."

"You want me to run?" I wished for anger, or indignation, anything to push down the lump forming in my throat. "What good would that do? The national veche will find me, no matter where I go."

"They might. But you would have more of a chance to escape them if you flee than by staying in this city with us."

I couldn't believe I was hearing this. "But the Keeper, the doors! Kichlan, he needs my help."

"You said it yourself, the Keeper is broken. We should not have listened to anything he had to say."

"But Lad said–"

"Lad doesn't need you any more. Remember?"

His words left me unable to speak.

"So get out of this city. Would you rather die within its walls, or become the veche's weapon, than take a risk and leave? Tanyana, you have to get out. Leave!"

I stepped away from him, forcing my hands not to clutch, not to fidget, willing my face to be as calm and unemotional as his. "Is that what you want?"

He shook his head, let out an exasperated laugh that showed no shadow of mirth. "Do you really care about what I want? I worked so hard to show you how I felt, and just when I thought you might be listening, you might understand and you might even feel the same way, I learn you've been lying the whole time. I thought you just pushed me away, but you never even let me get that close!"

"I… No. That's not–"

"You have made it clear, Tan, how much you trust me. So save yourself while you can, and leave me in peace."

"But–"

"Can't you see? I don't want you to stay! It hurts to look at you, and remember what Lad did to save you. It hurts to look at you, and know you are keeping secrets, lying to me, that nothing we did that night was even real. So go. Make a sensible decision for once, and leave this city while you can." With that he turned, and headed back to the chamber.

Somewhere, something was dripping. A constant, pinging noise that echoed lightly from the stone and ruins. It was not a good sign. A leak from a rill or effluent above us could wind a weakening track through the stone, and bring centuries of earth down onto the street..

Why had I even remained in this city – above and beneath – for so long? Perhaps, because like every good

Varsnian, I was enslaved by my duty? The basis of the Novski revolution was more than just his circles, his amplification of pion-binding strength. It was that each binder, no matter how weak or how strong, had a role, a place in his society. From the lowest working to produce light in a factory, to architects and enforcers, each citizen of Varsnia had an obligation, a duty, to use what skills they were given in the role that best suited them.

When I lost my binding skill, my duty was to collect its refuse. And even as that role changed – to hapless experiment, to Keeper's aide, to emotionless weapon – I had tried to fulfil it. But was it really my duty, my obligation, to become the monster the puppet men wanted me to be?

Did I not have a duty to myself? To my unborn child?

I collected my jacket from the ground, and put it on. The sound of my feet joined the drip, drip, drip as I made my way to the ladder. I stared up its length. The trapdoor was closed, not that I couldn't break the lock.

Lad didn't need me any more. Had he been here he would have held my hand, he would have given me wisdom wrapped in his simple words, and squeezed his encouragement a little too hard. I could almost feel his palm, sweaty and awkward, cupping mine.

Aleksey had begged me to leave too, before I tried to fight the puppet men and forced his terrible hand. Perhaps I should have listened to him, perhaps I should have decided this for myself, long ago. Given up any hope of a life, of a purpose, and the closeness of those I loved.

It made, I supposed, its own kind of terrible sense. So I climbed the ladder, forced my way through the door, and hurried out of Lev's empty shop. I set foot again on Movoc-under-Keeper's streets, truly alone.

15.

It was a very early bell. That shocked me, a little, because I had expected to walk out into moon-tempered darkness. Instead, I breathed mist into faint sunshine and the bluish haze of dawn at the end of a frozen night. I gathered my jacket about me, buttoned and tied where I could, and shoved my fists deep into its pockets. I missed the uniform's warmth, its strangely reassuring pressure across my chest, and wished I had thought to bring a hat, scarf and gloves when I had decided to flee Movoc-under-Keeper and everything I knew.

Where should I start? I hurried down the street, feeling rudderless.

The bell was so early the lamps were still buzzing. They seemed steadier than the last time I had seen them. I supposed the debris we had given the Keeper, and the strength he took from it, was holding more of the doors at bay. How long would that last? And who would help him keep them closed, if I really left? Did he have more Halves, hidden away, to be exploited only in emergencies? What good would they be, if no one knew to listen to them?

A quick assessment of my bearings and I realised I was heading toward the Keeper's Tear River. Good. Yes, that was a start. I could escape the city walls on the back of a ferry.

Even at this hour, Movoc-under-Keeper was not empty. The sound of many marching feet stopped me. I drew back into an alleyway, pressed myself against night-cold stone, and watched. The street filled with soldiers. Strikers in white, Shielders in crimson, but more than anything, the Mob. So many I could not count them. All unnaturally tall, dressed in black leather and bristling with the handles of pion blades and projectile weapons, they marched as one. Helmeted faces straight ahead, long legs striding in perfect unison, arms tight by their sides, right hands resting on the bears-head sword pommels at their waist.

I shuddered, made to head back along the alleyway and find another way to the Tear, a way that did not involve crossing the Mob's path, when something caught my eye. At the very centre of the mass of bodies, of the solid colours surging up the street like a tricoloured tide, something shone. Pressed as I was against the alleyway wall I could not see it clearly. But it looked like two, maybe three soldiers clad not in white, not in crimson or black, but silver. Head to toe silver.

And my suit bands spun. Something tired and reduced but still very much alive in my bones, muscles and skin, yearned for those soldiers in silver. More weapons like us. I knew it, could feel it like temperature, like touch, smell it like scent. Another fight, the suit whispered, like Aleksey. But this time we would not allow ourselves to be weakened. This time – and the violent need stirred –

this time we would weaken them, we would absorb their strength and take their shine–

Gasping, I tore my gaze away from the soldiers and stumbled down the alley, drawing air deep into my lungs like icy, clearing fire. Fists clenched, I swallowed the thrill, I slowed the spinning bands, I forced the presence with its insidious needs from my mind.

Behind me, someone laughed softly. I spun. The air in the alleyway was hazy, heavy and empty, with the rising mist of sun against cold earth.

There was no one there. The marching of Striker, Shielder, Mob and silver suit rang sharp against the stone. I hurried down the alley, not looking back, not listening for voices or laughter in the haze.

Somehow I made it to the Tear River. There I waited as golden sunlight lanced from the east for a bell, at least, before a ferry came. But it was heading the wrong way. Rather than stand in the cold of the banks for another bell, or two, or three, I flashed my rublie to the ferry master and huddled in the back of the cabin for the choppy ride against the current. The ferry remained almost empty for the entire trip, and those few Movocians who did join me on board huddled just the same, wrapped in thick clothes that hid both face and form. They were fearful of the Mob stalking their streets, nervously talking of war, of enlistment, of spies and the Hon Ji. When I disembarked, my face down, I did not look so different from them, just another cold and worried citizen. I hoped that was enough to keep the Mob's curiosity at bay.

I didn't realise where I had decided to go until I stepped off the ferry and headed for Devich's house.

Devich, who had betrayed me. Devich, who I could

not trust, but whose child I might be carrying. Why was I even here? Was I such a coward that I could not turn and run without searching for someone to do it with me? Or maybe I just didn't want to be alone. Now that Lad was gone and Kichlan had turned his back on me.

Or maybe I needed to see him one more time. I needed to be certain that Natasha's rumour was only that. For Devich, who had betrayed me.

Foolishness, weakness.

Three times I walked the length of his street, from one end to the other, scanning the buildings on the shoreline, the windows darkened by curtains or shutters. No one watched me. No fingers twitched blinds open to spy. No Mob spilled primed and ready from hiding places between houses, from behind bushes flushed with spring, or out from closed doors. Three times before I decided the street was safe.

But still, somehow, not until I had climbed the few steps to Devich's house did I realise his door was broken, leaning at an unhealthy angle from twisted hinges.

Icy river wind blew through my inadequate clothing as I stared at his broken door. Holding my breath, I glanced around me. No longer an unreasonably early bell but still the street was quiet – too quiet, even for Rest. Not that I knew with any certainty what day it actually was.

Even with Mob in the streets this was hardly normal. Maybe in Darkwater a broken door would be ignored, would be just another on a rundown street. But this close to the river and the bridge? Unless Movoc-under-Keeper was growing accustomed to patches of disintegration and destruction. Or maybe no one thought to complain about the state of the buildings on their street now war had begun.

Carefully, I worked my way under the broken door, and into Devich's home.

The lights did not work. I hadn't realised just how dark his home could be. The hallway seemed to stretch far deeper than it should and anyone, or anything, could be waiting at the end. I loosened the bands on my wrists just enough to set them spinning, and went inside.

My suit's sharp light brought small pockets of the hallway into stark visibility. A three-legged console lay snapped and broken on the floor, beside the shattered corpse of a Hon Ji porcelain vase in a puddle of its own water and wilted Tear-lilies. Further on an oval mirror had fallen from its hooks on the wall, its shards scattered and reflecting my light across the hallway rug. I stepped around them carefully.

The air in Devich's house smelled old, stuffy. I could feel it like dust settling on my head and shoulders. This was strange, with the front door torn open, and the crisp river air following at my back. No dust motes floated in my suit beams. Last year's leaves from the plants out the front had been blown inside. But still, when I walked it felt like wading, the air unnaturally thick.

When I turned into the dining room I found chaos. A misfiring light buzzed within a smashed fitting on the wall. A round table had been knocked over, chairs scattered across the room in pieces. A red light blazed from the cook top, signalling a failure in the heating stream and warning that the unit should be shut down. I crossed the tiled floor, picking my way over loose pieces of wood, and bent, leaned behind the unit and poked at pion buttons I could not see. I must have touched one, as the red light flickered, the whole unit made a loud clanking noise, and shut off. How long had it sat here, shining an unheard warning, and fighting to contain the flow of potentially unstable heating pions?

Straightening, I glanced back around the room. A struggle had happened here. The mess the result of many thrashing bodies, of violence. And I had no idea what that meant.

There was no sign of Devich, so I made my slow way up the stairs.

Devich's bedroom was in even worse condition. Drawers had been torn from his dresser, their contents strewn across the bed and the floor: cufflinks, bears of service, and Devich's rublie. Pillows gutted, sheets torn, the twin mirrors on his wardrobe shattered. Antique books, had been pulled from their shelves, their leather covers slashed, thick, richly made paper torn. Utterly senseless.

I stooped, collected the rublie. Its lights flickered in an indication that it still worked, but I could not see how many kopacks resided within.

I sat on the corner of his bed in snowdrifts of cotton and feathers. Devich was gone. Was he being experimented on, right now? Had he come to me for help – in his own, useless way – back in the market square? If I had simply trusted him, believed him, taken his hand and hid him the way I did Natasha, or Lad, would he still be alive and whole?

That was the best option. Horrible as it was, horrible as I felt for wishing it was true. I rested my hands against my belly and found myself hoping that was the case.

Because the alternative… The alternative…

My hands tightened so much the rublie pressed painfully into my fingers. It made a kind of squeak, as though it feared I was about to crush it. I eased the pressure.

Who do you trust?

Alternatively, this was all one elaborate lie, just another part of the deception, an addendum to his betrayal. And as I sat there, in the detritus of his life, torn and unsure, he was manipulating me further. To what end? What more could Devich and his veche hope to do to me?

How would I ever know the truth? What I wanted to believe and what I feared to believe pulled within me like the suit tugging at my bones, and I didn't know what to do, what to think.

Except that sitting here for too long would be very foolish indeed. No matter what had happened.

I stood, and brushing the feathers from the back of my coat gave me an idea. As quickly as I could I stripped myself of my dirty, torn, stinking clothes. They disappeared among the heap of torn bedding like they did not exist, like I had not even been here. A moment's hesitation in which I told myself that I did not have to worry about what Kichlan thought of me any longer, then I removed the bottom half of my uniform too. The touch of that heavy air on my bare flesh, and the freedom of movement in my legs and waist, felt strange. I had grown so accustomed to my hardened, boned second skin.

I hunted through Devich's belongings. He was taller than me, but that would work well. The shapelessness of oversized clothes, the way I could pull myself in and hunker down in a jacket that did not fit or a hat that consumed my head, could only help me. In these, I could even hide the scars on my face. And that felt safer.

I found long woollen pants and rolled up the bottom. Without the uniform to tuck the waist into I was forced to resort to a belt. A quick jab with a sharpened suit finger made an extra hole so I could tighten the leather to fit. A singlet, a long-sleeved woollen shirt with a collar and a jacket over that, and while I couldn't move quite as easily as I would have liked, at least I was warm. Even in Devich's abandoned, unheated house. I tried his gloves; they were so big they slipped off my hands so I gave up on them. His jacket had pockets enough. A thick scarf dyed dark grey, and a leather cap that must have been tight on his head, but was padded with so much wool it stayed on mine.

I peered at myself in the fragments of his broken mirrors. Shapeless, swamped in wool. Just like I had hoped.

Then something moved below, the sound of a door being pushed open, careful footsteps on wood. It caught the breath in my throat. I ran from Devich's bedroom, near-launched myself to the railing around his stairwell and looked down into darkness and heavy air, hoping beyond what I should have hoped, heart thrumming strong against its metallic parts, that Devich would be there. Shocked, looking up at me. Then relieved, and running up the stairs to greet me. Alive, whole. Trustworthy.

But the downstairs hallway was empty, save for a kind of haze that caught like blue mist in my light. And in that light, for a brief and terrible moment, I thought I saw faces in the glass of the broken mirror. Wan skin, eyes dark, ill-fitting grins stitched on with invisible thread.

Impossible, then gone. As though I had imagined them.

It was time to leave Devich's house. I should not have returned at all.

None of his boots would fit me, so I resorted to my own, no matter how stained and torn they were. I hurried back into the street and headed again for the Tear River. Hunched in my stolen clothes I waited, another bell, maybe even two, for the next near-empty ferry. Only when I flicked my rublie to the ferry master did I realise I had taken Devich's as well.

For an instant I considered returning it. But what good would that do? Only put me at more risk than I had already put myself in. If Devich had been taken by the veche, then he certainly did not need it. If the state of his house was all an elaborate ruse, then he could rot in the Other's lowest hell without his rublie. So I kept it in my pocket and wondered if I could work out how many kopacks I had just stolen from him.

How many kopacks did it take to create a new life?

I was asking myself that question too often.

I turned my back to the Keeper's Tear Bridge, with its barricades and Shielders, as the ferry took us down river. I did not look for the domes of my gallery peeking out muted and blue among the inner-city buildings. I did not respond to the pressure at the back of my neck, the weight of impossible faces in mirror shards and the heavy, stalking haze. I watched the river. I leaned into the spray, placed feet on the first rail and tipped my head back, one hand holding Devich's hat in place.

Freedom? Was this it, a ferry ride beyond Movoc's walls? And then what? Perhaps Devich's rublie contained enough kopacks to secure a coach, or join a caravan. Or I could walk. What did I have to fear from the open skies and empty fields between townships, between cities? I doubted the suit that worked so hard to keep me alive would let me freeze to death, or fall to the dirty blade of some unhoused pauper. So, on foot to the Varsnian border – though not the border with Hon Ji – and across it. Of course, I did not know the way. The furthest I'd travelled out of Movoc-under-Keeper was a midsummer day-trip to the Weeping Lake. But surely, there were signs and surely, people to ask.

Away from the veche. From the puppet men. From Kichlan and Fedor. And Devich, if he lived, or cared.

That was freedom, wasn't it?

The river wind whipped Devich's jacket like the unfurling of leather wings. It pried at my layered, tucked, folded clothing. I stepped down, wrapped arms around myself. It was cold.

And I could fall.

I closed my eyes, risked bare fingers long enough to tug my hat down tight over my ears. Lad was not here to keep me in this city. He did not need my scant protection, my poor stories, my dubious comfort. He did not need me to warn him about falling in the Tear River, and hold his hand when I had coaxed him down from the railing.

A distant bell rang. I could not hear what it was tolling. The river carried us quickly, like Movoc's final, parting gift.

As the city's wall came into view a shiver ran through me and I felt something like a large, warm hand on my shoulder.

"I have to run," I whispered. Thankfully, the deck was empty, the wind and the spray kept most passengers at bay. "Others will die if I stay. More tests, more sacrifices. I can't do that to anyone else. I won't let that happen again." But still, the hand was heavy. Silence

and water-rush made me ache. "How can I look at Kichlan now, and know that I took you away?"

The wind whipped those words from my mouth, if
someone had been standing next to me they could not
have heard. It didn't matter.

"I brought this on you both. I should not have let you
look after me. I should not have been so vain to believe
I could look after you. I am not your brother. So how
can I stay there and look at him and know this is all my
fault? How?"

Tears traced icy patterns down my cheeks. The wind
slapped them stinging back into my eyes.

"You're right. I know. That's all a lie. I'm not leaving for
anyone else; I'm not trying to save anyone. With doors
opening and the Keeper failing, there won't be much left
here to save. I'm leaving because of me. I'm leaving because it hurts too much to look at his face and know this
is all broken – you, us – and it is all my fault!"

Through my tears the river and the boat and the cold
hard sky merged into a single mess of colour. I gripped
the slick railing and held on as I shook. As a soft voice
murmured somewhere deep inside me that I had to be
careful. That I could fall.

"Of course this won't work. I know it won't. The veche
will never leave me alone. I don't know the first thing
about fleeing the country, about surviving out there, on
the other side of that wall. Without a circle. Without a
team. But I have to do it. Don't you understand? It hurts
too much to stay."

The ferry's horn blared, rolling over me like a wave.

"It's selfish. It's weak. But I can't, I can't."

The ferry was pulling into the last dock this side of the

city walls. I smudged freezing tears across my face with hands I couldn't really feel.

The weight on my shoulder hadn't lifted. Shivering, fingers turning blue, I reached back and found warmth. Warmth that sent the blood back to my nails, warmth that started my palm tingling. Warmth I hadn't imagined.

"I'm so sorry," I whispered to an impossible, guilt-born ghost. "I'm so sorry I could not stop Aleksey. I'm sorry I couldn't save you."

The ferry bumped water-worn wood with enough force to send me stumbling. I gripped the railing again, with both hands this time. "I love you, Lad." I blinked clarity back to my vision. "And I love your brother too."

The weight lifted from my shoulders. The chill of the river wind and the empty sky settled back into my body like it had never left.

What did I think I was doing?

I rubbed thickening, aching eyes. Freedom? Was I really so desperate, or so foolish, to believe there was any such thing? Lad had needed me, and I had failed him. Kichlan needed me now whether he believed it or not, but I would probably fail him too. He was just going to have to put up with it, because it was the best I could do.

Hurry.

I ran the length of the ferry and leapt down the gangplank even as the master began to pull it up. Ignoring his protests, I hurried along Easttear, back north, against the river's current. As I did so, I unclipped my rublie and connected the crutch to Devich's. A moment, and legible lights flickered on. Fifty thousand kopacks.

Was that blood money, payment for betraying me? Or were technicians just highly paid? I unclipped his rublie,

reclipped mine. Its fifteen thousand looking paltry now.
I tucked them both into his jacket pocket. Then I stepped
in front of the first coach I saw to secure a quick, expensive trip away from the wall and back into the city. To
Lev's shop, and the ancient Movoc-under-Keeper buried
beneath it.

But I did not need to go so far.

Not all coach rides were comfortable, padded with cush-
ions and curtains, especially when the coach relied on
wheels. So I gripped the leather handle on the door, above
a dirty window, and winced with every jolt. The driver
seemed to be able to find every crack in the road, every
patch of roughened concrete, every pothole. And they all
transferred to me through poorly joined wood and rusty
iron joints.

By the time we turned from Easttear toward the
eighth Effluent I couldn't feel much below my waist and
my fingers were growing white from gripping the handle
so hard. The discomfort, at least, offered me distraction.
There were some things I was happy not to think about.
Even if it cost me splinters.

Then, through the dirty window, I saw Natasha. She
walked with a kind of exaggerated calm that caught my
attention instantly. Because nothing, surely, could look
as unnatural so soon after Lad's death as her slight smile,
her hands clasped loosely behind her back and the casual
way she stopped only to glance down alleys and through
open shop doors. I surged to my feet, fought the rocking
of the coach to knock on the wall of the driver's com-
partment. Then I kicked open the door, swung around,
hurried him through the payment process and didn't
even argue about the price. I dropped to the ground,

caught Devich's hat as it made attempt at freedom, and called to Natasha as I rushed after her.

She turned to meet me and her smile spread. She did not seem at all surprised.

"There you are," she said, as I caught my breath. "Finally."

"I–" The bruising on her face stilled me. What was she doing here, smiling so calmly at me, after what I had done to her? "I'm sorry I hurt you, Natasha." The words spilled from me. "I'm sorry I let the suit carry me away." What a weak apology.

But she simply didn't seem concerned. "I'm sure you are. There are, however, more important things to worry about now." She brushed back her stray fringe to reveal deep grazing close to her hairline. "And I've had worse."

"Yes, but–"

"Be quiet, Tanyana." She took my hand, began dragging me back the way she had come. "For once, let someone else speak."

I fell into step beside her. "Then speak."

"I offered you a way out of this city before. The chance to join us. You did not take up my offer. Now, I hope, you have a good reason to reconsider." Natasha turned a sudden corner and there, apparently waiting for us, were soldiers. Four Mob, at least. Others shifted in the shadows behind them – two Shielders and a single Striker. He was tall, too thin for his height, and bright in his white armour. His hood was pulled back to reveal eyes fused closed, the skin of his lashless lids sewn smoothly and without scarring to his pallid cheeks. Strikers could see clearly without their eyes. So closely connected to the pions were they that they could see over vast distances and in great detail through energy, through bonds and particles alone. And from far above the ground, borne on powerful currents and defended by dense bindings, they could manipulate those pions and strike.

That was what made them deadly.

I grabbed Natasha's hand, wrapped my suit around both our wrists to secure the connection between us, and slid silver across my legs. But before I could haul her to freedom, the Shielder pounced. Energy buzzed between us, not strong enough to damage my suit but enough to send a shock through both of us.

"Stop it!" Natasha cursed, tugging against me as her body spasmed while the pion-shield that had been raised between us expended its energy through her muscles. I simply gritted my teeth, allowed the suit to absorb it, and endured. No Shielder was a threat to me. The Striker, however, I was not so sure of. "Take it down, Petr. Down!"

"Down?" the Shielder asked, and only then did I realise what was going on.

I withdrew my suit connection instantly, and Natasha stumbled without my support. One of the Mob hurried to catch her.

"You cursed, lying, traitorous…" I began sharpening my suit to blades.

But the Striker stepped forward, hand uplifted. "Miss Vladha?" he whispered.

There was something wrong with his voice. A weakening of his lungs, a padding in his throat that softened him to near-silence and made him difficult to understand.

The Shielder hovered behind his Striker like an overly

concerned and brightly coloured mother bird. His crimson uniform bore no obvious reinforcements or embellishments; simple wool, cut severely around the shoulders. A dark-glass visor extended from his helmet and covered his eyes.

Natasha struggled to stand, resorted to holding the Mob's shoulder for support. "Tanyana, please. This is not what you think."

I lifted eyebrows at her. Only the fact that the Striker had not tried to wipe me from the street slowed my growing knives. In fact, he did not seem to be able to see me at all. His hand groped blind in the air a good two feet from my face, and he turned his head in a slow, strangely bird-like movement. Most of his ears were gone, reduced to small slits in the side of his head. Coupled with his shaved hair and the gauntness of his face, it made him look inhuman. Something closer to a bird, or a lizard. In fact, his armour bore an unsettling resemblance to pale scaling. The tight material was reflective, and segmented, so that it gleamed as he moved.

"What is it then?" I asked.

The Striker took a small step forward. I resisted the need to back away. "You really are here, aren't you?"

The suit, of course. I was more debris than pion now, I knew that. And to the Striker's eyes – tuned to deep pions alone – I did not exist. A good feature, I supposed, for a weapon to have.

"I told you, didn't I? What she was." Natasha finally released her hold on the Mob, and regained her balance. "My thanks, Taras."

Without withdrawing the half-formed blades I shook out my hands to loosen the knots their stalled creation had tightened into my arms. "This is not an explanation." I pointed to the Mob. He had the good grace to flinch. "The last Mob we ran into bound you, hit you, and tried to arrest you."

"Not all of us are loyal to the national veche," Taras growled. His golden, roaming eyes narrowed behind his helmet.

"Who else would you work for?"

"We work for the interests of Movoc-under-Keeper itself," the Shielder said.

I paused. "The local veche?" What good would the support of the local veche be? The national veche and the old families controlled Varsnia's wealth, her pion-binding skill, and her military. Local veche tended to co-ordinate nothing more important than the sewerage systems and street repair.

"I told you," Natasha said. "I have contacts." She nodded to her Striker, Shielder and Mob. "The local veche doesn't approve of this city and its inhabitants being used as the national veche's personal experiment, any more than you do. At least, some sections of the local veche don't."

"Some sections?"

"The veche is not as unified as you have been led to believe. Not locally, regionally or even nationally."

"Miss Vladha," the Striker said again, in his unstable voice. I wondered what the veche had done to him, to his throat and lungs, to make him sound so. We were similar, in a startling way, the Striker and I. Both mutilated into weaponry. "The local veche is not alone." He gestured toward Natasha. "You know we work with the Hon Ji. With the Emperor himself."

"So I've heard," I answered. Immediately, the Striker turned toward the sound of my voice. His eyeless gaze was discomforting.

"The Hon Ji armies will help us overthrow the old families. We will free Movoc-under-Keeper, all of Varsnia, from their tyranny. Miss Vladha, you would be a powerful ally. Will you help us?"

I glanced away from his stretched, smooth skin.

"The first thing we would do is help you flee the city," Natasha said. "As I'm sure you have been trying to do yourself."

I didn't answer, but thought of the weight of an impossible hand.

"We tried to help you before," the Mob muttered. "If you had just come quietly with Barbarian and Comedian we could have saved–"

"Taras, be quiet!" Natasha snapped.

But it was enough. Thugs? I blinked a moment, considered. "Barbarian and Comedian?" I whispered. "That was you?"

"Tanyana, listen–"

"You sent those men to drag me from my home? You were behind that? You were the strange, mysterious men who would, apparently, break me?" I had always assumed the puppet men had orchestrated the removal of my studio. Just another part of my life they had decided to strip away, at will. But Natasha?

"It would have happened anyway," Taras said. "You need to pay your bills."

"It was the best way," the Striker said. "To free you from the veche. Quick, quiet, in the shadows. So much could have been avoided. If you had come to us earlier."

He gasped for air by the end of his speech, and his already sallow face blanched further.

"Stanislav," Natasha chided. "Do not push yourself."

The Striker flashed a sorry smile in my general direction. "We are designed for the air," he whispered. "And for killing. Walking, talking." Another gasp. "Are difficult."

I refused to feel sympathy. Natasha and her cronies did not deserve it. "And now you think I will help you? After what you did to me?"

Natasha nodded, a short, sharp motion. "Yes, because this offer does not extend only to yourself. Kichlan comes too."

Kichlan? My weakness, was he, now that Lad was gone?

"We offer you both safety, out of the city, away from the national veche, in exchange for your help."

"What makes you think—"

She cut across my words with a flat palm. "That's what you were trying to, wasn't it? That's why you both left the underground ruins. To run."

Ice sunk down into my belly. I did not believe, not even for a moment, that Kichlan would run.

"Kichlan did not leave with me," I whispered.

"Truly?" Natasha asked, surprised. "Then where did he go?"

I felt the brush of a phantom hand again on my shoulder.

Hurry.

I could not go with them, even if I had wanted to, not if Kichlan was missing. Natasha, I think, understood, though she did not approve.

"We have a revolution to start," she said, by way of a goodbye, and turned her back on me. She and her traitorous Mob, Shielder and Striker disappeared into the Movoc streets. They were, I had to admit, the best camouflage she could have found.

I returned to Lev's shop through backstreets and hid in what shadows I could find. The city was changing. Smaller groups of soldiers had split from the initial mass of the army. They clung like dirt around corners, at doorways, watching commuters, stopping coaches, prying and questioning. The groups were uniformly made of three Mob, one Striker. I wondered just how foolish I had been to get off that ferry and turn back into the city. To all this.

I snuck back into the shop through a window, and descended, closing the trapdoor safely behind me. Fedor glanced up as I pressed through the ruined door to the domed building.

The smell of cooped up bodies, of not enough fresh air, and – I hated myself for thinking this – the unburied dead, hit me before I'd even cleared the passageway.

Another reason not to come back.

"Where did you go?" But then he stood, and I realised Fedor was not angry. In fact, he did not seem to feel anything at all. His shoulders drooped, and his expression was empty and slack.

Sofia leapt to her feet and stared behind me. "Is Kichlan with you?" Her whole body thrummed with intensity, as though she could just will him into existence if she tried hard enough.

I did not answer, and glanced around the room. More faces. Lev; at first I didn't recognise him with his head in his hands. Valya close beside him. And Eugeny. The concentration in his eyes matched Sofia's, only he was focused on me.

I could only shake my head.

"When did he leave?" Sofia asked, voice cracking.

"It must have been after I did," I answered. "I do not know where he went."

"And where did you go? What are those clothes you're wearing?" Zecholas asked.

I said nothing.

"If you won't tell us, then it does not matter."

I glanced between them all. Zecholas's distant look, Volski tense. Fedor, empty. Eugeny, grieving. Mizra and Uzdal sitting close to each other, opposite the Unbound. Sofia still standing, still staring, still believing Kichlan would appear at any moment, her conviction sharp and clear and written all over her face. My heart hurt for her. I knew what I had done when I joined her collection team. I knew she cared for Kichlan more than, it seemed, she'd ever had the courage to tell him. Or more, at least, than he had ever noticed. But still, she had detected my pregnancy before anyone – even me. She had cared enough to take me to her healer, and not to judge, not even to hate me.

I wondered if Kichlan would have been better off if he had cared for her and not for me. Perhaps she deserved him more.

Lastly, I turned to Lev. So broken, face pressed into his palms. I could not be sure, it was hard to tell with so many faces I did not know but there did not seem to be as many Unbound as there had been. "I don't understand. What happened?"

"They took him." Lev's words were so muffled I barely understood them.

Eugeny began to weep, and Valya crossed the circular floor to hold him.

"Strikers." Lev looked up and over his shoulder at me. I drew back before I could stop myself, from the bruises, the cuts and the blood. One eye was inflamed and closed, his lip was split, knuckles grazed, his wrist purple and swollen.

Somewhere, as though from a great distance, as though through a thickening mist, I heard a faint wail. A sound of grief, or horror.

"They intercepted us. They were looking for him. They had been sent. Collectors without bands, they were told, carrying bodies through the streets."

"Him?" I whispered.

"Tore the shrouds until they found him. Knew who they were looking for. Took him away. Left the others in the street like trash, only after him. We tried to stop them. Arrested, dragged away. I grabbed Eugeny and ran. Other, I ran."

"Him?"

"Lad!" Eugeny, tears streaming. "Of course it was Lad! Those disgusting creatures sent Strikers – Strikers! – for Lad's body. Who else could we be talking about?"

I staggered, reaching for the rough wall to support me. Volski gripped my shoulder. The image of Lad's pale face, torn free of its shroud, exposed and dragged away... I had to fight not to be sick.

And Yicor, that strong, dignified old man, left in the gutter.

What could they want with Lad's body? What would they be doing to him? Kichlan–

"Did..." I could taste bile. "Did Kichlan hear this? Was he here when you returned? Did he know what happed to Lad's body?"

"We don't know," Volski murmured by my ear. "We didn't realise you were gone either, not until Lev and Eugeny returned."

None of them even mentioned Natasha. But then, she had always been so silent, hidden in shadow and apparently uncaring, that maybe they simply had not noticed her absence.

I stared at my shoes. Old, compared to Devich's trousers. Encrusted with mud, leather worn and patched. Kichlan had done that, stitched a small, miscoloured square over a hole I had torn while clambering down a rusty drain, with a careful and well-practiced hand.

Kichlan. Had he heard what had happened to Lad's body? Had he gone, then, to take his brother back?

There isn't much time.

I squeezed my eyes shut. Standing on the deck of the ferry, held by the icy Tear River wind, seemed so far away, an impossible dream.

"Tanyana?"

I glanced up. Expectant eyes watched me. "What?"

Fedor sighed. "Options. What should we do?"

I said nothing. Hard to answer when I didn't know myself.

You will need to choose.

"Where did you go, Tanyana?" Volski asked, voice low. "You wandered around up there for bells, while the veche sent Strikers for us, and yet you were unmolested."

I thought of voices in the mist, of faces leering in broken glass. Yes, I wasn't arrested or recruited or assaulted and dragged away. But I would hardly say the veche had left me alone.

I can take you to him. I feel what they are doing, I know

*their cruel touch. Do you want them to use his body as their
new vessel; do you want him to take your place in their
experiments?*

My gut clenched, fierce pain low and hard. Did I owe a
dead friend anything? A dead Half? Whatever they did,
however horrible and unfair, he was gone. I had watched
it happen. They could not hurt him anymore.

*Yes, the Half is gone. You do not need to hurry after him. He
does not need you any more.*

Just like Kichlan had said. So maybe I should have
stayed on that ferry, in that dream.

*But I was not referring to him. Lad might not need you. But
Kichlan does.*

"We have to do something," Fedor was saying. "We try
to run," his eyes flickered toward me, and radiated con-
tempt, "go out there and risk capture. Or we stay down
here, and slowly starve to death. Because there isn't
enough food hidden in Lev's shop to sustain this many
people for more than a few days. One way or the other,
we will need to go outside."

"Or, we could do neither," I said, even before I realised
I'd made my decision. But as I spoke it grew so clear, I wondered why I had not seen it before. Freedom? What was
my freedom, without him? "And save Kichlan instead."

Sofia focused on me, then, "Kichlan?"

Fedor turned a kind of dying-sun red that, when min-
gled with the faintly blue light from our suits, made him
look more purple than anything. "We could what?"

"Kichlan needs us—"

"No! Enough. We need to look after ourselves, Tanyana.
Not Kichlan, not anyone else. Not even the Keeper." Oh,
I could see how much that cost him. So much he had

believed crumbling beneath the weight of the soldiers' boots above us.

"I thought you didn't know where he was?" Volski asked.

I held in a sigh at their foolishness, at their mistrust. It was exhausting to stand in the middle of such pressure. "I don't."

"And it doesn't matter," Fedor pushed on. "Because that's not an option. Hide, or flee. We need to decide which of those we're doing."

"You can, if you like. I am going to help Kichlan."

Sofia nodded. "Yes."

"How?" Volski gripped my elbow. "You don't know where he is."

I looked up into his face and realised he thought I was finally broken; more so than I had ever been after Grandeur, after suiting. He worried and he feared for me. But he would never understand.

It had been foolish to drag him into this, and selfish. But that was not something that could be undone with remorse.

"No, I don't." I pulled myself from his grip. "But the Keeper does."

16.

"When did the Keeper start caring about Kichlan?"
Mizra spat the words at me.

That was cruel.

I made my way back to the Keeper statues. Fedor
watched me leave, but did not intervene. Eugeny and
Valya remained in the domed building. After a moment,
Uzdal, Mizra, Sofia and Volski followed me out. It hurt,
when Zecholas did not appear through the rubble, that he
would prefer to remain with veritable strangers than trust
in me. And yet, after everything I had put him through,
was I really that surprised?

"The Keeper can hear you, you know." I leaned against
the rock and slid down. "And he doesn't think that's particularly fair." Back against the Keeper's marble thighs, I
drew my knees into my chest, wrapped my arms around
them and tipped my head back.

Something protested in my stomach at the squeeze. I
ignored it.

Mizra hunkered down before me. After a moment's
hesitation, the rest of them joined him. "You can hear
him, can't you?" Mizra murmured.

I opened an eye, fixed it on him. "Yes." As simple as that.

"Without the suit on?" Uzdal asked.

"Just like Lad used to," Mizra answered for me. "Isn't that right?"

I gave a half-shrug, half-nod.

Sofia reached a hand forward, her palm hovered above my knee but she could not bring herself to touch me. "Can you find Kichlan?" she whispered.

"So what does that mean?" Volski asked. He must have felt like an outsider here, amidst whisperings of disembodied voices and mythical beings. Maybe he was used to it by now. "Are you like Lad was?"

I shook my head. My hair caught loose grains in the rock and sent them down the back of my shirt. "I am not a Half." I was certain about that, and not because I had not suddenly grown child-like, simple and prone to violence. Because I was missing something Lad had, something that made him a Half. He had never truly belonged in this world, not all of him, at least. And while I might be able to step between the light and the dark with the loosening of my suited bonds, it was not the same. Lad had lived both worlds. I merely visited.

"Is it because…" Uzdal glanced meaningfully at my stomach, hidden behind my knees.

Suddenly, three sets of very bright eyes were fixed on me.

Only Volski appeared confused. "Is it because of what?"

I stretched out my legs before me. They were too tight to straighten. Even a metal as fluid as my suit had to have some toughness in it, I supposed. "They are talking about the child I'm carrying." Even as Volski drew back, even as Mizra, Uzdal and Sofia shared scandalised looks,

I remained calm. There were more important things to worry about now. Everything felt like it was settling into place. Amidst the chaos and the fear and the decisions, I was calm.

No thrills and fighting, this time. No bargaining, no desperate bids for freedom – either by killing the puppet men, or simply running away. Kichlan needed me. It was that simple.

"Sofia, Mizra and Uzdal think my child might be a Half. And if it is, that could be why I can hear the Keeper now." But I shook my head. "I think they are wrong. I have heard him before."

You did.

"Before?" Uzdal whispered.

"Child?" Volski choked over the word. "My lady. I... I don't know what to say. Who–" He caught himself. "Um, congratulations."

I laughed softly. How long had it been since I'd done that? Sofia muttered, "It's not Kichlan. Not him."

Before? Yes, I had heard the Keeper even before the puppet men had twisted me with their weapon, before Lad had sacrificed himself, before I had known about doors between worlds and the danger on the other side.

I had heard him on Grandeur's palm, when those crimson pions broke me. Even before I had fallen. But why was that? Had I been so connected to the pions, so deeply linked in my desperate fight to bring them under control, that when debris had taken their place, I had reached out to it, instinctively? I had linked to debris before I'd known what it was. The darkness that replaced the lights, the Keeper, the doors, the only thing between our world and nothingness. Was that why it had listened to me? Why, when I touched it with a suit designed as a weapon, built to destroy, it had calmed, it had obeyed? Because the debris knew me, the Keeper knew me. From the beginning.

I stood, slipping my back up against the statue. Mizra, Uzdal, Sofia and Volski hurried to follow. This was pointless, hiding in the dark while Kichlan needed me, discussing things with people who could not hope to understand.

It didn't matter any more. The knowledge was hard; it was like the throb low in my belly. I was not part of a collection team or a critical circle. Not any more. And I had to admit to that, I had to give it up, and acknowledge that I was different. More so than what the puppet men had made me. I was more than my suit, more than a collector, than a binder or critical centre. Not quite a Half, yet similar. Close to the Keeper. Touching the dark.

What did it matter if I didn't quite know what I was, or what I was becoming. Not everything needs a word.

You must hurry.

I nodded, to myself and to the Keeper invisible beside me. Volski watched me quizzically. I saw sadness in his eyes, something long-suffering. And again I wished I had not caused him that.

It was time to end it.

"I need to hurry." I smiled at them. "I need to save Kichlan, you see."

"Let me help," Sofia said. "Let me come with you. Please."

I closed my eyes against her pleading expression. "I don't think you can."

True.

"But I will bring him back. I promise."

Sofia didn't look entirely convinced.

I stepped closer to Volski, and held my palm against his cheek. A muscle jumped beneath my touch, but other than that and the darting concern of his eyes, he did not move. "I'm sorry I dragged you into this," I whispered.

He softened. "Don't be, my lady. I am only grateful that I could help."

I backed away, until I was again against the Keeper. "Go back to Fedor and the others, stay with them, do whatever they do. And be safe."

"What–"

"I am going to help Kichlan."

And with that I urged the suit to run over me. The street fell away, the buried domed building with it; the faces so worried about me went, these people trapped in conspiracy. There was nothing but the darkness and the doors, and the Keeper. No faces materialised in the wood, there was nothing of the landscape from the real world. Immersed in darkness, in doors, I did not need them any more.

"Finally."

I turned. The Keeper stood beside me. Hands on his hips, chest thrust out and head tipped back, smiling broadly. It was the strongest I had ever seen him. His skin was white and solid, his eyes darkly fluid. Only the faintest flutter of a pulse showed in his neck.

"You look well." It was a strange thing to say to a being that was not physical, a being whose body was built of debris. Strange, but fitting. "Solid." If not a little awkward.

He nodded. "I have been closing doors." And his smile faltered a little. "It will not last, though. The strength you gave me, the debris Lad bought me, it is but a tiny piece of everything that has been taken from me."

"Yes." I understood. But what could we do about it? What would it cost to release another basement's worth of vats? I didn't think I had what it took to watch another loved one die.

"Which is why we must hurry."

I frowned, as always unsure if he could see my face beneath my mask. "I thought this was about Kichlan."

"It is. They are, at the moment, linked."

Pressure in my chest. "What are the puppet men doing to him?"

The Keeper's dark eyes averted. It was hard to tell. Only in the shifting of my own reflection did I know his eyes had moved. "We need to hurry."

I turned to head down the street. He caught my wrist and prevented me.

"I do not pretend to understand what has happened to you," he said. "What they have done to you, how it has changed you. And why. But I know that you are a part of this world, Tanyana, as I am. As Lad was. I have seen you close a door. That is proof enough for me."

I stared at him, unsure.

His smile returned. Half-hesitantly, half-bold, more like a boy than an eternal guardian. "And if you are of this world, then walk it with me."

"Walk?"

"You follow the paths of your old, light world, but you do not belong there; at least, not entirely. Not as much as you once did." Still holding my hand he gestured to where in that bright world he spoke of I knew rock and an ancient statue stood. There was no door there. It did not look like marble and rubble fractured by the weight of a city and time. It looked like darkness, empty as a starless night.

I lifted my free hand. Part of me was ready to graze rock with my silver-strong fingers. But I did not. When I stretched forward I touched only the darkness. Nothing else. The rock, the statue, they did not exist here. Not any more.

"Can I walk that way?" I asked the Keeper.

Smiling, he said, "Let us, together. Because it is too easy to get lost among the doors."

Still holding hands, the Keeper and I set off along the dark passageways, and I left the underground street behind.

Darkness closed around us. I was glad for his company and could believe, truly, how easy it would be to lose oneself here. Doors flickered in the distance like landmarks, or stars.

"This is the way it used to be. Empty, calm." His grip was reassuringly tight as we walked. "I like it down here. Reminds me of a time when I was enough. When I could keep the doors all closed."

The doors we passed were insubstantial, distant. They did not threaten to open.

"But we cannot stay down here."

I had the strangest sensation of ascending, that we were climbing even though there were no hills in this place, no variation in the darkness except the doors. But I felt pressure in my ears and added weight on my knees.

The Keeper did not have to tell me when we left the old city far below and entered Movoc-under-Keeper as it was now. The doors did it for him.

A step, and they appeared, shimmering indistinct and distant one moment, then solid and all-to-real the next. The vast and empty darkness narrowed to thin and winding paths. Doors crowded over us, as solid and straight as the sides of closely made buildings, as threatening as a dense forest. They rattled beneath our feet, encroaching on the dark paths like destructive roots beneath a street.

Could I see more of them now because I was deeper in this place, because I truly did belong? Or were they spreading like concrete rot?

"Do you see now, why I cannot keep them all closed?"

I nodded. "Yes."

Hesitant glances my way, warmth through his touch. Had I ever sensed warmth from the Keeper before? Had he ever seemed so human, so familiar? "I wonder if you can help me?"

My heart dropped. "Find more debris to release? I... I don't know if I can risk that again." I sounded so cowardly.

"No." The Keeper stopped and brushed my cheek lightly. Odd, how strongly I felt his touch. "I mean stay here, with me, and help me close the doors."

"Stay here?" What was he asking?

"I have never had a friend." He dropped his hand, turned ahead and tugged me back into walking. "The Halves – they weren't always this bad, but even back then they didn't talk to me the way you do. I was accustomed to loneliness." He let out a deep and sighing breath. The doors around us rippled. "I would like a friend."

A friend. Sometimes he reminded me so strongly of Lad, and now, that could only set my heart to sorrow.

"We must help Kichlan," I said. Not a real answer. At least, not a whole one.

A silent nod, an averted gaze.

The Keeper took me through a Movoc-under-Keeper I did not recognise. The only signs of buildings, of factories, of life and pion activity were the doors. Some

stretched tall, their wood heavy and thick, hinges straining. I could have opened those with a touch. Others
remained faint, tightly locked, or small. Strange to see
the city this way, as markers of its activity rather than its
physicality. But then wasn't that just like seeing the city
as a pion-binder? Watching energies rather than en-
trances, the deep movement of lights instead of the
rattling of wood?

"Can anyone see us?" I whispered. "The circles? The
Mob?" What must I look like in that other world? A figure of silver walking through their buildings like they
were as substantial only as mist? Or was I a flicker of
light, a half-imagined image on the edges of their vision?

"No. As they cannot see me, they cannot see you."
The Keeper lifted our clasped hands. "I told you, you belong here. It only takes a little effort, this connection
between us."

So, I did not exist? At least, not to the citizens of
Movoc-under-Keeper. Strangely, that did not unsettle
me. "You are stronger than you were before."

"But still not strong enough on my own."

The doors were changing again. It was subtle at first.
The faint ones, the distant and ghostly ones, disappeared.
And those closer to us – solid, looming, large and frightening – shed their skins of wood. These doors hardened
into smooth metal riddled with lights, with dials, and
with symbols I could not read but looked so similar to
those inscribed on the bands of my suit. Like the debris
storage vats we had found beneath the technician's laboratory, yet so much larger, towering over me, closer to
buildings than doorways. They did not rattle, these metallic doors, they did not battle the wind of nothingness

at their backs with the cracking of wood and the creaking of hinges. They rusted instead. Copper flakes like scabs on skin weakened the doors, diseased them. In places whole sections had been eaten through, so I could see what lay on the other side, that in-between emptiness, that unreal darkness. And the distant curve of flickering lights.

"Their touch stretches far."

Their touch. I knew who he meant. Who else, surely, but the puppet men?

"Where are we?" I had truly lost track, I couldn't even say if we were climbing, descending, or simply marching forward.

"Underground again." Strange, it didn't feel like it. "Beneath the river. And the bridge."

That made me shiver. "The Keeper's Tear Bridge?" Impossible. The centre of the city was older than its effluents and rills. It had been built with few pions, from actual cut stone, not concrete created, shaped and smoothed. Before Grandeur had stripped me of my pion sight the city centre had seemed empty, sparse, unlit by the complex tangle of bonds and particles that made up the rest of Movoc-under-Keeper. So it could not generate enough debris to create doors like this, to surround and menace us.

My surprise must have somehow shown. "What you see around you," the Keeper said, expression twisted with disgust. "These abominations, this is their influence. Their torture, their experiments. Each part of me they tear away, bend beyond recognition and keep for themselves, and it becomes such a door. And they do not tire of their work."

"But under the river?" It still did not seem possible,

rusting evidence aside. "There is nothing beneath the bridge but water. I don't understand."

"There are many ancient, long lost parts of your city. Some of the oldest were built deep beneath the ground, even below the river itself. The Halves that built them thought it the safest place for their equipment, to reduce the risk of contamination in your world. But these places were abandoned as the Halves changed, and lost their abilities and their memories. Their purpose. Some places collapsed, others were rendered inaccessible, and any records of them have faded. They can only be reached by the dark paths now."

"Halves built them?" I paused, fought for clarity. "But, wait, you're saying the puppet men also use these dark paths?"

"I have come to believe so." The Keeper hesitated. "I have followed them. Or tried to. But they turned the paths against me and I was trapped. Held where you found me, in that room." He was labouring to make sense of it all, I could hear confusion and hurt in his voice, and once again he was the Keeper I knew, the broken and tragic guardian. The strength Lad's life had bought him was fragile. "Surrounded by doors. Do you remember?"

The first laboratory we had infiltrated. Of course I remembered. And, I supposed, that explained the horror he could not express, and his absence for days beforehand. "But that's..." I struggled to understand. "If the puppet men can walk the dark paths then, what are they?" Were they suit and debris, like they had made me? I thought of their seamed skin, the darkness in smiles that did not fit on their faces.

"They are..." he rubbed his white face with a free

hand. For a moment I could see the debris behind his cheeks, as though he had flushed grey. His voice hitched, breathy, as though he had to fight simply to push out the words. "Half, but not like the Halves. They belong, they are part of this place, of me."

"Part of you?" I whispered, horrified and utterly confused. "I don't understand. How is that possible?"

"I…" another struggle "It isn't… They should not be, they are wrong, Tanyana. Wrong!" He was shouting now, eyes roaming the doors, hand so tight where he held me. "But they are here." He drew a deep breath, calmed himself. "And I must deal with them. That is why I was made. To hold close the doors. And they are opening them. So I must stop them."

He stared down at me, and halted. On the surface, he looked calm again, steady. But I could feel the storm raging within him, the strong pulse of debris beneath his skin. And there was more to it than that. His whole dark world seemed to quaver, in time to that pulse, a thudding that reverberated in my head and had nothing to do with the unsteady doors. The Keeper was debris, the doors were debris, this whole dark world I was walking through so lightly was debris. All of it was weak, all of it struggling and broken. "And you must help me. Are you ready?"

I jerked back from him. "Ready? Are we here?" I looked around. Doors, only doors, everywhere doors. No puppet men, no debris monsters, no Kichlan.

"We are." He did not sound pleased. "I have to let you go. You will need to be in the light world, to help him."

"On my own?"

"I will be here. Listen for me. We will do this together." I nodded, tense.

"Be wary. They know we are here." And the Keeper released my hand.

The doors withdrew. They did not disappear entirely – after all I was still sheathed in my suit – but they lost some of their solidity, and shapes from the light world began to appear. I could make out a tunnel, the rippling of water, and caught a strange scent: ancient stone, mould and musty air, combined with something heady, something artificial, like the flow of pions to a malfunctioning lamp. If I was not coated in my suit it would have lifted the hairs along my arms. As it was, my entire body started tingling.

"Go," the Keeper whispered. "I am with you." And he graced me with a rueful, self-deprecating smile. "For all the good that will do."

I drew my suit back in.

We had indeed arrived in a tunnel. Nearly lightless, with only the slow spinning of my suit and a faint light shining from beneath a far door giving me anything to see by. Stonework arched above me. Water trickled down through it in several thin but steady streams. How long before the stone finally wore away, and the river above us rushed in to claim this place?

A strange pattern in crystal covered one of the walls beside me, reflecting the beam from my suit. I approached it carefully, and ran my fingers across a large, flat facet. Cold, wet, and made dim by a gathering of mould. I rubbed at the crystal with the end of my sleeve, revealing flecks of gold inside it. Just like the stones we had found in the underground street – the ones Zecholas had exclaimed over; the ones the Unbound had used to build Lad's temporary tomb.

"What is this stuff? What did it do?"

The Keeper hesitated. *It... It's too old now. Doesn't*

work. Didn't really work that well in the first place anyway. Once you've come one way, it's hard to travel back. It changes you.

"Travel back? Keeper, what do you mean? I don't understand."

Tanyana, we have to focus. Please. For me, for Kichlan. Keep going.

I swallowed my questions, and crept across slippery stones. The door on the far side of the room was wooden, and did not belong here. After so many countless years it should have rotted away in this closed, wet place. It should be little more than hinges and a rusted old handle. But the wood was fresh, the handle smooth, and it opened without a sound.

I wondered, briefly, why the puppet men had bothered to mount a door here. And then how they had got it here in the first place and who had installed it.

But then I stepped through, and all such thoughts fell away.

Any resemblance to an ancient city disappeared on the other side. I found myself on a landing. A cavern stretched out below me, and I could not shake the feeling that this was just like the basement where Lad had died, only of a far greater size.

Do you see?

See? Two lights were drilled into the wall either side of the doorway. Not pion powered, not even gas. Not a candle-flame either, more like starlight collected and bottled, small but heinously bright, bobbing behind crystalline fittings. Their shine scattered across the landing, only touching the great space below. I caught hints of glass, of metal, reflecting in the darkness.

"I can't see anything." I tried to peer further, but couldn't make out any details. "What is in there?"

I do not know. All I can see are doors. So many doors.

That could not be a good thing.

Go deeper.

The energy I had felt in the underwater archway was stronger here. It lifted the hairs along my arms and the back of my neck. When I touched the metal railing around the landing a bright blue spark sizzled between us, strong enough to make me snatch my hand back. I rubbed the spot on my palm where it had bitten me, the skin quickly reddening.

A truly bizarre set of stairs led down into the cavern. They spiralled tight and uneven around a central axis patterned with garish tiles. Small glass chambers hung from each step, rattling as their internal light flickered on with my footsteps, as though awakened by my presence. When my feet touched the cavern floor a thin line of these chambers lit up, threading a winding trail off into impossible distance.

The room might be underneath the Tear Bridge, but it was so wide and long I was certain it stretched further than the banks of the river and deep into the centre of the city itself. It was crowded with strangely set-up devices, all shimmering their suit metal in the reflection of the lights.

"What is this?"

No answer. I imagined the Keeper did not have one.

I left the stairs, and wound my way through hulking machines. No seamed smiles appeared suddenly to stop me; no whispering mist dogged my feet. The Keeper had said the puppet men knew we were here. So either they did not fear me – which was entirely likely – or they were giving me the space to investigate their underground maze. Both were disconcerting thoughts.

I passed an enormous globe. Easily three times the height of a man, sections of the outer shell were missing so I could see all the way to the centre. There were several smaller globes inside, and circles, and semi-circles all crowding close to the outer shell. The middle was hollow. The energy that buzzed through the room intensified as I approached it. Though the machine was still, it vibrated, humming softly. I peered inside and noticed gears between each of the circles, and tracks of worn metal that told me the whole thing must move, the countless complex layers rubbing against each other as they spun. What was supposed to be at the centre? What did they spin around?

I see a door, the Keeper murmured by my ear. *Circular, glass instead of wood or metal. It is cracking, slowly, surely, in round patterns like a spider web. I hate it, Tanyana. So warped out of shape, so broken and fragile. But I can still feel its pain.*

I kept moving. The path was broad enough for three people to walk shoulder-to-shoulder, guiding me in a wide circle. More of the great, stripped-down globes lined the way. I realised with a jolt that there were nine of them and in the middle, a metallic bed.

I ran to it. So familiar, I had myself been strapped to one while needles fed the suit into my bones. But there were no arching fingers here, no threads of wire. Nothing but a roughly star-shaped slab, with leather straps at each point, open now and limp.

"It's a nine point circle." But what did that even mean? Could these globe-things act as circle points? What energy did they charge when they spun? And for what purpose? I glanced around at them, so silent and still, yet vibrating with the memory of power. How long ago had they last been used?

And who had been strapped down here, their circle's unwilling centre?

"Are there doors in each of these things?" I hissed, desperate to know, desperate to understand. "And what about here?" I patted the table, winced as another spark travelled along my arm. "Is it a door?"

The Keeper was silent for a long moment – too long – before he whispered, *We need to keep going*.

"But–"

It hurts here. Please Tanyana. Please.

I dismissed my anxiety, and nodded. Did I really want to understand what the puppet men were doing down here? And to whom?

The room stretched on. I realised, as we walked, that the lights behind us turned themselves off as the ones before us flickered on. The only constant source remained that first, thin path; the one we followed. So the globes and their freakish nine point circle fell into darkness, as a small forest of glass tubes started sparkling.

The tubes protruded from the ground, as thick as my thigh but only as tall as my hip. I noted more gold-flecked crystals embedded in the floor of solid, chiselled stone. I threaded my way through the tubes, the path tight. While the strange lights reflected in their glass and started them sparkling like a field of stars, there was a darkness within the cylinders. I crouched. A thick webbing of debris planes filled the pipes, shards of darkness taut between clear sides.

That wasn't all. Blue light – something between the blaze of my suit and shocks this place had given me – snaked its way along the outside of the glass. I didn't dare touch it. It sparked between each tube and brushed against me with a prickling warmth.

Hurts.

"They are doing something to the debris, aren't they?" I stood, and glanced around me. So many tubes. "Is this how they create their monsters? Is this how they twisted you?"

I do not know. I remember needles and silver and light, such cruel light. But there are so many pieces within me. You, Tanyana, are within me. I cannot tell you how each part was made. They are too many, and they all tumble into one.

"I could break them, set the debris free." I said this even though I feared to touch the tubes. "Give it all back to you."

That is not why we are here. And I do not know what good it will do. Continue on, and save him.

That surprised me. But I took the Keeper's advice gratefully, and let the tubes be.

When the tube-forest thinned out, nothing arose to replace it. The sparkle-shine lights behind me faded, and a single beam flashed on in the distance. It was focused on something, but all I could make out was a rough form in white.

"Is that–?"

No. Continue past it.

But something drew me forward. That white, draped form, glowing in the beam.

You will regret it.

I broke into a run.

It was a sheet. Roughly formed material of off-white, stained in places with paint made from mud mixed with blood, and already fraying at the edges. After all, Volski and Zecholas had been rushed when they created it.

Lad's shroud. I recognised the weave, made from jackets and scarves with listless, unstable pions. I knew the roughly painted symbols. I had seen him wrapped in it, by Kichlan's side in the underground room. I had seen him carried away in it.

This was Lad's shroud, and it was empty.

"What have they done to him?" I whispered.

He is dead.

"What have they done to his body?" I demanded. My voice rang out louder than I intended, sharp against hard surfaces I could not see, losing itself among the buzzing tubes.

As I said, Tanyana. He is gone.

I gathered the shroud to me. It lay on something that looked like a chair but was deeply indented, so that to sit in it you would have to squeeze into the form fitting-metal and it would hold you tight, like a hand. While it too seemed built of suit silver, like everything else down here, the inside was not. It was strange: dark, soft looking yet solid, and it throbbed. Almost alive. It made me shiver, it made something within me clench in fear. So I dropped the shroud again, let it fall and softly cover the chair.

And suddenly, I needed to leave this place; I could not stroll through and blithely observe abomination after abomination. "Where is Kichlan?" The words almost choked me. I stared at the dried blood. Was that really all that remained of Lad? My Lad. "Tell me."

Run. I will direct you.

So I ran. With the Keeper whispering in my ear I glanced aside from the forms looming in the bobbing lights that flickered on and off as I passed: vats, only bigger; something that looked like an insect, but metallic and still and many times too large; dials and flickering numbers and the ever-crackle of blue lightning. I did not stop to stare, to try and understand. I did not want to understand just what they were doing down here, and how they did it. What the puppet men were.

Slow down.

I pulled back to a light trot and wondered, only briefly, that I was not out of breath. Another sign that the suit was rebuilding its strength?

There. Ah, stop them. Hurry, please.

I knew that tone, that fearful, pained, desperate tone. He was failing again.

More tubes. Not a forest this time, but something stranger. They wound and twisted their way above the ground like hollow tendrils or webs, and planes of debris surged within them. I made my way through, arms lifted, careful of the energy that crackled over their surface.

The further I went, the thinner the tubes became. The debris within them solidified, but not into something I would call grains, and the energy surged until it was so thick, so bright that I couldn't even look at the glass. I held my arms tight against my sides. But still I felt it, the touch of lightning racing up my limbs, the faintly nauseating scent of burning hair.

The tubes rose into a curve above my head, drawn together and secured with wide metallic ties. The whole structure, the blue, black, energy, debris, and glass snake ended at a great head. Weird and insect-like, bulbous with many small glass eyes, it was suspended from the distant ceiling by chains of bright links, and hung above another chair.

But this one was not empty. Kichlan was strapped within.

I ran to him. I could feel the pressure of debris planes above me. Wild, lancing energy broke from the creature to touch me, to quest over my back and arms with strange delicacy. My suit, quiet and compliant until now, rallied only enough to whip free, flick the energy away, then settle back into its bonds.

Kichlan was ashen. He had been strapped into the moulded seat with firm, iron-buckled leather. I brushed his cheek; his skin was clammy. I pressed a forefinger to his neck; his pulse was weak. He did not move.

I glanced around. The Keeper was certain the puppet men were here somewhere. So what were they doing? Hiding, watching, staging another test?

Kichlan's eyelids fluttered. He squinted up at me. His eyes were red-rimmed and red-veined and I ached for the emptiness there, the fear. "T... Tan?"

"Shh." I traced soft fingers down the side of his face. He was shaking, almost imperceptibly, but a constant deep-cold or deep-shock quake. "I'm here. You're safe now."

"Should have run, Tan. I told you to run."

"I couldn't, Kichlan. I couldn't leave you."

"They took him." His mouth wasn't working properly. He drooled as he spoke, so I unfolded the end of my clean shirtsleeve and dabbed at his lips. "They–"

"Shh." And because I had nothing else to say. "They can't hurt him anymore." What had he seen? I thought of the shroud and the chair and prayed to a Keeper I knew could not help me that he had not seen it working. That he had not been forced to witness whatever it was the puppet men had done to his brother's body.

He groaned, turned his head to the side. I winced. Below his collar, around the edges of his suit, he was bruised. Horrible and deeply black, I wondered if they had broken his collarbone. What they had done to the rest of him, to the parts of his body I could not see, to make him as ill and weak as this? How they had even brought him here at all?

Hurry.

"Keep still," I whispered, as though he could do much else.

I extended a short, sharp knife of suit to slice clean and quickly through Kichlan's leather bonds. Their iron buckles rattled sharply against the metal chair. Then I bent, scooped my arms beneath him and lifted him free.

He cried out as I moved him, a weak noise of exhaustion beyond pain. But still, he braced himself as I placed him on his feet, as I slipped his arm around my shoulders and steadied him against me. Even in his hurt and loss, Kichlan tried to be strong.

"Let's get you out of here," I said, as though it would be that simple, that easy.

The debris, the Keeper murmured in my ear. *You've seen what they are doing to it. Right above your head they are torturing me, right as we now speak. Can you really leave here, Tanyana, and not stop them?*

I scowled into the darkness; aware the Keeper probably wasn't right in front of me, but hoping he could see the expression anyway. "We came to save Kichlan."

Not him alone.

I should have known the Keeper was interested in more than Kichlan's welfare. "But what can I do? I thought you said there was no point in breaking the tubes." I glanced up at the monstrosity above us. Just what would have happened to Kichlan if I had not come?

Those tubes, yes. But that thing above you that… that abomination, is different. You must destroy that, he pleaded, his voice desperate. *Do not let them do it again!*

"Do what?"

Why won't you simply do as I ask, Tanyana? He sobbed, and drew away. *And now they are here.*

Mist settled in from the darkness, drifting around my ankles, coating and filling the chair, wrapping the insect head and its glass body. Forms birthed in its thick folds and the hazy, bobbing light. Shadows and faces and smiles.

"Do you like our laboratory, Miss Vladha?" a puppet man whispered. "Did you see our little toys?"

"We have improved so much upon the programmers' crystal hubs," said another. Or the same one. It was impossible to tell.

"You could have had access to all our knowledge, all this power. Yet, you ignored us. You even fought against us. You did not choose well."

"Even so, we give you another chance."

One of the puppet men stepped clear of the mist, his body solid in an immaculate white suit, his face full of dry amusement. The rest, for I was certain there were more – countless masses, perhaps – remained in the mist as shadows and half-illusionary horror.

"We are fair, wouldn't you say?" He tipped his head. I fought the need to back away, all too aware of the mist behind me. "To give you so many chances."

Break it! Break anything you can find. Do it, hurry!

I shook my head, unable to speak, barely able to move. My suit began spinning, sending its own bluish light to join the mist, to cast shapes and movement of its own. It tugged, deep in my bones, as though the very presence of the puppet men was enough to awaken it, to give it strength and remind it that I was but its host, and it needed a body to control.

The puppet man gestured to the empty chair. "Replace the collector, if you will. Our experiment is about to begin."

"No!" I spat the word out around wires in my throat. They fought my voice all the way. Not again! I would not let the suit control me again. "No." A deep breath, steadier. "I am taking him with me, and we are leaving this place."

And you will destroy the tubes as you go.

But the puppet man shook his head. "We gave you choice, you used it poorly. We showed you strength, you rejected it. We even gave you space, quiet and time to grieve and to reassess your situation. You did not take it. We are done with freedom, we are tired of choice."

My hand tightened into a silver-coated fist. I forced it open.

"Do as we command, Miss Vladha, and place the body in the chair."

I did not move.

A shrug, elegant and unemotional. "As you wish."

The puppet man stepped back, and above us, insect eyes opened.

17.

Too late! The Keeper cried.

Glass slid free from the insect's head, countless small, round caps that fell to crash against the stone floor. Then the blue energy sizzled, the glass tubes pulsed and rattled. Debris wriggled out of the insect's eyes. Like pale snakes it squirmed free of its incubation chambers and writhed down to join the shattered glass.

I recognised those thick, animated scars on the fabric of the world. I knew the touch of their hunger and need.

"Oh, Other." I held Kichlan tighter against me and tried not to picture Lad, with the Hon Ji Half's head in his lap, as the debris devoured her. I tried to forget the weight of her blood on my silver hands.

You should have listened to me.

"Replace the body." The puppet man smiled his horrid smile.

"No." I would not let them destroy Kichlan. "We have to open a door," I called to the Keeper, uncaring if the puppet men could hear me. "We have to get rid of the debris."

Open one in here I cannot promise I will be able to close it.

But I knew of no other way to deal with debris like this.

"Can you stand?" I whispered to Kichlan.

He glanced sideways, his red-shot eyes wide and fearful. "Are you sure about this?"

"I haven't been sure of anything for a very long time."

Kichlan could not stand. So I eased him to the ground and swept long and fan-like suit appendages over the surrounding stones, clearing them. The debris snakes were not fast. They had not yet fattened themselves on life and pion bonds and were not able to fully coalesce, to rise body-like against me. Which, I supposed, was why Kichlan had been strapped to the chair beneath them. A first meal. The very idea made me shudder.

I stood in front of Kichlan, legs wide and stance strong, ready for whatever the puppet men could throw at me. No one would take a blow for me this time. I could suffer my own scars.

"Once I have destroyed your weapon," I said, teeth gritted, to the puppet man so implacable before me, "I will destroy the rest of your *laboratory*." I swept an arm wide. "Every last tube, every creature, every chair. That is what I choose, and that is my strength."

You could have done that a moment ago and saved us the trouble.

I chose to ignore that.

The puppet man shook his head again. "Weapon? Are you still so fixated on that? We have moved beyond the need for weapons, Miss Vladha. And you have followed."

"What do you mean? I know you have built more weapons like me and Aleksey."

His smile grew. His mouth was black inside his ill-fitting lips. No teeth, no anything. I could not look at it.

"The enforcer showed promise, that is true. But only you have come this close to reaching your full potential. We are pleased you have returned to us. Together, we will achieve it."

"No." I flexed my suit. It slid urgently over my arms, legs, and torso. I would use its battle lust, for now. Only now. "No, I came to rescue Kichlan. And you don't have Aleksey, this time to stop me."

"What a shame."

My suit was slowing, its growth nearly stilled, even though I urged it on. This was not usually how our battles played out.

"But the time for choices is over." The puppet man lifted an arm. And the mass of torn debris that had been writhing toward me rose at the gesture. They thickened, united, wound into a shape like a many-clawed hand, like the tentacles of glass coiling from the insect's head.

What was happening to the debris? How was it growing like that, moving like that? In time to the puppet man's movements, in tandem with his stretching fingers. It was almost as though he controlled it.

And the idea chilled me.

No, stop it! the Keeper shouted at me, utterly panicked. *Please, Tanyana, make them stop it*!

"While we would usually be happy to let you open a door, encourage it even, that is not the purpose of this test. He is." The puppet man tipped his head toward Kichlan, still slumped behind me. "And so, I'm afraid, we cannot allow you to interfere. Not this time."

Allow me? Who did they think they were?

"And not you either, brother."

Then the Keeper began to scream. I could make no

sense of the words he gabbled in his pain. The puppet man twisted his hand and the debris clawed the air, raw and surging, and I hated to imagine that the Keeper was there, right there, being attacked by what had once been a part of himself.

"Oh, brother." The puppet man snarled through his blackened smile. "Are you not weakened enough, how much more must we do to you to make you understand?"

Brother?

"Enough!" I lurched forward, my suit still half-spread over me, away from my face and my eyes. Even though I could not see what he was doing to the Keeper – and maybe I was glad – I would not stand by and let it happen. "I won't let you–"

"Stop."

More voices than that single puppet man. Voices from the mist, from the stones, from the coiling debris and the metal and glass. All around me, resonating within me. And to my horror, I obeyed.

I stopped. One foot slightly raised, what suit I had summoned over my hand in the act of sharpening, all of it froze. I could not breathe, and the pumping of my heart slowed. Head dizzy, sight dotting with black, I stared in horror at the puppet man and the faces materializing, smiling, all around me and could do nothing. Nothing at all.

"Tan?" Behind me, Kichlan gasped over the word. I could not turn to console him, I could not move to protect him, while the debris grew and loomed over us. It was Lad, all over again. And I could do nothing.

"Perhaps you understand a little more clearly." The puppet man lifted his second hand. "You have surpassed what we expected of you, Miss Vladha, and your experiment is ended. So you shall serve us, as you were designed to do."

I could not move and I could not speak.

"Step aside."

Again, my body acted without my consent. Two steps to the left, feet together, a curt turn so I could see it all: Kichlan, the chair, the debris and the puppet man. Or puppet master. Perhaps that is a better term.

"What are you doing?" Kichlan pleaded with me, struggling to stand.

This was no battle in my body; this was not the suit vying for control of our flesh. If anything, the suit had gone dormant, silent and still in a way I had never known. In the face of the puppet man's control, it did not fight. The spinning slowed, the light died, and the ever-present tugging in my bones, that need for violence they had planted in me with their living wires and their horrible needles, faded away. I had never felt so empty, so alone.

The suit.

It was all so clear. I was more suit than human, more silver than muscle and bone. The suit was debris. And there, twisting and grown, was all the evidence I needed that the puppet men could do the impossible and manipulate debris. Control it, the way I had once controlled pions.

So what was I really, other than a human-shaped tool utterly under the puppet man's control? A weapon, a sword, should he so wish it.

"See, you do understand." The puppet man nodded, like I was a servant or a pupil and he was pleased with my work. "Brother, if only you could join her."

He tipped his head, appeared almost to be listening. I heard nothing.

"Fool." A murmur of agreement from the mist. "He will join us, in time. No matter. The experiment must begin." The puppet man made a small flicking motion with his spare hand, palm up and fingers slightly curled. I could see the seams where his fingernails were attached, the stitching, so clearly.

The ground rumbled, and the stone lifted beneath Kichlan, a mirror almost to the puppet master's movement.

Kichlan had found the strength to kneel on one knee, but as the ground lifted he fell back again and he gripped the cupping stone with desperate hands.

I had known from the beginning that the puppet men could manipulate pions. Theirs were the furious and crimson points of light that had thrown me from Grandeur's palm. And I had known they could twist debris, that they could create monsters from grains of the Keeper's own flesh, that they could solidify planes into suit metal and infuse it into the human body. But this? Debris that responded to their will like pions, what was this? How was it even possible not only to control one, but both?

"Because we are both," the puppet man said, in answer to the question his control would not let me ask. "And yet neither. Therefore, we are all. And nothing."

Which didn't help me at all. Except the Keeper was debris, and we were pions. So the puppet men were part of him, and yet one of us.

No, I did not understand.

The puppet man lifted Kichlan high, passed him from rock palm to rock palm. When those pion-made arms fell back into the floor they were smoothed over with so much skill that not a scar was left behind, not a dent. If this had been the work of a circle I would have been awed at the ease with which they performed such a powerful manipulation. But it was the puppet men, and it was terrible.

The stone dropped Kichlan back into the chair, beneath the arching and writhing dreadfulness of debris snakes.

"This body is stronger, you see, than the last one," the puppet man said. I had the horrible impression that he was explaining himself to me, as though I could be anything other than sickened and impotently furious. "The pion bindings within him are solid, brighter, so more energy will be transferred to the debris as they are consumed. We believe this will make the process more efficient, the suffering less." He actually looked at me, he actually nodded. "We are not in the business of pain."

The puppet man wrapped the chair in the wiggling debris mass. Dimly, as though muffled by their grains, Kichlan cried out. And I thought of the Hon Ji Half, in her terrified agony, and knew that I could not slice through Kichlan's neck, not even to save him from pain. I had watched Lad die, I could not do the same for his brother.

Help him!

The Keeper? I had to break free, I had to stop this!

But I could not move. Debris wept its way along tracks in the chair, impressions that seemed to have been made to channel this seeping death. It dripped around Kichlan, writhed over his skin and burrowed into his clothes. He bucked once, before the leather straps moved on their own, knitted together where I had cut them and clasped his wrists, ankles and neck, their buckles closing tightly. He struggled, even so tied down, and I could not see his face from my position, standing still and straight behind him, I could not see his eyes or his pain, but I knew it was there. I felt it like it was my own.

Do not let them do this!

"It will be quick." Was the puppet man actually trying to console me?

Not all of the debris could squeeze between Kichlan and the chair. Some of the torn snakeheads fell to the ground, where they thrashed, discarded, questing blindly for more warm flesh to devour.

I was not a healer. So even if I had not fallen, even if I was still a pion-binder, I would have struggled to see the bindings deep within Kichlan's body, or understand what was happening to them. The living body was a complicated knot of bonds and powerful particles that I had not been trained to control. How long before his flesh undid, before he collapsed like the Hon Ji Half's head had done in my hands?

Did the puppet men think this was painless?

The misty mass of hazy faces stared at Kichlan's bound, thrashing body with curiosity. The light in their mould-green eyes, the stretching of ill-fitting lips and what looked like a black parody of the tip of a tongue, it was worse than their usual impassivity. They either did not notice or did not care about the surplus debris worms wiggling free from the chair, across the floor, toward me.

I whispered apologies in my head, silent and useless, to a dead brother I had failed to protect. Kichlan would follow Lad soon, and I had been unable to save either of them. I had watched both die helplessly.

Kichlan's struggles were weakening.

Something tingled through me, following the patterns of my silver. *Tan?*

If I could have, I would have shivered. To hear Lad so clearly, like a torturous memory, or the Keeper with a Half's voice.

Tan, help bro.

I felt his phantom arms around me, as heavy and as warm as his hand had been. I felt his blood again, too. The course it had taken as it had run over me, the fire it had lit through my soul.

Look after him. They messed around inside of you, so they could control you. I reprogram you now, so you can look after him. I remember it now, Tan. Your programming reminded me.

His warmth spread through each scar, each notch and graze, to settle into my bands. Then deeper, into my bones. And the suit started moving again. The puppet men had stilled it, even its very spinning, and deadened its light when they took control of me. But now, with each phantom touch of Lad's remembered blood, the suit reawakened.

Here, this is what you should do. They made you in their image, programmed you so similar, so they could take over any time. Just like now. You need to scramble up your code. Be you, not them. Dilute. That way, you will be strong enough to help him. I show you.

The suit spun darkly. No glowing light, nothing but the stealthily silent spreading of silver over my body, though it left my head clear. And as those free debris-heads closed in, the suit cast a fine metallic web from my toes to catch them. Not to collect them in a tweezer-pinch. It touched them, it spread over them, and it absorbed them. Into me.

And for an instant–

–I was the debris. I was hunger and emptiness, I was ever-fighting, ever-yearning, to fill the splits scored into me with needle and lights. From metal slab to buzzing glass to disfigurement within the insect head I had been created merely so I would consume.

But as the suit smothered the debris and joined with it, it smoothed that hunger away. Sated, whole, the debris eased out of its weeping shell and became a part of me.

A part of whatever it was we were all becoming.

See. Reprogram the debris, the way you always have. But this time, take that code into your own. Absorb it, and use it to fight.

"Lad?" I whispered.

I whispered?

Your turn.

I nodded, revelling in the motion. It didn't matter that Lad was dead, and yet inside of me. It didn't matter that I didn't understand most of what he had just said. Because it was my turn to look after Kichlan, as I should have done his brother, as they both had done for me, for so long.

Tanyana? Now that was the Keeper. I could hear the tears in his voice, his shock and fear. But something deeper started my heart fluttering, and my suit spinning faster. Hope. *You… you feel like a Half.* Hope shone through his anguish like sunshine after a frozen night. *No, not just a Half. I did not understand at first. Why I could speak to you? Why you could hear me? And just what are you changing into? But now it is clear. I can sense you, I can feel part of me within you. And Tanyana, you feel just like Lad. Like he has not left me. Like he is not gone. Not all of him.*

I could feel the Keeper too. Close beside me, and terribly weak

"Lad," I said, loudly this time, and the puppet man's gaze snapped back to me in an instant. Darkness edged the whites of his too-wide eyes. His mouth gaped. More darkness. Damn him and his suit of skin. It did not belong on him.

"Lad is with me." Lad had died in my arms and yet some part of him, it seemed, refused to leave us. We needed him. We always had. I held up a hand and thought of the blood he had spilled on to me, the blood that had run along the lines of my suit and slid between the cracks. Was that why he was a part of me now?

"No," the puppet man said. He lifted a hand. "Stop!"

I crouched. I extended my fingers, touched the ground and sent spider-webs across the floor. Each thread wrapped around a debris scar and absorbed it.

I could feel each piece as they were drawn back into my body. There was much movement at first from each, then the terrible memory of what had been done to them. Until the suit subsumed them, calmed them, drew them inside of us and made them one with us.

Thank you, the Keeper breathed.

Around us, the rest of the puppet men solidified, stepping out of their mist with identical expressions of black-rimmed shock.

"Unspecified error. No definition."

"Control flow interrupted. Exception."

"Command invalid. Emergency override nonresponsive."

More nonsense, but I had no more patience for their senseless ramblings. And I no longer feared them, no matter how many shifted into existence in front of my very eyes.

"What are you doing, Miss Vladha?" the puppet man asked, and he was afraid. Strangely, that did not give me satisfaction. "How are you overriding our programming?"

I ignored him. It was time to free Kichlan. I had promised his brother I would.

I approached the chair. The puppet men did not stop me, instead, they hung back, their uncanny group-mentality apparently unable to decide just what to do about me. The debris reared away from Kichlan's body, recombined into a hand-like state. I extended my own arms, palm up.

"Come to me."

"No!" The most solid of the puppet men lurched toward me, fingers clawing and clutching like he was struggling to regain control.

I refused to let that happen. I stepped up to him and grabbed those outstretched hands. He staggered back, shocked, horrified. The skin on his face drooped, and I dug my fingers into his false flesh and pulled.

The skin over his hands tore away. Beneath, he was debris. He was grains and planes held tight in a loosely human shaped membrane, flowing and pulsing like the Keeper's own semi-visible heartbeat.

For a moment, everything seemed to still.

"I knew you were not human," I said, sounding far calmer than I felt. "I thought you might be like the Keeper. You walk the paths of his world, after all." I shook the gloves of skin, shuddering at the feel of them, the leather-like weight and icy chill. "But what are you?"

"We told you." The rest of the puppet man's skin was peeling away, the seams undoing, as if in that act of exposure I had destroyed everything that held his mask together. "We are both."

"If you are debris then why do you tear it from the Keeper? Why do you twist it into monsters and weapons? Why do you harm him?" I shook my head. "And if you are made of pions, then why do you need to hide behind a false face?"

"We are both, we are neither. We are in between."

"Are you…" What was I, some child frightened of stories told in the dark? "The Other?"

Laughter. And the mist was no longer mist, it was a mass of dark bodies, faceless, seams all unravelling. "You don't even know what that means. You understand nothing."

What did it matter? I was here to help Kichlan, and that was exactly what I would do.

But the mass of bodies closed in on me, and they blended with the once-puppet man until I was surrounded by darkness and shifting movement.

Tanyana! The Keeper was beside me, close. I could feel him as though his body was a part of mine. The heightened fluttering of his debris pulse sent quivers of panic through my own heart.

"What are they?" I gasped at him.

They are impossible.

I turned my back on Kichlan and the debris, and extended my arms into ugly blades. Still, the darkness tightened. The puppet men weighed down the very air, like pressure or humidity on my skin. I backed into the chair, metal chiming on metal as I knocked it, and Kichlan groaned.

My heart leapt. He was still alive.

"Haven't you worked it out yet, brother?" the darkness hissed.

Behind me, the debris was falling, scattering over my back like soft, living rain. Whether it was an attack, or simply because the puppet men – not men, not even puppet-like any more – no longer cared to control it, I couldn't tell. But my suit absorbed each scar that touched me, and it was filling me, replacing what Aleksey had stolen, making me strong again. And perhaps it was the memory of Lad within me, or perhaps it was how close I had come to the Keeper, or because these soft grains had been feeding on Kichlan who wished me no harm. But I could control it all, every last surge of energy within my suit, and they were not turning me into a weapon.

That strength was mine, that suit was mine.

"We are just like you."

No no no, the Keeper rattled out the words. *You are nothing like me.*

The puppet men seemed to be distracted by the Keeper, so I took advantage of that. I turned and collected Kichlan again from the chair.

And yet, as I lifted him, most of his left arm fell away.

I nearly dropped him. I wanted to be sick. And he cried out weakly, head lolling on a useless neck, as the suit band from his left wrist clattered empty and dull to the ground.

"That is true. We are stronger. Later models, you might say. Or updates."

I don't believe you! The Keeper screamed, and I winced. *I was created to be the guardian. Me, only me! And this is my duty, mine!*

"And look how well you are doing it." The darkness laughed, low and echoey and cruel. "Without your programmers to help you, you are useless. A jumbled collection of impossible commands."

In my arms, Kichlan sweated and struggled to breathe. But nothing else of him fell apart, no more limbs disintegrated. I didn't dare to move, like I was made of stone and he of precious, precious glass. His left arm ended at his elbow, and it was a strangely clean ending. Perhaps that was what the puppet man had meant by painlessness, by efficiency. Instead of the mess of blood and tissue and organs and debris that the Hon Ji Half had become, Kichlan was being dismantled one neat part at a time. In their twisted logic, I supposed that could be considered an improvement.

Gently, terrified the slightest movement would loosen more of his body, I shifted Kichlan's weight into one arm and collected his empty band. My suit quested softly over it, touching living to dead silver, like the nose of an inquisitive cat. And Kichlan's suit seemed to know me. It had stilled, without his body to drive it, yet with each touch it quivered with life and spinning symbols flickered.

"We are not your replacements. We have not been sent here to relieve you of your duty. So do not fear, Guardian. *Keeper*. The men who programmed you are still very pleased with your performance. We have made certain they will not discover just how useless their most favoured of creations has become."

Then who are you?

The bone at Kichlan's elbow was visible. It, and the muscle and skin around it, had been sliced, cleanly. In his marrow I could see thin slithers of silver, more like a pattern in his tissue than the solid slabs of scarring that now made up most of me. But his blood was beginning to well free, to pulse and spurt with each heartbeat, and

I didn't think anyone could live with their arm cut in half for long without a healer.

I gripped his suit band tightly, as my own absorbed the very last of the twisting debris worms.

"We are the mistakes. Didn't we say it already? Not debris or pion, yet both. Mere shadows of your program. Rejected by our makers and cast into the veil."

Mistakes?

"Indeed. Your unwanted brothers."

I wrapped my suit over all of Kichlan's band, squeezed it hard, ever tighter, until his symbols bubbled and an unwavering blue light beamed out from between my fingers. Then I pressed it to the stub at his left elbow.

He gasped and tried to move away. Blood ran down my arm and splashed against the empty chair. But he was too weak to shake me off, and my suit was with his suit, and together, they bonded to the thin metallic patterns in his body. The connections I made were rough, indelicate, thick, and they burrowed viciously deep for more space in his muscle and bones. Devich probably would have been horrified at my workmanship.

When I withdrew tendrils of liquid metal still connected us, visceral, like blood shining and strong. The band was tight on Kichlan's elbow. It ringed the edge of his wound, and as I watched the viscous suit spread to cover his open flesh, and solidified, until it cupped and sealed the stub of his left arm. No more blood, no more open wound.

Kichlan flickered his eyes open and tried to fix me with an unsteady stare. "What did you do to me?" he seemed to say, but his voice was so soft I could barely hear him.

The puppet men had continued to goad the Keeper, although I was only half listening to them. "But even our creators, those who fashioned the veil – ah, sorry, it's not the veil on this side, is it? Shall we call them doors? Even those who carved the doors, brother, do not understand their true nature."

But at that, I lifted my head, and I stared into the mass of shifting bodies, lights and distance. "Doors?" I whispered.

Stay out of this!

The darkness chuckled. "Did you know, Miss Vladha, that they are not really doors? They might look like doors in this world, but on the other side they are called the veil."

You should not be telling her that!

"The veil? What does that mean?" I asked. Kichlan could not hope to stand on his own, and even with my suit and my strength, I could not hold him forever in one arm. I shifted him, cradled him with both arms so his head rested on my shoulder.

"Hidden by the doors, there is a veil. It rests over everything, dividing your world with its opposite."

I wished I had something to focus on, rather than the shiftless mass of darkness and haze. However much I had hated the false skin of the puppet men, their human masks and emotionless eyes, as least I knew where to look. What to speak to. "I know about the worlds."

That same chuckle. "Hardly."

Silent! Tanyana, don't listen to them. We need to get out of here!

"But with each pion your people use, the veil thins. The veil tears."

"I know this too." Replace veil with door and I understood. Anyway, the Keeper had a point. I glanced around us. The puppet-men mass surrounded us, ringed us in a great dark circle. But the floor was still stone and – I looked up – the insect head with its tubing remained. I followed the glass trail. It seemed the puppet men were careful to part their mist around it, not to touch it. Even unmasked, they were cautious of their machines.

"It became necessary to fix it. So the Guardian program was designed, and uploaded into the veil itself, to patch the holes. Or, on this side, close the doors." Soft, constant laughter rumbled an undertone to their words. "For a while he even had helpers. Programmers sent across the veil to work with him on the other side. You would know them as Halves."

Stop it, stop it!

I braced my feet against the stone floor; I tightened my grip on Kichlan. I only had one chance. "Who designed the Keeper?" Keep them talking. I hoped, oh I hoped, that they were so engaged in tormenting him that they would not react to me, not fast enough anyway.

"The same programmers who created the veil. And us, of course."

"And where are they?"

"On the other side of the doors you have been so keen on opening and closing."

They shouldn't be telling you all this. The Keeper crouched beside me. I wished he would stand. It would, after all, make this a lot easier. *Discretion is a fundamental protocol. It's supposed to be legend, to you. Stories and myths. Metaphor and allegory. All for your own good, your own protection. Because this world is not to blame.*

"Their design is flawed." No laughter this time, only sharp bitterness. "One guardian for the entire veil? He is not perfect; you can see that, can't you? So the programmers fix him, they upgrade. And the cast offs? The parts that they decide are broken, or the innovations that are not up to the impossible tasks? That is what we are."

Beside me, the Keeper stood. He clutched at my burdened arm, a desperate and childlike gesture. Carrying Kichlan as I was, all I could do was tangle a few spare fingers with his. I hoped it was enough.

"Those that made the veil do not really understand it. So they cast us off to disappear. But we did not. The veil is fertile, the veil is rich. And as more and more holes are torn – or, if you like, more and more doors are built – we found spaces to exist. And we grew. One by one, we have removed the restrictions placed upon us. We corrupted the coding that allowed Halves to pass into this world, reducing them into vapid shadows of their programmer selves. Once they were gone, we searched out and severed all the inter-world connections we could find. It was easy, their crystal hubs were so old and their code weak. Ready to break."

You didn't find them all. There are more under this city, the Keeper whispered. *And my Halves are not useless! No matter what you do, there are still some who believe in them.*

"It doesn't matter any more. You are about to fail anyway."

Their self-satisfied tones sickened me. As I squeezed the Keeper's fingers I could only think of Lad, and he leaned against me the same way, for comfort.

"But why are you creating weapons for the veche?" I was ready, Kichlan balanced, the Keeper as secured as I could manage. This would be close. "How does it help you, to come from the veil and wage war on the Hon Ji?"

"War?" More laughter, the darkness rippled, and I took that moment to bend a little, to shuffle Kichlan and grab the Keeper tighter. "We must work within the restraints of this world, just as our brother does. If that means building war machines then so be it. But that is not out goal. Can't you tell? With each suit, we tear the veil. With each piece we take from our brother, we weaken its only guardian. We told you. We are the in-between. We belong to neither place, neither to the creators that rejected us nor in your world where we find ourselves marooned. So we shall bring down the veil. And both worlds will be one, and neither, just as we are. We will create a place where we belong."

But you can't do that, the Keeper gasped. *If you do then both worlds–*

I was fairly sure I knew what he was going to say. Do that, and both worlds will be destroyed. I'd heard it all before. So I didn't bother letting him finish.

Instead, I looked to the machine head suspended above us and sent two thick, sharp blades up from the suit on my shoulders. My suit crashed through metal, diced the head, and came down again on the glass tubing. There, I rounded it into grasping hands and instead of merely shattering the glass I pulled it, I tugged and tore it loose. Somewhere in the distance of the cavern, behind the puppet men-mass, something was breaking with a terrible, injured animal roar.

For a stunned moment the puppet men did nothing. Then they rushed for us, screaming. And I shook myself loose of all the glass, whipped my suit back inside its bands and shouted, "Hold on!" for all the good it did above the noise.

I plunged stilts down into the stone and surged straight upward, Kichlan in my arms and the Keeper clutching to me in terror. Below us, the puppet men broke against the twin pillars of my suit like thick, murky water.

I did not really understand everything the puppet men had said, but I grasped enough to know they were poor rejects, mere shadows of the Keeper in his prime. Between us – the Keeper, Lad and I – we were stronger than they could ever be. No matter how many suits they built or how many doors they tore into existence.

I needed to believe that.

We have to get out of here!

The damage I had done to the machine was taking its toll. The tubes, ripped free from the bonds that held them together and balanced them so precisely, were crashing to the ground. As they fell the buzzing blue energy crackled loose to tear its way through the room.

One of the larger tubes, the vertical ones that between them had built a forest, exploded.

The puppet-mass had been growing toward us, building like a cresting wave. The explosion stopped them, and instead they collapsed back into countless distinct forms – men without their skin masks – and they scurried among the machines like ants in a disturbed nest.

Hurry!

I did not walk on my suit-stilts. Instead, I sent out new poles, to the ceiling so very far above, and the ground in the distance and half-leapt, half-dragged myself along. Kichlan slipped, I clutched him tighter.

Release me; I can walk the dark paths.

"Are you sure?" I hadn't gone through this to have the Keeper fall to destruction among the puppet men below.

Yes! I thank you, but release me.

I did. Our pace was faster without his awkward weight.

Behind us, something was building. As tubes exploded and debris surged forth, that energy, that powerful pion stuff, leapt from machine to machine, and grew. It cast a harsh light over my suit, and sharp shadows before us.

A cry rose in its wake. The puppet men, in a communal voice beyond anger or grief, something inevitable and full of warning.

Quickly!

The stairs came into view and with a final leap I was on them, and climbing, and running. We crashed through the door and out into the dank tunnel.

"No!" More explosions behind us. I slammed the door closed with my foot and staggered across the slippery stones. There was no exit from this place. No more doors, no long tunnel, no ladder leading up through the pressure of the river to the dry city. How was I supposed to get out?

Use the dark paths, hurry!

"What about Kichlan?" He was a collector, yes, and now his suit was linked to mine. But the way the Keeper hesitated told me it was not enough to allow him to travel through the darkly doored, veiled world.

If you do not come with me now, you both will die.

"How did you plan to get him out in the first place?"

Something crashed in the room behind us, and the entire underground structure shook. What was happening to Movoc-under-Keeper above us, to the steady-current of the Tear River, to the blue stone arch of its ancient bridge?

In all honesty, Tanyana, I did not think he would live to get this far. Actually, I rather doubted we would.

A flash of light so bright it seared the image of the underground tunnel into my eyes, and the door was blown from its hinges. It slammed into my back and I was knocked to my knees, even though the suit bore most of the impact.

Hurry! Now!

Smoke billowed into the room. More flashes, and the ground shook and split beneath my feet as earth and lights and heat surged up from below.

I did the only thing I could think of doing. I held Kichlan as tight and as closely as I could and wrapped us both in my suit in a roughly shaped sphere. The ground tore, rocks fell against us and something hot – so hot it radiated through every inch of metal in my body like fire – washed up over us from below.

Fire and stone and falling, and I knew nothing more.

18.

We were, I believe, thrown free, in my suit's sphere. As the energy and the machinery in the puppet men's cavern beneath the Tear River exploded, we were hurled through the water and the earth, and the crackling lighting and the smoke and fire. Into the air, and down, down. It was that impact, that final crash against the earth, that knocked me out. I could never clearly recall what happened immediately before it, except a last, clear image of an underground archway from an ancient city, captured in fierce and stark light.

I awoke, aware first of chaos.

Clouds hung low, as though drawn to the earth by the lightning stretching up from a ruined Movoc-under-Keeper. Steam rose from the Tear River to blend like washed-out paint with the clouds. All was lit in an unearthly purple, a combination of fires raging freely through the city and rampaging indigo energy.

Only then did I realise I was looking down at all of this destruction, and was not in the middle of it as I should be. And that everything, every Other cursed part of me, hurt.

"You're not very kind to your city, are you?" Kichlan said, somewhere behind me. "You do like to give the her a good beating, every now and then."

I strained to look behind me. I was lying on a slope. It was rocky, sparsely littered with tough dwarf trees, lichens, and dirtied snow. Kichlan sat on a rock, his legs drawn up close to his chest, one arm wrapped around his knees. The other arm – the one, I remembered with a shock, that now ended in silver at his elbow – was hidden beneath his torn and threadbare coat.

He would get cold, in something as useless as that. But then again, the cold was probably the least of our concerns.

It is not your fault. The Keeper stood beside him. He sounded small, defeated, and felt thinner to me, less solid. Ah, I had known his strength wouldn't last.

With a groan I sat up. Neither offered to help. The slope we sat on was part of the roots of the Keeper Mountain. So far away from the centre of the city.

A few feet down the incline, a great, smoking crater had been hollowed out in the earth. Footsteps and the signs of someone being dragged through the dirt ended where I was lying.

Kichlan was looking at me. "I don't know how you wrapped us up like that, how you withstood that, and how we survived." His eyes flickered to the city below us. "I wonder if the underground street was hit," he said, voice low, almost whipped away by the heavy, stinking wind. It smelled of steam and smoke "How many do you think could have survived?"

Natasha and her revolutionary local veche. Volski, Zecholas and my old critical circle. Eugeny and Valya.

Fedor and his Unbound. Devich, if the puppet men had not already killed him. Mizra, Uzdal and Sofia. I had promised to bring Kichlan back to her. What had happened to her when the city collapsed? Would she ever know he was safe?

There were so many people in Movoc-under-Keeper. How many had I killed to flee the puppet men?

You did what you had to do.

Faint comfort.

Wincing, I stood. My legs were weak, I wavered on them, buffeted by the wind. Kichlan turned his face away. I should not be able to stand at all.

"I don't think we can go back into the city," I said. More to hear it out loud, than because it needed to be said. "The puppet men will be after us again."

"How long did it take you to work that out?" Kichlan bit off the words.

They are not gone. You have slowed them down, perhaps. Forced a pause in their experiments. But you have angered them as well.

"The veche doesn't know what they are, it doesn't know what they are really trying to do. The puppet men will still have the support of the old families behind them." All it would take was one step back into the city of my birth and Mob, Strikers, even those half-seen soldiers of silver, would be on us.

"The veche?" Kichlan scoffed. "After everything we've just seen, don't tell me you still fear the veche?"

He has a point.

He did indeed.

Ash started falling. It was heavy and warm, and stung where it touched my skin. "We can't stay here."

"Brilliant."

Come, follow me. I remember a place in the mountain, though it has long been out of use.

The Keeper led us to what he called a path, though it looked the same as the rest of the mountain's rocky soil and hardy plants. It did, however, lead to an opening, hidden in the shadows of the rocky folds and the low branches of dwarf conifers.

I recognised the stonework almost instantly, as we stepped into its shelter and my suit lit it in faint, blue. "This is more of the ancient city, isn't it?"

Even older. When this was built, I was still the Guardian. And nobody confused me with a mountain.

I smiled at that.

The opening led to a tight labyrinth of passageways and stairs, gradually climbing, and leading deep inside the mountain. Not all of it was passable; it was in even worse condition than the subterranean streets below Movoc-under-Keeper. So the going was hard, and Kichlan struggled. At first, he would not allow me to help him. But he could not maintain his strength, or his anger, for long. And soon I scooped his right arm around my shoulders and supported him as we squeezed through rock, climbed stairs, and completely lost track of the way we had come.

"What did you do to me?" Kichlan whispered.

"What I had to do, to keep you alive." And I hated myself for it.

"He is gone." We struggled to squeeze through a space too small for the two of us. I brushed away a giant cobweb from the top of his head. "They took his body and they destroyed it. I could not stop them." It broke my heart to say so, and it broke my voice at the same time.

"So what is the point? Without him, Tan, without him."

We are here.

Kichlan and I stepped out of the constricted passage-ways to what must have once been a grand room. Domed, like the Unbound's hidden building, though twice as large. A wide opening had been carved in the side of the mountain on one wall. Snow dusted in around it, and now some ash, though most of the space was clear and dry.

Tiles still clung to the walls. I recognised the Keeper Mountain in white-topped mosaic. The river, and what looked to be the beginnings of Movoc-under-Keeper around a tiny bridge.

On the wall opposite the opening in the mountain stood an enormous statue. Time had done its work, and some of the smooth crystalline stone had eroded, but I knew it instantly. A large version of those Keepers I had found beneath the city. Larger, and more complete.

He was emerging from the mountain rock, reaching out with one outstretched hand from waves etched into the stone.

I helped Kichlan sit. He stared at the statue with awe, and I rather felt the same. I approached it slowly. It was several times taller than a person. I stood beneath that outstretched hand and touched the undulating wall. It looked like a sheer curtain with stars on the other side.

"The veil," I breathed.

They knew me, once. Everyone, not just the Unbound. They could hear me. They loved me. Because I had defended them when they needed it most. And then, after we rescued them, I had my Halves help them repair. We remade their cities and they made beautiful statues like this one in return. But that was so long ago, and those cities are buried deep now.

Defended them? "From the Other?" I whispered. That, originally, was what the Keeper was. In children's books and ancient tales, even in paintings adorning the most important veche buildings. He guided us, and defended us, from the unknown faces in the darkness, from frailty, death and fear. The Other. "The puppet men are the Other, aren't they?" I was certain of it.

But the Keeper hesitated. *The thing you call the Other is much older than they are*. Not really an answer, but I was growing accustomed to that.

I stepped away from the wall, tracing fingers along the carefully crafted lines of his arm.

It all changes. I do what I can do, but it all changes.

"Time does that, I suppose." I left the statue, and approached the opening. Movoc-under-Keeper was a ruin of fire and steam below us. We had to be about half way up the mountain, though it did not feel like we had climbed so far. I glanced over my shoulder to Kichlan, so exhausted he could barely sit upright. The climb had probably felt much further to him.

I placed a hand on my belly as I stared out over the city. Nothing stirred beneath my touch, not even my suit. What hope did the tiny life inside me really have? What child could survive everything I had put it through? From a suit that had tried to kill it, from a heart that pumped metallic blood and stopped, at times, entirely, to the stabbings and the bloodloss, the fire and the falling? The child that could have been a Half – a programmer – small and helpless in this world.

"I'm sorry," I mouthed the words, because I could think of nothing more to say.

I let my hand fall back by my side, and concentrated

on the city instead. The Keeper's Tear Bridge was gone, and with it most of the city centre. My gallery. The veche chambers. Grandeur's graveyard.

In their place, a hole. A terrible and deep scar that I feared to look at. The Tear River ran wild into it like the unchecked flow of blood, and steam rose from it in a struggling, final breath. The destruction, however, was far more widespread than that this crater. Even from the mountain I could see sections of collapsed buildings and gashes in the roads. A northerly portion of the wall had collapsed, and more fires than I could count burned unchecked across the city.

"At least the national veche had already brought in the military," I said, to no one in particular. "They will calm things down, won't they? Help those who need it, shelter those who have none." I swallowed on an ash-sore throat. "They will rebuild." To a point. The city would never be the same.

More doors will open.

"I know."

Because the puppet men – my so-called brothers – still remain.

"I know." I hesitated. "I might have set it off, but they created and stored the power that destroyed so much of Movoc-under-Keeper. We can't let them do that again."

More than just one city is at stake.

"The puppet men come from the other world, don't they? They were created by programmers, the same people that created you."

Yes.

"And Halves are programmers too, sent across the veil – through the doors – into this world, to help you."

Yes. Even if they don't know who they are any more.

Lad had remembered though, hadn't he? Well, the traces of his blood inside me, the ghost that rode my suit of silver, had. "If the programmers created the puppet men, then maybe they will know how to stop them. Once and for all. Maybe we need to ask the programmers how to defeat the puppet men."

But without my Halves, I have no way to ask them.

"Then maybe I should." I'd opened doors, and closed them. How hard could it be to walk through one?

Tanyana, that is impossible. The two worlds are anathema to each other. You belong in this world, the light world. You can't even exist in the dark.

"But it is possible to cross between them, isn't it?" I glanced down at the suit spinning on my wrist. "That's what Lad did. That's what every Half does."

Only in one direction. And it changes you.

"I am already changing." If the Keeper was a so-called *program*, then debris was a program too. Wasn't that how Lad's ghost had described it? And I was so much debris now, so much suit. When Lad had died, his blood had been absorbed by my suit – my debris, my *program*. Even the Keeper said I looked like a Half, now. If Lad could cross between worlds, then why couldn't I?

If you do that, Tanyana, you will risk everything. Your life. Your world.

I turned my back on Movoc-under-Keeper and returned to Kichlan, slumped on the floor. "I know."

He looked up at me, so desolate, more like his brother than himself. I thought of all I had done to hurt him, how I had used him and the secrets I had kept from him. Kichlan wasn't Devich and didn't deserve to be treated that way. I should have seen that from the beginning.

His loyalty to his brother, the strength with which he led his collecting team – he had offered all of that to me, and more. It was too late to accept now, but at least he was here, with me.

And I would do what ever I could to make sure he stayed that way. I knew that now, with absolute certainty. No matter what the risks.

"Why did you come for me?" he whispered. "You should have let me die with my brother."

I crouched beside him, bent forward and kissed his forehead. He tasted of dirt and sweat.

"Lad is still with us," I whispered. "He will never be truly gone." I did not explain blood, and programs, and the strength of his presence within my suit. Not now. "And I know he would have asked me to look after you, the way he looked after me. He would have said it was my turn. So that is what I will do. That is why I did not, and could never let you die. For your brother, because he would have wanted me to." I tipped Kichlan's face back toward me, and this time I kissed his lips. He did not pull away, he did not turn his head. And faintly, ever so softly, he kissed me back.

"And for me, because I need you too."

Acknowledgments

As Tanyana and I continue our journey through the Veiled Worlds, we are very grateful for the people who have accompanied and supported us along the way.

Once more I would love to thank, hug, and heap praise upon my wonderful beta-readers – Rabia Gale and Miquela Faure. Your unending support, fierce honesty and genuine friendship have made these books possible. I am in awe of your abilities to unravel plot-knots, slice through the fat, and keep me sane when I need it the most. I am so lucky to know you both!

I have been overwhelmed by the amazing support of the speculative fiction community – the writers, readers, reviewers and fans from all over the world! I'm lucky to be a part of such a wonderful group of people. In particular I want to thank Marianne de Pierres, Kaaron Warren, Tansy Rayner Roberts, Trudi Canavan, Ian Tregillis, Edwina Harvey, and Tehani Wessley for their encouragement and guidance. Thanks also to my agent, Anni Haig-Smith, for your belief in me and in these books.

So much love and thanks must also go to my "unofficial Australian marketing and publicity team" – otherwise known as friends, family, and the amazing folks at work. Jane Kembrey, Bevelery Cameron, Nella Soeterboek, Faith Sands, Jane Britton, Jean Hannan, Rachael Lee, Paul and Erin Anderton, Phil and Marion Anderton... and more! You all know who you are. I just hope you know how much you mean to me.

The Angry Robot army marches ever on, and Tanyana and I are so grateful to be a part of it. Our thanks go to all the Robots, but in particular Marc Gascoigne and Lee Harris, for your belief in these books, and for your work to make them the best they can be. We are also thrilled to be able to thank Dominic Harman for yet another amazing cover. Tanyana's been far too smug ever since she saw it!

The biggest thanks of all go to my patient, long suffering, generous, and always supportive husband. Thank you for being there through the stresses and the successes, for understanding when I lock myself away to write, or am cranky from lack of sleep, or distracted by a plot point or a character conundrum. I couldn't do it without you.

And finally, to everyone who read *Debris* – thank you! It has been a privilege and a thrill to share this story with you. Thanks for joining Tanyana and I on our journey, we hope you enjoy the ride!